Sita's Sister

Kavita Kané is the best-selling author of *Karna's Wife: The Outcast's Queen*. She started her career as a journalist and is now a full-time novelist. She is a post-graduate in English literature and mass communications and a self-confessed aficionado of theatre and cinema. Married to a mariner, she is a mother of two teenaged daughters and currently lives in Pune along with Dude, the friendly Rottweiler, and Babe, the unfriendly cat.

Sita's
Sister

KAVITA KANÉ

RUPA

Published by
Rupa Publications India Pvt. Ltd 2014
7/16, Ansari Road, Daryaganj
New Delhi 110002

Sales Centres:
Allahabad Bengaluru Chennai
Hyderabad Jaipur Kathmandu
Kolkata Mumbai

ISBN: 978-81-291-3484-4

Fourth impression 2016

10 9 8 7 6 5 4

Typeset by SÜRYA, New Delhi

Printed at Rakmo Press Pvt. Ltd, New Delhi

To Kimaya and Amiya, who taught me that the daughter
is the mother of invention

CONTENTS

PROLOGUE: THE FOUR SISTERS   1
THE TWO PRINCES   6
THE SWAYAMVAR   26
THE LOVERS   43
THE REJECTION   58
THE FOUR WEDDINGS   76
THE CITY OF AYODHYA   91
THE SISTERS   104
THE CROWN PRINCE   119
THE EXILE   134
THE FAREWELL   149
THE DESPAIR   166
THE INTRIGUE   179
THE MOURNING   196
THE MEETING   209
THE SEPARATION   226
THE RIVALRY   241
THE WAITING   259
THE ABDUCTION   273
THE WAR   283
THE RETURN   292
EPILOGUE: THE LOSS   308
ACKNOWLEDGEMENTS   310

PROLOGUE: THE FOUR SISTERS

'That girl seems to have vanished into thin air! Where is she?' Urmila could not contain the exasperation in her voice. Where *was* Sita? They were playing hide-and-seek and like always, the fun had dissipated from the game and it had become a mission to locate her elder sister. Her hideouts were as self-effacing as she was; Sita could come up with the most unexpected hideaways which took hours to track down.

Urmila found herself getting irritated; she was tired, her feet were hurting from running down the marbled corridors, climbing the pillared staircases and, the most trying of it all, searching for the hidden girl in the vast woodland that her father proudly called the 'family's garden'. It was a private forest. King Seeradhwaj Janak, her father—the pronunciation of which name was easy for Urmila as she was used to reciting Vedic verses every day—might be one of the most prosperous kings and a respected scholar, but the environs he loved most were the expansive tree-studded greens that housed a million flowers, the little girl thought part sourly, part affectionately. It was her favourite haven too—one in which she could duck easily and remain untraced for hours together. Like Sita was doing right now...

Urmila's aching feet reminded her that she was digressing and she had still not found her hiding sister. She was *not* going to accept defeat—Urmila's tiny, stubborn chin rose belligerently. If she could mine out her cousins Mandavi and Shrutakirti (condensed to Kirti by her as she found the name a tongue-twister) from their respective hideouts—a tall-trunked, high-branched tree and a chest—she snorted derisively, she should be able to track down Sita too. But Kirti was just seven, two full years younger to Urmila's wise nine, and Mandavi was the same age as she and they had been easy to uncover from their hiding posts. Sita, however, was a year older, and *that's* why she managed to select the most fetching places to hide, Urmila seethed. Behind the rising annoyance, however, was a tremor of worry that was shaking Urmila from her feigned anger. Where *was* her sister? Sita might be a little timid, but she was very strong in the face of mishaps and crises. Had she fallen? Had she hurt herself but was stifling the cry of pain lest her hiding hole was discovered? Had she fallen unconscious? Was she bleeding? Where *was* Sita?

'You worry too much about her, Urmi, nothing has happened to her!' Mandavi's sharp voice cut short her perturbing thoughts. As always, Mandavi had astutely voiced her inmost fears. 'Come, quick, let's go to that hall upstairs—that's the only place we haven't checked.'

'But we are not allowed to go there...,' lisped Kirti, her big eyes widening.

'Yes, and Sita being such an obedient girl would not break the rule. Why would she hide there when we have been forbidden to go to that wing of the palace?' Urmila said uneasily knowing *she* would not hesitate to break any such rule. For Sita, she was ready to earn her father's wrath.

'I want to go to father! Let's tell him we have lost Sita...' Kirti was going to burst into tears any moment now.

'Cry baby!' Mandavi laughed scornfully.

'No, dear, there's nothing to be scared of,' Urmila bent down and gathered her little sister close, giving Mandavi a quelling look. She could hear her youngest cousin's heart thudding noisily, her slight body trembling against hers. 'Why don't you go to Ma and tell her we are here? And bring along uncle too...'

'Urmi, we'll get into trouble...' Mandavi said warningly.

'We are already in deep trouble,' Urmila retorted, her voice hardening, the fear spiralling fast to engulf her.

She saw Kirti scrambling away as fast as her short, plump legs permitted her.

'Let's go find Sita,' said Urmila, taking Mandavi's hand.

The two small girls ran up the high steps of the wide, curving stairway in a hurried rush to locate their missing sister. They had to find her soon, Urmila thought furiously, as she peeped into each room and found it dismayingly empty.

'She's not here in this room too...!' Mandavi looked shaken, her face white. Urmila could hear the tears in her voice.

They came to a huge, carved door. It was the door to the room the girls had been warned never to enter: the sacred hall. It was shut, but not locked. The girls stood looking at each other, undecided and wavering. Would Sita be inside? That thought propelled Urmila to push at the door. It did not budge. She pushed it harder, with all her hope, might and urgency. Mandavi pressed on with her slight shoulders. They felt the door move and slowly swing open. The girls rushed in, their eager, scared eyes scanning the long, pillared hall.

'She can't be here! How could she have got inside if both of us together couldn't open that door?' Mandavi whispered urgently. 'Let's leave fast...before we are caught!'

'No!' Urmila's hand snaked out swiftly to catch hold of Mandavi's wrist. 'We have tried every room, every nook, every corner...she must be here. Sita has to be here!' Urmila said chokingly, the tears welling up in her eyes and throat. 'Sita!

Sitaa!' She screamed, her voice hoarse with despair. 'Come out...please! Where are you?'

Her voice echoed distantly bouncing off the high domed ceiling. Her eyes barely noticed that the hall was extraordinarily long, lined with a row of carved chairs on either side, along the column of pillars. Urmila was staring far ahead. At the far end of the room was a throne, perched high over a long flight of steps. At the end of the steps and just in front of the throne was a low-lying long table on which was a huge iron box and peering into it was...Sita!

'Sita!' Joy and sheer relief gurgled out as a squeal from Urmila's throat. She ran towards her sister, wanting to hug her fiercely. But she stopped. The sight before her was too much to behold. Were it not for the solemnity of the occasion, Urmila would have laughed aloud; it seemed that ludicrous. Sita was holding an enormous bow in her hand—it was gigantic, considering Sita's elfin frame, towering high above her. But she was holding it effortlessly in one hand; peeking inside the massive casket in which the bow must have been previously placed. She was obviously searching for something.

'I can't find my play ball,' cried Sita, looking distressed. 'It must have fallen in here when I climbed into this box to hide. Oh there! I found it!' She almost swooped on the ball, which lay in the inner niche of the armoury box, the huge bow in her small hand swaying dangerously.

'Be careful,' Urmila shouted instinctively.

As an answer, Sita carefully placed the tall bow back into the confines of the strong box with one hand and, skilfully scooped out the ball with the other. Noticing that the table—which was actually an elongated cart—was slightly askew, the meticulous girl that she was, Sita promptly straightened it with a nudge of her knees.

'How did you do that?' blurted Mandavi, her eyes shining in

wonderment. 'It looks sooooo heavy...it must weigh a tonne!' She was gazing at Sita with newfound awe.

Sita shrugged lightly and said, 'Let's go...we are getting late. Ma will get worried!'

Suddenly realizing the reason of their presence in the hall, the series of events came rushing back to Urmila and flooded her with trepidation. She was about to retort tartly when her angry words were silenced by the sight of her parents and her uncle at the bottom of the steps. Her heart sank—now for the collective reprimands, she thought in dismay. But the harsh words were not uttered. Instead, all three adults seemed thunderstruck, carrying the same frozen expression on their faces which Mandavi had had a few moments ago. That of sheer awe.

Her father walked slowly up the steps, his eyes filled with a strange expression. It was more than amazement; Urmila could not figure out what, or possibly she did not know the right word to describe that emotion. She saw him folding his hands and bowing his head in...reverence. Her mother and uncle followed suit, folding their hands in veneration as well. But why, Urmila looked puzzled. Why did they have that look they reserved for the deity of Goddess Gouri in their beautiful temple in the garden?

Urmila did not have an answer. But she was more thankful that she had escaped the stern rebuke from her parents. She sighed happily and ran to her sisters.

THE TWO PRINCES

'We have unexpected guests,' proclaimed Mandavi with elaborate enthusiasm.

But her dramatic declaration failed to evoke the response she desired. The three other girls allowed her words to drift meaninglessly in the sun-warmed room and continued with what they were doing. The oldest among the four, Sita, was distributing the morning prasad after having returned from her customary ritual of visiting the temple of Goddess Gauri early morning. Sita's sister, Urmila, was getting ready to mix some fresh colours in the palette and settling down to her morning hours of marathon painting. The canvas was still blank; she hadn't painted a stroke. This meant Urmila was troubled; and it must be about Sita, Mandavi deduced perceptively. That girl worries too much about her sister.

The quiet, efficient Shrutakirti, her younger sister, was competently assisting both her cousins—getting out the colours for Urmila while helping Sita with her pooja thali. They were a picture of contrasts. Sita—elegant and ethereal, whisper-slim and delicately framed, always meticulous and impeccably dressed, she was a girl of few words. Shrutakirti was smart and striking with her long, thick mane of curly hair framing a small, sharply cut face, illuminated by her large, dark intense eyes. She was the youngest of the four sisters but was the tallest of them all, though all the four girls were quite tall. But Kirti, right now, seemed to almost tower over the feisty, voluptuous Urmila. Urmila's fetching roundness blunted her height. She was like the colours she was blending so dexterously—warm, vibrant and sparkling, her quicksilver temper included. She had an effortless easy-going manner that made her very agreeable. Mandavi, who looked every bit the proud princess, envied Urmila's facile charm. The scene in the room was a familiar sight for her and Mandavi realized that there was an endearing, emblematic quality to their everyday mornings. There lingered a certain sense of contentment in the sameness and she felt a sudden urge to dispel it. Her opening words had evidently not made an impact as each of the girls continued doing what they were busy with.

'I heard from the maids that two young and handsome princes of Ayodhya have arrived here,' Mandavi persisted in her usual loud, authoritative voice, '...and that Uncle has invited them to stay at the west wing of the palace.'

'How many times have I told you not to overhear maids gossip?' Urmila said perfunctorily, without paying any serious attention to what Mandavi was saying, blending the reds furiously with the yellow. As she helped Urmila help get the right tone, Kirti suppressed a smile, a gesture that did not go unnoticed by Mandavi, throwing her immediately on the defensive. Whenever Kirti and Urmila got together, Mandavi felt absurdly left out, a sliver of jealousy snaking insidiously inside her. She idolized her cousin and believed she was closest to her as they were almost the same age. Kirti was her kid sister; she was not supposed to intrude into the elders' domain. Mandavi's possessive streak went on an erratic overdrive, propelling her into an unreasonable irritation.

'But one gets to know so many things from them!' She snapped, but without vitriol. 'News you wouldn't get to know otherwise. One needs to be sufficiently aware and armed of information, as they say, an ear to the ground, and eyes in the wall. You can't isolate yourself in the palace,' she sniffed delicately.

Mandavi was svelte and sylphlike and as tall as Urmila, but here the similarity ceased. Mandavi always stood tall and straight, sinewy and strong—courtesy her astonishing equestrian skills unlike Urmila's curvy, sensual softness which made her appear more diminutive. Urmila had an open, vivacious countenance, her oval face accentuated by a pair of wide spaced, big, flashing eyes, a trim, pert nose, full rose-bud lips which curved often and generously in a potently appealing smile and which none could resist. Mandavi appeared somewhat stern, with her solemn, steady eyes and straight lips which rarely deigned to smile, giving the impression of deliberate aloofness and an air of cold aristocracy.

Right now, her lips were pursed, dagger-thin, in indignant argument, 'That's what affairs of state, and those of the palace, are all about. You have to have your sources—you nourish them and they nourish you. Otherwise how would we cloistered princesses know what's occurring in the world beyond our tapestried, high-windowed chambers? Like charity, gossip starts at home—and so does politics! And anyway, these maids always have the most delicious things to tell you...it's idle entertainment,' she smirked wickedly.

'They talk, you listen; it should be the other way round, dear princess!' Urmila reminded her.

'I seriously wonder how they come and tell you anything,' said Kirti curiously. 'Mandavi, you seem so frightening and formidable otherwise! Do you gift them generously?'

'Oh, hush, girls!' Sita laughed and pushed a morsel of the prasad in Urmila's mouth. 'Talk sweet, dear,' she said affectionately.

The four young girls engaged in such banter all the time.

There was no malice in it, not a shred of meanness. They were simply disarmingly frank with each other; brutally blunt sometimes. And why wouldn't they? They were sisters, after all, and there was no need to be nice and good all the time.

Urmila gulped down the prasad hurriedly and turned to Mandavi, 'And anyway, what's so unusual about guests coming over? Don't forget, the philosophy conference which father hosts each year at Mithila is on. Moreover, there will be a lot more coming in as Sita's swayamvar is just a week away! The palace is already brimming with people.'

Sita smiled complacently—the mention of her imminent marriage did not seem to excite her. Nothing seems to excite her, Urmila thought apprehensively. Sita was one of the most exasperatingly calm and unexcitable people she knew—always composed, clear-headed and mild-mannered. But it was her wedding, and wasn't the bride-to-be supposed to be a little more animated about one of the most momentous events in her young, unadventurous life? Mandavi had been right when she called them the cloistered princesses. They were largely that, although they were well versed in the Vedas and the Upanishads, politics, music, art and literature. They had journeyed fabulous worlds, traversing unknown frontiers—but all in the mind, sitting in the verandahs and chambers of the palace of Mithila which overlooked the distant horizon of an undiscovered world. However, they had accompanied their father to all the conferences and religious seminars across the country, experiencing a world no princess had been allowed to visit. But Urmila yearned for more; she wanted to see more places, places she had heard about through her growing years... But she knew that she, too, would be married off after Sita's swayamvar. Marriage did not hold much interest for Urmila but it was a social discipline she would have to conform to. She would rather seek knowledge instead of a suitor.

The thought of the swayamvar brought Urmila back to the

present—to their pretty, colourful bed chamber in Mithila. She stared at her elder sister intently. Sita was looking exquisite as always; slender and delicate, her long neck curved gracefully so that she appeared willowy and taller than she actually was. In azure blue silk—her favourite pastel colour—she looked pale but not an unhealthy pallid. She was very fair, her skin almost translucent and stretched across her high cheek bones, her thick brows highlighted her slightly slanting eyes; her heart-shaped face was suffused with a perpetual serenity and demureness. Despite the gentleness, Urmila knew that her elder sister had an indomitable will and strength of purpose, but she masked her emotions so smoothly that not a wrinkle furrowed her fair brows.

'Sita, aren't you happy about your wedding?' Urmila asked abruptly. 'You seem so...so aloof, so nonchalant about it—it's not normal!'

'What do you want me to do, cavort in joy?' Sita questioned with a soft laugh, 'I know it's my wedding and, of course, I am elated about it...'

'Then show it! You don't look too thrilled...or even remotely excited as brides often are!'

'I am happy, dear, for how things will be. It is all planned, so what is there to be so anxious about? The man who manages to break the famous Shiv dhanush shall be my husband. It's very simple,' she explained sedately.

'Break the Shiv dhanush?' Mandavi expostulated, with a shake of her head, 'Just because you could wield it so easily as a child, Uncle wants some superhero to do the same? That bow is more than eight-and-a-half-feet long and so heavy that it needs around three hundred people to lift it! It needs an enormous trolley to cart it around and again another three hundred people to push the cart to move it an inch! And Uncle has announced that whosoever wants to marry Sita can do so only after stringing the bow. I can't imagine anyone even shifting it, forget lifting it!'

'That's exactly the point, don't you see?' Urmila asked quietly. 'It has to be an extraordinary man who can do that—and indeed, it is going to be an extraordinary man who will marry Sita!'

'You have answered your own question, Urmila,' said Sita amiably. 'And that's why I am so calm about my wedding! I trust father...'

Urmila gave Sita a sharp look. There was always an air of quick, quiet acceptance about her. She was rarely confrontational like Urmila; and though it was a swayamvar—to marry a man of her choice—Urmila knew Sita was bound by her father's decision.

But who would be that man who would achieve this monumental feat? And would that man be good enough for her good sister? The thought had been niggling at her relentlessly ever since her parents had planned Sita's swayamvar. Urmila sighed; she couldn't stop worrying about her elder sister. Sita was the gentlest, kindest, sweetest person; so achingly, implausibly nice that she seemed like a beautiful angel come down to earth. She was really an angel, her father always reminded her. She had been named Sita—the furrow—after the channel of love and hope in which her childless parents had found her as a bawling baby. This had happened while they were ploughing the fields as a part of the yagna they were performing. The beautiful baby had touched their heart and soul and the childless King Seeradhwaj, Janak of Videha and his queen Sunaina had promptly adopted her as their first daughter. Janak, the philosopher-king that he was, believed that 'sita' was actually the most poetic description for his daughter—a metaphor for verdancy and fruitfulness—and an unending blessing coming from the soil—the bhumi. She was earth's child—warm, rooted and life-giving.

Urmila had been born a year later, a foil to Sita right from the start. The two cradles had rocked in perfect harmony since childhood as smooth and strong as the bond that was to blossom between the two girls. Completing the circle of love and laughter were Mandavi and Kirti, their younger cousins, the two chirpy daughters of the widowed King Kushadhwaj, the king of Varanasi and the younger brother of Seeradhwaj Janak.

'...And so about these princes...' continued Mandavi, her authoritative tone breaking through Urmila's anxious thoughts. 'The older one is Ram and Lakshman is his younger brother, and they are here with Rishi Vishwamitra.'

'Sage Vishwamitra?' Sita echoed, the surprise apparent in her voice.

Urmila was intrigued. Vishwamitra was not a person whom anyone could meet easily. He was one of the most renowned and revered rishis of the country—a brahmarishi—a sage who has understood the meaning of brahman, the ultimate reality, and has attained the highest divine knowledge, brahmajnana. The story, from what Urmila could recall, was that the rishi was previously a king. He was earlier known as King Kaushik who clashed against none other than the mighty Rishi Vasishtha, a brahmarishi and the royal priest of the court of Ayodhya, and was routed. This defeat made him realize that the power obtained by penance was far superior to military strength. The humiliated king relinquished his kingdom and began his pursuit of the supreme and spiritual knowledge to become a bigger rishi than his rival, Sage Vasishtha, and took on the name of Vishwamitra. After many trials and tribulations and the severest of penance and austerities, the sage at last received the title of brahmarishi from Vasishtha himself.

Though Vishwamitra had changed his vocation, he could not change his essential nature; like the glorious king he formerly was, the brahmarishi maintained his regal hauteur and arrogance and was greatly feared for the same. The mightiest kings trembled before him. So why had that mighty sage come to her father's kingdom, wondered Urmila? And who were the two princes with him?

'But why are they with Rishi Vishwamitra?' Urmila could not help asking. Sita nodded eagerly.

Urmila's questions were swiftly answered by her voluble cousin, who was still gushing about the young princes of Ayodhya.

'It seems Sage Vishwamitra asked King Dashrath of Ayodhya for the help of his two sons, Ram and Lakshman, to kill some demons who were disrupting his penance in the Dandaka forest. I don't remember their names...' she frowned. 'Oh yes, the she-demon Taraka and her sons Subahu and Mareecha. These demons were very powerful and none could kill them. But these two young princes did! Mareecha escaped but they killed both the dreaded Taraka and Subahu.'

'But why have they come *here*?' Urmila asked sharply. Was her father in trouble with the influential, irascible sage? Had he sent the princes as a silent warning? Was tension brewing between Mithila and Ayodhya? Urmila couldn't stem her troubled thoughts.

'Oh, nothing. They are here just to enjoy themselves!' Mandavi shrugged airily. 'It seems the revered sage wanted the princes of Ayodhya to meet the famous King Janak of Mithila, my renowned uncle!' she guffawed.

'Don't be so flippant, dear!' chided Sita good-humouredly. 'You must have found out why they are here through your sources...'

Mandavi nodded, 'But seriously, Vishwamitra came to Mithila to attend the yagna uncle is performing for which he has invited all the rishis of the country. You can well imagine his delight when Vishwamitra paid an unexpected visit!'

'So these two young men with the rishi are here to visit Mithila...?' said Kirti softly. 'Or are they here for Sita's swayamvar?' she asked flatly.

Kirti had incisively voiced Urmila's doubts but she knew there was more to it than what was apparent. She glanced at Sita who was frowning and seemed to share her apprehensions.

That morning was not their usual morning. Sita, who had been unusually silent during the past few days, was late in returning from the temple. Her cousins had gone off to help her mother in the wedding preparations. And instead of joining them, Urmila was waiting for Sita to return. Where was she, Urmila could not stop fretting. She wasn't in the kitchen, her favourite haunt, Urmila had checked. A full two hours later, the otherwise splendidly calm and collected Sita entered the room, her usually pale face ashen. She looked visibly flustered and was making it worse by trying to hide it.

'Why are you late?' grumbled Urmila, 'I have been waiting for you when I am supposed to help Mother with the jewellery and Father in compiling his texts for the visiting rishis. Where had you disappeared...' Urmila's indignation trailed off when she realized her sister was barely paying attention to her. Urmila watched her roaming around the room restlessly till she could not take it anymore. She got up and took Sita's hands in hers. They were cold and trembling.

'What is it?' she asked gently. 'You haven't been yourself lately. I noticed it but decided to let you be till you thought it right to disclose. Is there anything? What took you so long?'

Sita did not answer immediately but looked at Urmila with the wide, frightened eyes of a trapped doe.

'What's wrong?' Urmila repeated, her sister's fear was beginning to affect her too, but she refused to panic.

'I just met him again...!' blurted Sita, with an uncharacteristic fumble.

Urmila stared back at her vacantly, not comprehending her words. Sita made another effort to explain.

'I just met Ram, the prince of Ayodhya, in the garden. And his brother Lakshman,' she added hastily.

'And?' Urmila pressed kindly.

Sita blushed prettily, and profusely. The otherwise eloquent Sita, who could smartly retort with lucid clarifications or recite a quick couplet of poetry, seemed to be at a loss for the right words. All she did was play with her fingers. She needn't have explained. Urmila took a quick, informed guess. And measuring Sita's altering expressions and emotions, Urmila felt a huge sense of relief, and delayed delight. Had Sita finally met her man?

'It's so extreme,' said Sita with a sigh. 'It happened three days ago. I was on my way to the Gauri temple as I always do every morning—and imagine my shock when I saw him...er them, standing right before me in the garden. I was in my own world, dreaming as usual, and almost walked into them!' she laughed self-consciously.

Responding to Urmila's enquiring look, she rushed quickly, 'They bowed and introduced themselves and said they were collecting flowers for the puja to be performed by Rishi Vishwamitra...'

Urmila did not interrupt but allowed her sister the luxury of time in explaining the most heart-stirring episode of her life which seemed to have whipped up such an emotional upheaval in her.

'...And all I could do was stare at him and finally I nodded politely and fled without saying a word!'

'Sita,' wailed Urmila, in mock despair, 'you didn't!'

'Oh that's why I am feeling so foolish now. What must he have thought of me? Some wide-eyed idiot who didn't have the etiquettes befitting a princess!' Sita groaned in self-admonishment.

'A wide-eyed, lovelorn idiot,' Urmila corrected teasingly.

'Don't!' Sita begged. 'I have never felt so utterly stupid and incompetent before! And how did you guess it was love?' she demanded indignantly. 'Here I am trying to assimilate my feelings and there you go, already jumping to this ridiculous conclusion!'

Urmila remained silent, her smile encouraging Sita to divulge further. 'Oh Urmila, what do I do? I don't seem to be able to understand anything for the past three days!' she said, in open bewilderment. 'I saw him again today and I ran from there and have been sitting on the verandah steps for an hour trying to catch my breath and get back to my senses. I can't seem to think straight. There was a strange, strong pull I felt for him which I simply could not wish away. It was magnetic, mesmerizing... It is a spell I can't seem to break off!' she cried as if in pain but there was a serene glow about her, the first flare of love shining in her eyes, lighting up her face.

It took Urmila's breath away. She could merely stare in amazement at the plight of her sister. Could one meeting be so potent? So completely overwhelming? So irresistible, overpowering and devastating?

'Will you please come with me to the temple tomorrow morning?' Sita asked in a small voice. 'I know you are not too fond of visiting the temple but I guess I shall feel a lot braver if you are there...'

'...In case you bump into him again?' Urmila said mischievously. 'This time, please improvise, and plan, write and memorize what you are going to say to him.'

'No, but I shouldn't be meeting him, should I?' Sita asked suddenly, getting up in nervous apprehension. 'I should not be. I am supposed to be getting married in a week's time and what am I doing thinking about a stranger? Why can't I stop thinking of him?' she cried in self-mortification. 'This is madness! What am I thinking of?' She said in utter despair.

'Calm down, Sita, you have done nothing wrong!' Urmila

shook her elder sister gently. 'You are getting agitated and self-flagellating for an imagined crime.'

'You can't stop going to the temple because there may be a slim chance that you might meet him, can you? So let's take tomorrow as it comes—we go together to the temple and I shall pray for you too!'

The dawn was soft and pink, leisurely changing into flaming yellow and oranges as the sun rose late into the winter sky. Mandavi and Kirti were surprised to see Urmila accompanying them to the temple and insisted on knowing the reason. Urmila could not think of a quick retort or a reply that would assuage the collective curiosity of her probing cousins.

'Getting rid of my sins,' Urmila murmured tactfully.

'How did you get religious suddenly?' Mandavi demanded. 'You are more the freethinker—who doesn't believe in rituals and rites. Or is it that you have caught Sita's fever of searching for a groom?'

Sita coloured a delicate pink. 'That's a downright tasteless remark!' blustered Urmila.

Mandavi grinned wickedly. 'In fact, I think all the three of us should pray for the most suitable husband from henceforth—after Sita, we will be in quick reckoning!'

The early morning prayers and aarti done, the four girls collected the prasad and started to walk back to the palace. Running down the temple steps, trying to warm herself against the morning chill, Urmila started walking briskly through the fragrant, flower-laden garden. She stopped abruptly when she heard Sita gasp softly beside her.

She looked up and there they were, standing tall, still and silhouetted against the fast rising sun, as if they, too, were waiting for them to come into full view. And Urmila realized why Sita had been feeling guilty—there was a strong trace of stealth and a furtive anticipation at each step which got them closer to the two waiting youths.

'Oh, there are the two princes of Ayodhya!' Kirti exclaimed animatedly.

'Hush!' Mandavi whispered furiously.

Oblivious of the sotto voce exchange of words behind her, Urmila was more keen on observing Sita's expressions. She had faltered and fallen back, her head lowered, drawing the shawl closer. Urmila realized she was leading the pack with her sisters and the retinue of maids trailing her. Now it was up to her to either ignore them or walk past...but that would be blatantly discourteous. The other alternative was to stop and greet them. She decided upon the latter.

The two young men were already bowing their heads, their hands folded together in salutation. She did the same and hoped the girls behind her were doing the same as well. 'Greetings! Welcome to Mithila!' she said politely. 'I am Urmila, and here are my cousins Mandavi and Kirti, and my sister Sita.'

'Greetings to you ladies,' Prince Ram said softly and smiled. 'And good morning again, O princess of Mithila,' he said looking straight at Sita. Urmila could almost hear Sita's heart breaking with joy. 'I am Ram and this is my younger brother Lakshman.'

Urmila glanced swiftly at him in polite acknowledgement. The other man bowed stiffly, and unlike his brother, his face was immobile, frozen in cold hauteur.

'I had heard Mithila was one of the most beautiful cities of the country but I refused to believe that there could be a city prettier than our lovely Ayodhya. But I was wrong; Mithila is beautiful. And so are the people. And the kind hospitality of the king and the queen,' he said pointedly, with a gracious smile.

It was not mere polite conversation or idle small talk; he was praising Mithila with genuine conviction. His charm did not ring false and his easy, affable sincerity was heartwarming.

Ram was as handsome as he was renowned to be. Tall and athletic, a bow or a sword would have become his stature more than the basket of flowers he was carrying right now. Yet he did not appear ludicrous, carrying it with an easy grace and dexterity. However, one could not say the same about his brother. Lakshman stood rigid and unsmiling as the short conversation flowed between Ram and her. He looked distinctly impatient, his lips curled in slight annoyance. He was as tall as Ram, slimmer and more lithe and unbelievably handsome in a craggy way; but without the likeable, pleasing good looks of his elder brother. He had a saturnine, chiselled face with a thin, crooked nose and deep, smouldering eyes, but the perpetual, glowering frown marred his handsomeness. He stood taut and wired, as if ready to spring at the slightest pretext. He suddenly looked at her with his dark, piercing eyes and she felt herself go warm, then cold. It was not his eyes, darkly luminous and jet black, but it was the regard. His gaze seemed to go right through the bone. Urmila shivered. What a decidedly odd, unlikely pair. She saw he was bowing stiff again as if to get away from the chatter as fast as he could. She bowed her head, her eyes frosty, and turned away from the two brothers, but not before she caught a look being exchanged between Sita and Ram. Urmila took her sister's arm and pulled her away, and the four girls continued their way back to the palace. They walked in discreet silence, hesitant to talk in the presence of the whispering maids.

The moment they were in the safe confines of the inner chamber, the mood altered noisily.

'So that was the reason for your unusual presence at the temple, you wanted to meet the princes!' Mandavi accused Urmila.

Urmila bristled. The encounter with the younger prince had left her in a decidedly volatile mood and Mandavi's comment fuelled the fire within her. But before she could explode, Sita came swiftly to her rescue. 'It was I who dragged her out—I didn't want to go to the temple alone. I wasn't sure if the two of you would wake up on time as you slept late last night looking up the wedding feast menu,' she explained smoothly.

Urmila was reassured but just for a short while.

'Presumed innocent,' riposted Mandavi sweetly. 'But thus we got to meet the young princes at last. They are both fine looking...' she paused dramatically. 'But did you happen to notice it too, Kirti, that there was this...ahem, little something unfurling right under our noses? And our sisters here actually believe we didn't notice anything amiss!'

There lingered a long silence in the room, with each expecting the other to start talking. Finally, Sita broke the uncomfortable stillness, stifling the room. 'I really don't think I want to confer about the princes,' she said stiltedly. 'The fact that they are still here makes it clear that they have been invited by father for my swayamvar. This means they are my suitors; so it's best I do not discuss them,' she enunciated each word with a certain forcefulness uncharacteristic of her. But she laced it so beautifully with dignity and elegance that they were shorn of any aggressiveness. That was the magic Sita had, Urmila thought, marvelling at her sister's composure when she knew she was breaking from within. She watched her quietly leave the room, leaving a trail of another painful silence.

'What's with her?' asked Kirti quietly. 'And Urmi, please don't tell us it is prenuptial nerves. Besides, Sita is too composed and well-behaved to throw tantrums.'

Urmila remained silent, her lips thinned in a stubborn line. She would not talk for Sita. Mandavi immediately recognized her mood.

'Don't say it, Urmi,' she said. 'But I think I know what Sita is going through. She's clearly upset about her wedding...and her feelings. We shall not intrude. If she wants to confide in us, she will.'

'She will...but only to Urmi,' nodded Kirti astutely.

'So that's that!' Mandavi commented wryly.

'So that's not that!' retorted her younger sister. 'I am sure we shall meet the two princes again on our way to the temple tomorrow. So, is Sita planning to stop visiting the temple till her wedding day?'

Urmila knew the reply to Kirti's sardonic question but she had no answer to the uneasy feelings kindled at the mere mention of the word 'princes'. And that one prince in particular with his intense, blazing eyes.

Sita was in a worse state than the last time when they had had a similar conversation. But this time Urmila had her private fear to deal with, too, and it would take an effort on her part not to reveal her feelings to her sister. But the spin was, Urmila thought with dry humour, that now she just might be able to identify with her sister better in their common emotional affliction. Sita, anyway, had worked herself into such a state that she would not have noticed her younger sister's turmoil.

'Did the others guess?' she asked frantically, the moment Urmila stepped inside the room. 'Did you tell them anything?'

'I think they are getting a fair idea...' Urmila started slowly, '...and they will eventually make an intelligent inference but I assure you, I haven't and will not divulge anything,' she promised.

'I know you won't! You are so fiercely loyal and honourable! But right now my feelings are neither...and I hate myself for being so transparent about it,' cried Sita. 'But with each passing day, I so dread the day of my swayamvar! I have fallen in love with a man whom I know nothing about! And what if I were to marry some other stranger who manages to lift that heavy bow? I tremble at the thought...how can I marry some man when I love another?'

'Is that why you are getting so hysterical with worry?' Urmila laughed dismissively and went up to her older sister. 'Now listen to me carefully. The man you have fallen in love with at first sight is no stranger—he is the prince of Ayodhya and the world is singing praises of his feats, his valour, his goodness and his good looks, of course!' she teased, hoping to bring a smile on her sister's worried face. Sita dimpled engagingly. 'Think clearly, Sita. There must be a reason why Rishi Vishwamitra got him to Mithila. And now, since he has been invited to stay on for your swayamvar, I am sure he is the suitor who will win your hand; he is the one who will break that bow! He is *your* prince, princess!'

'Is he? Will he be mine?' Sita smiled tremulously. 'Will your words really come true? I don't know what I'll do if...'

'Shh!' Urmila placated her elder sister reassuringly. 'My words will come true...you will watch them happen! So, enjoy this day and the days to come—they are going to be the best!'

Urmila noticed her words were having the desired effect on Sita. She looked a lot calmer. Urmila was taken aback when a pair of slim arms was flung around her and she was folded in a close embrace. Sita was rarely effusive about her feelings; and she never cried.

'O Urmi, what will I do without you?' sobbed Sita, the words flowing as swiftly as the tears down her cheeks. 'You have an answer for everything...'

Sita could not go on as the enormity of the circumstances slowly dawned on her. For the first time, she was aware of a new harsh reality—that she would be separated from her younger sister and she would be leaving her soon for a different world. Urmila might have been the younger sister, younger just by a year, but for Sita, she was her anchor who secured her to a comforting veracity of her own existence. Urmila was her lifeline, she was her soulmate.

As their adopted daughter, Janak and Sunaina had fawned on

Sita to the point of being slavish. She had been embarrassed by it, squirming uneasily at the gratuitous affection lavished unduly upon her. Her upbringing had not been normal; she could not recall a single instance when she had been scolded or frowned upon. Urmila had suffered all of that and taken it with a brave smile on a trembling chin. Sita had been hailed as Janaki, Janak's daughter, when it was Urmila who was his daughter and the sole proprietor of that name. Sita was Maithili, the princess of Mithila, when it was Urmila who should have been crowned with that title. But never had Sita seen Urmila resentful about all the favours showered upon her, when she was deprived of them. Sita had never dared to discuss this with Urmila as she might not have liked it. She had kept quiet and taken in all the outpouring of love and adoration without letting anyone know how she felt— that it still did not make her one of their own. It left her, instead, feeling like an outsider. She could never forget that she was a foundling; and that she was indebted to them forever. That feeling of obligation was enormous; a burden she silently carried and could never shrug off. However, Sita could not remember even one instance when either her parents or her sisters had ever made her feel unloved.

Instead, by bestowing too much, they had made her feel too special. All of them but Urmila; she was the only one who treated Sita 'normally'—like a sister would another. Urmila had screamed at her, pulled her hair, pinched her, argued bitterly and each time, it had been Urmila who had earned the ire of her parents. Praise was reserved for Sita, though it was invariably Urmila who picked up the Vedic verses more quickly than her sisters.

Sita recalled each of these moments and they made her angry—all of them had been undeniably unfair on her younger sister. Her younger sister...Sita repeated the words in her mind with renewed fondness; Urmila had always been the veritable older sister all through their growing years—strong, fiercely protective like a tigress shielding her from everything, guiding her, helping her, consoling her. Her parents' love had been smothering and the sweetest memories she carried was of her younger sister. Each tender gesture was like a picture painted lovingly in her mind—Urmila hugging her tightly each night before going to sleep to dispel her nightmares, kissing her tears away when she had fallen from a branch or like this moment, trying to show her a better world than she could ever imagine. Sita wondered in sudden despair how she would be able to disengage herself from her sister's comforting existence, her rooted reality which she would have to extricate herself from.

Urmila was close to tears herself, but she kept them in check, refusing to crumple. Sita suddenly seemed to have realized the enormity of the situation but for Urmila, her sister's impending marriage had been a torturous thought, an unpleasant eventuality. Her sister was going to get married; she couldn't find herself feeling gorgeously happy about it. That dull ache in her heart would not let go of her. The thought of parting was more excruciating than the happiness of the occasion. Was she being selfish? No, she was just so dejected, Urmila quickly self-analysed. She was having an agonizingly bittersweet time: excited yet secretly sorrowful while she prepared for her sister's grand wedding. But the presence of the intruding prince was mercifully distracting.

For five successive days, it happened the way Kirti had shrewdly envisioned—they kept meeting the two princes at the garden each morning. But conversation expanded into nothingness, filled instead with the customary silent greeting and cursory smiles; and evocative looks. Each time Ram smiled, Sita bowed her head to hide the rising colour. Was it bashfulness, discomfiture or plain guilt of the secret love she harboured for this man?

Urmila was feeling similarly wretched. She tried to hide the awkwardness by bowing her head lower in courtesy but each time, she hated herself for trying to steal a furtive glance at the younger brother. And each time, she found his hard eyes on her, his open, unblinking gaze, washing her in a flood of mixed emotions. Urmila was proud of the fact that she was not shy but she found her nerves suddenly failing her and the intended words freezing in her mouth. She felt her throat and mouth go dry and her tongue instinctively moving sensuously on the parched lips. What was she doing, she thought desperately, watching his expressions change. Her face flaming, she moved away, turning her face from him and from a new, overpowering reality she was finding difficult to assimilate.

She felt a reassuring grip on her upper arm. She turned to meet Mandavi's steady gaze. She knew.

'Isn't Prince Ram wonderful? He is so kind and courteous!' gushed one of the maids.

'Yes, but why does the younger prince frown constantly? He seems to be always angry and scowling,' giggled another.

Mandavi's stern look silenced their chatter immediately and forbade further talk. Urmila could feel his eyes boring into her retreating figure and she felt a frenzied urge to turn around and look at him. But she did not. She found herself waiting for the next morning to see him again.

THE SWAYAMVAR

Urmila's words seemed to have worked their magic on Sita; she looked neither impassive nor morose, the twin emotions that had been afflicting the bride-to-be the previous week. She was her expected composed, collected self, wearing a bright smile.

She was sitting down, her slim hands resting on her lap, her eyebrows slightly raised in expectation, her self-assured smile in place. She tugged at Urmila's hand and whispered, 'Urmi, as you always do, you promised me a new hope.' And her eyes, discreetly through her long lashes, travelled to where Ram was sitting in the huge raj sabha where the swayamvar was being organized.

The hall was exactly the same as Urmila remembered it. Long and stretched as she had found it when she had dared to enter the forbidden place so many years ago. Urmila hadn't had the courage to step inside it ever again. Even now, through adult eyes, the hall appeared vast and overwhelming. The long rows of high columns, the high domed ceiling from which dropped down a most exquisite, huge chandelier flickering the side walls with strange shadows, even as the late morning light entered the room through a series of long windows in the aisles. And in the middle of the long hall, was the Shiv dhanush—worshipped by her father—the divine bow of Lord Shiv given by Sage Parshuram to one of her father's ancestors to look after while the famous rishi performed his penance. Rishi Parshuram was known to be very fond of the Rudra bow as it was presented by Lord Shiv himself to the rishi for his penance and devotion. Keeping this in mind, Urmila's ancestor and many after him had vigilantly kept the bow in safe-keeping for many decades. That bow remained locked in a strong iron casket in a latched armoury room where no one was allowed to enter—a rule that Sita and she had dared to break once and had never been able to forget their reckless temerity ever since. It was eight and a half feet long and had to be carried on an eight-wheeled carriage and dragged like a temple chariot even if it had to be moved within the hall. Today it had been displayed in public and King Janak had declared that whoever could string this bow of Rudra would marry his elder daughter, Sita. The sight of the great dhanush still made Urmila wonder how Sita had managed to lift it using her tiny, ten-year-old wrist. The sight had been blinding and Urmila shivered at the memory.

The image of her father bowing and looking up reverently at the little Sita flashed through her mind and Urmila felt a strange knot within her. Was Sita special? Or more specifically, did she have special powers? Urmila had not been able to clear this doubt which had bothered her all through her growing years and today, she was again faced with the same question. Her parents had resolutely considered Sita unique and extraordinary but Urmila had always assumed it was because Sita had been an adopted child and hence the shower of ceaseless attention and affection. But their love had always been deferential—it was almost close to worship. That is why Urmila was never jealous or angry; she simply felt awe at her parents' veneration for her elder sister. Urmila found this distinctly odd coming from her parents who were in other ways the most intelligent, sensible beings, devoid of any superior airs or fatuous truculence, often associated with royal hauteur.

Her father Seeradhwaj Janak was, besides being powerful, a hugely popular king and was affectionately called simply King Janak—the family name of the dynasty which had been ruling Videha for so many centuries from Mithila, the beautiful capital city. Urmila still found his popularity quite overwhelming and as a child she used to beam with a certain smugness when the crowds cheered and bowed their heads in collective homage wherever he went. But her parents had reigned in her pride by teaching her lessons in humility. Privileged did not mean special; just fortunate. And fortunes could change in a flash, they warned.

Janak was a striking personality—tall, thin, aristocratic with a long, hooked nose and a neatly trimmed silver beard which showed his age truthfully. His face was creased, not with worry, but with light age lines marking years of wisdom. Janak was no ordinary king; he was a renowned rishi as well, the favourite pupil of the famous sage Yajñavalkya, the author of *Shukla Yajurveda*, as also Sage Ashtavakra, from whom he learnt about the soul and the true nature of the self. Janak was the royal sage, rajrishi, who was well-versed in the Vedas and shastras and as spiritually advanced as other rishis. He was a king who believed in the discipline of action and selfless philanthropic service to mankind. He never turned away from his responsibility of administrating the kingdom of Videha with kindness and humility. And today, while the yagna was still going on, Janak was hosting a different ceremony—the swayamvar of Sita, graced with the presence of the bravest and most famous kings of the country.

Urmila looked at her sister more closely, trying to recognize the special powers within her. She was sitting with her arms folded, her head tilted to one side, as she often did. Not in her favoured light pastel shades today, she was instead attired in rich, deep yellow silks, adding a golden glaze to her etherealness.

Unlike most princesses who looked lost and weighed down by the heavy, elaborate, glittering gem-studded jewels at their wedding, Sita, with her delicate gold-filigreed ornaments, was the very embodiment of earthy elegance. This was the swayamvar of the princess for whose hand kings, emperors and princes from within the country and even outside were competing against each other.

Thinking of faraway lands, Urmila's eyes sought out a tall, strapping, lumbering figure amongst the host of kings present in the hall. It was that of Ravan, the emperor of Lanka, whose presence had created a furore in the raj sabha. She spotted him soon enough, sitting close to her father. She wondered what he was talking about so seriously with her father. But he was supposed to be an exemplary scholar too, Urmila acknowledged, having done her homework well, with valued inputs from Mandavi as well, on all the suitors vying for Sita's hand in marriage.

Ravan was an accomplished scholar, keenly knowledgeable in the Vedas, music—he played the veena splendidly it seemed—and abstruse subjects as assorted as astrology, architecture, Ayurveda and political science. He was said to be the mightiest of all kings and it showed lavishly. From the sparkling jewels, dripping about him and his resplendent crown which dwarfed her father's simple one to ignominy, Ravan looked as dazzling as all the gems he was splattered with. He was immensely tall, almost gigantic, dwarfing all those around him. He looked and seemed powerful, his massive shoulders magnifying the effect. He was handsome, Urmila acknowledged with a discerning eye, but not regularly good looking. It was his overpowering personality that was so arresting that set him apart from the others. He was renowned—he knew it, he looked it and amply showed it. He had brazenly announced that he would be the first one to string the bow, silencing any protests and ruling out any opposition or contest.

Urmila heard Sita gasp and she patted her hand reassuringly. She saw Sita's eyes wander towards Ram, sitting at the opposite end, between Vishwamitra and his younger brother. Urmila had promised herself that she would not glance at Lakshman, hardening her heart and her resolve to keep her eyes away from the brooding prince throughout the swayamvar but she had broken her self-imposed decree in just a matter of minutes.

'When will the ceremony start?' she mumbled, her edginess escalating.

Beside her, Sita appeared serene and poised, but her hands were clenching hers hard as they watched Ravan amble towards the bow. Ravan, like Ram, was an unanticipated visitor and her father and the other kings and princes had been none too pleased at his arrival. But courteous civility prevailed and protocol followed. Ravan was given the first chance to string the mighty bow.

He sauntered across with an air of aggressive defiance and unconcealed arrogance. But he bowed chivalrously before her father and Sita, before he folded his hand in silent veneration. With eyes peacefully shut, his hand folded and his head bowed, Urmila saw him murmuring a mantra. He must be praying to Shiv, she thought. Ravan considered himself Shiv's most faithful devotee.

Saying his brief prayer, Ravan bent down to lift the mighty bow, clasping it firmly in his big hands. It did not move an inch. There was a thick silence. He gripped it more firmly this time and tried to heave it; it did not budge. He tried yet again; he could not nudge it. The most powerful king in the raj sabha could not believe his eyes. He gave a roar of rage and used both his hands to haul it up but he was left grabbing hard at the bow instead.

To Urmila's flamboyant mind, it was a rather funny sight to see such a big, conceited king with his massive frame and his gems-blazing crown bent low on his knees, grappling ineffectually with an inert, horizontal bow that refused to be moved around.

Urmila bit her lip, enjoying the sight of the fallen king. Her dancing eyes went over to the others in the hall. Most looked perturbed. Ram, she noticed, was watching silently, his face composed, a slight frown furrowing his eyebrows. His companions, though, looked evidently amused. Vishwamitra had a small grim smile while the younger prince was suppressing a devilish grin, his eyes for once sparkling, not with jaded annoyance, but with unconcealed laughter. It changed him completely, making him look younger and amiable, flooding his face with unmitigated charm and a glowing cheeriness, wiping out any trace of his characteristic frown. Urmila was mesmerised at the transformation.

Mandavi nudged her warningly. Urmila looked down, her face scarlet, the bubbling smile immediately drying up. Had she been staring at him too long? Ravan was apoplectic with unbridled anger by now. He was still struggling with the bow and after another agonizing hour-long minute, he finally surrendered. He looked up, and had the grace to look regretful but his next words tainted the fleeting graciousness.

'With folded hands, I admit defeat that I cannot move the sacred Shiv dhanush,' he said superciliously. 'I must have fallen short in my penance to Lord Shiv that I could not do what I was asked to. But this I do know, that if I cannot move it, none present in this room can. So, King Janak, do you wish your daughter to remain unmarried? Because no one in this room will be able to string the bow—it is impossible to even shift it. What sort of a suicidal condition have you laid for your daughter? Do you want her to remain a spinster?' he sneered. 'I would not wish that, sir, and despite everything, am ready to marry her.'

His sheer conceit took her breath away, as a tide of anger overtook Urmila. How dare Ravan insult her father and sister? Furious, she watched her mother's face go ashen in fear and worry. Her father remained calm.

'I regret that you were not able to string Rudra's bow, O king!

But as a Shiv devotee you would know that I shall have to continue with the condition I have placed,' he said firmly, his face tranquil and his eyes looking evenly back at Ravan. 'Have no fear, sir; my daughter will not remain unmarried and lonely as it would be truly an extraordinary man who will eventually wed her. I shall wait for such a man to string the bow.'

The anger in Ravana's glittering eyes suddenly died down and was replaced with contempt. 'You might have to wait for eternity or till your daughter grows old!' he snorted. 'We shall soon see...and I have no time now though I shall wait and watch till infinity for your daughter Sita to get married to some precious man who fulfils your impossible condition. Meanwhile, since I would hate wasting this visit, I would not mind marrying your other daughter; she is as ravishingly beautiful as the world claims her to be!'

Even her mild-mannered father was shocked at the words; he stood speechless with horror. Ravan had clearly uttered those insulting words to salvage his broken pride. They were the defeated words of a crushed man who had lost his esteem and ego in harsh public glare.

Urmila felt his lascivious gaze on her. His eyes glittered wolfishly in his cruel, dark face. His open, blatant look made Urmila cringe but she lifted up her chin fiercely. She looked squarely up at him, her eyes sparkling with unsuppressed fury and loathing. It was a long, livid moment. And from the corner of her eyes, she thought she saw an angry movement. It was Lakshman, being restrained by Ram. Sita moved toward her sister protectively. Ravan's eyes turned to Sita.

'This humiliation has happened because of you. I shall never forget this day, fair lady. I will remember this...' He said softly, the tone menacing.

And saying his last, lingering words, he stormed out, leaving behind a pall of gloom. The mighty Ravan having been defeated, many disheartened kings followed suit and quietly left the raj sabha without daring a chance.

'Shall we begin again?' said Janak, requesting the others to be seated. 'The man who strings this extraordinary bow shall win my daughter's hand in marriage. Only then...' There was a stern note of warning in his words.

Many kings, princes and nobles obliged and attempted lifting the bow. None could push it even an inch. All returned to their seats, mortified and defeated. 'I have been saying this over and over again that the terms of this swayamvar are simply unattainable!' Mandavi broke in agitatedly. 'By now at least thirty princes must have tried their luck...even the powerful Ravan couldn't do it!'

'Mercifully,' retorted Kirti. 'Did you see how he looked at Sita? And Urmila? He is an ogre, that man!'

'But that doesn't moderate our predicament, does it?' snapped Mandavi. 'Who on earth will be able to lift that bow?'

'The lucky man,' Urmila said sharply. 'And he will be able to do the impossible. Don't worry, just watch on...'

Her assurances were principally for her mother whose eyes turned bleaker as each defeated suitor walked wearily back to his seat. Sunaina's worst fears were getting confirmed—there was no one good enough to marry her daughter.

There was a mounting sense of anger and frustration in the raj sabha as well. 'Is your daughter so unique that you have set upon us this impossible task?' asked one prince, heatedly. 'I agree to what Ravan claimed—that if not Princess Sita, we are ready to marry your other daughter!'

'...or the nieces.'

'O king, your stipulation for this swayamvar is absolutely hopeless and you well knew it was certain to fail. You are insulting our pride, our respect, our capability! If not your elder daughter, we demand that we be allowed to choose the other princesses in marriage instead!'

'Yes!' yelled another in agreement.

'I want to marry Princess Urmila!' a shout was heard from the crowd.

The strident voices joined as a furious refrain, the uproar deafening.

Urmila felt a cold shiver run down her spine; the situation was fast getting critical. She could think of no way of diffusing the latent hostility; nor any measure to protect herself from the antagonistic suitors. How was she going to save herself from this impending predicament? But seeing her father's wan face, her trepidation was replaced by swift indignation. She knew she would have to battle it alone—for herself and her sisters.

There was a rush of movement and Urmila saw the man who had occupied her heart, thoughts, passion and emotion for all these days getting up slowly, his hand at the scabbard of his sword, his face a dark mask of cold fury—Lakshman.

'What sort of a swayamvar is this where the princesses are being humiliated at every step?' he started heatedly. He walked forward, turning on each king who had chorused the hostile din earlier. He looked like a prowling lion, circling his victims.

'O kings and princes, you are honoured guests invited by King Janak for his elder daughter's swayamwar. But where is your sense of honour that you speak so disrespectfully, so rashly? And before you declare anything, there is still another suitor who has not had a chance to show his skills yet. Pray, kings, let me introduce all of you to my brother, Prince Ram of Ayodhya, the eldest son of King Dashratha!'

There was an abrupt silence and the irate protests of the kings died down suddenly as Ram stood up. He bowed to Vishwamitra to seek his blessings and walked towards the bow. He saluted Janak to obtain his permission and finally he bowed to the queen and the princesses.

The room was eerily still with all eyes on the young prince in hopeful anticipation. Ram peered into the iron case and touched the bow reverently. With his right hand, he clasped the bow at the centre and gently pulled and picked it up as if it were a delicate garland of flowers. An immediate image of the slight, small Sita holding the bow in her right hand flashed through Urmila's elated mind.

Lifting it high, Ram proceeded to rest one end of the bow against his big toe; he bent it and strung it, quickly drawing the string back. Urmila heard Sita gasp with unsuppressed delight and saw Ram throw Sita a long, exultant look. Probably he was distracted, his focus momentarily diverted or he had under-estimated his strength but with a swift, overpowering force, he pulled at the bow and it snapped like a dry branch with a booming clap like a flashing thunder streak.

Urmila could not describe the expression on Sita's face. It was luminous; her eyes softly glowing and the small, shy smile radiating her enormous, irrepressible joy.

As the high-ceilinged raj sabha broke into a happy pandemonium, a visibly ecstatic Sunaina brought out the pooja thali.

Urmila knew her mother had been very worried for the past several weeks about Sita. She had forever had severe misgivings about the clause her husband had decided upon but she scarcely showed her growing scepticism to the girls. Was there such an exceptional man who would be able to string the intimidating Rudra bow and marry her exceptional daughter? She had got her answer at last. He was standing there in person, tall, fair and handsome. Ram, the prince of Ayodhya. Her worries had vanished and she meant to celebrate. She took the pooja thali from Urmila's hand and smeared vermilion on Ram's forehead.

'God bless you,' was all she could murmur through her glistening tears. Sunaina was not an emotional woman and the tears rushing out dispelled a disquietude that had wracked her all these long years. She had lived in the constant anxiety that Sita would be rejected because she was a foundling; that she would be spurned on social grounds. And that is why she had doubled her efforts to assimilate Sita into the royal fabric and had declared her as Janaki, the daughter of Janak, and Vaidehi, the princess of Videha. Urmila, like any jealous child, had initially been resentful of this favoured show of affection but her mother had taken her aside and explained the new reality to her. Sita was the adopted child, her elder sister and she was never to be allowed to feel socially or emotionally bereft. But she loved her as much and even more and she was never to forget that too. Urmila had been all of seven years of age when she had been so informed and from that day, she had bid goodbye to childhood and grown up suddenly to a wiser maturity. Sita was her sister, not her competitor.

As Sita placed the garland over Ram's handsome head, there was a thunderous disruption. Swivelling her head toward the sound of the sudden interruption, Urmila saw the figure of a tall, towering man, a rishi, silhouetted against the framed doorway. Even from a distance, Urmila could guess that he was angry...rather, incensed. As he walked purposefully towards her father, each stride echoed with a violent belligerence. He was very old but his straight back and powerful arms seemed to wipe out the years. He was fearsome in appearance, with long, matted locks, a bow on one shoulder and a gleaming axe in his other hand. And when he spoke, the high-domed room seemed to tremble.

'Welcome back, Rishi Parshuram!' said Janak, folding his hands in deep veneration. This figure of livid wrath was Parshuram, Urmila's heart sank in dismay, the immortal chiranjeevi rishi whom no one on this earth could defeat. He was that *Brahmakshatriya*—the first warrior Brahmin—who had received a parshu, an axe, as his weapon from Shiv as a boon, and from where he had got his famous, dreaded name. The man who had triggered a genocide on twenty-one generations of kshatriyas twenty-one times over to avenge his father, Jamadagni's senseless murder by kshatriya Kartavirya Arjun.

'Who dared break the Shiv dhanush?' He growled, turning his glittering eyes toward Janak. The very sight of the mystic bow pitifully broken into two pieces seemed to fuel his fury further. 'This bow was given to me by Lord Shiv and I had handed it to your forefather, Devrata, to be kept in safe custody,' his said in his rasping voice. 'But today I see it splintered and smashed into pieces...Who is the culprit, Janak? He will not escape my wrath!'

'I am the culprit, sir,' said Janak self-effacingly, trying to propitiate the angry rishi. 'I decided to keep this sacred bow as a test of worthiness for the suitors of my daughter Sita who were asked to lift and string the bow. None were successful, not even the mighty Ravan. But this young prince of Ayodhya, Ram, did it!'

'But why was the bow the object of contest? Did you not know it was hallowed?' the rishi thundered.

'Yes I did, sir,' her father said steadily. 'But many years ago, Sita, then a child, while playing with her sisters, had accidentally picked it up—so easily...'

'It otherwise took a hundred people from the palace to move it...' her father continued in polite earnestness, '...and taking this incident as a good omen, I decided to make the bow the coveted prize of her swayamvar. He who could string the bow could marry her. But it would take an incomparable man to do that.'

'And my brother is that unparalleled man, the only one to pick up the bow when others could not even move it,' intervened Lakshman, stepping forward and bowing courteously to the enraged rishi. 'But in the process of being strung, the bow snapped in half since it was old...' he elaborated in explanation, attempting to make him see reason.

His remark, instead, infuriated the sage even more. His face flushed red, the blood rushing to his head and gleaming eyes. Urmila saw him flexing his fingers and re-arranging his hold over the axe. Grasping the dangerousness of the situation, she was quick to understand that this would lead to bloodshed. Parshuram would not hesitate to kill Lakshman. She had to intervene. No one dared to confront the rishi when he was an imposing inferno of rage but Lakshman had done the unthinkable.

Urmila could feel the fear leaping at her throat; she was gripped by an unknown terror for the man she loved...there, she had said it! In her most horrifying moments, she was admitting to it at last. Her heart beating wildly, Urmila knew she was ready to face the full fury of the rishi—anything to save Lakshman from the bloody fight from which he would never escape alive. Quaking inside but with unfaltering steps, she went up to Parshuram and with her head bowed, her eyes beseeching, her hands folded, she sought his blessings.

'We are indeed blessed by your visit,' she started softly, her eyes steady. 'Sir, you must be tired...please take a seat and rest.'

Saying this, she bent down to touch the sage's feet, hoping desperately her ploy had worked in distracting the angry man. The rishi instinctively murmured, 'Bless you, princess. May your husband live in your lifetime!'

Realizing the full impact of his words, Urmila stepped back, hoping frantically Lakshman would now be safe from the rishi's wrath and his brandishing axe.

The sight of Lakshman, with his faintly arrogant expression, though, refuelled the rishi's rage. 'You audacious young man, how dare you dismiss the bow so impertinently? I can easily behead you with my parshu!' He shouted, swinging his axe.

A surprised but a likewise belligerent Lakshman retaliated and took out his sword, ready to tackle the rishi. But when the rishi turned to confront Lakshman, he was unable to lift his axe, and his arm froze. The rishi looked amazed and a sudden comprehension hit him. He was being held back by his own words. There was a frozen second of realization as the impact of his words sunk in. He turned to Urmila, but before he could say or do anything further, Ram interceded.

'O, greatest of all rishis, I am the reason for your just anger,' he stated, bowing before the sage. 'Please forgive my brother, he is innocent. He is only trying to protect me as he always does, and will lay down his life, before any harm can befall me. But it was I who strung the bow, and in my carelessness, broke it in two. And by doing so, I won the fair hand of the fair princess. O sir, please forgive me for my rashness, please give us your blessings.'

The great Vishwamitra rose from his seat. Seeing him, Rishi Parshuram instantly mollified and bowed low to his grandfather, touching his feet in due reverence. 'Yes, grandson, please pardon the young men for their recklessness for they now seek your blessings,' entreated Vishwamitra. 'You are a famed Brahmin. Having killed all the kshatriyas you have avenged the death of your father, my nephew, Jamadagni, my sister's son. You went back to your tapasya, as is the natural order, to cleanse yourself from the vengeful wrath. Then, pray, why are you bloodying your hand again by proposing to kill this young prince who is much loved by all and is to be the groom of Janaki, Janak's daughter? Please refrain!'

Parshuram folded his hands in supplication. 'Forgive me grandsire, I now realize these princes are your protégé. You are the one who has taught them the devastras, the celestial weaponry of bal and adibal. You have trained them in philosophy and advanced religion, and guided them to kill the most fearsome of demons like Taraka and Subahu.'

'And led them to this hall for the swayamvar of Sita. For Ram to see the Shivdhanush,' smiled Vishwamitra gently. 'There was a reason.'

But Parshuram's face hardened visibly, unmoved by his grandfather's plea. 'I have been hearing paeans about this young prince. If this young man is so supreme and unrivalled as you insist, that he could break the Shiv bow, I challenge him now with my other bow, the Vishnu bow—the one given to my father Sage Jamadagni by Lord Vishnu. Vishwarkarma, the holy architect of the Universe, made two exactly similar bows. One was given to Lord Shiv and the other to Lord Vishnu. This is the bow as powerful as the one you just broke. I challenge you to string this bow. It will be a test of your skill and strength and if you succeed, I shall honour you by giving you a chance to fight a duel with me!'

'I accept your challenge, sir. Please give me your bow,' said Ram and reached out to seize the bow of Vishnu from the rishi's unwary hands. He swiftly strung it, placed an arrow and pointed it straight at the rishi's heart.

'Now what will you give me as a target to this deadly arrow in exchange for your life?' He asked calmly.

Rishi Parshuram looked stunned, his eyes incredulous, his mighty arms listless as if sapped of their strength. The mystic parshu crashed to the floor from his limp fingers with a loud clatter. And what followed was a spectacle that left all onlookers speechless.

The elderly rishi was a changed man. Bowing low, almost on his knees, paying homage to the young prince of Ayodhya, he was a subdued man, drained of his glory, arrogance and fury, and radiating from him instead was a kindly serenity now.

'I now realize who you are. You, my lord, are my superior, my successor,' he murmured in great deference. 'From now on, I devote my tapasya to you. I shall return to my hermitage at Mahendra Parvat and continue my penance. Let the arrow which you have now aimed consume all my powers, my tapas, and let it all go to you.'

With these last words, Parshuram reverentially walked around the prince and left the raj sabha, a far cry from his dramatic, strident entry a little while ago. Deferentially, Ram, with the Vishnu bow still in hand, pointed the arrow up to the sky and shot it straight above, cutting a lightening swathe through the dispersing clouds.

Everyone in the hall went still. Sunaina was the first to break the strained silence.

'Shall we continue with the ceremony?' She said gently, a pleased smile back on her face. Taking the cue, Ram and Sita, as a couple, bent down to touch her feet and seek her blessings. Janak, the much relieved father, made a quick announcement. 'My dearly loved child, my daughter Sita, shall be wedded to Prince Ram of Ayodhya!' He proclaimed and the rejoicing began outside the palace walls too.

Urmila was still trembling from the close shave and darted a quick look around her, hoping none had noticed her escapade. Now that she had acted upon her mad impulse at the raj sabha, she had exposed her feelings. And while Lakshman had saved her from a violent predicament, so had she, snatching Lakshman from death. In saving each other, they had, inadvertently, professed their love for each other, a love they had denied for long, even to themselves.

Had anyone noticed this? Her father was smiling. So was her mother, and her cousins looked excited, clustering around Sita. Sita was a pretty picture of bliss. Ram stood tall and pleased, and behind him she saw a pair of smouldering eyes watching her intently. They were not furious, but fierce; they looked tormented. She could see them darkening with an indiscernible emotion; she could not figure what but she felt a curl of pleasure. Nervously, she tucked a wick of hair behind her ear, her eyes staring at him unseeingly. And in the midst of the joyful revelry, everything went still around her. They hardly spoke to each other, preferring to let silence define their association, their relationship, their love. But it wasn't a union of silence between them; he seemed to speak to her with a look. He seemed to make love to her with his eyes.

A distant voice broke the lingering, lengthened spell. 'Dispatch the swiftest messenger to Ayodhya to tell the good news to King Dashrath and to invite him for the wedding!' She heard her father announce.

After a swift conference with Rishi Vishwamitra and Shatanand, the royal priest of Mithila, her father pronounced the date of the wedding. It would be the auspicious day of the Uttara Falguni nakshatra. That was just a fortnight from today.

THE LOVERS

It took about three days for the messenger of Janak to reach Ayodhya to confer the good news. Dashrath promptly sent back a message expressing his delight over the happy turn of events. And it took another three days for the messenger to return to Mithila bringing back the reply from Ayodhya. Those six days were perhaps the longest, the most confusing, and the most defining days in Urmila's life.

Urmila could not escape her sisters' persistently probing questions. 'You scarcely let any of us know of your feelings for Ram's brother,' Sita started in an openly accusatory tone. 'While here I was pouring my heart out about myself and Ram, you preferred to keep it all locked up as some secret...' She looked visibly hurt.

'You were too upset yourself,' Urmila riposted with a tired smile. But she was taken aback; had she been so transparent about her feelings for him? She had been fantasizing and fretting about Lakshman for the last so many days and now her sisters seemed to be all aware of her clandestine ruminations. 'But what makes you think...' she started indignantly.

'Not think, believe! And for all his scowls and chilly silence, he seems to have eyes only for you. Everyone here can see that except you!' snorted Sita derisively. 'He clearly likes you a lot!'

'Like? Now that would be the tamest understatement! Lakshman is quite besotted by her!' squealed Kirti in glee. 'All through the swayamvar I couldn't help but observe those intense looks that both of them kept trading! Not to miss how both came to each other's rescue at the nick of time. If that's not love, what is?' she sighed. 'Urmi, you can't deny that! Sita, when you met Ram in our garden, both of you enjoyed an immediate mutual attraction. At that very same time, what we didn't realize though, was that much was the same with these two as well! Even before your swayamvar, Sita, they must have engaged in a silent, for-your-eyes-only-courtship that we failed to notice. It was you and Ram who well occupied our mind and attention, but I think the next potential couple are Urmila and Lakshman—long before we could ever imagine them marrying!'

Mandavi refrained from adding to the chaffing banter. She gave Urmila a long, hard look; Urmila's strained smile hid some inner conflict which she was not yet willing to divulge. For all her freely vented bluster and bravado, Mandavi knew that Urmila rarely revealed her intimate sentiments. You could almost call her secretive, masking her feelings beautifully lest anyone intrude into her inmost realm of hidden thoughts. It was a defence Urmila had evolved since childhood.

She could sense Urmila's anxious embarrassment. Urmila, who otherwise possessed a liberal sense of humour and was a sporting victim of relentless bouts of teasing, looked ill at ease. If Urmila's current discomfiture was anything to go by, it must be because of some strain. She was tense but she did not want to show it.

'What perfect marriage mediators the two of you are!' Mandavi interceded, coming to Urmila's rescue. 'What about me, dears? Don't count me out. I am the same age as Urmi, so at the correct eligible age too! But I refuse to be silly and fall in love like Sita dearest. I would much prefer a handsome prince served to me on a platter—his kingdom, horses, palaces and gems, his good looks, passion and all! All I would have to do is garland my perfect prince. No falling in love for me, it's too much heartache, too many tears!' she shrugged airily.

'Hmm, you are too headstrong and hard-hearted to fall in love,' agreed Kirti scoffingly but there was no spite in her words. 'But let's hope you never have to take back these very words!'

Sita looked impatiently at all of them. 'So, shall I tell Ram and Father and ask them to do the needful?' she asked sweetly of Urmila, her eyes shining with a sudden hope. 'Oh, wouldn't that be wonderful? A double wedding...think of it! And we'll always be together...two sisters marrying two brothers! It couldn't get better! Oh, Urmi, I am so very, very happy for you—and for myself! It's the happiest day of my life...I was dreading that I shall have to leave you, Urmi, but now I'll have both my favourite people around me forever!'

Beaming with unconcealed joy, she hugged her younger sister tightly and long, as if to never let her go. Urmila could feel the joy bubbling inside Sita and did not have the heart to diffuse the euphoria. She might be sure of her feelings for Lakshman but she was still not certain of his reciprocation, whatever the sanguine claims of her moony-eyed sisters. Urmila felt a hot flush up her neck; she could still feel the heat of his look. How it made her blush and shiver with pleasure. It was like a wave: drowning and drenching her in its passionate whirl and leaving her bereft in anticipation as it ebbed. She was still unsure about him. That self-doubting, niggling fear did not seem to leave her, settling as a tight knot in the deepest corner of her heart.

After the swayamvar, Ram had settled in beautifully with the family, his charm disarming, his affection infectious. In an odd way, Urmila found both her elder sister and Ram incredibly alike. A single definition could well describe them both. They were both good-natured, friendly, and always cheerful. Their love was true and unhampered by false pride and self-importance. Urmila watched fondly as she saw them smiling, chatting and laughing together.

Were she and Lakshman also alike in temperament just like Ram and Sita? Sita's gentle spirit enhanced, by contrast, Urmila's fiery, contentious nature and Urmila recognized a similar parallel between these brothers as well—Ram's eager friendliness and good nature counterbalanced Lakshman's stiff hauteur. Mercifully, Ram and Sita were spared the common affliction that both she and Lakshman suffered and shared—the prickly egotism that stopped them from expressing their feelings for each other.

She was always very physically aware of his presence around her—his voice, his searing looks and his scent—even when he was standing a far distance away, cold, aloof and stern-faced. It left her with a cold anxiety; had she, after all, just imagined all that was said and unsaid through those deep, unfathomable silences? Were those torrid, stifling looks that left her breathless merely a fabrication of her fervid mind?

She saw him chatting with his brother a little distance away near the deserted pathway leading to the woods. He threw back his head and laughed. It was a rare, delicious sight. He had a nice laugh. And a nice, strong neck. Urmila had attempted desperately for some civil conversation but each time he had firmly thrust her away. She did not know whether to feel amused or affronted.

She approached him slowly. He was alone again, Ram leaving his brother's company for Sita's. Pursing her lips in slight displeasure, she politely handed him a cool glass of lemonade and played the good host. He took the glass and their hands touched; she felt a jolt of hot pleasure and withdrew her trembling hands but he held on, looking steadily into her eyes. Surprisingly, it calmed her and she could say what she had been meaning to tell him since the day of the swayamvar. She had yet not thanked him for rescuing her that day. 'I cannot thank you enough...' she said, trying to break the ice, '...for what you did. Had it not been for you, the angry suitors would have reacted even more violently. I shudder to think what might have happened...'

'I didn't do much—I was just letting them know that they were depriving my brother of the chance he was entitled to,' Lakshman cut her off curtly. 'And if it is about showing gratitude, I guess I am obliged to do the same. Princess, your ingenuousness managed to avert a bloody confrontation between me and the great Parshuram. You saved me from his terrible wrath and I am still alive today. You saved my life and I am eternally indebted!' he drawled languidly, in a pompous, self-aggrandizing manner. He did not seem either gracious or grateful and Urmila felt illogically hurt. She saw him bowing to her exaggeratedly and sauntering away, rudely cutting off any further conversation.

What was wrong with him? Or had she drawn the wrong conclusion? Was he deliberately infuriating her or was he simply insufferable? Urmila despaired how she could have fallen in love with such a person. She could not fathom his contradictory behaviour. Did he love her? He made her believe so, making feverish love to her with his eyes in those rare, precious moments. She could not forget that glimpse of his tortured face at the swayamvar, his emotions naked to her, or his jealous fury when Ravan had insulted her with his lewd stare. She remembered how he had rushed to her aid when she was threatened by the enraged princes. Was this not love, she sighed. Then why did he insist on being surly? Did she remind him of his folly? Was he a reluctant man in love?

The very next morning, she was to again question her irrational fascination for this enigma of a man. It was time to go for the daily puja at the Gauri temple and Sita was late. It was uncharacteristic of her elder sister to keep anyone waiting and Urmila decided to check her chamber. The bed was neatly made and Sita was not there. Urmila decided to ask the cousins if they had seen her. They were nowhere to be seen either. The girls must be all together, Urmila thought. She re-confirmed with the maids and was informed that Sita had left with her handmaids for the temple. Urmila cursed herself for being late herself and quickly hurried to catch up with her sisters.

She had walked for almost a furlong and entered the denser part of the garden when she spotted Sita. She was alone and Urmila was about to call out for her when she saw Ram walking down from a distance. Walking a little ahead of him was Lakshman, his steps brisk and alert. Suddenly she saw him pause, his right arm extended, warning Ram to stop in his tracks. She saw Lakshman swivel around, catch sight of the approaching Sita and without a moment's hesitation take aim at her and shoot her down with his arrow.

Urmila stood rooted, she could not scream; rage, fear and grief leapt at her throat. She saw Sita falling down in a bloodied heap, her hands clutching at the arrow piercing her heart. She screamed and ran toward her but Lakshman's compelling voice tried to stop her. 'Stop! Don't go near her!' she heard him shout urgently.

In agonized frenzy, she ignored his warning and continued to rush toward her wounded sister. Urmila heard the sound of running footsteps behind her and before she could whirl around, she found herself trapped by a band of powerful arms. She tried to wrench away but Lakshman was holding her down by her left arm, pressing her hard against him. 'Can't you hear me?' he rasped. 'Stay away from your sister!'

Urmila watched as Sita writhed in a pool of blood—the puddle spreading fast under her body.

'You killed her! Why? Why?' she spat at him.

She saw a dagger hanging at his waist as he still grappled with her, and snatching it with her right hand, she tried to thrust it in his neck, his shoulders, his back—anywhere she could reach and hurt him grievously to allow her to escape from his restraining grasp. But before she could stab him, he had pinned both her wrists, forcing them down so hard, that she was forced to let go of the dagger, seeing it fall weakly from her hands, its blade glinting in the early morning rays. Flashing a look of unbridled fury and loathing, she found herself staring back at his darkening eyes, his craggy face barely a few inches away from hers. She could feel his hot breath on her throat; he could sense her hatred and anger.

She wanted to scream at him, but the wordless scream was stifled in her dry throat. It was full of bubbling sobs instead, the tears coursing down her face.

'She is not Sita, Mila!' she heard him say softly, almost gently, his eyes tender. Urmila's eyes widened in shock. 'It's someone else in her guise,' he whispered, his face close. She squirmed as she felt his lips move on her skin. 'And I shall let you go if you promise not to attack me again with that brandishing dagger so that I can find out who did this,' he released her saying that, letting go of her wrists suddenly. Feeling strangely bereft and free from his warm hold, Urmila slowly straightened herself, her fingers rubbing her bruised wrists. She saw him stride purposefully toward the fake Sita and stood tall above the struggling body.

'Who are you?' he asked quietly, the venom in his voice deadly.

He got a gurgle for an answer. Lakshman did not wait for a reply. He smoothly shot a relentless arrow in the person's midriff. Urmila flinched as she heard a loud, agonized scream like the last, failing cry of a dying animal.

She heard fresh footsteps and looked up to see Sita dashing toward her, followed closely by her cousins. She sighed in quick relief—this was her Sita! Lakshman raised his arm high in warning, and the girls stopped running, standing close to Ram, who had been watching the spectacle mutely all this while. All of them were gazing down at Sita's lookalike. She was still gasping for breath, struggling to resume her original form. He was a demon, a dying, desperate demon.

His last shriek had got the guards and Janak hurrying to the site as well. Janak recognized the demon and was not surprised.

'Who is he, father?' asked Urmila urgently. 'What is he doing here?'

King Janak hesitated, he was hoping to brush it off but the intense stare of several pairs of questioning eyes forced him to elucidate. 'This man here is Banasur. He had sent me a message warning me against Sita's swayamvar,' he started slowly, 'then I received another message just yesterday to cancel the wedding. I guessed the demon clan did not want this marriage to happen but preferred to ignore it as a mere threat. I never could have imagined that he would come here to kidnap Sita. Or worse, kill, either Ram or Sita, or both!'

'That's a little difficult with Lakshman around!' said Ram heartily, clearly trying to ease the bleak mood. '...and as usual, my brave little younger brother saved the day for all of us!'

Janak was overwhelmed with gratitude. He turned to Lakshman and bowed to him. 'You have not just saved my daughters and my son-in-law; you have given me a new life. How would have I faced the world, my family and myself? You, young man, have averted a tragedy...and I shall be eternally indebted to you!'

Lakshman was evidently embarrassed but seeing the king overcome with feelings, he tried to reassure him. 'I did what I should have,' he said kindly, trying to assuage the king's face. 'We are family now and it is our duty to look after each other,' he affirmed, bowing before the king but not before sweeping Urmila a sardonic glance. She flushed; it was her turn to look embarrassed as she mentally relived their riotous confrontation a few minutes ago. She had jumped to an unfair conclusion, the consequence of which could have been tragic had it not been for Lakshman's quick presence of mind and his swift decisiveness in that moment of crisis.

'Sir, you should have let us know of these threats. You should not be worrying about your daughters any longer,' said Ram, his face grave. 'It is our responsibility to protect your family now. From here on, I promise to take care of all of you—and not just Sita.'

In the midst of their talk, no one had paid attention to the wounded demon. Before they could realize, he in his last effort, made a dash for the thick woods. Urmila expected Lakshman to prevent him from fleeing or wounding him further but he stood immobile, his eyes fixed at the retreating figure. She gave him a defiant, questioning look.

'Why did you allow him to escape?' she demanded.

'Princess, I think he got the right message, which he will convey to the people concerned,' he said softly. 'Unlike some...'

He deliberately left the sentence unfinished, the words hanging in the air accusingly. He stooped down and picked up his dagger which had fallen in the grass and put it back in the empty scabbard at his trim waist. 'Aha! This devious little thing with which you were ready to kill me! For what? Think!' he whispered softly, raising a quizzical eyebrow and walked away from her.

Urmila flushed in disconcertion, clenching her fists. She had barely recovered from the rough embrace as he had gripped her close, hard and warm against him. With a start, Urmila realized he even had an endearment for her. Mila, he had throatily murmured with passion blazing in his eyes. Urmila rolled the word in her mind—Mila, something that has been found and received, she said with relish.

But their conversation had left her fretting at his cryptic words. What was he trying to tell her? That she had been ready to kill him for her sister? She could not wipe away that tearing, troubling thought—had she elected her sister over him?

Urmila hid the red welts on her wrists wearing some extra bangles. Thankfully, none of her sisters noticed but she could not help but unconsciously touch the bruise each time she met Lakshman. He caught her once and threw her a knowing, sardonic look. It was taunting: questioning her about her feelings for him yet pushing her away from him. He insisted on staying away from her with aloof dignity, yet she often found him sidling a stray glance at her, as if he could not resist it.

Six days later, a messenger arrived from Ayodhya and Janak summoned the four girls for an immediate discussion. This was indeed not exceptional in the palace of Mithila. Janak always conferred, not just with his wife and younger brother, but with his daughters and nieces as well, before taking any major decision. It was a family tradition that all valued, appreciated and respected.

The moment she entered the room, Urmila anxiously examined the expressions and demeanour of the elders. They did not look grim enough; the news to be divulged would not be very bad. But her mother looked distinctly uneasy; the news to be divulge would not be that good either.

'King Dashrath expresses his delight over the good news of Sita's marriage to Ram,' Janak began, his tone amiable. He paused long as was his habit, often infuriating her impatient mother.

'But he has another request which, though very flattering, has left me in a quandary...' he again lapsed into a long pause. 'He has asked for the hand of the other three girls in marriage for his other three sons,' he said shortly. 'Chronologically, it is Lakshman for Urmila,' he paused watching the colour rise on his daughter's face; that meant a possible affirmative from his otherwise fastidious daughter. He smiled and that enigmatic smile told Urmila that her father realized her feelings for Lakshman.

'...Bharat for Mandavi and lastly, Shatrughna for Shrutakirti,' he continued. 'Since none of us have even seen the other two princes, he has duly sent across their portraits. You can, of course, look at them. What do you say, my princesses?' he asked, looking expectantly at each one of them. 'I have not given my reply yet for I wanted to know your opinion,' he said gently, but there was a ring of firmness in his voice. 'There is no pressure, please let me know how you wish it to be. It is up to you to decide. It is not mandatory that you abide by our wishes.'

'Is it your wish that we marry the princes?' Urmila asked succinctly.

'Honestly, I don't have anything against them. They are fine young princes—brave, noble and kind. I already know Lakshman. Frankly, I couldn't have found a better man for you, dear,' her father enthused. '...and he has stood up for you more than once, if I am right...,' he pressed on, his tone light, his eyes teasing, watching his daughter go vividly scarlet. 'So, he sufficiently qualifies to be a suitable son-in-law for me. He is infinitely better than any from that angry gang of princes who were out to seize you!' he said with mock horror. 'So, Urmila, do you agree with me that Lakshman makes for a fine groom for you?'

Not deceived by her father's light banter, Urmila knew he was seriously asking her to acknowledge her feelings, her free choice. She nodded slowly, her face breaking into a shy, lovely smile.

'Yes, I abide by your decision,' she said discreetly, but her heart was singing. She now had her parents' permission and her heart's sanction; it could not have been more legitimate.

'Now how about you, Mandavi? And Kirti?' asked Janak, turning to his nieces who were standing silently near Urmila.

Kirti walked to the tiny portraits of the princes kept on the carved table. She picked Shatrughna's portrait and stared at it for long. After a long minute, she quietly kept it down and nodded her consent.

'I can't fault him his looks. I would not mind marrying the prince,' she said, her voice firm.

'Are you sure? You have not even met him!' interrupted Mandavi sharply.

'From the stories I have heard, the four princes of Ayodhya are very alike—brave and clever, and above all, kind and respectful,' her younger sister argued wisely. 'I don't think I can get a better marriage proposal than this one. I accept.'

'Uncle, would it be ungracious of me to answer in a while? I need time to come to a definite decision. Honestly, I am confused...' Mandavi's voice trailed off uncertainly.

'Take your time, dear, you have a full day to make up your mind,' her father, King Kushadhwaj, assured her gently. 'Whatever your decision, we shall stand by it.'

'Yes,' agreed Janak. 'The decision is entirely yours. Let us know by tomorrow morning, dear.'

Sunaina had not spoken a word. Her brows were creased in consternation. She was a woman of strong opinions and did not hesitate to voice them. Her husband had profound respect for them and was often in agreement. That she had not uttered a word during this crucial conversation was not just unusual, it was worrisome. Were the senior members of the family hiding something from them?

Urmila decided to be upfront. 'Ma, aren't you happy with my decision?' she asked bluntly, staring at her mother.

Sunaina's worried face wreathed in a smile. 'Oh no, dear, not at all!' she exclaimed. 'I am as proud of Lakshman as of Ram being my son-in-law! And Bharat and Shatrughna are handsome young eligible princes that no princess in her right mind would reject!'

Mandavi tightened her lips, the subtle reprimand finding its mark.

'But you don't look as happy as you claim to sound,' Urmila persisted. 'I can sense a certain reluctance, some hesitation...What is it, Ma? What is troubling you?'

Her mother gave a helpless look and her doubt hardened. Janak interposed gallantly. 'Your mother has some reservations about this proposal...' he hesitated, his tone grave. 'Though the four princes are individually exceedingly suitable for each one of you, my little princesses, your mother is not too keen on the idea of four sisters marrying into the same family of four brothers. Her argument is that it would complicate the personal equation between you sisters, or your husbands respectively.'

Urmila suddenly recalled Lakshman's sardonic accusation that she had been ready to kill him for her sister and understood what her mother was worried about. Urmila knew her mother was not a woman controlled by sentiments; she was sensible even in the most trying moments of crisis. And right now, she was able to register her mother's gnawing misgivings. Sita was not convinced though.

'Ma, what could be better than us sisters getting married into the same family?' she questioned. 'That means we shall always be together—as sisters and sisters-in-law. What I had been dreading the most has been wonderfully averted! I shall not have to leave my sisters for my new family. Oh Ma, the most wrenching moment for any daughter on her wedding day is to say farewell to her parents and her home—to be separated from them forever. If I can take my sisters with me I would consider myself the luckiest of all girls! The thought of leaving you and father is breaking my heart...' she stopped, her voice tremulous. 'How could our staying together harm us? Will marriage lessen our love for each other? No, Ma, it shall strengthen it further, as no one knows us better. We love each other too much for anything or anyone to come between us.'

'And your husbands?' Sunaina asked sharply. 'If such a situation arises, and it will happen someday, sometime—before any one of you, where you are cornered into choosing between your husband and your sister, whom would you choose, dear?'

Sita looked perplexed. 'But why would it happen? My love for my sisters and my love for my husband would never clash, for, besides myself, both of them realize how deeply we feel for each other. Both would know that I love them unconditionally and both would think twice before causing such hurt. They would, rather, try to avoid such a crisis—something I can be assured of from my sister but not from a stranger sister-in-law. Oh Ma, having a sister for a sister-in-law is a boon! Don't ever worry about us. We shall look after each other beautifully, I assure you, I promise you!'

Sunaina smiled. 'I don't need your promise, dear. I am not doubting the affection you have for each other. It is the other way round. Will you be fair on your sister or your husband as the situation demands, or worse, will you be able to be fair on yourself for having to make that difficult choice?'

'Don't make it sound so ominous, Ma!' cried Sita. 'You are postulating a sequence of events which might or might not happen. I am confident they won't; we won't let it happen, shan't we, Urmi? Oh Urmi, say something!' she begged.

Urmila found herself at a loss of words. She wanted to say so much, her heart stirring with an uneasy intensity but she realized she agreed with both of them. Like Sita, she was certain of their love for each. But she could she drive away that unspoken fear that her mother was speaking of. Was this just their optimistic idealism speaking and would it hold true for the men? Would the brothers stand for each other and ignore their wives or would they be swayed by their love for their wives? The brothers collectively epitomised a transcendental bonding; would the sisters, as their wives, introduce a new polarity of authority and power?

Just a few days ago, she had been put to test on the choice she would make. And unthinkingly, blindly, she had opted for Sita, not believing or trusting Lakshman. In one insane moment, she had believed the worst of him and within that decisive second, her love for him had evaporated into hatred, which had not hesitated to kill him with his own dagger. In those terrible moments, Urmila had experienced the dilemma which her mother was so fearful about, and like her mother, Urmila did not like what it portended.

'What is to happen, shall unfold,' she sighed. 'Without intention, we are powerless in directing or determining what is to come. But in the present, let's not analyse and doubt the intensity of our love. I simply pray that we have the strength and convictions to make the right choice were such a situation forced upon us. And if it does, let us be brave enough to face the consequences!'

Her mother gave her a strange look, but Urmila also detected a trace of sadness which she found disconcerting. 'I am trying to warn you of what might await you, as a mother and above all, as a woman who has seen quite a few relationships change colour and conviction,' remarked Sunaina dryly. 'I know you well, girls. You are sensitive and sensible and I am so proud of you! I know you shall be strong enough to take the right decision and know how to live, and love.'

But for all her brave words, Urmila was not too sure about the terms their future would dictate on her and her sisters.

THE REJECTION

Mandavi, for all her pretentious claims, could not take her eyes off the portrait. Not that the portrait was a piece of art, discerned Urmila's critical eye, but the man in the portrait definitely was. After glancing at Shatrughna's miniature which Kirti seemed to be mooning over as well, Urmila concluded fairly that Bharat was the best looking of the brothers. Broad forehead, a pair of deep set eyes, a finely chiselled nose over perfectly shaped lips. He was incredibly good looking, a quality which any girl would find difficult to resist. Mandavi could not remain immune for long either and Urmila could well surmise that it would not take Mandavi long to accept the marriage proposal. King Dashrath had shrewdly known what he was about to accomplish when he had sent the portraits over with the letter. He knew the answer well before he finally received the expected reply in Janak's neat hand. The four princesses of Videha would be marrying the four princes of Kosala on the date already fixed. Just a week away and the twin cities of Ayodhya and Mithila burst into a frenzy of activity and euphoria.

Urmila found it wonderfully strange that just a few days ago, she was preparing for her sister's wedding and now she was going to be a bride herself! The sisters running errands till yesterday were today's brides-to-be. Getting pampered and fawned upon and being dolled and decked up was a delicious feeling; Urmila was enjoying the indulgence. The only dull spot was that she rarely got to catch a glimpse of the man she was soon to marry. She wanted to talk to him personally, and openly, about their official engagement but the series of pre-wedding events at the palace prevented her from meeting him. Neither did he make any attempt to seek her out. It was a disquieting feeling but Urmila tried to cheerfully brush it off as bridal nerves.

That morning her father had asked the four girls to seek the blessings of Rishi Vishwamitra, who it seemed, had been the chief brain masterminding the four weddings, silently and piously. As Urmila stood before him, she saw him in a new light. He was surprisingly very good looking but formidable with his angry, piercing eyes—a lot like Lakshman's, Urmila thought with mild amusement. He was tall and well built, his lanky frame accentuating a muscular sturdiness. But it was his eyes which often did most of the talking—they were often calm, with frequent flashes of humour and irascibility. Considering he had assiduously planned their romance, Urmila could well believe his incredible love story. The beautiful apsara Menaka, the celestial nymph, was especially brought from heaven by Indra, the king of the devas, to distract and seduce the rishi and break his severe meditative penance which was threatening the three worlds—heaven, earth and hell. She did, but only to fall in love with him as well. And he, too, fell in love with her. They got married but not to live happily ever after...

But there was nothing remotely romantic about him now— neither in dress, design or demeanour. Urmila followed her sisters as she touched his feet to seek his blessings. 'After the way you wrangled the blessing from the great Rishi Parshuram, I fear, dear, I am careful to measure my words!' chuckled Vishwamitra.

Urmila found herself blushing, hating her reaction each time the betraying colour flooded her face. His mocking words had brought a rush of memories of that fateful day when she swung from hope to despair, from fear to unmitigated joy. 'You are a brave child and in your unassuming, charming way, you shall win whatever you aspire for. But it won't be easy, dear. You are the strongest of the four; you shall reap what you receive; not reap what you have sown...'

Urmila looked puzzled. What was he trying to imply? Before she could ask him to elaborate, he continued, 'There was a reason why I came to Mithila, there was a reason why I stayed on here and there is still a reason why I wanted the four of you to marry the four young princes of Ayodhya. Time will tell all...' the rishi declared sagely, albeit with a certain conceit. It was as though it was he and not Time and Fate who had propelled the events. Urmila frowned. Was this a blessing, a back-handed self-compliment or a subtle warning of things to come?

She shrugged nonchalantly. She was not a superstitious person, nor one who particularly believed in ritual and rites, her father's philosophy and family's inherited pattern of though notwithstanding. Was she supposed to perform some yagna to propitiate an angry god, she wondered with a mirthless smile. As if reading her thoughts, the sage told her gently, 'It is not yagna, but dharma which you shall always have to uphold. It is how you nurture your relationships and your deeds that will see you through.You are the one who shall deliver them all to happiness eventually. Your love shall eventually succeed!' he said and Urmila caught a fleeting look of a sad, lost look on the sage's tired face. Was he reminscing his lost love?

Urmila was not sure if she was more confused or frightened by his eerie enunciations. But catching the kindly look on the sage's face, she assumed the best and felt reassured. However, she was relieved, as were her sisters, only when they finally took their leave and proceeded back to the palace. They almost ran back, their quick steps breaking into a slow sprint.

'He is a little scary, isn't he? Weird...' Kirti giggled.

'Don't be disrespectful!' Sita rebuked her.

'I am not being rude, but he really did scare me and I was wondering if I am doing the right thing marrying a man I haven't even met,' said Kirti wryly.' Everything seems to be going fine—too fine—and that is the reason for these unfunny jitters!'

'...And his words were hardly reassuring. Was he trying to warn us about something?' asked Mandavi, puzzled. 'But then why would he, he is the one who arranged this whole affair!'

'Hush, girls, look at the brighter side—be thankful to him that he gave us our life partners and helped us stay together—even matrimony could not separate us...' smiled Sita jauntily, driving away the clouds of doubt and depressing thoughts.

They walked silently, each lost in her own thoughts when, suddenly, loud, angry words broke the peace of the place.

'...This is unfair to all of us! Why doesn't he understand?'

It was a male voice and Urmila's keen ear immediately recognized it to be Lakshman's.

'Calm down, Lakshman!' they heard Ram plead, clearly trying to soothe his evidently irate brother. The brothers seemed to be in the midst of a heated argument and the passing girls could hear each word ringing clear through the window above. Courtesy demanded they moved away and not eavesdrop but the next words uttered by Lakshman rooted Urmila immobile.

'How can I remain calm when I keep insisting that I do *not* want to marry? Why am I being forced?' he asked furiously.

'If you don't, this is going to be embarrassing for all of us. Why are you being so stubborn?'

They were talking about her. Urmila felt a certain coldness creep into her heart and with each word he pronounced, it became harder and heavier.

'My marriage would be a lie, though an alluring one!' she heard Lakshman say. 'It's best if I don't marry. I am saving everyone from heartache, don't you understand, brother?'

'Tell her then...she might understand...' Ram sounded unconvinced.

'How am I supposed to tell her I cannot marry her?' There was frustration in his voice.

Urmila couldn't take it any longer; she could not bear to hear his harsh pronouncements. All she was aware of was a searing pain deep in her heart and she wanted to get away from there, from the onslaught of his savage words. She made a sudden movement, the dry leaves rustled noisily under her feet and there was a pause in the conversation above. She looked up and saw Lakshman looking down at her. There was a look of dismal incredulity on his face...and something more. But she did not bother to know. She turned around and started to walk away as fast as she could. Mandavi made a move to come with her but she shook her head violently.

'Please, no, let me be!' she barely managed to speak.

'Mila, stop!' called Lakshman from above.

She heard him but quickened her steps and made a mad dash to the woods—her childhood hideout whenever she wanted some private moments of solitude and solace. She was working herself up in a state and she did not want anyone, even her sisters, to see her like this. She was crazed with grief, the tears falling hard and fast, but not able to wash away the hurt and pain breaking her heart. She had got it all wrong. He had never loved her. He didn't want her. He didn't want to marry her—the rejection stung. And his repudiative words kept ringing feverishly, searing her mind, her soul, her very being. She felt discarded, thrown away in distaste and contempt.

She had been running long and was deep into the woods. But she well knew her way around. Her mother had warned her repeatedly about the dangers but this thick glade was her haven, her secret hideaway where she could bare her heart. She felt drained, her energy seeping out, her body wracked with dry sobs, she crumbled into a heap. Through her brimming tears, she could not see what was hurting her most—his rejection, her lost love, her shattered trust, her anguish or the humiliation. She couldn't forgive him; she couldn't forgive herself even more. What madness had made her fall in love with him, made her want him, trust him, cherish him? And the fact that she couldn't have him and, bitterly still, that he did not want her, burned her with a mortification more consuming than the licking flames of disillusionment. She had been ruthlessly forsaken, cast away for a reason unknown. Urmila hated wallowing in tears of self-pity but never had she experienced such a crushing, intense feeling of abandonment. She had never felt more lonely and bereft, more desolate and deserted.

She did not realize how long she had been sitting here. It was high noon now: she must have been here for hours. Urmila knew she had to return before her absence created a panic. But the thought of informing her parents that she would not be marrying Lakshman made her feel heartsick. How was she going to explain it to them when it was inexplicable to her as well?

A sudden rustling noise brought her back to another reality. Was it some animal? Urmila realized she had no weapon on her to protect herself. She frantically looked around for a hardy stick or rock or something to hurl at the approaching animal. She heard the sound of running footsteps and before she could rise and run, Lakshman appeared from nowhere. He seemed to loom large before her. He looked at her as if in a daze.

Both of them looked shocked and speechless; he relieved, she stunned. His face showed his fear and his quick relief at seeing her sitting crouched amongst the bushes. He wanted to rush and grab her by her shoulders and hold her close, never to let go of her soft body crushed against his but he restrained himself, recalling the words he had addressed to his brother. They had not been meant for her ears, but she had overheard them and Lakshman could never forget the stricken look on her face. And then she had fled from him, like a hurt doe, disappearing into the woods, hoping for a place to hide to lick her wound—which he had inflicted with his insensitivity and lack of foresight. He wished he had spoken to her earlier than she having to overhear the damning conversation with Ram; he wished he could snatch back those words.

He was standing so close to her that she could hear the wild thudding of his heart. The mere sight of him made her almost melt in the comforting warmth of his presence but she remembered why and where she was. She was not going to chase her mad dream again. She struggled within herself, the pain and anger rushing back, pushing out any soft thoughts of him. Lakshman stared back at her. She still looked grief-stricken, her eyes haunted, the tears drying into dark rills, ravaging her lovely face. He cursed himself for being the cause of that despair.

'How did you find the way?' she asked stupidly.

'I would have searched and eventually found you, Mila!' he said evenly, spacing the two syllables of 'Mi-la' with an unbearable tenderness.

Urmila was stung to the quick. 'Don't, don't call me that! Don't you dare again! You have no right,' she said forcefully, her fury rekindled. 'You know better than to keep up with this pretence! You didn't have the courage to tell me what I was entitled to. Coward!' she spat. 'What was that you said? Aha, marriage is an alluring lie. Well, so are you! A dishonourable man with dishonourable intentions.' Rage leapt at her throat, choking the words and she could not speak anymore.

'All I know is that my intention was never to hurt you!' he said simply, his craggy face falling into soft lines of gentleness. 'It is not as it seems, what you overheard was a part of a larger story. And I genuinely intended to tell you the truth but...'

'But what? You lost your nerve?' she asked contemptuously. 'Frankly, I don't care to know. I don't need your explanations. You are what you are; it was me who could not see through you. I was the fool!'

'So was I,' he said grimly. 'I didn't lose courage, I lost my heart. To you...and that's what made it so difficult. I loved you and wanted you so desperately...yet I dare not have you...'

Urmila gave a bitter laugh. 'Stop it. You can't fool me anymore! I heard you. You don't want me, that is why you don't want to marry me!'

'Don't doubt that, ever!' he said thickly. 'I love you, Mila. And I am saying this now as I am not afraid to say so. It was this fear of losing you that forbade me to never utter those words. You were too beautiful, too good to make me hope you would be accessible or accept my love. I have been in love with you from that beautiful moment when I saw you looking at me haughtily in the garden with that pooja thali in your hands. And nothing has been the same ever again. Not me, my peace of mind, my principles, my promises. You have taken away my heart, my pride, my everything...but what can I give you? Nothing but sorrow and heartache. I cannot promise you happiness. And that's why I cannot marry you. I shouldn't. And that is what I was telling Ram.'

Her scornful smile and bitter words died on her lips. The man who stood in front of her was a man possessed, controlled by the powerful force of strong emotions, torn in the conflict of his heart and mind, thought and reason, his love and his ideals.

'That is my quandary—I love you to distraction and yet I don't have the courage to marry you. Because I am a torn man, Mila,' he said despairingly. 'I had no intentions of marrying ever. For me, my life is being with my brother. He is my all. He is my friend, my teacher, my life, my soul. I cannot do without him—that's how I have grown up, that's how I have been made...' he shook his head in disbelief. 'They say I am so servile to him because my mother Queen Sumitra is not of royal lineage, but from a class of handmaids. I don't really care either way. She is the wisest woman I know and taught me right since childhood that Ram is my God and the purpose that justifies my existence is serving him, protecting him. Some people consider me his menial, and I don't mind it. He is the reason for my being. That's what I thought I was—a brother completely dedicated to his elder brother. That was my life's aim...till I met you...' he said throatily.

He gave her a look that still had the power to make her melt. 'I prided myself on the belief that I would never get charmed by any woman, which made my decision to remain unmarried relatively easy. I had never contemplated falling in love. But I did, and badly.'

Badly—an unusual expression to describe love. Or was that exactly what it was and would be? Urmila kept silent, unsure of what to say and what to believe.

'You were everything I had not predicted—lovely, intelligent, teasing, witty, strong and above all, so devoted to your sisters. I felt a certain affinity with you because, as is true for me, your siblings are the anchors of your life. I loved the way you were protective about your sisters, I loved that flashing look in your eyes when challenged, I loved your laugh, the way you furrowed your brows while frowning, that quick colour rising deliciously on your face each time we exchanged glances. I was a drowning man myself, taken by the tide. And then, as I found myself falling hopelessly for you, I felt a strange fear—was my love for you distancing me from my service to my brother?'

'Was that the reason for your unpleasantness?' she asked more in wonderment than recalled regret.

'Ashamedly, yes. Each time I saw you, I went insane; all I

wanted was to have you completely for myself. And each time I realized I could not give myself completely to you at all. I was livid when Ravan dared to even look at you, I could have killed him! When the princes at the swayamvar clamoured for your hand, all I felt was fury and jealousy and the fear that I would lose you. I wanted to protect you from them and the likes of men like Ravan. This realization made me force myself to recognize my feelings for you but I had no right to them when I could not acknowledge them in word and action to you.' He saw her flinch. 'And it was this frustration and anger that made me stay away from you, knowing full well in that bleak certainty that you could never be mine.'

'No, I am yours,' she corrected him quietly, uninhibited about revealing her feelings. '*You* are not mine.'

'I am. I am. I have never loved anyone so passionately, so blindly, so incoherently,' he sighed, drawing in his breath painfully. 'When I say I love you, Mila, I am sure about you but not myself. That *I* taunts me—can I love truly and wholly? Am I that strong to love you back? Am I that capable and deserving of love and loving? Shall I ever be able to make you happy? Am I worthy of your love? And I fall short. I am a man trapped.'

'Trapped in your own expectations, your own self-limitations,' she said softly, unperturbed by his argument. Her anger and hurt had suddenly dissipated. 'Loving is also giving; you are not ready to give yourself to me. But don't you see, I don't want your complete surrender. I love you but that does not mean I possess you, your beliefs and your loyalties. I assure you that I shall never come between your loyalty to your brothers and your family. Likewise, I shall not allow my love for you to be threatened by my love for my sisters and my parents. By loving you, my love for them will never falter, nor should yours.'

'But it would clash, we are marrying into a family,' he said impatiently.

He was sounding much like her mother, Urmila realized with a start, reminiscing the earlier conversation. Both of them were saddled with the same unwarranted burden of fear and trepidation.

'But that doesn't mean you stop loving one for another,' she said vehemently, 'or abandoning one for the other! That is no sacrifice!'

'I am afraid that is what I shall do if I were faced with that dilemma. I shall choose my brother each time.'

He saw her wince but continued relentlessly. 'And that is what I want to talk to you about. Were we to marry, I shall not be able to give you the happiness and full attention you deserve. That would not be fair on you and I don't want you getting hurt. There will be times when we shall have to choose and I shall unhesitatingly choose my brother each time over you. He shall always take precedence in my life, not you. And that is why I cannot marry you. I simply should not.'

He was being brutally honest; she didn't know whether to hate him for it or admire him. But this was the truth—he could love her only that much and not more. He had devoted his life to his brother and he could not accommodate her. Was it a gesture of rejection or resignation? Or was his self-deprecating manner winning her all over again with a dawning respect? Or was it helplessness that she could not give him up but grab at the thinnest hope? She was madly in love with this man but was she mad enough to marry him knowing all that he had confessed to her?

'I had meant to explain this to you but father's letter made things worse,' he looked restless. 'He assumes that I will get married, and now that he has announced our wedding to the world, I don't know how I can get out,' he gave a mirthless smile. 'But that would not be fair to anyone, especially you. I cannot do that to you—it'd be unforgivable!'

'But you are doing exactly that! You *are* forsaking me right now!' cried Urmila. 'I know what you are going through, your dilemma, but how are you going to explain to my father, to the world?'

'I won't hurt and humiliate you ever, I would rather kill myself!' he said huskily. 'I shall tell him the truth as well. '

'What? That out of fear that I may come between the two brothers, you are ready to abandon me?'

She made it sound so ludicrous that even Lakshman could not help giving a sad, twisted smile. He shook his head. 'You lovely temptress, as your name claims, you have me well and truly! You are now ensnaring me with your wit and words,' he sighed. 'But I fear I don't have the courage or the will to confess to your father that I cannot marry you as I am not worthy of you or your love. But I shall have to and he will understand. The world may point fingers at me and I shall accept it. But Mila, I cannot forsake your happiness for my principles.'

'And so?'

'Wives seek ambition for their husbands, often seeking their own fortunes through the husband's,' he answered wryly. 'Moreover, a princess always wishes to be a queen. And you won't become one if you marry me. You are, after all, King Janak's daughter, a rare scholar herself and no ordinary princess, while I will never be king...but the support for the king—my brother, Ram.'

'And you believe you are an ordinary prince?' she countered sarcastically. 'Either you are in doubt about yourself or you are doubting me—both are insulting to my sense of pride. Or is this another way of dissuasion?'

'I can never doubt you, Mila. But by marrying me your social position, too, will get compromised...I am no choice for you.'

'No, you still are my choice, regardless of your reluctance,' she retorted coolly. 'But *you* do have a choice—either break off the wedding and leave me to my fate or marry me, your loyalty to your brother notwithstanding. I accept you as my husband, do you?'

'Don't be so flippant, Mila. You know I can't leave you to your fate and desert you but will I ever make you happy if I marry you?' he said cupping her face in his hands. She found the gesture delightfully intimate. This was the first time he had touched her deliberately, as a gesture of tenderness, not in a tussle. He held her close and she felt a wave of pleasure wash over her. 'You don't realize what you are saying. I love you and my biggest fear is that I shall lose you and all because of me!'

'You will lose me if you don't marry me now,' she whispered brokenly. 'Oh Lakshman, can't you see that you are doing that right now in fearful anticipation of it happening in the future?' she said gently, placing her hand over his. He took her hands and rubbed his thumb absently on the inner side of her wrist. It was erotic, distracting her faintly from what she was saying. 'You are so scared of the time yet to come that you are ready to let go of the time we have now. You are depriving us of our present at the price of withholding our future. Are you so scared that you won't give us a chance? I know you love me. Likewise, I love you—for what you are and not for what I hope you to be. I know you will always remain devoted to Ram. I cannot prise you from him. I have heard so many stories about the deep love between you and Ram. The two of you are like Nara and Narayan—the twins who derived love and strength from each other. I accept that. I have to, if I want to have you. And I promise you, I shall never come between the two of you. Just as I know Sita shall never interfere between you brothers. It is that simple.'

'No, it is not. Mila, your words make it so,' he argued. 'And you do have a way with words that is hard to resist.'

'My words make it sensible too,' she smiled bewitchingly. 'And I shall prove them right with the right action, if and when the time comes. Right now, prince of Ayodhya, you have no choice but to marry this princess of Mithila and we shall live happily ever after!'

Urmila knew she was a woman of words. But she had never imagined she would use this skill to convince a man about what a good wife she would make, or how he would be the ideal husband for her, she thought with a grim smile. Now, returning to the palace, and noticing Mandavi's censorious frown, Urmila knew she would be at her persuasive best again. They, too, had overheard everything and had presumed the worst. She had to redeem him in their eyes and reassure her wary sisters that she had taken the right decision.

She was immediately assailed with a volley of words the moment she stepped inside her chamber.

'Are you fine now?' Sita looked anxious.

'Did you meet him?' Mandavi questioned searchingly.

Kirti took her hand in hers and made her sit down 'After you ran off, he followed you—he looked miserable. Are things fine between you both?'

The sight of the three scared faces so worried for her moved Urmila and made her feel cherished. These were her sisters. She could not afford to lie to them; she had to tell them the truth. Not all the details, she recalled with a blush and a smile.

'The fact that you are smiling again proves all's well,' said Mandavi with relief in her voice. 'But, whatever happened? Why didn't he want to marry you? After what he said and how he hurt you, I swear I was ready to kill him!' she spat.

Urmila squeezed her hand to reassure her. Under her aloof mask, Mandavi was fierce—not just the most possessive but also the most protective of her sisters. She would have gladly clawed his eyes out, given a chance. And that was why the air needed to be cleared urgently. It was up to her to restore his lost respect.

'I assumed the worst, so did you all,' Urmila said quietly. 'He loves me, I don't doubt that. But he does not want to marry me to protect me from heartache and disillusionment...'

'Disillusionment?' interrupted Mandavi sharply.

'Because he fears he cannot give me his all. He wanted nothing—neither love nor marriage—to come between him and Ram.'

She heard Sita gasp but she ignored it. 'He wanted to make everything clear and tell me the truth about exactly where and how I stand in his life. The other option, of course, was to call off the wedding. That was the option he was contemplating to save me from any future hurt.'

She was met with a still pause till Mandavi angrily got up.

'In this prioritization of his emotions, you are always going to be second place, is that it?' Mandavi asked indignantly. 'And you accepted?' she looked incredulous.

'Yes,' Urmila said calmly. 'I love him too much to let him go. I love him too much and accept him with all his conditions. And I love myself too much to suffer again that misery of being without him. I am lost without him and I am ready to take what I am left with. That one moment when I thought he had forsaken me, was the worst and I wouldn't ever want to relive it, whatever it takes—even subjugating myself! I experienced how harsh heartbreak can be...' her eyes clouded with remembered pain. 'It strips you of hope, pride, dignity, desire, trust and leaves nothing within you but just a dull, killing pain. I won't be able to go through it again...I simply cannot live without him. I could not give him up,' her shoulders drooped in silent defeat.

'You are a proud woman, Urmi,' said Kirti. 'Will your love not affect your sense of pride, your self-preservation? Will you be able to live with yourself? How can you accept a man who has sacrificed himself for another? Where does it leave you?'

It was a series of questions for which Urmila had just one

answer. 'Nowhere. Just leaves me with a man I love who is not mine. If love is supposed to bring out the best in one, I rest my case.'

'By giving up your self-respect?' derided Mandavi. 'How will you be able to accept this secondary status in his life?'

'I have always known what secondary is—I have grown up with it!' snapped Urmila and the moment she said those words, she regretted it. Sita had gone pale, her face transparent to not mask the hurt her irresponsible words had inflicted.

'Sita, I am so sorry, I didn't mean it the way it came out...' Urmila stammered, begging profusely. 'I was just trying to explain...'

'...What it felt like to play second fiddle,' Sita finished the sentence for her. 'I know what you have gone through all these years—consistently sidelined to pave way for me. I was undeservedly adored.'

'Don't ever say that!' Urmila retorted hotly. 'You deserve all the affection, all the applause; you are so wonderfully good, darling, that we pale in comparison. We know that. And I don't resent that.'

'I know. That's what makes it worse. You loved me doubly more instead!' cried Sita. 'I love mother, father and you but between the four of us love hasn't been distributed equally, has it? They loved me too much for your too little, even though you are their blood daughter. You never did mind, never protested and the guilt kills me...'

Urmila was aghast—had she done that to her sister? Was loving too much unfair?

'Don't, Sita!' she protested. 'Why are you holding yourself responsible for something you did not do, something which really did not happen? You were favoured because of your goodness, for your qualities, not because you were the firstborn! Or because you were adopted,' she added, realizing what was hurting her sister. 'And neither was I in any way neglected or ignored. What I was trying to say was that I came second in chronology...'

'No!' Sita shook her head fiercely. 'Secondary means being subsidiary. First it was our parents and now Lakshman! It is simply unjust!'

Urmila laughed lightly. 'Now, dear, you are mixing issues. Lakshman was making clear his supreme loyalty to his elder brother and trying to make me understand their relationship. And it is in my best interest to understand and accept it,' she added dryly.

'No, knowing you, you will sensibly compartmentalize the love; you will never allow one to dominate the other,' argued Sita.

'I find this entire notion of grading and rating love odious!' exclaimed Mandavi. 'It's demeaning.'

'No, it is accepting a certain reality, knowing how and where you stand,' shrugged Urmila. 'Mother was trying to explain to us the same thing Lakshman was so convinced about. It is not about ranking love; it is about circumstances and situations. At every point, we need to choose between those whom we love. It is a constant conflict but that does not mean we love one less than the other.'

'I understand what you are saying, Urmi,' said Kirti sagely. 'You would rather accept him for what he is, for what he can give, than lose him forever. But I appreciate his courage in being upfront and not mincing his words. Some may call it harsh; I say it was brutally honest. No one can accuse him of having set wrong expectations or misleading you. His intentions were entirely honourable. But good intentions are often not enough; however, you know what to expect now.'

Her last statement sounded oddly cryptic. Kirti, Urmila often observed, though the youngest of the sisters, was way mature beyond her fledgling years.

'Expect what?' repeated Mandavi.

'Somehow what he said pertains not just to you, Urmi, I think it applies to all of us,' Kirti said slowly, as if a new realization was slowly filtering into her.

'And that is?' prompted Mandavi, impatiently.

'The unusually strong bond between the brothers, it's like ours, we can't do without each other either,' remarked Kirti. 'Is that why Vishwamitra suggested to King Dashrath that the four of us would be the perfect match for his four sons? It fits, doesn't it? Even those warbled words we thought were a riddle were actually letting us on about the time to come...that all of us might face the same situation.'

'You are scaring me, Kirti, what are you saying?' cried Mandavi in restive exasperation.

'The love between the four princes borders on devotion, especially the younger brothers' dedication to Ram,' she said. 'They would do anything for him and vice versa. Lakshman's devotion is more overt, more visible, because he wears it as an emblem. The others, I am sure, would do the same, if the situation arose. There is this infrangible thread of allegiance that binds them together, and now what Lakshman is warning Urmila of, can be true for us too, Mandavi,'continued Kirti grimly. 'That if such a situation were to merge, where any of them would have to choose between his wife and the brother, it will be the brother they will opt for. It would do well if the wife always keeps this in mind.'

There was a long moment of subdued silence, each forced to face a new truth.

THE FOUR WEDDINGS

Urmila found a new meaning in Kirti's sombre words. She was swamped with a dampening feeling of apprehension. Nuptials were supposed to spell mirth and merriment but theirs seem to be a series of chronic chaos. Barely had Urmila managed to steer hers in the clear, that it was Sita's turn next.

Just when everyone was envying them their fairytale wedding, the royal priest, Shatanand, came in with some disturbing news. After perusing carefully the astrological charts of the four princes and princesses, he said everything was perfect but for one flaw. Ram, it seemed, had *mangaldosha*–the dominant influence of the planet Mars–in his horoscope which would not augur well for the marriage. The stout, brisk, old priest brusquely declared that it would be best to call off the wedding. That marriage, he warned, would bring mostly grief to Sita. His words, as expected, threw the family in a paralytic crisis.

Urmila had not seen her father look so devastated ever; he could not believe his ears. Janak greatly respected his royal priest and had an unfailing faith in his prophetic powers. But neither could he ignore the portentous significance of Ram stringing Rudra's bow. He was convinced that Ram was destined for Sita.

Just as Sita was for Ram. But the heavenly stars suddenly seemed to have gone against them, Urmila thought sourly. Sunaina was adamant about calling off the wedding. Janak was aghast—the groom's father and brothers were to reach Mithila the next morning. With what face was he to greet them?

'After what Rishi Shantanand has said, I refuse to take a chance with my daughter's future,' Sunaina told him resolutely, her lips thinning in an unhappy, straight line, a habit her daughter had inherited when she was particularly displeased. 'We should tell them the truth and I am sure King Dashrath would understand. He would wish the best for his son too.'

'Sita is the best thing for him, dear,' countered her husband, frowning in consternation. 'The Shiv bow is the proof, can't you see? It got them together. You saw how many young men attempted to string that bow, and finally it was only Ram who could do it. They are meant to be!'

'Then is the horoscope misleading? Don't you believe in our priest? He is never wrong! How can you take the risk?' his wife pleaded.

'The priests claim that if there is a condition placed before marriage as in Sita's swayamvar, the manglik dosha does not work. So rest assured, dear,' cajoled the wise Janak, hoping his words would convince his worried wife.

Sunaina was a rational woman, but fear is not; it can capriciously attack the most reasonable person. The queen of Mithila was no exception. Irrational fear had morphed her into an implacable mother, protecting her child from seen and unforseen harm. She was impervious to anyone's pleas, persuasion, requests or reason, Sita notwithstanding. But, to her consternation, it was Sita who opposed her the most fiercely.

'I cannot think of marrying anyone else. I consider Ram my husband, my lifemate,' she said quietly but her voice was hard and uncompromising, brooking no argument.

That is how Sita was, thought Urmila with an amused smile, at her characteristic strongest—brief and decisive. Urmila well knew her sister's demureness was deceptive. Sita was like a peach— apparently soft and delicate but hard and strong from within. 'But if you so insist that I do not marry Ram, I shan't marry at all. I would rather remain unwed,' she continued determinedly.

Sita said it firmly, in no uncertain terms, overriding any objection. Her mother could simply stare at her in open disbelief. Sita was her weakness and also the reason for her pride, a pride immense and inordinate. Sita could do no wrong, she was complete, without any fault or blemish.

'And what if what the royal priest has said comes true?' demanded her mother. 'He also mentioned that though a princess, you will largely live in the forest for most of your married life. What does that mean? Do you want to be unhappily married to him? And suffer?'

'I love him,' Sita said simply, as if that was an answer to all the questions and doubts her mother was likely to raise. 'If I am not with him, I shall be unhappy. I would suffer unimaginable misery. I have to marry him for myself, to make myself happy.'

Urmila was struck by her sister's words. They sounded familiar, similar to what she had said to her sisters in justification of her decision to marry Lakshman. Both of them were in love, wanting to marry the men they loved. Were they making an unsuitable choice?

Falling in love was far easier than staying in love. Urmila recollected those tremulous, treacherous days. Would then, living in love be a trying tale of trials or of triumph?

Urmila had not revealed to her mother the conversation she had had with Lakshman. She could well imagine her mother's reaction if she had. For the sake of her daughters' happiness and well-being, Sunaina would have calmly broken off the wedding, social mores be damned. She did not believe in rules and did not agree that one's behaviour needed to be governed by social conditions, customarily followed otherwise. She favoured a personal philosophy of individual progress and private freedom and choice. And that is where Sita had caught her—trapped her in her philosophy of personal liberty. She could not back off now.

Sunaina smiled wanly. 'It is your decision,' she murmured. It was a statement, not a question of which she knew the anticipated answer. 'So be it. And may you have the conviction to mean what you say. And the moral strength to brave it out.'

Urmila silently took her mother's advice though her mother was not aware she had given her one. She knew her mother's admonitory words to Sita were pertinent for her as well.

Dashrath arrived with his two younger sons in Mithila early the next morning. Mandavi and Kirti, as was their daily routine, went to the temple but were clearly distracted. They wanted to see Bharat and Shatrughna in person before the wedding the next day. Their prayers were answered—they saw them at the very same place where Sita and Urmila had met their soulmates.

'The garden seems to have become the exalted rendezvous of our collective romance,' giggled Sita as they caught a fleeting glimpse of the four princes returning from their daily puja. They too appeared to be indulging in the game of pretence—collecting flowers for the prayers was their pretext. Dashrath was with Janak in the palace and the two younger princes were conveniently with their older brothers, helping them out with the morning puja.

But the princesses were getting late; Sunaina was waiting for them to return from the temple to begin the haldi ceremony where turmeric would be applied on their bodies. Thus, it was just a momentary glance that could be shared between the brides-

and grooms-to-be before they garlanded each other tomorrow at the auspicious mahurat.

Urmila had had no time to look at the two younger princes, her eyes as usual were searching for Lakshman. He was there with his brothers...and a woman. She was laughing up at him. Even from a distance, Urmila could see that the woman with the lilting laugh and smiling eyes was breathtakingly beautiful. Who was she? Urmila's eyes narrowed, watching the two smiling at each other and she felt an unfamiliar stab of pain slicing through her. It was jealousy, bile green and unadulterated, and she didn't know how to deal with it. The more she suppressed it, the more angrily it flared, searing her with an irrational burst of rancour, resentment and anger.

Who was she, she kept asking herself repeatedly. Urmila knew she was being uncharacteristically unreasonable: the woman, she rationalized with distinct mental discernment, must be some relative, his cousin probably, but she could not shake off that wave of possessiveness that deluged her mind. She was unable to forget their laughing faces, their mysterious familiarity; it intruded into her peace, her sleep and all of her waking thoughts.

Vasishtha and Dashrath had meanwhile met with Janak, Vishwamitra and Shatanand to further discuss about the contentious mahurat. The three rishis warned the kings that though the mahurat of Uttara Falguni nakshatra was perfect for the couples, the stars were such that even if there was a moment's delay, the planets would change their position and the fortunes would not augur well for the four brides and their grooms.

Unaware of these dissuasive predictions, the four brides woke up to a dull wintry day to dress up in all their wedding finery. The sun was out but Urmila could still see the moon, the day seemed to be blurring into the inky night, blotting the sun and the warmth of the daylight. Each of the brides had worn a different colour. Sita was in her favourite silver gauze blue, Urmila in crimson, Mandavi in an emerald green and Kirti in turmeric yellow—all auspicious colours, Sage Shatanand observed with relief. The queen, mercifully, had gone conservative, for once, he told himself. He would have preferred all the four girls wearing red—the colour of fertility but only Urmila, his favourite disciple, was attired in scarlet and gold. But she had always been wise and correct, the guru thought fondly. He was a little worried about the princesses, though. The four princes were an excellent choice but their fates were too intertwined for them to enjoy individual marital bliss. He looked up at the sky—it was brumous, sullen, sunless. Time seemed to be standing still, though a little confused. He watched the wedding rituals coming to a close and it was time for the final phase. The brides were placing the thick jasmine and rose garlands over the groom's bowed heads as he had specifically instructed. The timing was important; the rest would follow smoothly.

Urmila was duly introduced to her father-in-law King Dashrath. He looked even more withered and ancient than her father. The immediate impression was of kindliness—a tall, handsome man with more salt than pepper in his greying mane, his eyes warm and kind. Yet there was nothing weak about him, there was strength not just in his slim, slightly bent figure, but in his face, firm jawline, hawkish nose and gentle voice. Urmila had heard nasty rumours that this mighty king was a slave to his favourite wife, the beautiful Kaikeyi, but now, looking at him, it was hard to believe it. He looked like a man in control, a powerful king of his land, the proud father of four handsome sons.

And each of his four sons was incredibly good-looking. Bharat resembled his father the most, there was a quiet serenity in him, even more than his elder brother Ram. His eyes were clear and tranquil, emanating a quiet authority, like Ram's. The twins, Lakshman and Shatrughna didn't look identical, yet there was a very close resemblance in their mood and mannerism. Shatrughna, though, frowned less than his twin and certainly smiled a lot more. In fact, he seemed quite a prankster from the perpetual devilish glint in his eyes and the fun he liberally poked at his brothers. His brothers indulged him. The sedate Kirti was going to have quite a handful, Urmila relished the thought with roguish delight.

'As it's a group wedding, are we supposed to stand in a queue according to order of age, popularity or height?' asked Shatrughna tongue-in-cheek. 'Ram wins in all except height; there, I guess, we twins are the winners!' he grinned, nudging Lakshman to head the waiting line. 'Come, brother, let's get married first and quick!'

No one could help smiling; Shatrughna dissipated the solemn air with his frequent one-liners throughout the ceremony. Giggling at his jokes, Urmila found herself staring again at the strange woman hovering around the brothers. Her smile promptly disappeared as she caught sight of the beautiful woman whom she had seen last morning laughing so comfortably with Lakshman. She was dressed in silken fuschia pink, the hot colour flowing warmly all over her well-rounded, hourglass figure. At a closer look, Urmila found her more beautiful and much older. She was standing close to the four princes with a silver thali and diya, authoritative and busy. She must be some relative, Urmila thought with enormous relief, feeling abruptly bouyant and pleased. But who else could she have been? Urmila had not been proud of that spurt of jealousy and possessiveness that had pervaded and overpowered her since the previous morning. Finding out that she was their sister, Urmila experienced a light, lifting moment of relief. And the thought made her break into her first genuine smile of the day. It started small, getting gradually wider as she perceived the sheer foolishness of her jealousy. She could not stop smiling, brilliant and radiantly, her eyes brimming bright with newfound bliss. The sight simply took Lakshman's breath away as he looked proudly at his bride. She looked the loveliest and definitely the happiest.

The beautiful lady was Shanta, the elder sister of Ram and the oldest daughter of Dashrath and his older queen Kausalya. She had led an eventful life unlike the protected princesses of Mithila. Though born as the princess of Ayodhya, or Kosala to be specific, she was adopted by Kausalya's elder sister Vershini and her husband King Rompad of Angadesh, a close friend of Dashrath. They were childless and once in light banter, the sister-in-law asked her younger brother-in-law that if he were so generous and a man of his word, would he give his newborn daughter to her as her child? Honouring the word given by a Raghuvansh kshatriya, Dashrath readily agreed and gave his only daughter, an infant, to his best friend and sister-in-law. And Shanta was brought up as the princess of Angadesh, far away from her parents at Ayodhya. Educated in the Vedas, arts, craft and music, Shanta grew up to be a scholar and a very beautiful princess who married not a prince, but a learned rishi—Rishyasringa, who was said to have saved her kingdom from a relentless famine.

Years later, as Dashrath had no children after Shanta, he decided to have another yagna to beget him a son to continue his royal dynasty. He then called upon his son-in-law Rishyasringa to perform a *putra kameshthi yagna* to beget progeny, and thus were born Ram, Bharat, and the twins Lakshman and Shatrughna— the four princes of Kosala.

Rishi Rishyaringa was present at the wedding and her father had been delighted to meet him, as he did when he met any scholar, smiled Urmila with fond regard. Rishyaringa was thin and ascetic looking but with a fire burning within him that shone through his eyes, flashing with profound knowledge and brilliance.

Right now, he was talking to Vishwamitra, intent and grim. Urmila wondered with a sinking heart what they were discussing, but the frown flew away as the rishi's expression immediately softened as he caught sight of his approaching wife, walking quickly toward him. Theirs was a love story as interesting as themselves.

Rishyaringa, before he met Shanta, had led a singularly isolated life, having never been exposed to any womanly influence including that of his mother, the apsara Urvashi, who had left him and his father Sage Vibhandaka, after giving birth to him. She had been sent down by Indra to seduce the rishi to distract him from his penance. Betrayed and hurt, Sage Vibhandaka developed hatred for all women, a belief he tried to pass on to his young impressionable son and saw to it that he was never exposed to the wile of a woman. The rishi took him away into the deep forest to lead a life of seclusion and meditation.

When Rompad saw his kingdom reeling from drought and famine, he was told that the only person who could save him from this predicament was any learned brahmin who had derived powers from the observance of severe chastity. And that person was Rishyaringa. But who would go to the forest and invite him to perform the yagna in the city? His father would never allow him to leave the safe sanctuary of the forest.

It was Shanta who came upon a brilliant scheme. Along with a courtesan, who would use her charms if necessary, the princess went herself to persuade the young rishi to perform the yagna for her father and save the citizens of Angadesh. She was careful to meet the unsuspecting rishi when his father was away collecting wood as she feared he would throw her out or worse, curse her or her kingdom. And as expected, when he saw the two beautiful girls, the courtesan and the princess, the rishi who had never seen a woman in his life, fell hopelessly in love with the latter. She persuaded him to come to the city to perform the agnihotra puja. The besotted rishi agreed readily. Fleeing from his angry father, he came to the city with Shanta and used his powers to bless and drench the dry land with heavy showers. As the yagna progressed and the sky darkened, so did Vibhandaka cloud with rage as he headed toward the city to get back his son. And as soon as the heavy clouds burst into torrential rains, Vibhandaka reached the capital to see his son getting married to the beautiful princess. He was swiftly calmed down by some quick thinking of the enterprising princess. It was Shanta who, prepared for the worst of her father-in-law's fury, had planned to appease him by presenting him with a series of thoughtful gifts and revealing the depth and sincerity of her love for his son. The old man was duly conciliated to give them his blessing for a long, happy and fruitful life.

Such was Shanta. Urmila saw her now, standing behind Ram, lovely and resplendent in her silks and glittering gems and regarded her with renewed respect. The rites were coming to a close and Urmila, through the corner of her eyes, watched Sita garlanding Ram. She was the elder sister, it was her right to lead. Taking cue, Urmila followed suit with Mandavi and Kirti. She was trembling but her hands were steady, as she placed the fragrant garland on Lakshman's strong neck, turning up a radiant face at him, her eyes as bright as fresh drops of dew. Without taking his eyes off her, he bent his handsome head, a crooked smile on his lips.

'You look the merriest of the brides! And so beatifically beautiful!' he murmured in her ear, 'or is it just me who makes you so?' he asked teasingly, his voice soft and husky as he brought his head down to garland her.

'No, it's your sister!' she whispered back wickedly.

He raised a surprised eyebrow, but she was not going to reveal more of her treacherous thoughts. 'Soumitra, my dear brother, this is your Urmila, isn't she?' beamed Shanta.

Urmila was surprised at the name she addressed Lakshman

with—Soumitra, the son of Sumitra. Shanta continued talking to her. 'I heard how you saved Soumitra's life from Guru Parshuram's killer wrath. It reminded me of how I managed to appease my furious father-in-law!'

Urmila flushed swiftly, hating the colour seeping into her face but she need not have worried.

'But I have never seen a more angelic bride, so heady with happiness than yours, Soumitra!' gushed Shanta. 'You are absolutely exquisite, my dear, and may you always be so ravishingly happy!'

'Mila, this is Shanta, my sister, and dear sister, you seem to be the reason for my bride's gorgeous glow!' introduced Lakshman sardonically, holding Urmila's hand openly, while touching the inside of her wrist in a slow, circular motion with his thumb. Urmila felt a frisson of pleasure and did not make any attempt to shake his hand away.

'Me?' asked Shanta, puzzled.

'Yes, sister, what's the spell you have cast on my bride?' he asked innocently.

Tingling with the sensuous sensation on her wrist, Urmila blushed more furiously. More so, as she remembered with renewed mortification her jealous rage which had devoured her the whole of the previous day. She managed to greet her sister-in-law with a sheepish smile.

'Not me, no, dear brother, methinks it's the spell *you* have cast on your Mila! You clearly seem to be on very dear terms of endearment,' said Shanta, pointedly looking at their hands and sailed off, smiling, to greet her other sisters-in-law.

Urmila pounced on him. 'Oh please, stop embarrassing me!' she hissed.

'I think I can guess what happened... Was your artistic imagination at work again...?' whispered back Lakshman, his eyes dancing mischievously. 'There was this lovely woman I saw last morning in the garden...' he began.

'Please!' she begged in a hoarse whisper, her face as crimson as the deep silk she was wearing.

'...and that was you! Why the jealousy, Mila?' he asked, his tone suddenly serious. 'It is mostly irrational, and stems from insecurity. Are you unsure about me? Then I hope I shall never make you suffer that overriding vulnerability ever again. I am yours. Always,' he added huskily.

Urmila was overwhelmed as she gazed into his softly burning eyes: he was giving her a promise on their wedding day. She could not turn away from the intensity of his look, the intensity of his declaration. It was only when he gently held her by her wrist and lead her toward her parents, that Urmila, seeing them, hurriedly bent down to seek their blessing. Her new husband followed suit, obediently, the expression on his face, sufficiently subdued.

The four brides had wed their four princes and the city of Mithila exploded into euphoria and festive fervour. The same would be happening in Ayodhya, thought King Dashrath, a warm feeling seeping into his tired bones. He could not have been happier. Today he would be returning home with four daughters along with his sons.

He felt a tap on his shoulder. He turned to see a pale Janak, accompanied by Sunaina, Vasishtha, Vishwamitra, Shatanand and his son-in-law Rishyaringa huddled in a worried cluster.

'I have some unfavourable news,' said the king of Mithila, looking troubled. 'The appointed mahurat of the Uttara Falguni nakshatra has long gone, we don't know how. There was some sort of a miscalculation.'

Dashrath's heart sank. 'You mean we skipped the auspicious nakshatra?' he asked incredulously, not expecting an answer. He gathered his answer from their bleak expressions; the outcome was irrevocable. He looked at his royal priest, Vasishtha, for some solution and saw the pessimistic shake of his head.

'It seems the gods were not in favour of the nakshatra as it would guarantee the marriage between Ram and Sita to be successful,' explained the priest.

'But why?' demanded a perplexed Dashrath. 'Why would anyone, even the gods, not want my son and daughter-in-law to have a happy married life? How have these young innocent souls harmed anyone to start their new life with such a bad omen?' he cried in anger.

He was visibly upset and his voice had risen higher than he, and the others, would have wished. The four newly married couples overheard the old king. Watching the smiles disappear from the radiant faces of the four brides, Sunaina was aroused to an impatient anger. And the latent fear arose again within her. Her initial hesitation had proved correct; she wished she had had the power and the will to have broken off the four alliances when her intuition had prompted her to do so. And as much as she wished she had been proved wrong, Sunaina knew all she could do was pray for her four daughters whom she loved the most in the world.

'The gods wanted to postpone the marriage of Ram and Sita because if the wedding would have taken place on the exact Uttara Falguni nakshatra, the marriage would have run smoothly, ideally blissful,' explained Vasishtha, his face serene as if he knew what was going to happen next. 'The irreprsible Narada suggested to the gods to send Chandra, the Moon God, as a dancing nymph—an apsara before the wedding mahurat. Transformed as an apsara, Chandra Dev attended this very wedding here and enchanted everyone with the dances. He fooled and distracted us, the weather changed and meanwhile the planets changed their positions. The gods are celebrating now that they have succeeded in what they had so meticulously planned.'

'But why?' repeated the bewildered Dashrath in impotent anger.

'Because it is what Fate desires—a decree designated beforehand,' said Rishyaringa quietly. 'A happy marriage between Ram and Sita would not enable the events which are meant to develop. It is part of an elaborate, systematic scheme of things to unfold. Let it be, O king, and value the present moment.'

Urmila watched the solemn faces of all the four sages and knew that they knew more than what they were telling. She felt a twinge of apprehension—what was it that awaited her and her sisters? Were they all being pushed into doing things beyond their control? She felt the warm clasp of her husband's hands and felt safe all over again. Freed from further anxiety and her confidence restored, Urmila sought out her mother. Even from a distance, she knew her mother was worried but was making a brave effort not to show it. She went up to her and touched her shoulder lightly.

'Mother, this happy day shall not unfold an unhappy future, a braver one perhaps,' she said softly. Her mother smiled back weakly. That's how it had always been with the two of them. Urmila holding on as much as she could and finally rushing to her mother's lap, seeking comfort in its warmth and the wisdom in those gentle eyes and, in turn, giving her mother all the support she could muster. They were each other's anchor.

'Yes, you will be able to do it, come what may,' murmured Sunaina, and placed a soft, sad kiss on her daughter's forehead. 'Don't worry about me. With you there to look after your sisters, I have no reason to fret. But there is a new life waiting for you which will test you at every step. Just be yourself—listen to what your mind says and follow your heart. They will eventually tell you the same truth. And above all, my dearest daughter, look after Sita and your cousins. Remember that the four of you are sisters, now sisters by marriage too. Let that equation never change the love and trust in your hearts. You might not know, Urmila, but you are their strength, their guiding force. Like you were, and are, for me. You have mothered me as often as you have your sisters. I shall miss you but each time with pride that I am the mother of such a daughter. Don't look back, look forward. Go, my dearest.'

Urmila felt a lump in her throat, her lips trembled and she turned away from the warm glow of her mother's love toward her sisters standing behind her—her eternal companions now and for ever. Sita seemed unfazed at the guru's ominous pronouncement, a collected, small smile on her lips. The glacial, expressionless Mandavi seemed colder, and Kirti's face had an expression of wonder and astonishment; she was stunned. The bewilderment was giving way to a sense of approaching dread. In their heady notion of love and romance, were the four sisters idealizing their future as well? Life had been easy till now, brimming with love and laughter; was their fortune going to change for the better or...Urmila shook her head firmly: she would not be discouraged.

There was an expression of inner serenity, a wisdom to face all that was to be on the faces of the four brothers. They were bound by a common belief—an immense faith in themselves. Even the otherwise volatile Lakshman looked unruffled by the portentous mutterings around them. He gave her a slight nod, his eyes fervent, consoling her in his reassuring way. It wasn't going to be easy, he seemed to say, but they would make it.

THE CITY OF AYODHYA

She caught sight of the golden domes of Ayodhya from a long distance. There were four of them, like upturned lotuses, shimmering in the daylight. As it drew closer, the palace of Ayodhya glittered overpoweringly in all its brilliance, expanse and grandeur. Urmila and her sisters had never before seen an edifice of such blatant magnificence. Its imposing proportions were disconcerting. She wondered how many days it would take for her to get familiar with its vastness. It was nothing like the palace of Mithila which, in comparison, seemed like a stately villa, standing tall in the cool hills, simple and sedate in the centre of the foliaged wooded garden. And she was already missing it. It had taken more than three days to reach Ayodhya and now, dwarfed by the dazzling palace looming in front of her, she felt like a stranger in her new home. Its grandeur made her feel lost and insignificant.

It must be nervousness, Urmila chided herself but at the moment the only comfort she could draw was from the warmth of his body; she drew closer to Lakshman, her hand faintly touching his. He clasped them in silent assurance. Urmila glanced at her sisters; were they feeling as anxious as she was? She did not know but the fact that they were with her made her feel a lot better.

The welcome showered on them reflected the facade of the palace—elaborate and ostentatious—yet cold. Urmila soon found herself face to face with the three queens, each so starkly different. The first to greet them was Kaikeyi; she was evidently the chief queen. At that moment, Urmila believed those malicious rumours of King Dashrath being slavishly besotted with this queen. Kaikeyi was stunning in her beauty and youth, and her loveliness was enticing—it was difficult to take one's eyes off her.

But there was a tiny physical flaw in her exquisiteness. The little finger of Kaikeyi's right hand was grotesquely twisted; it seemed broken and wasted on her fair, pretty hand, but there was a story of love and valour behind it. Famously, Kaikeyi had accompanied her husband in the battlefield—a rare, unusual feat—against the powerful king Sambarasura. During that battle, Sambarasura's arrow broke the wheel of Dashrath's chariot and another of his arrows pierced the king's armour and lodged in his chest, leaving him fatally wounded and bleeding profusely. The queen, acting as her husband's charioteer, quickly repaired the broken wheel by using her little finger for the axle while manoeuvring the chariot away from the battlefield, nursed the wounded king and got him back to fight the war. The twisted finger was a constant reminder of that fateful day and the queen flaunted it proudly, not embarrassed by the deformity.

As was the correct protocol of ceremony, Ram and Sita lead the way and were the first to be greeted with the customary aarti. Kaikeyi performed it in such a way that it left Sita out. All the warmth was reserved for Ram; Sita was getting the cold shoulder.

'Welcome home, Prince Ram, and may the sun always shine on you,' she said warmly, her eyes shining with soft fondness. Sita was bestowed with a frosty glance. The air grew tense, robbing Sita of her smile. The sisters looked on bewildered and bemused, not knowing what to expect next.

Urmila was so shocked at this biased reception that she could only stare in disbelief. She felt Lakshman stiffening next to her, his fists clenching and she realized she was not imagining the imperious dismissal by the queen for Sita.

It was her turn next and she felt Lakshman's warm hand in hers, gently chafing the inside of her wrist with his thumb. It was meant to be a gesture of reassurance, to abate her nervousness but it did more than that. Urmila prepared herself for the glacial treatment from the royal mother-in-law and involuntarily squared her shoulders belligerently and looked straight into the eyes of the queen. They were warm and welcoming.

'Urmila, as your name says—you are where the heart meets the soul and what a lovely couple you both make!' she gushed. 'The most beautiful princess of the land, I hear. My dear, I have also heard you are as fiery as our dear Soumitra here,' she said embracing them both with a warm smile, but glancing warily at Lakshman. She affectionately called him Soumitra, too, but was there a certain apprehensiveness or contempt in that look? 'And that you have all the qualities deserving of a princess, nay, queen, O daughter of King Janak, Janaki, and princess of Mithila, Maithili...'

'I am neither,' Urmila corrected emphatically. 'It is Sita who is called Janaki and Maithili, Mother.' Her tone was almost defiant.

'Perhaps, but it's yours by right,' said Kaikeyi smoothly and turned affectionately to Mandavi. 'My Bharat's bride—as fair and lovely as marble, and cool as the marble too...'

That subtle snide did not go unnoticed by Urmila. The queen certainly had a way with words. Mandavi looked at her mother-in-law impassively, not an emotion passing on her lovely, unsmiling face. She had caught onto the uncongenial vibes as well. Kirti, again, was given a carelessly casual welcome but not as hurtful as the one bestowed upon Sita. More than Sita, it was Urmila who was smarting from it. And what had she, Urmila, done that she alone had been favoured with unreserved warmth? It was bewildering and discriminating. Was it meant to drive a wedge between the sisters or was it a show of strength, a power game?

All through the proceedings, no one dared to reprimand the queen for her graceless behaviour—neither the other two queens nor her husband who looked on with an indulgent smile. Either he was oblivious to the undercurrent or he preferred to ignore it. Being neutral did not mean being fair, her mother had once succinctly told her. And encouraging favouritism was far worse. The king of Ayodhya seemed a case in point. Amongst his sons, it was clearly Ram who was his favourite and Kaikeyi was the special one amongst the queens. Whom would he choose between his favourite son and favourite wife? Or did he really believe that such a prospect would never arise, seeing the younger queen's obvious partiality? That threat seemed palpably close now...only if Ram had decided to take offence and spring to his bride's defence...

Urmila soon became aware of the fact that like she was observing each member of her new family, she was also being scrutinized very closely. It was an old lady with weedy hair and small, sharp eyes with greed in them who kept hovering around Kaikeyi. The princes treated her deferentially even though she was not part of the royal family. Was she the queen's favoured handmaid? Her stature was higher than that certainly, as was evident from the way she spoke brashly and ordered the other maids around. She had a lot of weight to throw around, Urmila thought nastily watching her corpulent waist and fat arms, taking an instant dislike to her. Her name, she soon got to know, was Manthara and she had a limp because of a back curvature, which made her stoop heavily. She was tall and very fair like her mistress. Like mistress, like maid: both arrogant and petty in the limited power they wielded.

Kausalya tried to undo the deliberate damage inflicted by the younger queen. She was all warmth and kindliness and gradually made the brides feel at home. She was regal without the hauteur of the younger queen. Plump and much older, she brooked no challenge to Kaikeyi's beauty. And she well knew it. Kausalya was a dignified lady who reacted to life, as to her youthful, beautiful competitor, with a tolerant smile.

But the person whom Urmila took an immediate affinity to was Sumitra, the youngest queen. She barely spoke a word, her presence was equally quiet. She did not boast of the imperious beauty of Kaikeyi or the gushy effusiveness of Kausalya. But it was the depth of her emotions that was touching. She was ethereal, fair and pale, her eyes soft and sapient and slightly slanting, her high cheek bones giving her an air of being a goddess of wisdom and tranquility. She simply hugged each of the four princesses with such genuine affection that Urmila felt, loved, wanted, respected and at home for the first time in this new place.

Home, she strangely found this word hollow of its warmth. She was filled with a cold anxiety of being suddenly vulnerable, a feeling she could not fathom.

The city of Ayodhya welcomed the four brides with cheer and charm—something Urmila was not feeling right now. She was smiling to reciprocate the kindness of the people but within the palace, the walls seemed to be closing in on her and her sisters. She was especially worried about Sita after the ungracious treatment meted out to her by Kaikeyi. She wanted to meet her in a quiet corner but there was no such place or opportunity. And she firmly reminded herself that Sita had Ram now; he was there to protect her, like she had Lakshman.

Lakshman had seen Ram's injured look when Sita was insulted

but Ram had preferred to remain silent and wished his bride to do the same. But Lakshman harboured no such expectations from his bride. He was as displeased as Urmila and both simmered in their indignation, each understanding the other's ire and trying to placate each other through wordless, reassuring glances. Along with their individual fieriness and their fierce loyalty for their family, what bound them together was their immense patience and power of endurance—never for themselves but for each other and their siblings. He could well imagine, and understand, what his wife was going through; her sister's insult was her vilification too and that doubled the ignominy and pain. He wanted to console her and felt guilty that he could not make her first day in her new home the most blessed day of her life. He noticed her pallid face and could not but compare it with her radiance at their wedding at Mithila. He wished he could bring back that glow. Right now he knew she was desperate to talk to him, but prudence and protocol restrained them from doing so.

'Why is the queen mother so displeased with Sita?' she whispered urgently when she managed to grab a chance to snatch a quick conversation with him.

'She'll cool down, don't worry. Chin up!' was all he could whisper back and giving her chin a teasing tweak instead, he hurried to his father who was calling him. As the day darkened into dusk, she found herself feverishly waiting for the night to fall with the sprinkle of twinkling stars.

The awaiting night fell late. Late in the evening, after all the rituals were done, the brides were led to their bed chambers. Or rather palaces, Urmila corrected herself with dry humour. There were palaces within the main palace and each of the brothers had one as had the three queens. For the wedding festivities, each of them had been redecorated with much artistic care, courtesy Shanta's aesthetic eye and endeavour. Like the palace, this wing which was to be theirs, was overwhelming with its visual extravaganza of bubbling fountains, carved arches, winding stairways and filigreed balustrades.

However, Urmila was in no mood to take in the architectural grandeur of her palace; she had eyes only for him. The day had been fraught with unpleasantness and she wanted the night to be better, the best. All she had wished throughout the long, trying day was that she could be with him, talk to him, feel him, have him close to her. And now alone in their bedchamber, filled with the fragrance of rose petals sprinkled carefully on the huge white silken bed, she had that opportunity at last.

He was waiting for her and the moment he glanced up, Urmila, unable to restrain herself, ran to him and threw herself into his arms like no bashful bride would have ever done. She hugged him convulsively, her fingers sinking into his broad back. She looked up into his black, smouldering eyes, then softly kissed his shadowed cheeks, nose, his crooked smile and his lips. They were full and warm, the heat between them making them hot and scorching. She heard him moan deep in her mouth and felt his hand cupping her breast, the fingers of his other hand in her hair, urgently unbraiding it to let it fall loose over her shoulders. He threw the hairpin down.

'I want you like this!' he breathed thickly.

'I love you, I love you, I love you...let me say it,' she murmured madly. 'I love you!'

'And I so love you, my Mila,' he groaned, sinking his head into the softness of her neck, breathing in the scent of her exposed skin, her thick, flowing hair, inflaming him wildly. This was the girl he had loved and lusted for so long, his Mila, he thought fervidly, as he pulled her slender waist and pressed her harder against him—his sensuous woman, his sultry enchantress. And she was now in his arms, kissing him wantonly, her lips hot and hungry. She was his bride, his wife, she was his at last. He roamed his hand possessively over her silken, pliant body, kissing her, devouring her, stroking her with a passion of frenzied liberation. Through his hooded eyes, he watched her face fervently as she abandoned herself, to the heady sensation deluging both of them, their arms, their bodies entwined, moving in mounting ecstasy. When the moment crashed on them, he placed his lips hard over her mouth to drink in her spasmodic cry of abandonment.

Time seemed drawn, and later on, rested in satiated rapture, he saw her gazing at him. She looked languorously beautiful, still breathing heavily, her hair spilling over the silken sheets, her bare, soft bosom heaving, her lips swollen, her face glistening and flushed a warm peach. In her expression he read desire, excitement, tenderness and something else that he knew must be love. He felt a surge of emotion and he gathered her back carefully in his arms, savouring her lusciousness but cautious not to crush it. He felt blissfully calm, stroking her hair gently, running his finger on her bare back. I love her, I want her, I have her, he thought, and I have never been happier.

They remained long and restful in each other's arms, listening to their slowing heartbeats, their bodies cleaved together. Then, he felt her stirring against him.

'What does the queen have against Sita?' Urmila murmured languidly.

He could not help smiling; she will not let go. He felt her wriggle against him, straightening up to look at him closely.

'No one can dislike Sita. She's the easiest, loveliest person to get along with. What has she done to earn her dislike?' she persisted, her chin resting on his chest, staring at him in the moonlit darkness.

He ran a hand over his eyes and sighed in resignation. 'It is nothing personal she has against your sister,' he began. 'If I can gauge Mother Kaikeyi and the situation correctly, she is miffed because your sisters are not the best choice of brides she would have handpicked for us brothers. She had been bride-hunting for long and had big plans for us—particularly Ram. She wanted the very best for him...'

'But Sita is the best!' Urmila retorted with asperity.

'Again, knowing Ma Kaikeyi, she is dismissive about Sita because she is an orphan, not the true princess of Mithila, like you are. That's why she made it blatantly clear whom she favoured more. Ideally, you were more eligible for Ram, and not me. I am but a lackey prince!' he said solemnly, without losing the twinkle in his eyes. 'That's why the barb about you being the deserving queen...' he laughed.

'Oh, I don't want to be queen, I want you!' she flashed back indignantly. 'This is most distressing!'

But Lakshman had more to tell her. 'My father must not have had the time and opportunity to include her in the final decision and that must have really riled her. Her opinion was not sought. Don't worry, she will come around. She is a very emotionally transparent woman who believes in making her feelings known clearly to everyone. She is disappointed and I am sure your sisters will be able to woo her with their respective charm. Like you have already done!' he chuckled throatily. 'And, dear woman, you can start to work your charm on me again, or do you plan to debate all through our first wonderful night together?' he drawled, pulling her down against him and brought down her face hard against his lips without giving her a chance to argue further.

But Lakshman had underestimated Kaikeyi's ire. Matters had turned for the worst the next day. The insults got more vitriolic and less subtle. It was apparent that Kaikeyi, for reasons known and unknown, refused to accept Sita as Ram's bride. She had put forth the proposal that they must find him another bride and get Ram remarried. Dashrath had apparently agreed to her suggestion.

Urmila was flabbergasted. She rushed to her sister's chamber. Sita was alone, as still and silent as the empty room. Ram had been called by his father to discuss some matters. Urmila could correctly guess what that would be—Sita and their marriage.

Her sister's stricken face flared up her temper anew. 'How dare they do this to you?' started Urmila furiously. 'You shall not take it silently anymore, Sita! The barbs were mean enough and should have been stopped. They have the audacity to think of remarriage dismissing you as if you were some trophy to be replaced! I won't have it, Sita...'

'And neither will I,' Sita retorted grimly. 'I have married Ram and I know the man I love. He won't abandon me. Ever.'

Urmila looked at her uncertainly. 'He is discussing this with his parents. What if he gets coerced into taking another wife? This family does have such a tradition!' she reminded her sharply. 'Our father-in-law has done it before—on the pretext of begetting a child. After Shanta was born from Kausalya, he had no reason or right to bring Sumitra or Kaikeyi as his queens. But he did. And the other queens accepted this quietly.'

'Yes, it happens in many royal families but it won't happen with me!' said Sita. 'I shall not allow it. Never!' she added fiercely. 'I know what Ram's reply to his parents will be, but if he does agree, I shall see to it that it does not happen. On what grounds can they do that? That the marriage did not occur at the auspicious hour? Or that Ram has a mangaldosh? Well, then it should be me who should be protesting the loudest! Four weddings took place that day; are they going to annul all four and send us sisters packing home? Or are we expected to sit placidly and watch our husbands take a new set of brides?' she said scornfully.

'Do they seriously take us to be such tame girls who will scurry to obey?' scoffed Urmila in grim agreement. 'Haven't they realized yet that we are the daughters of Janak and Sunaina, who have been taught to uphold their pride and be courageous? They are so used to being obeyed without any questions that this palace seems to revel in some sort of a benign autocracy. The king said marry the four princesses, and the sons obediently did, without a murmur of protest,' she said. 'Now the king decrees Ram to marry again! This is tyranny!'

The arrival of Ram followed by Lakshman made her stop. Ram gathered the scene and seemed unperturbed, looking straight at his wife. His smile of reassurance dispelled all misgivings. Urmila made a move to leave, intending to give the couple their privacy, but Ram stopped her.

'Wait, listen to what I have to say. I know you must have been worried about your sister—about all of us,' he said calmly. 'My father asked me if I wanted to remarry. I unconditionally said no; that the question does not arise. I love Sita and I can never leave her, not for another woman, not for anything. Do you believe I would have abandoned her or I shall in the future?'

Urmila was not prepared for this blunt, hard question. 'As a man who loves his wife, you would not,' she said equably. 'But perhaps your other roles—as the eldest son, as the prince of Kosala, or as the heir apparent to the throne—they would have made you think otherwise and made you do so.'

Her reply had been equally straightforward, but Ram took it with a gentle nod of his head. 'As Sita's husband and the three roles notwithstanding—of which one is questionable—I would not abandon Sita. I would never remarry,' he replied stoutly. 'Never can I do that, especially when we have been brought up by our mother Kaikeyi to believe that having more than one wife is akin to a sin. It is a crime—unfair and unjustifiable—on your spouse, your loved one. It was she who taught us how to respect a woman. We were warned against even thinking of bringing more than one wife into this palace. My father did it in the past and all the three wives have suffered because of that decision. Who would know it better than our three mothers? We, their sons, have seen their silent pain. They endured more out of royal dignity than charitable tolerance. But it was Mother Kaikeyi who taught us how to love, respect and be loyal, especially to our life partner.'

Urmila was surprised at his words but still look unconvinced. 'Then why did the issue of remarriage come up? What has Sita done to suffer this ignominy?' she insisted. 'Why the snide remarks, the discourtesy that she was welcomed with?'

'Because very simply, Mother Kaikeyi was worried that my mangaldosh and the delay of our mahurat might work adversely for me. That it would eventually kill me,' said Ram quietly. 'She was worried and this miscommunication happened because things happened too fast. It was an anxious, worried mother you saw reacting, Urmila. Please don't harbour any ill feelings towards her. She overreacted and vented her ire on Sita, whom she naturally assumed to be the cause of the problem. I am here to apologize not just to Sita but to you and your sisters too, as inadvertently I have been responsible for the hurt and unhappiness.'

'No, dear son, you need not apologize on my behalf,' a voice sharply interrupted them. Kaikeyi was standing at the doorway, beautiful and regal, her face softened with guilt and regret, much to Urmila's disbelief. 'It is I who misconstrued a lot of things because of my ego and temper; and as a mother, a queen and elder of the family, it is inexcusable. Ram has a more kind explanation for my irresponsible, insensitive behaviour, but I realize I have done indefensible damage,' she turned to Sita. 'I have hurt you with my thoughtless behaviour and no words of regret and apology can mend the wound. But if you can, dear daughter, please forgive this old lady her transgressions.'

Saying so, she folded her hands in silent appeal. Sita looked distinctly uncomfortable; so did Urmila. The moment was awkward and getting disconcertingly stretched.

Sita's next words thawed the discomfiting silence. 'As a mother you wanted to see him safe, happy and unharmed and thus wished to get him remarried. There is no question of you asking us for forgiveness,' said Sita. 'No mother wishes any harm to befall her child and whatever you did was to protect Ram. Please do not be further upset about this.'

Urmila could only look on with shock and wonder and a grudging respect for the queen. If Kaikeyi had been prejudiced about Sita, Urmila could be accused of the same. Watching her humbly apologizing to the younger woman, Urmila felt a twinge of penitence on having nursed biased thoughts about her and Ram. It was her turn to beg for pardon.

But Ram's next words stopped her again. 'No, don't think of it, Urmila. You had a right to question my motives and that of my mother. You were defending your sister. And I know very well the extent you would go to protect her. Can I ever forget how you had whipped out Lakshman's dagger to kill him? You didn't spare him either! So who am I?' he asked in mock horror, genuine enjoyment twinkling in his eyes as he recalled the incident at the palace garden of Mithila.

Sita and the queen look puzzled but noticing Urmila's heightened colour and Lakshman's widening grin, all the queen said was, 'Oh she is a bloodthirsty knife-brandishing warrior too, is she?' she chuckled. 'I won't be too inquisitive of what happened but, aha, this girl can make my Soumitra smile! And what could be better than that—a spouse who can bring out the best in you?'

The tension had eased considerably making way for a fairly jaunty mood. All seemed almost normal: they were all smiling again. Kaikeyi gave her a long look and with a smile that did not quite reach her eyes, said gently, 'Urmila you remind me of myself of so many years ago. We are, though you may not agree, quite alike. Welcome home once again, princess!'

Was that a compliment or a passing regret, Urmila wondered in rising bewilderment, the answer to which question she would get fourteen years later.

THE SISTERS

'Why does everyone prefer Ram to Bharat?' asked Mandavi squarely, leaving her sisters surprised but unprepared to either reply or ponder over the blunt, insensitive question. They were no longer four sisters discussing the four princes of Kosala, but four sisters-in-law debating about the brothers-in-law. But Mandavi had always been tactless.

They were sitting in Urmila's paved patio. She had made it a shady, sylvan glade, very much like the one back home. It had been her puny attempt to recreate the sprawling, wooded garden of the Mithila palace she was chronically missing. Magnanimously open to the sky, ensconced between the bedchamber and the morning room, it fostered an intimacy and soon became the favoured venue for the sisters to meet. They would get together to catch up and chat, albeit for the briefest interval—a pact the girls promised not to break.

Urmila, characteristically, countered her cousin's query with her own. 'Now where does that come from?' she asked cautiously. 'How does it matter to us? Or has someone been talking too much?'

Mandavi could detect the tartness in her voice. 'No, it's just my observation of the last so many days since we arrived here,' she shrugged, trying to sound casual. 'Universally adored.'

'Deservedly or undeservedly, is that what you are trying to imply?' asked Kirti shrewdly.

'Certainly deservedly—he is always so gentle, warm, kind and friendly and of course, *so* dutiful,' emphasized Mandavi, and Urmila, like Kirti, wondered if her sister was being malicious. Sita was oblivious, smiling, pleased at hearing praises being heaped upon her husband. 'He seems to be everyone's favourite—right from his father to all the three mothers, his sister, the nobles at court, the servants, the public...hmm, just about everyone!'

'But for Manthara. She detests him—like poison,' said Urmila astutely. Noticing Mandavi tightening her jaw, Urmila's suspicions were confirmed.

Sita laughed. 'No! Oh, it was such a long time ago! It seems as a naughty kid, Ram had hit her with an arrow on her hump. She spanked him for it, of course!'

'And never forgot it ever since!' retorted Urmila. 'And interestingly, an act for which Ram and the brothers were packed off to some school for disciplining them.'

'But she is such a sweet lady, Urmi, she taught me one of the choicest dishes Ram relishes!' said Sita. 'And she was delighted that I love to cook; she has handed me her favourite recipes which I plan to master this month. She is a culinary wizard! Why do you say she hates Ram, when she sees to it that his favourite dishes are prepared every day!'

'And you are impressed?' asked Kirti, amused. 'Sita, you are either too good or too naïve. You can't see the evil in anyone, and that's not good, especially for you! Urmi is right. I think Manthara resents Ram.'

'Why do you keep saying that?' Mandavi demanded. 'She seems a sweet, old lady who exasperatingly chatters a lot, but she seems a good sort.'

'She doesn't chatter, Mandavi, she gossips. She is a vicious rumourmonger,' countered Urmila with a frown. 'She is trouble, and a troublemaker.'

'You and your fantastic imagination,' scoffed Mandavi, 'that's an extravagant exaggeration.'

'What has she been telling you?' Urmila asked suspiciously.

'Just this and that; idle maid talk,' answered Mandavi airily, 'but why this friendly interrogation?' she sounded more belligerent.

Urmila, though slightly surprised at her truculence, did not allow it to affect her. 'Just that I see her with you more often than she is with Mother Kaikeyi,' she replied evenly. 'So what does she say, our sweet old lady? Come on, it's been so long since we gossiped, didn't we?'

Mandavi looked mollified. 'Oh, typical childhood stories about the four brothers. Bharat in particular, of course,' said Mandavi with a fond smile. 'Lots of anecdotes, snippets from here and there—she's old, she tends to digress and ramble. Like, how Ram used to bully his brothers who so openly adored him.'

'Oh, did he?' exclaimed Sita, in amused surprise. 'I thought it would have been Lakshman. No offence, Urmi, but he's so aggressive and curt! I know that it is mostly a facade—to hide his innate reserve. But everyone quakes at his sight and no one dares to talk back to him! Everyone at the palace is scared stiff of him, including Kaikeyi. Even she thinks twice when he's around!'

Urmila smiled indulgently. Two months down, she knew her husband well enough and was secretly amused at how most considered him to be this dreaded horror. He could be taciturn to the brink of being menacing; words rarely spoken but like a whiplash if they were uttered as a retort or reprimand. He was a lot like her but Urmila knew how to cushion her words with delicacy and discreetness when needed. Lakshman would make a poor diplomat, but the most loyal of allies.

The couples seemed oddly similar in nature and notion. They

were all comfortably alike. Just as Sita was perfect for Ram, Mandavi was for Bharat: both were always calm, cool, collected to the point of being slightly dispassionate and detached. Kirti's quiet sagacity was a foil to Shatrughna's boisterous frivolity, his comic-serious sense of humour to her solemnity. But both, though being the youngest, had a distinct mental discernment and accumulated wisdom that was way beyond their age.

Shatrughna was quite unlike his twin in many ways but what was common between them was the fierce loyalty each had for his older brother: Lakshman for Ram and Shatrughna for Bharat. Urmila found it strange that they were not as close as was supposed and expected from twins; they seemed more attached to the respective older brothers. And though, Urmila had deduced, matters were not too amicable between the two senior queens, it did not affect the brothers. Their bonding was deep, open and strong. They were indisputably close, and vehement about it.

Mandavi responded to Sita's observation about Lakshman with a distinct thread of spite. 'No, but Lakshman's hardly a leader!' she said dismissively. 'He just follows Ram and obeys whatever the big brother says. He's his shadow. Just like Shatrughna is of Bharat. It's amazing that both of them prefer to tag along with Ram and Bharat respectively! They have no individuality. That's what I mean—Ram and Bharat are born leaders!'

Urmila again felt a flash of irritation and pursed her lips in quiet displeasure.

'It would be more correct and polite to call them inseparable companions,' snapped Kirti, her face flushed. 'They are not servile as you are implying; they are simply very close!'

'Why do you keep harping about Ram and Bharat?' asked Sita sharply. 'What are you saying, Mandavi?'

'She's saying what Manthara has been telling her,' Urmila said pleasantly, silently fuming.

'That is why she started off with that peculiar question of Ram being preferred over Bharat,' cried Kirti. 'It is Manthara who has been spooning this daily dose of poison to her as a fortifying syrup, but the talk is not as sweet as it appears!'

'I am intelligent enough and have a mind of my own! Or does the truth hurt you to the quick?' bristled Mandavi.

Urmila was shocked at her sister's virulence. The air was thick with an inexplicable animosity. This was no casual chatter: they were seriously squabbling, Urmila realized with growing dismay.

'What truth?' asked Sita, her face pale.

'That there is a definite competition between Ram and Bharat. And if matters come to a head, Lakshman will choose Ram and Shatrughna will obviously go for Bharat.'

Sita was shocked into speechlessness. Kirti pursed her lips, suppressing her indignation.

'Why would the brothers split up? What competition are you talking about, Mandavi?' questioned Urmila, genuinely puzzled now but treading cautiously, lest she gave vent to her own rising ire. Mandavi was being particularly nasty, and worse, insinuating. But she reminded herself of her mother's warning—that it would not take much to tilt the equation among the sisters.

'I am not talking about the upcoming archery contest between the four brothers to be held next week,' scoffed Mandavi. 'It is this unspoken, unacknowledged rivalry between Ram and Bharat which has been there since they were born.'

'And how is that? And why Ram and Bharat in particular?' asked Sita, more curious than annoyed.

'Because Ram is the son of the eldest queen—Kausalya and Bharat the son of the king's favourite queen—Kaikeyi—and both are eligible for the throne,' explained Mandavi. 'The twins don't count as they were born of the youngest queen and both are not duly bothered—they have left it to these two brothers.'

Mandavi was telling the story of the birth of the four princes but with a twist. After the birth of Shanta from Kausalya and having given her for adoption to his friend and brother-in-law Rompad, Dashrath was childless for years. One day, during a hunting expedition, he met the young, vivacious Kaikeyi, the lovely princess of Kekaya and fell in love with her. He married her on the condition that their firstborn would be the king of Ayodhya. But they remained childless. Eventually he married Sumitra, the princess of Magadh, his third queen, hoping for the son he yearned for but was disappointed again. Desperate, and on the advice of Vasishtha, and with the help of his son-in-law, Rishyasringa, King Dashrath performed two yagnas—the *Ashwamedha* and the *Putrakameshti*. At the end of the yagna, Agni arose from the *yagnakunda* and gave the king a jar of kheer to be consumed by his three wives which would beget him sons. He asked Kausalya and Kaikeyi to share the kheer with Sumitra. Sumitra got a morsel each from Kausalya and Kaikeyi, thereby giving birth to twins. Kausalya bore Ram and Kaikeyi gave birth to Bharat. This is how the four brothers were born.

'The throne?' asked Sita in shock. 'You are talking about the brothers aspiring and fighting for the throne! Impossible, they wouldn't dream of it!'

'They don't have to dream; it's a reality that's going to dawn sooner or later,' said Mandavi bluntly. 'They are princes after all and one of them is going to be the king—the choice is largely between Ram and Bharat...' she shrugged.

'So that is what was eating you up since the beginning! That is why you asked that irreverent question about why Ram is preferred to Bharat?' accused Kirti. 'Well, I will tell you, Ram should be king; not because he is the son of the eldest queen but because he's the best in every way—as a person, as a prince, as a warrior and most importantly, because he is so hugely popular—something which Bharat can never aspire to! Sorry to say, dear sister, most find him so boringly good that he seems a trifle dull!' she added hotly, not bothering to sieve her words either.

Mandavi blanched with cold anger, her eyes frosty. 'No, dear, Bharat *will* be king. Lakshman and your husband are not in the competition anyway; they are too servile, as Manthara says, and possibly because your mother-in-law is not a princess of Magadh as she claims, but of suspect parentage,' she continued relentlessly, ignoring her sisters' expressions of speechless outrage. 'I repeat, Bharat *will* be king, not Ram. Ma Kaikeyi's father allowed his daughter to marry King Dashrath on only that condition—that her son shall be the king of Kosala,' she pronounced glacially. 'And the word of honour is very important in this Raghu dynasty. King Dashrath cannot go back on his word. He will have to crown Bharat as king.'

'And you his queen, of course?' asked Urmila quietly, keeping her tone and temper even, not allowing herself to forget her mother's warning plea. 'Is that what this is all about? Is that how Manthara managed to convince you, Mandavi?'

'But yes, dear, you would wish it otherwise, wouldn't you?' said Mandavi with deceptive sweetness. 'You would rather have your dear elder sister be queen than your cousin...and what they say is so wrong, blood is certainly not thicker than water!'

Urmila gasped in horror; Sita looked as if she had been physically struck, her face ashen. All this while, Urmila had been deliberately leading the conversation to extract the truth out of Mandavi. But she had not expected so much venom to be spewed. Manthara seemed to have worked thoroughly on her sister.

'Stop it, Mandavi! This is outrageous!' cried Kirti furiously. 'You have been despicable throughout this conversation, constantly disparaging our husbands and now you stoop so low to say such a wicked thing! How could you?'

Before Mandavi could retaliate from the vitriolic assault of her sister's words, Urmila intervened. 'Please, girls, don't! We are fighting!' she said angrily, bringing the two girls to their senses. 'We have fought before as well but this is so hideously vindictive!'

she cried. 'What are we fighting about—who'll be queen, who is superior, who ups who? How does it matter? Did we ever think this way? We were always sisters, never cousins, never queens and princesses. Oh, what's wrong with us?'

The plea in her voice stopped further argument. Mandavi looked shaken. So did Sita and Kirti. It had been a moment of mad viciousness; each lashing at the other.

'It is Manthara who is so wrong for us,' continued Urmila, her tone gentler. 'I wasn't doubting you, Mandavi, but trying to warn you that she's dangerous. Her motives and methods are questionable. She is toxic. With her sweet venom, she brings out the worst in us—our insecurity, our latent fears, our petty jealousies. She is deliberately harmful, sowing distrust and ill will. You saw what she has done to us? That's why I was worried. That's why I was probing... By now, hopefully we have all realized how effectively her poison has played up...'

Mandavi look wretched and turned to Sita, 'Your goodness might prompt you to forgive me but I don't think I can ever forgive myself for what I said...'

Sita's face was crumpled. 'No, it is what you believed that is so hurtful... As an adopted sister, was I always an outsider for you, Mandavi?'

'Sita, like Mandavi, Manthara has worked on you too, do you realize?' said Urmila softly. 'By ingratiating herself to both of you, she has played one against the other.'

'She certainly never made me forget what an unfortunate orphan I was, brought up with my selfish sisters!' agreed Sita, with a mirthless smile.

Mandavi nodded her head slowly. 'She made me feel that as I had married the best, I deserved the best—from being the princess of Varanasi to being the queen of Kosala...how could I have been such a blind egotist?!'

'Is that what you wanted to be—a queen?' Kirti asked in surprise.

'Yes,' confessed Mandavi, her voice suddenly low. 'I always hoped I would marry a king to be his queen and not remain a princess all my life. That is why I was hesitating in marrying Bharat...'

'And you only agreed when you were convinced that Bharat had a fair chance to be king!' Urmila could not hide the incredulity in her voice. Mandavi had always been the most ambitious amongst them, sharp and politically astute, but she would not have believed her to be so excessively materialistic or so deceptively manipulative.

'Guilty as you think me to be,' said Mandavi candidly, reading her sister's thoughts. 'I am not very proud of myself right now. Yes, it was my dream to be queen one day but not at the cost of my sisters' happiness. I know you girls don't believe me, but I mean it. I was wrong. I was led to hope, and allowed myself to hope, that I was the destined queen as Bharat's wife...'

'We do believe you, Mandavi,' said Sita. 'Don't be so hard on yourself. I was gullible too, and inferred the worst.'

Mandavi gave her a hard look, turned on her heel and spun away, rushing out of the patio. Sita called urgently after her, but she did not stop.

'What did I say wrong?' asked Sita in bewilderment.

'Give her time,' Urmila said gently. 'She is upset. And so are we.'

With one of them having gone, the three girls sat together in protracted silence, drawing consolation from each other. They were still shocked at the wickedness of Manthara and how their individual involvement with her had exposed their wickedness as well.

Urmila simply wondered who would be next in line to be seduced by Manthara's evil talk.

She did not have to wait long. Manthara was visibly enthused about the contest between the four princes where they would display their martial skills. But she was visibly disappointed when Bharat refused to participate in the contest, citing the reason that he could never compete against his brothers. It was after much cajoling and at Ram's request, that Bharat allowed himself to join the contest in the spirit of sportsmanship.

The day of the contest dawned as clear and unclouded as the results were going to be. Everyone was clearly rooting for Ram. Dashrath beamed regally. His three queens by his side looked on eagerly, each uniformly proud of the four princes, or so it seemed. Kausalya's face held an intense look of hope and expectation—her son would not fail her, it seemed to say. Sumitra looked supremely serene as if knowing what would happen next. Kaikeyi was the most animated—enjoying the contest and applauding heartily.

The sisters preferred to flock together though Mandavi seemed stiff with them. She remained with them for a while and then joined her mother-in-law. Was the contest reminding her of her harsh words? She had not spoken to them since that awful day and Urmila was getting anxious at the deepening coldness between them. She looked neutral, as she always did, her face expressionless and taciturn.

As far as the competition was concerned, it was ridiculously tame. The brothers looked half-hearted in their attempts and the contest was so brief that it ended as soon as it began. It was the mild-mannered Bharat who excelled and gained the first position, but much to everyone's surprise—and obvious delight—it was Ram who was announced the winner. Vasishtha soon revealed the alleged discrepancy. The four princes had been put to test in more unsubtle ways as well. The guru had made one of his students pose as a distressed citizen who, in the thick of the contest, begged for help. Ram had quickly obliged, leaving the competition mid-way, rushing to the man's rescue, relinquishing the first position to his brother. But this gesture declared him the winner. And a precursor to the throne, Urmila thought with a smile, watching the clamorous applause for Ram and the stark disappointment on Manthara's face. It was the dawning reality Manthara feared most, and was so furious about.

That evening, Urmila could not resist teasing her husband about his poor show at the contest. 'It was such a sham! Who were you brothers trying to fool?' she asked with a laugh.

'Our dear parents,' he chuckled. 'We were dead against it—especially Bharat—but Manthara managed to convince Father to organize it. I guess she wanted to show the people of Ayodhya who is the best among us. And yes, you are right, it was a charade for our parents' and Manthara's benefit!' he said, unpinning her bun rolled tightly at the nape of her neck and running his fingers through her loose hair. He did that so often, and each time, as he watched her mane tumbling down, he looked at her as if he was undressing her. Urmila was pleasantly disconcerted but a thought struck her—Manthara again. She had planned the whole show though it had not ended as she would have liked.

Urmila was not allowed to think any further as she sank willingly in his arms, feeling his hands and lips working on her deliciously...

The next morning Urmila was surprised to see the old hunchback in her palace's front hall.

'Got some sweets made by Princess Sita for you,' announced Manthara, bowing. 'She is busy in the royal kitchen, serving up this new recipe I taught her but she sent me right away to give it to you. Have a bite!' she requested brightly.

'Delicious!' Urmila said perfunctorily, sampling a tiny morsel. 'But then, it always is. Sita is a natural!'

'Yes, she is a bright and quick learner, and so patient,' beamed the old maid. 'Why don't you visit the kitchen, princess? I shall teach you too.'

'Because I do not like to cook,' Urmila replied pleasantly. 'I would rather paint.'

'Oh that smattering of colour? It's lovely, of course, but that doesn't make the man happy when he's hungry, does it?' she cackled. 'I say the way to a man's heart is always through the palate! Didn't you notice the glow on Ram? It's all because of the fabulous fare Sita serves him every day. Such a talented girl, and so sweet and loving! Just the right choice for our dear Ram. It is fortunate that he has her as his wife. His soon-to-be-queen,' she added slyly.

Manthara took Urmila's silence as acquiescence and continued with her toothy smile. 'That girl is real lucky! An orphan who was found by none other than the king of Mithila himself...and so a foundling grows up as a princess like you. But unlike you, by marrying Ram, she'll become queen, smart girl.'

Urmila was not ignorant of Manthara's insidiousness. Her remark was double edged insinuating that Sita was an opportunist and Urmila had not been able to do what she had—get herself a better catch. She remembered what Mandavi had said about Lakshman and Queen Sumitra being servile and felt an anger stirring within her again. Suppressing an angry retort, Urmila cut her short curtly, 'That will do, Manthara. Thank you,' she said dismissing the maid.

The brusque dismissal had the effect Urmila desired; it was a tiny vindication. Manthara went crimson with fury.

'Don't try that tone on me, young lady!' she shouted, her lined face mottled red. 'I am the queen's head maid, her wet nurse since she was a baby. So you will show me some respect! I am not one of your servants running errands or serving you! What inflated pride! No wonder everyone likes Sita more than you, you haughty princess! She is the more loved, more popular princess of Mithila, not you, though you might be the natural daughter of King Janak. Why, even your own parents, I hear, love her more than you!'

Urmila, taken aback by Manthara's outburst, did not deign to react. The words did sting, however much she had prepared to remain unaffected by them. The wily Manthara had succeeded in hitting her where it hurt most. Did that mean that she, too, was susceptible to an unacknowledged insecurity? Was she secretly envious of her elder sister?

Manthara had touched a raw nerve. In a quick flash, Urmila reminisced all those instances when her parents had favoured Sita and not her. But, surprisingly, she had been angry with her parents and never with Sita. She could never vent her annoyance on her sister because, each time, she saw Sita squirming as uncomfortably. After each of those instances of childish unpleasantness, it was Sita who apologised frantically, consoling her, comforting her and taking the sting away from her anger. And now this woman was forcing her back into that world she had long forgotten, the memories flooding her troubled mind.

Urmila realized she might have earned herself an implacable enemy in Manthara. Not that the vicious old lady was a friend to anyone but herself and her self-interest.

'Nor can you use that tone on me, Manthara,' she retorted icily. 'You have explained so well who you are—the maid of the queen. Let me remind you who I am—a princess and the wife of the most feared prince in the palace. And pray, henceforth, do not dare to step into my palace without seeking permission. As told earlier, you may leave. Right now!'

Watching Manthara leave in a fit, Urmila hoped she would not try her wile on her again. She had barely managed to sigh in relief that she heard a commotion.

'What the hell!' she heard Lakshman's angry exclamation. 'What are you doing here? I have told you before, Manthara, I do *not* want you anywhere near my palace or my wife. I hope this is the last time I see you here. Now leave!'

With amazement, Urmila saw Manthara muttering copious

apologies and weakly explaining how she had come for an errand and scuttled away before Lakshman had anything more caustic to say to her.

'Why was that harridan here, Mila?' he asked her sharply, more curt than he meant to be. Urmila did not resent his tone; clearly he disliked the old maid as openly as she did.

'As she said, to make me taste some of the savouries prepared by Sita.'

'And?' he asked shrewdly. 'Manthara is no errand girl to pass on messages or sweetmeat. She had more on her mind.'

'And her tongue!' Urmila concurred with a laugh. 'As I didn't subscribe to her wily winsomeness, she bared her claws, and was leaving in a huff, when you chased her away so effectively. *That* was some sight!' she giggled.

'Oh good,' he looked relieved. 'I thought I would have to warn you against that troublemaker. But you did well and seem to understand her quite well, my smart little woman!' he smiled affectionately, a gleam of pride in his eyes. 'But seriously, she is the devil, stay away from her.'

'But she won't stay away! She'll meddle and manoeuvre and manipulate—that's why she's so scary—the things she can do...' she shuddered and Lakshman drew her close.

'Relax, she won't harm you,' he said comfortingly. Urmila hugged him tighter.

'I can handle her,' she looked up and said cheerfully. 'But how has she been able to stay here for so long?'

'Because she is like a mother to Ma Kaikeyi. She brought her up.'

And he recounted a strange story. 'Queen Kaikeyi's childhood was as intriguing as the queen herself,' he said. 'As a young girl and the only sister to seven brothers, she grew up motherless, in the care of her wet nurse, Manthara, who served her devotedly. Her father, King Aswapati had banished her mother from his kingdom, Kekaya—a deed unheard of but not without a reason.

'Aswapati had a strange boon; he was able to understand the language of the birds. But he could not reveal what they said, for, if he were ever to do that, he would fall dead that instant. One day, the king and his queen were strolling through the palace gardens when Aswapati happened to overhear the conversation of a pair of mated swans. The conversation so amused him that he started to laugh loudly. His wife was unnaturally inquisitive, wanting to know what had amused her husband. And she insisted he tell her, knowing full well that if did so, he would lose his life. Incensed and hurt at his queen's insensitivity, he banished her from his palace and kingdom. The little princess Kaikeyi never saw her mother again and was raised by Manthara who accompanied her to Ayodhya and she stayed on.'

'In such a short time, she was able to poison the mind of both Sita and Mandavi, so I cannot imagine the damage she must have done in all these years!' observed Urmila.

'That's because you sisters are still new here,' he said. 'Fortunately, everyone knows about her insidious ways and fake charm. She doesn't fool anybody. In fact, everyone hates her, poor woman, and barely tolerates her because of Ma Kaikeyi.'

Manthara had an irrevocable power over the queen and she must have worked her evil on her as well. How had Kaikeyi managed to promote herself from a second consort to the chief queen, a title enjoyed so far by Kausalya? How did she eventually get to be the king's favourite? From whatever Urmila had witnessed, the equation between the queens was coldly cordial, the undercurrent of hostility staunch between them. Clearly, Manthara must have been instrumental in fracturing their relationship. There was no doubt about it.

People like Manthara did not remain idle. They were parasites; preying on their host's fear and anxiety, slowly destroying them. So who would be her next victim?

THE CROWN PRINCE

From the filigreed veranda, Urmila could see the entire expanse of the manicured garden surrounding the palace. It was as pretty as the structured landscape she was painting. All the sights around her were designed to give the impression of perfection—well-trimmed hedges, neatly lined trees and the grand palace that arose from the green bowels of that garden. Urmila knew that this was not the truth. In the last few months, she had seen the ugly cracks in the facade. They were deep and cavernous, hiding a lot more than they showed. The beautiful palace held a host of not-so-beautiful intrigues. There was the wicked old Manthara who was spreading her poison, the king was old and worried having a spate of nightmares he was terrified about. The four princes, however, remained unaffected by the guessing game of who the crown prince would be. They were their usual loving, laughing, lively selves, brightening up the palace, helping their father with the royal duties and administration.

The most unhappy person in the palace seemed to be Kausalya... She did not miss a chance to complain loudly about her plight. She reminded Urmila of a wretched soul, living in her world of darkness—very much like her chamber—a dark, gloomy dungeon, with thick curtains, the sunlight rarely streaming in bringing warmth and cheer. And in here, she had a grotesque pet—a vicious-looking parrot, in a golden cage hanging close to her bed. And all he called out was, 'Fie the enemy!' something he had clearly picked up from his mistress. And the loquacious red-beaked bird repeated this in shrill tones, ringing eerily in the palace of Kausalya. This was a taunt meant for no one but the beautiful Kaikeyi—her rival who had usurped her power and position in the king's heart, and in his bed.

Urmila avoided stepping into that wing of the palace, finding herself frequenting the chambers of Sumitra instead. It was she Urmila felt close to as she was almost like her mother, whom she missed every single day. She was kind but unfussy unlike Kausalya who hovered around like a protective, fiercely possessive hen. She did not speak much and believed in something done as opposed to something said. She was always calm but her placidity could not be misconstrued as timidness. She could be firm and staunchly resolute, almost stern, again like her mother. She was erudite and had an incisive wisdom, just like Sunaina. It was her calm sagacity which had drawn Urmila to her.

And matters had improved vastly with Kaikeyi since their first disagreeable meeting. She was immensely different from what Urmila had once thought of her. As Lakshman had correctly surmised, she was a candid person—clear in her opinions and very direct in her manner and speech without subtlety or evasion. She was informal and uncontrived, sans the royal reserve or secretiveness. The sum of this made her immensely likable and she was hugely popular with people in the palace and the subjects alike. Though she possessed a formidable fury, she was also generous and earnestly fair—especially in her love for the four princes. Unlike Kausalya whose world revolved around Ram, Kaikeyi was not as blatant about her love for her son Bharat. For her, the princes were all sons of her husband and she loved all of them equally. She knew each of them very well and treated them accordingly. With Ram she was openly affectionate, more than she was with Bharat; with Lakshman, she was careful as he could be irreverent at times but she respected him for his unwavering loyalty to Ram. Bharat was a quiet and soft-spoken person and with him, she was tender and protective. With Shatrughna, she was as warm and generous as she was with Ram, matching his boisterous humour with a hearty laugh and her brand of dry wit. But to Urmila's discerning eye, she was partial to Ram—probably because he was the most likeable of the four brothers. Or possibly because she knew her husband loved Ram the most—Dashrath simply could not survive without Ram. Kaikeyi loved her husband so much that she generously accepted all that was his.

If Dashrath was obsessed with Kaikeyi, she too doted on him. And Kausalya could never forgive the younger woman for that, as she had, unwittingly, distanced Dashrath from his other wives. The senior queen was often heard claiming that though Kaikeyi might be Dashrath's favourite queen, Ram was his favourite son. That equation was supposed to balance out the inequality amongst the queens but it could not douse the embers of resentment. Instead, over the years, it became a raging fire of ambition in Kausalya's heart to see her son crowned king.

Matters were not too great between the four sisters either with Mandavi keeping a cool distance from them. Urmila had tried several times to speak with her but she remained steadfastly aloof, maintaining a bare cordiality with them. She had stopped meeting them since that morning and made no attempt to liaise further. Urmila was fuelled with a firmer determination to dispel these newly sprouted yet deep-rooted differences at the earliest possible. Misunderstandings were malignant: they spread and seeped, corroding one's mind and eating into emotions. Their showdown had turned ugly: the spillover messy and uglier. But Mandavi was unapproachable, not allowing her a chance to reason or express regret. She was like a wall, blocking them from her world.

Urmila could not but compare the four sisters with the four brothers. They, too, must have suffered this sort of a misunderstanding. How had they handled it? How did they manage to stay so symbiotically together? Urmila knew the unspoken answer. It was the deep mutual trust they had for each other. It was not mere love that bound them: faith and respect ranked higher. Had they failed each other in these regards? Urmila was feeling wretched: Mandavi and she had been very close. Could a silly, egotistical fight mar all that bound them together? She knew it was not ego, but something else that had built the wall between them, though she could not gauge exactly what. Urmila despaired helplessly, as she vacantly painted in the upper room not noticing the messenger from Kekeya entering the palace.

She continued with the painting she had recently started. It was a scene of her wedding. She had planned it on a scale as grand as the wedding itself. She was not making much progress though, the worrying thoughts kept intruding relentlessly. Painting, for some, was a distraction from their troubled world, but not for her. She could not paint when she was troubled. All she could do was to stare at the blank canvas, her thoughts clamouring within her.

'Why are you grimacing?' She had not noticed her husband enter the room. She looked up with a start.

'Oh have you heard the bad news?'

'Bad news?' she repeated, uncomprehendingly.

'Ma Kaikeyi's father, King Aswapati, is precariously unwell and since he could not make it for the wedding, he wants to meet Bharat and Shatrughna with their brides,' informed Lakshman. 'Worse, there has been an enemy attack on their kingdom and Bharat's maternal uncle, Prince Yuddhajeet, hopes for help from his nephew. They are leaving right away. I just met Bharat...'

'Mandavi and Kirti are leaving without meeting me?!' she exclaimed.

'There wasn't much time, everything was so rushed and unexpected. They must have left by now...'

'Oh, but I must meet them! I have to! They can't leave...' she got up agitatedly, throwing the brushes down in a noisy clatter.

'Mila, wait!'

But she was already out of the room, rushing down the stairs towards the left wing of the palace, the residence of Mandavi. She was running now, past astonished looks, verandas and passageways. Suddenly the way to her sister's palace seemed too long. All she could think of was to meet her sisters before they left for Kekeya, thousands of miles from Ayodhya. She would not be able to see them for months together. She was breathless when she reached the flagstoned portico of Bharat's palace. They were nowhere in sight. Had they left? Was she too late?

She looked around desperately, catching sight of the royal minister, Sumantra. 'The younger princes just left for Kekeya, princess, on the swiftest horses we have,' he informed diligently.

'And the princesses?' she asked hopefully.

'They left almost immediately in the chariots with the soldiers.'

Her heart sank. She turned back, walking slowly to her room, the world suddenly turning grey and dull. Urmila wanted to weep, more out of frustration. She hadn't been able to speak with her cousins before their departure and did not know when she would get a chance to do that next. This thought flooded her with a sudden, constricting sense of desolation. She was used to them going away for brief visits to Varanasi to visit their father, her uncle Khushadwaj, for vacations, but this time it was different; they had gone without even a goodbye. She could not forget the unkind words Mandavi and she had last exchanged and she felt more miserable, feeling the prick of hot tears behind her eyes.

She met Lakshman in the hallway, just outside their chamber.

'Mila, what's the matter?'

One look at her crumpled face, and Lakshman guessed what must have happened. She had not been able to see off her sisters. And she had taken it badly.

Seeing him and hearing the anxious urgency in his voice, Urmila could not control herself, the anxiety of the last few days threatened to burst through a flood of tears. Her shoulders sagged and she found herself going to him, in his arms, her head resting on his chest.

He held her close in the comforting circle of his arms for a long while, her face buried wet against his chest. Urmila did tend to cry easily, but it was often in frustration or a bout of temper, rarely grief or hurt; those were too private to be revealed. She could handle the biggest crises but it was the little irritants that moved her to angry tears. These silent tears reminded him of her weeping—disconsolately and alone—in the forest soon after he had heartlessly spurned her. She was not crying with the same anguished abandonment that had wrenched his heart and conscience, but she was crushed with some grief that he did not know of. Clearly, it concerned her sisters.

'Hey, they'll come back soon...they haven't gone forever!' he said softly, removing the pin from her hair comb and running his fingers through the long mane that had cascaded down. 'Granted, Kekaya is very far off, but I think they should return within a month.'

'I guess I am overreacting...and see what you have done! I will have to tie my hair again!' she sniffled, slowly regaining her composure, even looking slightly embarrassed. 'It's not as silly as it sounds but we had an awful altercation some days ago and things have been getting worse between us...and now that she is gone, I can't resolve the matter for a long, long time!'

'A squabble?' he looked surprised. 'But knowing you, you would have apologized quickly, the peacemaker that you essentially are. And no, that's not a compliment!'

He saw her smile mirthlessly.

'...And that you haven't managed to do so, *is* a matter of concern. Do you want to tell me about it?' he asked quietly.

With much deliberation, she recounted all that had gone wrong between the sisters. At the end of her tale, Lakshman looked equally grim.

'Why didn't you tell me before when I caught Manthara right here last time?'

'What could you have done?' she countered helplessly. 'I thought it was between us sisters and we would be able to solve it soon enough. I didn't want to come to you with our little fights and problems...'

'This *is* serious,' he shook his head. 'The old maid is back to her old ways, and clearly has done more damage than imagined,' he said darkly. 'I'll look into that, but of course, a misunderstanding is best cleared with immediate communication.'

'But she refuses to even talk to us! She has been avoiding us since that day!'

'Either she is still angry and hurt...or she is ashamed,' he said slowly.

'But she behaved so because she was subjected to a cunning manipulation forcing her to think otherwise!'

'Exactly! She realizes that and hates herself for it. And possibly could not bear facing all of you?'

Urmila's frown cleared and her face broke into a small, relieved smile; she was amazed at his perspicacity. He barely knew Mandavi but he had gauged the situation correctly. She saw a new side of him; his astute intelligence manifested in his insight and acumen to draw sound conclusions. And also that side of him which made her talk to him about her insecurities freely, understanding her vulnerability as no one had. With a pang, she knew she loved him completely. That every moment she shared with him, got her closer to him, each fulfilling and consummate.

'Mila, now I hope and pray you don't ever regret that your husband can never be king?' he grinned. Her seriousness saddened him, and he wanted to tease her out of it, hoping to make her smile again.

'You know I would love you madly even if you were a wandering mendicant!' she lightly punched his shoulder. 'And considering your wise snides, you would well handle the department of law and justice or be the devil's advocate—you are better with words than feelings!' she retorted with a laugh. 'Do you brothers, too, have such disagreements?' she asked the question the answer of which she had been so eager to know.

'Of course, we do!' he shrugged. 'But yes, it strictly remains between us—that has been the mutual understanding right since we were little, boisterous boys! Shatrughna and I, being peas of the same pod, always react furiously to crisis. We are more emotive. Ram is the thinker, always fair and thinking of the effect and the result, hardly of the causes. Bharat is the calmest and gentlest. But he would make an implacable enemy because he never forgets, never forgives. Both of us, especially, often see the situation differently but the trust and respect we have for each other invariably dissipates the tension.'

Urmila understood, their close bond was characterised by an unusual rationality based on mutual comprehension, discernment and empathy. She had learnt to accept that Lakshman was Ram's eternal companion, his alter ego, but watching the two brothers, it became visible to both Sita and her that Ram could not do without Lakshman either. Lakshman seemed to be an extension of Ram—his brother, fellow, friend and confidant. Ram trusted and loved Lakshman the most, even more than Sita, Urmila sometimes suspected. Like her, Sita knew this and accepted it with dignified grace.

'But I guess it depends on the circumstances too,' continued Lakshman solemnly. 'Ours brought us together. What could have created a fracture in the family, has instead, strengthened us; Manthara and her devious designs being one of them. She tried her very best to create a rift between us but we saw through her, by default through our mothers, who could not handle it well between themselves,' he said.

The mood had subtly changed. It was he who was more sombre, wanting to talk but hesitating to reveal further. Urmila slipped her hand in his, prompting him with a gentle 'Yes?' It was more a push than a query; she knew what he was going to say but he was discussing his inner turmoil with her for the first time. He held her hand, rubbing his thumb abstractly over her inner wrist.

'It has been difficult for all of us growing up with mothers who resent each other,' he admitted with a long sigh. 'Matters were more volatile between Ma Kausalya and Ma Kaikeyi—my mother tried to be a mediator but she ended up being neither here nor there. Now she prefers being neutral; not that her opinions matter anyway,' he said dryly. 'And it is in this power struggle between the two queens that Ram and Bharat got inevitably caught and still do. That's what Manthara was trying to feed into Mandavi's mind, that it was Ram versus Bharat. Sadly, it is.'

'And it doesn't affect them?'

'No. Because it is not in their minds, it's on the minds of their mothers and probably some others. Ma Kausalya wants her son to be king. So does Father but the promise he gave Aswapati is making him anxious. Besides, Ma Kaikeyi is his favourite wife. But Ram is his favourite son. He adores both of them. It is not going to be easy...that is why he keeps having those nightmares that are giving him sleepless nights. He is in a quandary. But none of us will ever, *ever* go against each other,' he said it with a savage passion. 'We have seen it happening with our mothers, we do not wish to repeat it, relive it, ever.'

Little did he know that he said it sooner than he imagined the situation to take a turn for the worse.

It had been a week since Mandavi and Kirti had left for Kekeya, and Urmila was feeling their stark absence. Sita was often with Kausalya or in the kitchen polishing her culinary interest with Kaikeyi and Manthara, both excellent cooks. She barely had time to chat with her. Lakshman was with Ram, busy with the arrangement of the raj sabha to be convened that day. All the ministers, neighbouring kings and political allies would be present for it.

This left Urmila with a lot of time to indulge in her twin pursuits: studying and painting. She had no desire to join her sister in the royal kitchen. She was happier wielding the brush than the ladle: a fact that did not endear her to many here. Kitchens were too hot and noisy and a simmering cauldron for gossip. And with Manthara around, it was bound to get spicier. There, she grimaced, she was thinking of the trivial and could not concentrate on her work. She was glad to put aside her brushes when Lakshman entered the room.

He came up to her and promptly removed the hairpin from her coiled coif, undoing it to make her hair come tumbling down. It had become his established custom, his gesture of affection she had got used to so well. And each time, he made it an intimate, sensual gesture, his eyes roaming possessively as her hair cascaded down. 'You know that I cannot roam around with my hair loose, it's socially unacceptable!' she sighed, picking up the hairpin to tie her hair again. But he held her hand.

'Don't. Whenever I get time to catch a glimpse of you through the rushed day, I'd like to see you with your hair wild and flowing. That is when I get my Mila back, not the Urmila of the world.'

Urmila did not argue; he was all smiles. 'Father just announced at the raj sabha that Ram will be crown prince. It was a unanimous decision, of course,' he said. 'The ceremony is scheduled for tomorrow.'

'What?' Urmila sounded incredulous. 'So soon? But why this unprecedented haste?' she looked as bewildered as she must have sounded.

'It's father. He insists on having it tomorrow morning. It's the month of Chaitra and he wishes no further delay.'

'But...Bharat and Shatrughna are away. And should he not invite King Aswapati, my father and Shanta for such an important function? Why the hurry?' she persisted. 'Or is it because he is making the most of Bharat's absence?' she prodded shrewdly.

'Yes, like he possibly orchestrated the old king's ill health from here!' he said laconically.

'Don't waste your sarcasm on me, just let me know what's happening!' she retorted.

'Mila, there's not much time. Everything's a flurry and here you are cross-examining me as if there is a plot afoot!' he flared irritably. 'I had come here to inform you that you are to prepare Sita for the ceremony. Ram and she will be fasting today and there are a whole lot of formalities to be completed...'

'That'll be done,' she replied, still ruffled. 'It's not that I am not happy about the news as you seem to suspect but the abruptness of it is certainly shocking!'

'Father has been having these ominous dreams since the last few weeks and he is thoroughly shaken and troubled by them,' Lakshman looked perturbed. 'You make it sound like a cold-blooded plan. It is not. He's worried sick. He is scared that he might die soon and he wants to coronate Ram as crown prince before any tragedy befalls. These are the fears of an old, troubled father, Mila, not a plot. Do you think Ram is not worthy to become king?'

'How can you think that?' she said indignantly. 'I was just taken aback by the headlong haste. To an outsider, it would seem like a scheming plot. Does Ma Kaikeyi know about this?' she said slowly.

'No. Not yet. Ram just informed me and Ma Kausalya. Sita and my mother were present there too. The haste seems unprecedented but for once I agree with Father—the yuvraj's coronation has to be done quickly. I, for one, want it to happen as early as possible.'

'But why? Don't you trust Bharat?'

'I do. But he is his mother's son and don't underestimate Manthara,' he replied evenly. 'She just might put ideas into his head like she must have been doing so all these years. She calls him yuvraj, if you noticed, never Bharat. His is a young, impressionable mind; he might get swayed under his grandfather's influence, or that of his mother. Ma Kaikeyi can be dangerously stubborn—he might succumb to her insistence.'

'...But she wants Ram to be king, not Bharat!' exclaimed Urmila, rising to the queen's defence.

'That is what she says but does she really mean it? After all, this is politics, a game of power and position. She wouldn't like to relinquish it. Moreover, there is a remote possibility that Bharat may rebel and question the decision. It is a risk Father hopes to elude. I guess that is the reason why he is making most of his absence, and the fact that he is neurotically afraid.'

'But it appears devious even when it is not. This doesn't seem fair. How are you going to explain it to Bharat when he returns? Won't he be hurt? I don't know how to put it, but I have mixed feelings about this. I am glad Ram will be king but there'll be trouble...'

'Exactly. And that's what we are trying to avert. Just hurry,' he said impatiently. 'Get your sister ready quickly. The rituals are to start soon...'

Slightly irritated with her, he left the room. But a bigger worry was gnawing at her: Kaikeyi had not heard the news yet, Urmila told herself uneasily, as she walked rapidly towards Sita's chambers. Had King Dashrath discussed this issue with her beforehand, since he had promised her father that it would be her son who would be heir apparent? Or had he gone ahead without her knowledge and consultation? The last time he had done that and not included her in choosing the brides for the four princes, she had thrown a royal tantrum and threatened the peace of the palace and the happiness of the newly-wed brides. Urmila hoped fervently that the old king or Ram had apprised Kaikeyi by now, or God forbid, Urmila stopped in her tracks, giving an involuntary shudder...it would be devastation.

The moment Urmila entered the chamber, Sita heaved a sigh of relief. 'I was wondering what to do. I was going to come to you and let you know what Ram just conveyed to us. He is going to be coroneted crown prince tomorrow!' she exclaimed, but there was no happy excitement in her voice.

'Where is he?'

'With his mother.'

'Ma Kaikeyi?'

'No, Ma Kausalya,' replied Sita.

Why had he not yet paid the younger queen a visit, Urmila thought nervously. It would have been better if he had broken the news to her personally—as a happy son would to his proud mother. There was no doubt in Urmila's mind that Kaikeyi would be equally glad to hear the news. This inexplicable delay in revealing it to her made it appear needlessly surreptitious. Urmila hoped it would be the father or the son who broke the news to her and not her old nursemaid. Urmila shivered at the thought.

'Are you cold?' Sita asked anxiously. 'But it's so warm today! I am glad that you turned up,' she brightened up visibly. 'Ma Kausalya has told me a list of things I am supposed to do—and I don't know where to begin!'

'For one, you have to start with the pre-coronation fasting today!' Urmila told her affectionately. 'The other things I shall get done. You need to sleep on a bed of grass tonight. The Narayana puja should start soon so we need to get you ready. What are you wearing? Your favourite yellow? It's an auspicious colour.'

'I am missing Mandavi and Kirti,' Sita interrupted her ramble of words. 'We could and should have waited for them...'

'Don't let us get into it,' Urmila tried to brush it off airily. 'We barely have any time to chat, there are so many things to be done.'

'Exactly. Why this sudden decision?' demanded Sita. 'Ram did not have the time to explain it to me but all he said was that he was obeying his father's wishes. It's all so rushed. And I can't help but remember Mandavi's words. She was so sure Bharat would be king according to the promise given by our father-in-law to his father-in-law. It was on that condition, that Ma Kaikeyi's son would be the heir apparent, that he allowed his daughter to marry King Dashrath. Then how is Ram being made crown prince?'

'You know the answer, Sita. Because he is the ideal choice—he is the eldest son and is popular with everyone. He is good, kind, virtuous, brave and noble. He is loved by his subjects. And, besides, his father wishes him to be king. It was a unanimous decision taken by the ministers, gurus and the citizens. Everyone knew it would happen one day. And that day is tomorrow,' explained Urmila, the words ringing hollow to her.

'I wish they were here!' repeated Sita. 'Matters would have been more sorted. How am I to face Mandavi when she returns? I feel guilty; it's like snatching what she aspired for...'

'Now don't be silly!' interjected Urmila sharply. 'Sita, I agree that you were taken aback by this sudden turn of events but do not dwell on such irrelevant thoughts. You are Ram's wife and, as his consort, you become the queen. It is simple.'

'We sisters don't seem to be together anymore, do we?' Sita looked forlorn. 'Things are no longer the same after that fight...Mandavi cut off from us completely, she and Kirti left for Kekeya without letting either of us know, and now they are not here for one of the most important events of my life. They should have been here, Urmi.'

'Let's not brood over it. What Mandavi believes or what she wishes for, does not matter right now. And anyway, they were largely not her words; she was being slowly vitiated by Manthara, all of us know that now.'

Manthara, Urmila felt a chill up her spine. The present setup was perfect for her to play mischief. Where was she?

'Have you seen Manthara?' she asked casually, not wanting to arouse Sita's suspicions. 'I could do with her help. She must know all the procedures and formalities.'

Sita shook her head. 'No, I haven't seen her since morning. She must be with Ma Kaikeyi.'

Urmila fervidly hoped not.

THE EXILE

It was not yet dawn, the sky still dark and cloudless, but from the palace windows high above, Urmila could see that the streets of Ayodhya were illuminated, with people starting to throng the city, the narrow lanes filling up fast. Like her and all the others they were waiting for the ceremony to begin—they were waiting for their king. He had not yet stepped out from his chambers.

Everything was ready—the holy water in jars, the curd, honey and clarified butter in golden bowls, the aromatic fried rice, the sacred grass and flowers arranged neatly in filigreed gold plates and silver trays. Outside, there was a procession of horses, bulls, elephants and chariots with white flags accompanied by cheerful crowds walking alongside; the music of drums, cymbals and trumpets renting the early hours in erupted merriment. The palace was festooned with gaily coloured floral garlands. Flickering oil lamps, adorning every corridor and arch, added a luminous brightness to the gaiety. Hand-drawn rangolis marked each step and hallway of the palace. How she and the senior queens had managed to plan out each detail and decoration, Urmila wondered tiredly, running her hands over her burning eyes. She had not slept through the night and neither had the others.

Everyone was ready. Ram was dressed in white silk robes, looking regal and solemn. In her rich, deep turmeric silk sari, complementing the heavy gold jewellery which initially she was averse to wearing, Sita looked every inch the golden queen. Urmila looked down at herself—she had bundled herself in an onion pink embroidered silk thanks to Sumitra, who had forced her to leave Sita's side and ordered her to dress up for the occasion.

Vasishtha had reached the palace with his procession of disciples for the maha puja, bringing with him the holy waters of all the holy rivers in golden vessels. So were the generals, ministers and noblemen of the court. Kausalya, bursting with fiery pride and unsuppressed joy, and Sumitra, sedate as always, were sitting at the yagna, waiting for the king. Both the queens were in ceremonial sparkling white and dull gold...but where was the third queen? Urmila felt a coil of uneasiness stirring within her. Kaikeyi had not yet appeared on the scene nor was Manthara to be seen anywhere. She glanced at her husband. Lakshman had barely managed to get ready but in his royal blue, he was the very prince she had fallen in love with—handsome, frowning and unsmiling. He, too, was worried as she could see. Why were the king and queen taking such a long time to make their appearance?

Ram and Sita were ready for the coronation. Kausalya was pouring ghee into the sacrificial fire, invoking blessings for her son. Vasishtha called Sumantra, the royal minister, and said, 'The preparations are all done. The holy fire has been started. Please go and call the king. The people are waiting for him.'

Urmila and the others were surprised to see a white-faced Sumantra return quickly without the king. Instead, he had a message from the king for Ram. He had been summoned to the king's chambers.

There was a still silence as Ram, alongside a grim-faced Lakshman, hastened after Sumantra. Everyone was wondering what was happening but none dared to voice their doubts. Sita slipped her hand into Urmila's and they held each other tightly; both anxiously awaiting an ambiguous, unfavourable outcome. The knot of fear was getting bigger, billowing deep inside her. Urmila saw Kausalya looking worried. Sumitra was already beside her, calmly chanting the mantras.

The thickening crowd outside was also getting impatient and restless, wondering about the unusual delay. Were the rites taking longer than usual? Was the ceremony to be more elaborate than otherwise? Little did they know what was happening in the inner chambers of the palace.

Ram returned almost half an hour later. Urmila noticed immediately that he was without any of his royal insignias. The white umbrella and the retinue reserved for the yuvaraj were missing. There was a calm resoluteness on Ram's face but his eyes looked uncharacteristically sad. Her husband, in contrast, looked white with fury. Her heart sank—the worst had happened.

Kausalya got up with unrestrained relief and led him to the seat meant for the yuvraj. He stopped short and said, his tone clear and soft, 'That seat is too high and unmerited for me, mother. I have come back with my father's commands that he wishes Bharat to be given the throne and that I should leave immediately for the Dandaka forest for fourteen years. I am not a crown prince, mother, but soon shall be a hermit living in exile in a forest,' he said. 'I came here to tell you this. Give me your blessings, mother.'

Kausalya looked dumbstruck, her face ashen. She would have crumpled in a heap had not Lakshman and Ram held her steadily. Sumitra rushed to her side as did Sita and Urmila. Lakshman politely requested the others to leave, citing a change of plan, the announcement of which would be made later.

'What are you saying, son?' she said weakly. 'What is happening? How can you leave us? How shall I live without you?'

'These are my father's wishes, I have to obey them,' said Ram quietly, his face stoic and expressionless. 'And I believe that it is my dharma, my duty. How can I break my father's word?'

Urmila could see that Ram was deliberately impassive in his manner, keeping his emotions in check. Was it to protect his mother from further anguish? He was leaving behind a mother who was old and weak and who had been living in a world of darkness for as long as Ram could recall. Her heart full of pain, frustration, fury and vengeance, she was surviving on the single hope that one day she would be the queen mother when Ram would be king. And even as Lakshman exploded in naked fury, Urmila saw Ram containing his pain and masking it with a smile.

'A fourteen-year exile!' exclaimed Lakshman furiously. 'What crime have you committed that you have been given such an extreme punishment reserved for the most vile offence? Or is it to have you out of the way for Bharat to take the crown?'

Ram simply shook his head and tried to pacify his angry brother. But he refused to be appeased. 'My old father has lost his head over his young wife! And only a weak-willed man could do what he has done!' he seethed contemptuously. He turned to his mother. 'Do you know why he has made this sudden pronouncement? Because he was forced to acquiesce to the two boons he had given to Kaikeyi when she had rescued him during the battle against Sambarasura!'

Urmila was numb. Her brain, stunned at the sudden turn of events, could scarcely unscramble the episode Lakshman was referring to. King Dashrath had offered Queen Kaikeyi two boons when she had saved his life so impressively in the aforementioned battle. She declared she would keep them for a later day. That day was today. She had asked for the impossible—a throne for her son and exile for Ram.

Lakshman was beyond seeing reason. 'How can my father forget his dharma as a king and be just a husband listening to his wife in matters of the court? His personal decision can't influence royal affairs of the state.' he lashed. 'Ram, you say you are doing your filial duty but I am questioning his role, his status and his right as a king, not as a father or a husband. On what grounds is he sending you away? You have not committed any crime; he has, by denying you your right to be crown prince and convicting an innocent man—you—to be sent on exile for fourteen years! You have no reason to be bound by the promises made by our father to his wife. As the prince of Ayodhya and the kingdom of Kosala, as the prince loved by his subjects, as one who is brave, kind and fair, you have a duty towards them. You know you can revolt and will be supported by everyone—the nobles, the ministers, the army, the people. Say it brother, and I shall do it!'

Lakshman paused, his fury unabated but his voice calm. 'You can. But you won't, dear brother, will you?' he said savagely. 'You would rather accept the injustice and go for that exile because, for you, filial obedience is above all. You would never disregard your father's promise. It is our family tradition, right?' he countered bitterly. 'And they both—Kaikeyi and Bharat—know that you would not dream of disobeying Father's wishes. That was the clever plan; and they won!'

Ram had kept silent during Lakshman's tirade, allowing him to vent his pain and the fire raging within him. 'You would not have been half angry or hurt if this had happened to you. Why, if I know you well, dear brother, you, too, would have quietly obeyed our father's orders.' asked Ram quietly. 'This anger stems from your deep love for me. You don't want me to suffer. Lakshman, you are my other self, my very soul in another body—how can you react differently from me? Why this senseless anger and indignation on my behalf? I have no desire for the throne or for power. I take his decision as a new opportunity for myself. If not as king, as a hermit, I shall get a chance to go to the forest and serve there.'

'But what about all of us here—your mother, your wife, your brothers?' interjected Kausalya, her voice choking with emotion. 'How would we live without you? And why? Because my husband is bound by some pledge he made to his ambitious wife?' she asked with vicious wrath. 'I won't allow it! I have suffered enough over the years but not anymore! I shall not part from my son! I won't allow you to leave us...you cannot disobey your mother either!' she sobbed, clinging to Ram in desperation. 'Be kind, son, take pity on me... How will this old mother live without her son? Take me with you!'

It was a terrible, moving sight: the mother hugging her child, holding on to the last vestige of sentiment and sanity. Overwrought, Urmila turned to Sita. She was standing straight and motionless, her eyes dry. She kept silent, her fists clenched.

'Mother, you have to be with your husband, my father. He needs you now more than ever, in his hour of pain and grief,' Ram gently wiped the tears from his mother's cheeks. 'Be kind to him, mother, for what he did; he had no choice. I have seen him—he is helpless and lying in bed, disconsolate and moaning. He is my God, mother, and I can never disobey him. His words and commands lead me to my destiny. Oh mother, this is fate, else why would someone as loving as Mother Kaikeyi ask for those boons now? Don't hate her either; she is doing what fate is making her do...'

'Don't blame it so conveniently on fate, brother!' broke in Lakshman harshly. 'Call it fate or Ma Kaikeyi's folly, but are we to look on helplessly and give in to fate? Ignore and swallow the injustice? Suffering injustice is also a crime, brother. As princes and warriors, it is our dharma to remove evil and establish justice. I am going to do just that—are our shoulders meant to embellish and simply showcase the bows and arrows and swords? I would take on all those who have conspired against you! Either by taking to arms or through argument. Will no one speak to the king and the queen? Why are we accepting their unjust order?' he asked in frustration. 'Why doesn't anyone say anything? Let Bharat be king if they so wish but I shall make one last attempt to persuade them to not send Ram to the forest. I shall go and beg them, implore them, grovel at their feet if need be...'

He made a move to rush out of the room before anyone could stop him. But an unusual, softly spoken request brought him to an abrupt halt.

'Would it make a difference, dear?' asked a soft, gentle voice. It was Sumitra. 'My son, I am proud of you. And this proud son of mine would lower his pride for his brother and beg at their feet for mercy but would they hear you? Would they listen to us? To reason? Ram is correct—this turn of event is a twist of fate. There is more to it than the pain and anger you are feeling right now for your brother. You want to fight for him, give him the justice he has been denied. Then, support him in what *he* wants, not what you want for him...'

She paused and Lakshman understood what she was saying even before she had finished the sentence. 'You read my mind, mother, as you always do...' he said softly, the anger suddenly dissipating from him. With a marked change of expression, he turned to his brother. 'I am sorry for the words of anger and irreverence against our father but I cannot bear it when you are harmed. And now I realize, you are not hurt, you are, in fact, welcoming this opportunity to see a new world. In that case, please take me with you in this wonderful journey. We have always been together; we are, as you said, one soul in two bodies. So, do not refuse me, Ram, because I shall follow you nevertheless. You cannot stop me.'

Urmila was struck numb, the implication of his words hitting her fast. He was leaving her to go with his brother for fourteen years.

Ram was not surprised, but he did not approve of what he

had heard from his brother. Frowning, he looked worriedly at his brother and then at Urmila. Lakshman did not turn around to look at her. His back was to her, straight and unrelenting. She got the message—he would go to the forest, with or without her consent.

'No, you will not,' countered Ram forcefully. 'You and Sita have to look after the family when I am not here. They need you more. Your place is in the palace, not in the forest. It is my punishment which I have to bear alone.'

'Oh the great follower of dharma, you have given a fine speech!' Sita's strident voice cut his sharply. 'As a wife, let me repeat my dharma to you. I have to be where my husband is; I have a right to share your love and happiness but also your unhappiness, duties and misfortunes. I am to share everything with you—a wife is first and foremost the companion of her husband, at his side always, loving, supporting and guiding him. So, there is no room for discussion here; I will go with you to the forest. And please do not insult me by saying I am a princess and that for me my world is the luxury of the palace. The forest will be my luxury henceforth. You cannot abandon me. You *cannot*. I am your wife and I am with you wherever you go. Parting from you will be more cruel than death.'

There was no plea in her statement; it was articulated with a succinctness that was stinging. But Urmila was horrified. Sita in the forest? She would be an incumbent for them in their mission, and worse, she would be exposing herself to unknown danger. Urmila was about to protest but bit back her words at the last possible moment: she could not interfere between husband and wife. It was their decision. She looked at the two queens, hoping they would stop Sita. But, instead, Kausalya looked pleased with her decision. 'Just as a good wife should be!' she said proudly. 'I give you my blessings, dear. Help him in his endeavour.'

How could Sita be of any help to them in the forest, wondered

Urmila. Rather would she not be making herself and the brothers susceptible to harm, injury and risk?

Both Lakshman and Sita had made their intentions clear: they would be accompanying Ram and there was no room for any argument. Lakshman had forsaken her and Sita was going to leave the palace with Ram. The two persons whom she loved most had left her, without a moment's hesitation. Suddenly, she had had enough of the scene in front of her. Her heart constricting painfully with conflicting emotions, feeling suddenly unwanted and bereft, Urmila silently slipped out of the room, but not unnoticed as she had thought she would.

Urmila's first instinctive reaction had been a flood of hurt for being rejected by both her husband and sister, followed by a deep and bitter anger. They had not considered her at all, each intent on getting what they wanted. She felt betrayed, left out and let down. Her grievance was more against Lakshman than Sita. For Sita, there was reserved an envy—another unfamiliar feeling—that she could accompany her husband to the forest; Urmila could not. Her husband had rejected the option outright. There was the guilt for harbouring such disagreeable scepticism towards the people she treasured most; why was she thinking such terrible thoughts about them? And then came the volcano of grief, like molten lava, exploding and scalding each sense, every thought on how she would be wrenched away from the man she loved for fourteen years. A man who did not love her enough, who could betray and forsake her yet again. He did not need her, her heart wept.

'Mila, don't!' she heard him say hoarsely. 'Please don't hate me so!'

She turned instinctively on hearing his beloved voice, unable to mask the stark despair in her eyes. He winced.

'Don't hate me for what I have done,' he repeated. 'Forgive me, if you can. I know I have failed you!'

There was a lump in her throat; she could not speak. She did not want to speak; she did not trust herself. The sight of him was so precious...soon it was going to be rare, no, absent—she would not see him for years now. She was drinking in the sight of him uninhibitedly, without anger or pride. She timidly stretched out her hand to touch him, scared he would soon disappear. She felt his smooth skin under her trembling fingers, looking straight into his eyes. They were as anguished as hers—tormented, tortured and torn between the two loves of his life. It struck her that they did not have too much time. He would be leaving soon. There was no time for anger and rancour, for pain and regret, for hatred or forgiveness. All she could do was love him.

'I love you,' she breathed softly. 'Go.'

'Yes, I have to. But not with you thinking the worst of me. Mila, I love you. But you think I don't,' he said, his fingers unconsciously loosening her bun at her nape, the hairpin dropping at her feet. 'Never, Mila, never think that. I cannot prove what I feel for you but don't condemn me. Can you feel how you fill my heart, my being, my very soul?' he swallowed convulsively. 'You are in me. And that's what I shall have when I am without you for the next fourteen years.'

'Then why can't you take me with you?' she asked sadly.

She said it before she could stop herself as she knew the answer. It was a futile request. Lakshman was going out of his own volition with Ram, he had not been banished. He was going with his brother as his soldier, his bodyguard, and a soldier does not take his wife to the battlefield. Urmila knew she had to harden her heart for herself—and for him. She looked at the darkening sky from her window, black and bleak, refusing to break into light, ushering the dawn of a new day.

'I cannot take you with me because I love you too much...not too less as you think,' he was saying tenderly, holding her hands and turning her wrists out to stroke them absently with his thumb. 'It's not easy in the forest. Ram is taking Sita because he knows he will be able to protect her. I am going as his guard, so how will I be able to look after you or protect you? And more importantly, you are safer here in the palace. The forest is not a safe place, and it's not just the physical hardship I am talking about. I know you can suffer that gladly. Dandaka is now especially dangerous with the demons, having captured it, throwing out or murdering the rishis, disrupting their penance. And you have seen how treacherous they can be, Mila! Don't you remember how they entered the Mithila palace and took the form of Sita? Everyone was fooled. Even you! Then how can I take you with me to such a place and expose you to danger?' he said violently. 'I would go mad with worry just imagining you coming to any harm! No, Mila, I would rather part with you for these many years than endanger you even for a moment! Possibly, as Ram said, that's what we are destined for—to fight the evil there and not sit easy on the throne of Ayodhya.'

His face was tortured, his eyes glistening with pain. He looked at her. She looked lovely and forlorn. Her silence drove him crazy. He did not miss the plea in her heart, her silent, softly despairing appeal, breaking his heart, almost killing his resolve. 'I can never forget how Ravan and the other princes looked at you at the swayamvar and I would have killed each of them for their temerity! And in the forest, if not protected, a woman is anyone's for the taking—it's an animals' world with no rules, morals or societal restrictions. How can I ever take you there?'

Urmila clutched at his hand, and said tremulously, 'Go, Lakshman. I shall not stop you...' she choked.

'You won't be alone here, Mila,' he continued gently, reassuring her and himself. 'Mandavi and Kirti will soon join you. And you are so strong—the strongest woman I have ever known. You are

Urmila, one where the hearts meet...' he said softly. 'It is you who binds all the sisters together with your patience and wisdom. Please do it for me now. Look after my broken family,' he implored. 'And let me go to the forest for I am not sure if I would be able to protect you as your husband. My work and goal would be to safeguard my brother—the king of Ayodhya and his queen. My duty is to protect the future of Ayodhya. That's what I have been born for...'

'But what about my future?' she wanted to scream in mad despair but it came out as a silent plea. 'I don't have anyone but you! Oh Lakshman, I need you!'

She didn't say it but her moist eyes reflected her hopelessness.

He could not bear it anymore. He crushed her to himself, holding her close, feeling her supple, warm body against his, resting his head in the softness of her neck, his agonized face buried in the lingering fragrance of her thick hair—his solace from the world. She was, as her name described, his Urmila, the enchantress, his beating heart.

She clung to him, never wanting to let go. She could feel the heat of his hard body, the burning lips on her skin, and she moved closer to him, absorbing his spicy smell, the hardness of his mouth, the softness of his full lips, taking in each detail, each moment of his physicality. He was breathing laboriously. She sensed the battle raging within him, his struggle with himself and his desperate endeavour for self-control.

'This is so difficult for us. Make it easier for me, Mila. Make it easier,' he whispered against her lips. 'You are my strength but also my weakness.'

She stood still, listening to the wild hammering of his heart, his agonised words bringing her back to the harsh reality. He would have to go. She would have to leave him. With cold deliberation, she broke away from him. His arms dropped loosely at his side, his face crushed. It was up to her now. She had to be strong, stronger for him as well. One wrong word from her would undo their happiness.

'Love is very close to hate, it doesn't take much to turn loving to hating,' she said slowly, looking hard into his darkened eyes, moist and soft. 'I love you...but I don't recognize you anymore. I cannot but hate you for forsaking me. You have spurned me for someone else, something else. You say you love me but you cannot remain with me here in the palace and instead opt to go with your brother. For fourteen years,' she emphasized each word. 'It is he who has been exiled, not you. Why should you accompany him? He has Sita with him—the kind soul that she is, and the dutiful wife,' she added deliberately. 'He is strong and capable enough to look after himself and Sita. Why do you need to go with them?'

Lakshman did not reply, he was staring at her in silent appeal. 'And how can I make it easier for you when it is you who has taken the decision?' she continued ruthlessly. 'I wasn't considered at all, was I? I have known it since I fell in love with you, married you and came here. I knew I would be forsaken—your brother comes first. Yet, am I asking for the impossible? That you don't leave me alone here? Don't say I am needed in the palace to look after your old parents. They have Bharat and Shatrughna, Mandavi and Kirti. You either take me with you to the forest or don't go there, stay back for me.'

She knew she was extracting the impossible from him. She heard him taking in a deep, ragged breath. 'You know I can't do either.'

'I knew you would refuse me, again,' she said flatly. 'That is what your love is—hurtful and rejecting. You don't love at all, Lakshman, you cannot love! You were right—you should have never married. You never did love me; even our marriage was forced upon you. It was a convenient arrangement that the other sisters got married to the remaining brothers. I was foolish to convince myself otherwise! All thanks to love! Or to whatever is left of it...' she deliberately left her sentence unfinished; as incomplete as she felt right now, as incomplete as she would be from now on.

Urmila went on, his stricken face licking a fire within her. 'And anyway, I couldn't have done what my sister has done. I am relieved that I don't have to go with you and I am thankful that you did not propose so. Look at me, Lakshman!' she looked down pointedly at herself in her shimmering soft silks and gems. 'I am a princess, born in leisure and luxury. Would you expect me to spurn this to chase you in your misguided, wild adventure with your brother eating berries, walking barefoot and cooking meals for the two of you?' she scoffed, hoping she had laced her words with the exact amount of scorn.

She saw him flinch and she felt a sharp stab of sorrow as she realized she had succeeded in her attempt to hurt him as much as he had inadvertently hurt her. 'You cannot stay back for me because your brother is more precious than your wife. You are not like your father to listen to his wife, are you?' she taunted. 'Will deserting your wife and serving your brother make you more noble? Then, let me hate you for that. Let me hate you for the forthcoming fourteen years—that endless chasm you have driven between us. Let me hate you as passionately as I loved you. Now, go!' she choked, turning away from him.

But he did not leave immediately. Urmila could feel his eyes on her back, as if waiting for her to turn around. She did not; she dared not read the loathing in his eyes.

'So be it, Urmila,' she heard him say. He had not called her Mila, she noted immediately. For the first time he had used her full name in private—Urmila—meaning the enchantress, the meeting of the hearts. Urmila, meaning, waves of passion. But she felt passion slipping out of her, her spirit drained, filling her instead with waves of anguish followed by numbness. She felt nothing. Her soul seemed to have been wrenched out of her, her listless, spiritless body, standing alone and upright, her back turned to him.

He seized her hand and forcefully thrust her fallen comb into her numb palm. Her face turned down and in a shadow, she kept her eyes away from him; she could not allow him to see her anguish.

She heard him changing in the next room. Moments later, he came into the chamber again, stripped of his silk robes, jewels and crown. Bare-chested, handsome and stark in his rough bark clothes, he still looked a prince. They were in complete contrast now; she in her glittering finery and he in his humble attire. He barely glanced at her; she drank in the last sight of him. And he left without a word.

You can hate me for all I just said. I hope I have made it easier for you now, she thought bleakly, made it easier for us, to hate rather than to love each other for the next fourteen years of separation. Would hatred be easier than loving?

THE FAREWELL

'Aren't you going to bid your husband goodbye? And your sister?' asked a gentle voice.

Urmila wearily turned her head. It was Sumitra.

'Come, child, I know it is difficult. But let's go to Kaikeyi's palace where the three are bidding their final farewell to the king,' she said, embracing Urmila tenderly. 'We have to have the strength...'

Urmila allowed herself to be led by the older woman to the lotus-domed, thousand-pillared marble palace of Kaikeyi, with its rich inlay in gold and gems. Despite her own crazed state, she was taken aback at what she saw there. At first, she could barely see him. The room was dark, lit partially by some oil lamps. Soon her eyes got accustomed to the dim light, and she saw the palatial room with its thick curtains blocking away the sunlight.

The king was lying weak and prostrate on the huge round bed, his eyes dull and shrunken deep in the sockets, twin pools of despair. And he was weeping uninhibitedly, with no restraint, pride or shame. It was a piteous sight; a powerful king lying powerless, sobbing in his son's arms.

In stark contrast, Kaikeyi stood tall, beautiful, strong and proud. She was not in her usual resplendent attire though. Her robes were crumpled, her hair loose, and without a single piece of jewellery on her. Without the glitter of gems and jewels, she did not look less glorious though. Her face was ablaze with a strange passion, hard and unrelenting. The usual softness, amicable smile and naughty twinkle in her eyes were all wiped out. She was unrecognizable.

Ram was embracing him, troubled but trying to pacify his disconsolate father. He and Lakshman had changed into the bark dress reserved for hermits residing in the forest. But both still looked like princes—young, handsome and with a regal aura about them.

'Don't go, son,' cried the old king. 'You are not in any way obliged to the thoughtless pledge I made to my scheming wife—that undeserving woman you consider your mother and love and respect so deeply!' he added scathingly, his eyes glittering with loathing at Kaikeyi. 'As a prince, you can challenge my command and seize the throne. Do so, son.'

'That's some fine advice coming from the just king and father, who would rather be unfair to his one son and trample upon his rights,' said Kaikeyi scornfully. 'What rights are you talking about? That Ram seize power and throw you and me in prison while Bharat is absent? What bravery, what courage coming from this royal house of the Raghuvansh!' she gave a brittle laugh.

Lakshman flushed. 'Let's not talk about decency, mother,' he said grimly. 'It is our decency that allows you to speak and do what you can. You know Ram would never go against his father's wishes, yet you are sending him on exile. That is cowardice, and plain wickedness. And you shall pay for it the moment we step out of this palace, mark my words.'

The queen turned a deep red. 'How dare you? But I see you are as subservient as always—following your brother like a servant to the forest,' she said spitefully. 'And I can see Ram's devoted wife, of course. But Sita, why are you still in your royal finery? Didn't you see your husband and brother-in-law in their bark dress? That is what you are to wear.'

The older queens were shocked into speechlessness but Urmila moved in, quick and curt. 'Not that the change of dress would make any difference to Sita—she would still be Ram's queen in the forest,' she said, her voice trembling with rage against this woman who was the cause of this untold misery, the reason why she would be parted for fourteen long, treacherous years from the man she loved. 'What difference would it make to her what she wears in the forest while we live in the comforts of the palace, Mother? This beautiful palace where a mother separates an old father from his son, a husband from his wife. Irrespective of what she wears, she will be at her husband's side, suffering the discomfort with a smile. Just like his brother will do. That's not being subservient, Ma, that's undying loyalty, the strength of supreme love. Ram has Sita and Lakshman with him in the forest. Who do we have, Mother, in this palace with all the wealth and power at our disposal? Just each other—four lonely women and who do you have? Your old faithful, Manthara, your maid?'

Before Kaikeyi could snap an angry retort, Ram intervened and said firmly, 'Mother, I have no desire for the throne or power for any argument. I shall take my leave and all I need is the blessing from my father. Urmila, please get Sita dressed in the bark robes.'

Urmila snatched the forest garment from Manthara's eager hands, flashing her a quelling look. She looked down and stared hard at the clothes. They were rough, scratchy and abrasive. Like how their life would be henceforth.

'How do I put them on?' Sita asked shyly. 'Neither Urmila nor I know how!'

Sita's innocence was charming; it made Ram smile. He took the rough fabric from Urmila's hand and demonstrated to both of them how it was to be worn. Urmila took Sita to the adjoining room and helped her into the bark dress, tying it at her shoulder as Ram had demonstrated earlier. She looked lovely unornamented, her face shining with eagerness and expectation, her long neck bare and graceful without the strands of necklaces and thick gold cords weighing it down, her arms slim and shapely sans the trinket and bracelets and bangles jangling at her wrist. Her feet were bare—soft, slight and slender—and Urmila could picture them treading on the treacherous, hard ground of the dark jungles of Dandaka.

She cringed inwardly, a stab of guilt piercing her, recalling how she had resented her just a few hours ago. Sita had Ram; she would have neither Lakshman nor Sita. They would not be there for each other from now on. Dread clutched at her heart.

'You are disappointed in me, aren't you, Urmi?' asked Sita, misinterpreting the expression on her face. 'I should have stood by you and asked Ram and Lakshman to take you with us as well. But I was so involved in convincing and arguing with Ram that it never struck me that I had ignored you altogether. As your older sister, I should have pleaded your case...'

'It doesn't matter now,' Urmila sighed wearily. 'It would not have helped anyway. Just like you are adamant about going with Ram, no one can change Lakshman's mind. Also, both of us know by now that the two are inseparable,' she smiled. 'You or I couldn't have done much. And it's for the best, at least I won't be worrying about you, Ram and Lakshman will take good care!'

'And you? What about you? That's what's bothering me...of course, Mandavi and Kirti will be here...'

'Shush! Stop worrying. The palace is not a dangerous place!' she laughed shortly. 'I have everyone here...'

'Except Lakshman,' said Sita quietly. 'That is what is gnawing at me...I could not stop Lakshman or have you with us. You may try to hide it from me but Urmi, I can feel what you are going through...' she said helplessly. 'But, do you know why Lakshman could take such a hard decision? Because he has faith in you. I think he believes in you more than in himself. You are his tower of strength, like you have inadvertently been for us sisters. I might be the oldest but it was you on whom we relied for support and comfort. Lakshman does the same. He could never have left the palace in its current devastated state had it not been for you. He knows that you will be able to hold fort and bring the family together some time, some day...'

'No, not till all of you return...' Urmila shook her head, '...that is when everything is going to be good again. These fourteen years are going to be a test for each one of us. The pain and suffering is inevitable, but it will be valuable. It teaches us a lot in many ways,' she said wryly. 'And, Sita, please I have a request. Don't ever discuss me with Lakshman, don't do anything that would remind him of me,' said Urmila, her eyes steady, her voice steadier. 'That is my sincere appeal to both you and Ram.'

Sita looked completely flummoxed. She moved closer to her sister, clasping her hands firmly in hers. 'Don't make me feel so ashamed, Urmi, that I won't ever bear to look at myself in the mirror. You make my exile a simple task compared to what you are doing. Not only are you going to be separated from your husband for the next fourteen years, but you don't want your husband to even think of you lest he digress from his goal to serve his brother. I bow to you, sister, for your vanvaas, your exile here in the palace shall be way harder than mine in the forest. Give me your strength and I know I shall succeed too.'

Sita hugged her and Urmila felt herself close to tears, her eyes hot and burning. She could not collapse now. It was the first time they were going to be separated in all of their eighteen years together and the pain of separation was almost incomprehensible now.

'Take care, always, Sita,' she hugged her back. 'You are so naive, you believe anything and anyone. Don't go by appearances, dear, please don't. There'll be many such Mantharas in the forest as well. Let Ram and Lakshman lead the way and you follow them, as closely as possible. It will be a different world.'

Sita simply nodded her head and Urmila said, 'Go safely and come back safe.'

Ram and Lakshman were waiting for Sita. Lakshman threw Urmila a strange look. Urmila flushed remembering the cruel words she had thrown at him.

'I am deeply grateful, Urmila,' said Ram as Urmila made Sita stand next to him. 'And not just for dressing her up,' he smiled faintly. 'I leave my old parents under your care, and I know they could not have been in kinder hands. You are a remarkable woman—extraordinarily brave and strong. Yet, it is me who is depriving you of the company of your husband, your happiness, for which I cannot be absolved. '

His words made Urmila cringe in embarrassment, she could not boast of the strength he claimed she possessed. 'No, it is for a higher calling, a nobler mission, you are taking my husband. He will always be there for you—in your good times and especially in your hard times,' she smiled, but Ram could hear the tears in her voice.

It was time for them to leave. The dawn had broken, bringing with it the anguish of the next day. The people in the streets were restless and fervid, angry at the rumours they were hearing. Ram was their crown prince, not Bharat. And why was their beloved prince Ram being sent on exile for fourteen years?

'Get the chariots ready and take them to the frontiers of the kingdom, Sumantra,' ordered the old king, his voice weak and trembling. 'Tell the commanders to take the foot soldiers, horses, elephants and along with the army, take the things necessary for the stay in the forest. Men and money should not be spared...'

'Are you planning to give a bankrupt kingdom to my son, without an army to protect it and people to rule?' Kaikeyi interrupted furiously. 'Is this a picnic you are hosting in the forest?'

The harshness of her words again shocked and angered those present in the room including the courtiers, rishis and the royal members of the family. Lakshman looked disgusted and Kausalya quailed in distress.

Ram, ironically, was the intercessor, as usual, trying to diffuse tempers and salvage a sinking situation. 'I have no need for all these royal embellishments,' he refused firmly. 'After giving up the throne, I have no desire for power or wealth or comfort. I am wearing the bark garment and like a hermit, who needs the bare minimum, I shall lead a life of frugality as is expected of me in the exile. I take your leave now, father, and I have your blessing. I leave behind my mother Kausalya, and Lakshman's mother Sumitra and wife Urmila under your care. They are three selfless women who will be suffering the worst pangs of parting and separation. Be kind to them when we are no longer here.'

And he bent down to touch the feet of his father. Sita and Lakshman followed suit, touched the king's feet, then their foreheads, and placed a hand over their hearts, bowing low to await his blessing.

'My dearest Ram, I know that even in the forest, you shall bring glory to our royal ancestors. Return in all that glory. But before that, forgive this old man for his folly and his sin,' he said brokenly. 'By fulfilling my promise, you, my dutiful son, will not allow dishonour to blot my name and that of our line of kings. I am proud of you, my son, but please don't be ashamed of me.'

Ram embraced his father, more as an act of consolation than mere affection. For the old king, however, his last wish was that he retained the respect in his son's eyes. He would not have been able to bear that shame. And Ram obliged, his love and respect for his father shining in his eyes, apparent in each gesture.

Kausalya performed the customary aarti for Ram and Sita, to bid them farewell and blessing them for their safe return. She had grown old overnight, as gaunt and haggard as her husband, the wearing effect of anguish and suffering already telling on her. 'Is my heart made of stone that I am still alive to see this day?' she wept bitterly. 'But do as your father has commanded and come back in full glory like the glorious son you are!'

Ram and Sita, in their bark clothes, walked to Kaikeyi. His face serene, Ram said calmly, 'Farewell, Mother, I am happy that I can fulfil your wish.' Saying that, he bowed and touched her feet, and the younger queen mother warily touched the top of his head to offer her blessing. Sita followed Ram's lead but Lakshman stood still and straight, refusing to bow and turned to the other queens. Kaikeyi flushed. Ram merely nodded his handsome head. Lakshman grimaced and bent low to cursorily touch her feet to receive her blessing.

Sumitra was bearing the brunt of the grief with a brave heart and a braver smile. She was the picture of optimism—soft-spoken and kind—propping each one of them with a gentle word.

Lakshman bent down to touch her feet for her blessing, and uttered just a sole word, 'Ma .' She embraced him, kissing him on his forehead, and said, 'I have always been proud of you but today, my dear son, my head cannot look higher. What you have done, no brother has done for another and from now on, it is you who will be the epitome of fraternal love and loyalty, an ideal for generations together. It wasn't duty but love which has made you accompany your brother and when love surpasses duty, it is salvation. You have made it your dharma. Look after Ram and Sita vigilantly and may you be blessed with the strength to do so. Henceforth, Ram is your father and Sita your mother and the forest is Ayodhya, your place of the future. Go happily, Soumitra, God bless you.'

Urmila felt small witnessing the scene in front of her. Their love was crowned with pride, honour, sacrifice, and above all, happiness. There was no place for maudlin self-pity or wasted sentimentality; it was poetic, almost sublime, exalted in expression and experience.

Sumitra handed the aarti thali of diya, flowers, betel nut and vermilion to Urmila, insinuating it was her turn to perform the aarti for Lakshman. She took it, with steady hands and an unsteady heart, fearing if she would be able to brave the contempt in his eyes. She dared not look into his eyes. But she had to. They were dark, piercing and...tender. Or was it the flickering diya which had softened his expression, wiping the loathing she had been expecting to see in his eyes?

'Do you think I would fall for that little charade of yours?' he asked under his breath. Urmila looked stunned, pausing momentarily.

'We could never hate each other. And hate certainly would not have been able to sustain us for the separation of the next fourteen years. It's our love which will, Mila,' he continued in a whisper, barely audible to her ears. 'And it's the memory of our full, sustained love which will never make us feel alone or lonely. You'll be with me always as I shall be with you, my Mila, my Urmila, my eternal enchantress, my woman of passion and strength.'

She felt herself basking in the warmth of his tender look. She smiled slowly, the love emanating from every pore of her body. She needn't say it; it was there in her eyes, in his eyes, everywhere. And her smile widened at his irreverence; trust him to snatch a conversation with her during a solemn aarti.

'And yes, smile that wonderful smile of yours which makes the world—and me—fall in love with you each time. I want this image of your smiling face forever, but not without your temper!' he added with a wry smile. 'Smile and never shed a tear of grief—promise me that.'

She nodded, 'Come back, dear warrior, as you would from a war,' she said, her eyes brimming with fiery pride and glistening with love, as she applied the vermilion on his forehead, '...safe and unharmed, glorious and unconquered.'

She bent down to touch his feet as was the custom, but he stopped her by holding her hard by the upper arm. 'Don't ever! I am not worthy,' he said shortly, no longer in a whisper but loud enough for all to hear. He turned to the others and addressed them. 'If I am being praised so profusely for being the devoted brother, I fail as a good husband, who is leaving behind his bride,' he paused to look back at her and said with an intensity that matched the burning passion in his eyes. 'O Urmila, will the world ever know of your inner suffering, your divine sacrifice? But my heart, full of shame and gratitude, knows what you are doing in silence, through your brave smile, your generous heart. Eternally, your Lakshman will be grateful to you and be proud of you. I go now and leave you alone but I leave my soul, my heart, here with you.'

Urmila clasped her neck, her throat constricting with bubbling emotion. Lakshman continued, talking again to those in the room 'As a husband, I should have taken care of her, looked after her, been here for her and protected her. I am doing none of that but leaving her behind to look after my old parents when as a good son I should have been doing so. I have failed as a husband and as a son. I bow to my mother and my wife and humbly ask for their forgiveness for falling short of that duty and devotion.'

Urmila was close to breaking down, her heart bursting with incredulous happiness and sadness. His mother looked overwhelmed and the others were visibly impressed. And as the room burst in quiet applause, Urmila felt his hands holding her wrists—and just for the quickest second she felt a delirious sensation—he was chaffing the soft, delicate skin of the inner side of her wrist with his thumb. It would be for the last time. He let go of her hands abruptly and turned on his heel, not looking back, to join his brother and Sita in the chariot which was to take them to the border of the kingdom of Ayodhya where the Dandaka forest started. Their fourteen-year exile began today.

Kausalya had got some goods and eatables for the journey and Sita hastened to keep them with the quivers and the bows stacked in the chariot.

'Why do we need these?' asked Sita in amazement. 'We are going to the forest as ascetics, not warriors! Why should we accept violence and these weapons of violence? Do you go as a recluse or as a kshtriya, O Ram?'

It was a moral question Sita had challenged Ram with at the outset of their journey, Urmila observed with an immense sense of pride for her sister. How justifiable was this display of prowess; wasn't non-violence a better option?

Ram looked at his wife with affection and admiration. 'Agreed, but the duty of a kshtriya is to protect the helpless—and the rishis in the forest we are going to are helpless against the insane violence of the demons. These weapons are to protect them, and us, if need be,' he smiled.

Meanwhile, the crowds in the streets grew louder and fuller, and had started following the chariot carrying Ram, Sita and Lakshman. 'Don't go so fast!' they implored, running behind the moving chariot 'Go slow, we want to catch the last sight of our beloved prince.'

Urmila saw Ram instructing the chariot to stop, and her heart skipped a joyous beat. Was he turning back home with Lakshman and Sita? She heard him speaking loudly and clearly, to the vast sea of people which had submerged the chariot. 'I am going to the forest with Sita and Lakshman to do what my father has ordered. For me, my father's word holds utmost importance, so please do not stop me, O citizens of Ayodhya,' he enunciated each word with clarity and strength. 'I know and respect the great love you reserve for me and I shall be happy and grateful, if you have the same love and respect for my brother Bharat from now on. He will be your king as appointed by my father...' There was an immediate uproar of protest and Ram's next word silenced the angry clamour. 'He is younger but he is good, wise and kind, having all the qualities of a good king. He is brave and strong and shall always protect you. He is your king, so give him your love and loyalty. I leave for the forest now, and have your blessing. Please give the same blessing to my unhappy, old father and my brother Bharat.'

And with these last words, Ram requested Sumantra to start the journey. Urmila saw the chariot move slowly through the thick throng, the people refusing to let their prince go. They followed him, many running after the chariot. From her palace window, Urmila saw the chariot gradually gather speed, leaving the crowd trailing behind them, a resounding lament of anguish echoing through the breaking skies and darkening the gathering clouds. As she watched the chariot become as a distant speck against a cloud of dust in the widening horizon, Urmila heard a wail from inside the palace.

Her father-in-law had collapsed, covering his face with his hands, as if trying to hide his face from the world or not wanting to see what he had just witnessed. His beloved son had left him and he could not take it anymore. Kaikeyi rushed to help him get up.

'Don't touch me, you venomous woman!' he shrieked in rage. 'From this moment, I disown you! I hate and loathe you, O sinful wife. You are no wife of mine now and I renounce you!'

Kaikeyi blanched, struck as if he had hit her. Her hands dropped from him.

'Take me away from her palace, Kausalya! Where are you?' he cried plaintively as Kausalya rushed to his side. 'Take me to your room. Let me die there, for now I know I shall die... O Kausalya, where are you? Where are you, my Ram?' cried the old king, rubbing his eyes, blinking through the tears rolling down his sagging, gaunt cheeks. 'Why is the world so dark to me now? Is it because my Ram, the light of my life, has gone?' he asked piteously, staggering precariously and stumbling.

Urmila swiftly caught him on time, before he crashed to the marble floor. The three queens helped her hold him straight, but he was unconscious. As instructed, he was carried to Kausalya's palace and he lay there for several hours, as silent and inert as the day had suddenly become, stretching long and interminable.

Urmila could not believe that so much had happened in such a short time. Just a few hours ago, she had been dressing up her sister for the coronation. Just a few hours ago, she had been with Lakshman, in his arms...she tore the image from her mind's eye, forcing her eyes to shut and open to see a new, bleak world. Everything looked the same, nothing seemed the same.

She had been in Kausalya's chamber before, not as often as Sita though. It was not as flamboyant as Kaikeyi's but grander than the Mithila palace nevertheless. It was dark and gloomy but right now, it looked defeated and sombre. Even the parrot in her room had stopped squawking. He was removed from the chamber lest he disturbed the fitfully sleeping king. Kausalya looked completely crushed, sitting beside the prostrate king, her lined face anguished and exhausted, her eyes bleary and unfocused with grief.

The king woke up several hours later, late in the day. He was barely conscious. 'Where is Ram? Where are you, Kausalya? I cannot see...let me touch you, are you there?' he whispered, his eyes open but unseeing.

'He has gone blind! O Lord, what more now?' cried Kausalya,

gripping his frail hand tightly, both of them coming close again in their grief and seeking strength from each other. The king's sight had gone as surely as Ram had from his life.

'How am I to console him when I cannot console myself?' she sobbed. 'How am I to live without Ram? And what words of solace can I offer my husband?'

It was only Sumitra who could give some comfort to the distraught Kausalya. 'Why are you mourning, Kausalya? What is there to grieve about?' she asked, her tone gentle but firm. 'You have always been proud of your son, so be proud of him now too. He will always be king—if not now, later—but by going to the forest and living a life of a tapasvi, he is doing what no prince has ever done before. That is what makes Ram unique. He is meant for greatness. Recognise it and be proud that you bore such an exemplary son. Which son would relinquish the crown just to obey his father's word? Which prince would renounce the kingdom to guard the king's honour? Ram is a hero—be proud of him, don't grieve for him. He is meant for glory and greatness and a higher salvation. Lakshman saw it in him, and decided to follow his footsteps to be with him in his new difficult path. He will see to it that Ram and Sita don't come to any harm. I am proud of my heroic son and shall not waste tears of grief but instead wait for that great day when they return glorious and unconquered as my brave daughter-in-law Urmila said. Look at her, she should be grieving too. They have just been married and she will be away from Lakshman for the coming fourteen years...can't you see her plight? Yet she has not shed a tear of self-pity.'

Urmila felt a twinge of embarrassment. She did not feel she had accomplished much or performed a great deed—she had accepted the situation with as much dignity and sagacity she could manage.

The wise woman that she was, she heard her mother-in-law allay Kausalya with further words of reassurance. 'Kausalya, you are a mother of an exceptional man, behave accordingly. You should give strength to your ageing husband and the other women in the palace, but breaking down thus does not befit a queen, nor does it befit the mother of a hero.'

The king continued to lapse between consciousness and unconsciousness in brief spells through the day, his health sinking and his will and eyesight destroyed. But his hate and rage toward his young wife could not be doused. He refused to meet her, forbidding her with the most cruel words he could muster.

'Go away, wicked woman, who has brought ruin to my son and family! How could I ever fall in love with you and your scheming ways? I must have been mad or intoxicated. What an uxorious fool I have been and the world will now laugh at me for that! You are a temptress, an evil serpent, a monster, a witch!' he said, pushing her hand away as she tried to arrange the pillows more comfortably for him. 'Do not pretend to care when all you wanted was the throne for your son. I, the king of all kings, the father of a good son, grovelled at your feet, I begged you to take back your terrible wishes but you turned away and threatened to kill yourself! And now you are surely and slowly killing me...or is that part of your bigger plan? To have me dead, so that mother and son can enjoy the crown and the throne?' he asked viciously. 'How could you do this to an old father in his last, tottering days? How could you do this to Kausalya and Sumitra? Forcing them to stay away from their sons while you bask with your son in power and glory? How could you separate a bride from her young husband, the pure-hearted Lakshman who, out of deep love for Ram, accompanied him in his fourteen-year exile? Can you not see the selfless love all around you? That was how my family was, how you were...I will never forgive you or him. But why do I berate poor Bharat?' the old king cried. 'If I know him well, he will be as repulsed as all of us are from your evil intentions. He will hate you and be ashamed of you. Oh foolish woman! He loves Ram truly, as once you pretended to! I wonder if he will ever agree to your terms, but if does accept the throne, Kausalya and Sumitra, please see to it that these two evil people are nowhere near my funeral. I do not want him to perform my last rites. If he does my obsequies, my departed soul and spirit could never accept it—so please stay away, merry widow!'

Kaikeyi took in his wrath stoically: she did not allow herself to be affected by it.

Instead, she ordered Sumantra to inform Bharat to return to Ayodhya as early as possible and to start making arrangements for his coronation; it would be grander and not a haphazard, hurried one like the one organized for Ram, she bitingly added.

'How I am or how I should be, does not matter. What you do, does,' she retorted unruffled. 'You had given me two boons which I had foolishly forgotten about and asked for after so many years but which I have got after much effort, drama and tussle. In the process, I have earned your ire and hatred and everyone else's,' she shrugged, looking pointedly at Kausalya. 'So be it. You call it evil manipulation, great king, but I call it self-preservation. How could you make Ram crown prince when you had once promised my father that it would be my son who would be heir apparent? Why was Bharat sent off to Kekeya so conveniently and the coronation announced during his absence? And how come Ram's coronation was planned under a shroud of secrecy and I was not even told about it?' she demanded, her eyes flashing. 'You broke my trust, not me. O great king, do not preach to me about ethics and morality when it was my son and I who would have been victims of your political designs but for my timely action,' she said contemptuously. 'As Bharat's mother, I protected his rights which he was being deprived of through your pretence of biased love and kindliness. I saved my son from injustice and in the bargain, if Ram has been subjected to it, it's only fair. And ironical.'

Urmila, even in her dull anguish, still could not believe the drastic transformation of the queen. She was unrecognizable— gone was her warmth, her affectionate lovingness and her integrity. All for political power? Who had corrupted her?... And before she could finish the question in her mind, Urmila knew the answer. There was only one person who had the wile and the natural endowment of chicanery to persuade the kindest soul to such evil. Manthara.

THE DESPAIR

What had Manthara told Kaikeyi that she got persuaded to do the unthinkable? That old, wily woman was nowhere to be seen near the sick king's bed. It had been four days since the king had given up food and water, and he was fast sinking. Instead, Manthara was with Kaikeyi who had been forbidden to enter the chamber. They were occupied with preparations for the coronation ceremony of Bharat. Messengers had been sent to Kekeya to bring him back but without letting him know the true reason for his premature return.

Urmila got to meet Manthara soon enough. Or, rather, the old maid made it a point to come and meet her. 'Queen Kaikeyi has called you to oversee the arrangements of the coronation puja,' she announced. 'You would know best since you almost did one for Ram recently,' she added nastily, with cloying sweetness.

'I have to check on the king's medication every hour, so please let the queen know I will not be able to assist her in any of the preparations,' retorted Urmila, her tone tart. 'Besides, Ma Kausalya is not feeling too well either, so I have to look after her, too. And while you see yourself out, Manthara, tell the maid

Mrugnaini to keep the water for boiling and not loiter around, gossiping and spreading malicious lies,' she continued smoothly, turning her back deliberately on the old woman.

She heard a sharp hiss of breath. The old woman's eyes became fixed in an incredulous stare, fury climbing all over her mottled face. 'You arrogant girl! You still dare to talk to me in your high and mighty manner!' she screeched. 'Who are you, insolent woman? Just an abandoned wife at the mercy of Queen Kaikeyi and Bharat. You will have to obey them, not your other mothers-in-law who are best seen tending to the dying king. They cannot protect you or your absentee husband whom you were so proud of! Where is he? He left you for his brother! And it's a joke that you once so loftily claimed him to be the man most feared in the palace! Bah! Where is he now? Fetching roots for his dear brother or pressing his tired feet?' she asked, malice dripping from every word she uttered from her toothless mouth.

Urmila remained unruffled, secretly pleased that she had managed to anger the crooked old lady and shake her from her smug diplomacy. 'I am not in a habit of discussing my personal life with maids,' she said icily, with all the arrogance she could muster. 'Nor am I Ma Kaikeyi who foolishly believes whatever you garble. You are just an old, disgruntled woman who is happy seeing others unhappy. And you know precisely how to make the happy unhappy. You may leave, Manthara. Now. With that dim witted spy of yours—that good-for-nothing Mrugnaini. You have them installed everywhere, haven't you? Kamini at Mandavi's palace, Pranjali at Ma Kausalya's; you breed them well—all as ratty and rotten as you.'

Manthara went white, her deviousness had been exposed, but she stood her ground, her voice rising shrilly and her eyes reflecting a peculiar, murderous glassiness. 'Last time you and your insolent husband threw me out of this very room,' she spat, 'this time you shall hear me out. What did you tell Mandavi, Kirti and Sita about me that they started avoiding me? They used to give me the respect I deserved till you put some unfunny ideas into their heads. Do you think you are very clever, that you are the leader amongst your sisters? You can never beat me!' Manthara's face was congested purple in spite. 'I'll have my way...I *am* having my way! See how things are falling perfectly into place. Just like I managed to create a rift between the queens, I shall see to it that you sisters fight in the palace for the next many years. Mandavi will return and she will be queen as she so desired, and that will distance her from you and Kirti. Sita is already out and I can wean Kirti away from you. After all, she is Mandavi's blood sister, not yours. You are just a sad, lonely figure who will have no one to turn to, neither your sisters nor your precious husband! Vengeance is mine, dear!' she cackled in sadistic pleasure, her eyes shining with hate and happiness.

Urmila answered calmly, 'What vengeance are you talking about, Manthara? Vengeance against whom? Us or Kaikeyi? For, you have caused her the most harm. And you call yourself her well-wisher!' she scoffed. 'You are her worst enemy. Does your conniving brain still not realize that you have just a few days to shout your triumphs? Fear the day when Bharat returns. Not only will he not accept the throne but he'll throw you out and hate his mother forever. You are smug that Bharat will obey his mother and be the king. But that just shows that you don't know him at all. He might be your favourite but he doesn't favour you. He tolerates you for his mother's sake—just like all the others in the palace do. Fortunately for you, Bharat is as noble as Ram and will never hurt you but be careful,' she warned. 'Also, I have just one question for you—you talk about devising a rift amongst us sisters and the queens, but could you do that with the brothers?'

Urmila paused, waiting for Manthara to reply. The wizened old lady was uncharacteristically silent but there was a faint gleam in her eyes, a glimmer far back in a dark tunnel.

'You cannot. You failed there. You must have tried several times; that is why the blatant favouritism for Bharat—not just because he was Ma Kaikeyi's son,' Urmila continued softly, 'but because you needed him as a weapon to hurt the princes. And you took his silence for acquiescence. He was silent out of respect for you, Manthara, as you were like the grandmother he never had. And you have betrayed his trust too. Just like you did with Ma Kaikeyi. You made her demand her boons. Not only did you remind her of them but also the long-forgotten promise King Dashrath had given her father.'

'But the king did go back on that promise, did he not?' barked Manthara. 'My Kaikeyi was beautiful, young, clever, brave, the most eligible princess of the country—why would she marry an old king? But she did because the foolish girl fell hopelessly in love with him. And I made her father put that condition as a last resort to safeguard her interest or she would have gladly agreed to anything!'

'It was you who influenced Aswapati!' said Urmila. 'You made him extract the promise from King Dashrath and he readily agreed hoping to have a son from Princess Kaikeyi.'

'Yes!' said Manthara viciously. 'He married her only to have a son. And when she could not give him one, he callously went ahead and got Sumitra as his third wife. A shock the poor princess could not bear and that's why I had to weaken the new bride's postion. Fortunately, she, too, could not beget a child and I started spreading rumours about her lineage...it worked mainly because Sumitra was such a quiet, timid kitten,' she laughed disparagingly. 'So uninteresting and dumb—just a pale shadow selflessly serving the elder queens without thinking of her own good or that of her sons! Why, she was stupid enough to encourage even the twins to dote on Ram and Bharat as she did on the queens!'

Urmila clenched her fists, her face tight with spreading anger; she could not believe this woman's atrocious wickedness.

'But it was always Kausalya who was the biggest rival being his first wife and Kaikeyi needed to usurp the status as quickly as she could and fortunately, that war against Samabara of Vaijayanti turned in Kaikeyi's favour,' recounted Manthara, preening over every memory. 'I persuaded her to join the battle—as she was such a fine warrior—to woo over the king all over again. She excelled on the battlefield and saved his life. With that one favour, she enslaved him for ever. Kausalya finally had to forfeit her right as chief queen. Kaikeyi soon became his favourite consort as I had planned. And everything was fine till Ram was born...'

That the king adored Ram from the day he laid eyes upon him although he had three other sons must have worried Manthara; and it was that insecurity that made her resent Ram so passionately. And over the years, the resentment turned to virulent hate, laced with a gnawing fear that this was the one person who could upset all her neatly laid plans.

Manthara spread her hands sadly but her smile was cunning. 'Everyone loved Ram—he had some magic about him and all succumbed to him—even Kaikeyi, foolishly so!' riled the wicked woman. 'She completely doted on him, always oh always, forgetting that Bharat was her son! Her son was to be made king but that silly love made her forget that promise her husband had once given her father. The king, too, had conveniently brushed it aside, sending poor Bharat to Kekeya often so that he does not grow too fond of Ayodhya. I used to remind her, reprimand her for sending her son away so often to her father's place and neglecting him but she kept saying she had no problems with Ram being made king as he was the rightful heir being the first born. Silly woman, first blinded by her love for her husband and then for Ram!'

The old woman was now openly boasting, not bothering to mask her emotions. She said in her heavy clogged voice, 'And then, after a lot of thinking, I found one chink in that armour of love—Kaikeyi's distrust for men. Thanks to her father having abandoned her mother so many years ago, she was always suspicious and doubtful of her husband's love. That is how I made her hostile to Kausalya and Sumitra, pitting them as rivals,' smiled Manthara craftily. 'All I had to do was fan that distrust at the right moment. And the hurried coronation was the perfect excuse to whip up all of Kaikeyi's latent insecurities.'

Urmila saw how Manthara had perfectly designed and designated her plan and felt physically sick.

Manthara was gloating and gleeful. 'Kaikeyi has always been emotionally gullible. She had complete faith in Ram; to shatter that immense faith and love, I had to put the fear, that deep, bubbling fear into her again that Kausalya would regain her power and position if Ram were to be made king. Then, Kausalya, who despised Kaikeyi, would hit back at the first given opportunity. She could, and gladly would, even put Kaikeyi and her son in prison or worse, make her subservient to her! That thought terrified Kaikeyi and she was ready to do everything that I said to save her from that unimaginable plight!' the old woman crowed, readjusting the gold-knobbed walking stick on which her body rested.

'And then I added to that fear by pointing out how the king had hastened the coronation of Ram during Bharat's convenient absence, planting a seed of doubt about his motives,' she smiled slyly, 'and how he had not bothered to inform her about it. I kept telling her that the king and Kausalya had fooled her and plotted against her and her son Bharat...and from that moment onwards, Kaikeyi became my little Kaikeyi again, whom I could mould as I wanted!' smirked Manthara, her face wreathed in a flat, white smile.

Thick cunning played on her wrinkled face. 'She begged me to get her out of this net which was closing upon her and I showed her the way out of the nightmare—to ask for the two boons the king had once promised her.' she shrugged. 'And I told her how to go about it too—throwing a tantrum, sulking, threatening to kill herself and all the drama that was necessary to force the king to agree. Oh, she performed beautifully! And it all happened exactly the way we wanted it. Of course, I did not expect Sita and Lakshman to follow suit—which made it all the better, for, frankly dear, as you said, I am scared of Lakshman's terrible temper and his loyalty. He could have spoiled the whole plan and revolted against Bharat and the king or Kaikeyi. Ram would never dream of it! That he went with Ram was a blessing!'

Everything was falling well into place as Manthara had envisaged—but for one. Bharat. Would he ever agree to his mother's proposal masterminded by Manthara?

The king was sinking fast. Since the day Ram had stepped out of the palace, the king had slumped in despair and despondency. Fevered and semi-conscious, he kept crying for his son to return. Everyone was worried and it was Sumitra who took one quick decision. 'Call for Shanta, quickly,' she told Vasishtha as Sumantra was not back from the forest yet. 'I think she should be with her father now. He does not look too good.'

Sumantra returned from the forest six days later. His return saw the city in a pall of gloom; there was still a lingering hope that they would return. With Sumantra's return and his narration of how the princes were, the king's last hope was gone. Ram had left, and with him had the king's will to live. He lay still and listless, his mind torpid, harking back to his days with Ram.

Kausalya broke down, swinging between grief and frustrated fury as she turned savagely on the languishing king. 'Why do you bother to know the details from your minister when it is you who sent him to escort your son to exile?' she flared. 'It is you who commanded my innocent son to go on a fourteen-year exile—a punishment reserved for the worst criminals. It was you who so meekly agreed to your wife's wishes well knowing they were criminally unfair and...cruel! It is you who took away my son from me. It is you...' her voice broke. '...And all for that mad love for your dearest wife! What sort of a king are you who gives boons to his wife so that her son supercedes the throne while mine—the heir apparent—is thrown out of the kingdom to live in the jungles. You let go of a good son and a good king for the sake of some hollow promise that you made to an ambitious wife. That's what the world is saying and laughing at you, while all I can do is weep for my lost son! Why? Why, do I have to suffer this?' she spewed her anguish.

Like the others, Urmila was stunned by her virulence. Her exploding fury must have been very deep-seated and relentless to not care for a dying man. Sumitra made a move to stop the cruel flow of words but the king turned his head towards the eldest queen, his eyes wet and vacant. 'You are suffering this, dear, for my mistake, my foolishness...and my sin, and the curse which is coming true...' he whispered tremulously. 'Have pity on me...'

His trembling voice bought the queen back to her senses. She clutched his emaciated hands in quick remorse. 'I am sorry, forgive me for my angry words...you haven't committed any sin. It is that woman who first stole you away from me and now my son!' she wept. 'I have nothing left, but this grief which we have to bear together while she lives happily with her son and the crown!'

Her grief was edged with her hate for Kaikeyi: throbbing and inexorable. The king shook his head, 'No, it's not Kaikeyi's fault either, it is mine. I have sinned. Why would a woman who was so fond of Ram suddenly turn against him so heartlessly? It is the curse working on us,' he said hoarsely. 'That curse of the old parents of Shravan is upon me now...'

'What curse are you talking about? What sin?' asked Kausalya fearfully, dreading the worst. Was the king's wandering mind making him ramble senselessly?

'I can see death approaching me and in these last moments I can only think of that sin I committed when I was young, brash and immature,' he sighed, the breath rattling in his throat. 'I was famous for my skill of using my arrow on moving, invisible targets just following their sound. One rainy evening, I had gone hunting to practice this art of mine on the banks of River Sarayu in the forest, hoping that some thirsty animal would come to drink water from the river. I heard the sound of water lapping and I aimed my arrow at that gurgling sound. The arrow correctly found its mark. But it was an incorrect target. Instead of a dying cry of an injured animal, I heard a loud, heart-wrenching, human scream that rent the stillness of the night and my very soul...I can still hear it!' he sighed. 'I rushed to the spot to see my kill; it was not an animal but a young boy, covered in his own blood, his chest ripped apart by my unthinking arrow. I can never forget that gruesome sight and it has come back to haunt me! He could barely breathe, the blood gurgling from his mouth. I went close to him to help him, to apologize, to beg his forgiveness but all he could gasp was a request to take some water for his old, blind parents whom he had left under the shade of a tree in the forest. It was then that I noticed the upturned pitcher of water. His parents were very thirsty and they needed the water urgently and saying that repeatedly, he died in my arms.'

The king was weeping, the tears silently coursing down his sunken cheeks.

'It was an accident,' said Sumitra gently. 'You did not mean to kill him.'

'That can be no consolation, my sweet Sumitra. You are saying this to comfort a dying man, I know, but...' paused the king, swallowing convulsively. 'But I had just killed a bright young boy—as old as my Ram—devoted to his parents...and all I could think of at that time was how I would face his parents. I had to take the pitcher of water to them—I couldn't have run away from that dastardly deed. And so, fearfully, I went to them. They were waiting under the tree as he had said. I gave them the water but dared not speak. And finally, gathering all my moral courage, I confessed to them of my heinous crime. I begged for forgiveness though there was no pardon for such a terrible sin. They were speechless in their grief, weeping inconsolably till the old man turned to me and requested me to take them to where the body of their dead son lay...' the old king continued shakily, his sightless eyes seeing his past which had returned to torment him. 'They sat down beside him, felt his bloodied body all over and broke down—two helpless old parents crying over the body of their young son. I was filled with guilt and self-loathing and wished the old parents gave me some punishment, some repentance. With my help, they performed the funeral rites of their son. The old father said to me, 'You have committed this crime in ignorance but it is still a crime. The grief you have given us is unbearable. We cannot live without our son. And though you shall live, may you suffer the same pain we are suffering now and may you die of the same grief of having parted from your beloved son.' And saying those terrible words, he and his wife jumped into the funeral pyre to be with their son. My sin is catching up with me now. Their curse is coming true. Let me die mourning for my son!'

The tears had dried and cracked on the old king's lined face, the lines of anguish more than those of old age. He was breathing heavily, his breaths coming in short gasps making it difficult for him to speak.

'Don't speak any more. Rest,' said Sumitra moistening his dried, chapped lips with some water. 'Why are you mourning, O king? Ram shall return, victorious and famous, greater than ever before. You couldn't have witnessed a prouder moment. So, dear king, don't burn in this relentless grief and consume yourself. Wait for that shining day—it will recompense for the suffering of the coming fourteen years.'

'Fourteen years?' grimaced the king in a vain attempt to smile mirthlessly, his face ravaged in pain. 'I cannot live without my Ram for another day. I cannot see but I can see death so near and I welcome it. It is better to die than live without Ram. He is my life, my soul...'

Urmila felt a sob in her throat, turning away from the crazed grief of a desperate father. Kaikeyi was not there to see that pain which she had inflicted on her husband; she was not allowed in his room. Without any thought, Urmila rushed out of the king's chamber and found herself running towards Kaikeyi's palace. The festive preparations were on for the coronation ceremony. Bharat was to arrive within a day or two.

Urmila barged into the inner chamber of the queen. She was surrounded by baskets of flaming orange marigolds to be used to decorate the entire palace.

'How can you sit here so prettily while your husband is dying there?' Urmila blurted unthinkingly, beyond care and caution. 'What are you made of, heartless queen, that you can think of all these sweets and savouries...' Urmila gestured wildly at the closed baskets of sweetmeats in the room. '...when your husband has given up food and water for the sixth day today? He'll die, he's dying...' she choked, the bile of bitterness burning her throat. 'And you know only you can stop this nightmare...you can still tell Sumantra to bring back Ram. The king will live on with that hope. Please, Mother, hate me for my impudence but please avert this tragedy. Save the king. Bring back Ram...let Bharat be king, but please bring Ram from the forest!'

'The king is being childish...it is his way of sulking,' shrugged Kaikeyi, with a dismissive smile. 'It is his way of showing he is angry with me. He'll come around!'

'Have you seen him? He is fast sinking... Oh, Ma, please, go to him, give him that assurance that you are sending back for Ram from the forest and he'll live...I am sure he will. Please, Mother, please, stop this tragedy! It will devastate our family!' she implored.

Urmila had her hands folded, her head bowed. It was an act of complete supplication, her righteous anger replaced by plain desperation.

But the queen remained unmoved, her face frigid in hostility. 'Did the queens send you to me?' she asked icily.

Urmila looked at her uncomprehendingly. 'The queens?' she shook her head. 'Why would they? They are besides themselves with grief watching their husband die. It is me and my silly, hopeful heart which has got me down here to you...'

'Or are you saying this to get your husband back?' asked the queen with a sardonic smile.

Urmila felt herself going warm as the hot flames of fury were rekindled. 'How can you do this? Has ambition made you blind?' she lashed back. 'I am trying to make you see what you cannot—trying to avoid a tragedy that will ruin us all! Lakshman went because he loves his brother. Just as Bharat does so devotedly. He will never accept the throne. He will hate you for what you have done...he will blame you for his father's death and the world will call you your husband's murderer!'

'She's threatening you, O queen. How dare she talk to you in this impertinent way?' interrupted Manthara hastily. 'Don't believe a word she says. She is, after all, Sumitra's daughter-in-law and Lakshman's wife, the man who would be the first to revolt against Bharat and you!'

'Keep quiet! You vile woman!' snapped Urmila, turning on the old maid. 'I am speaking to the mother of Ram, Queen Kaikeyi, and manners demand no one interrupts. So, stay silent!'

She turned to the queen again, her eyes pleading. 'I have not come here to quarrel with you and I apologize for all my impertinence. Can't you see, Ma, it is not worth it? How can you believe that anyone would dare harm you or Bharat if Ram were king? Don't you know Ram? Would he ever allow anyone, even his own mother, to even speak disrespectfully to you? That is what you are scared of, aren't you? That Ma Kausalya will become the queen mother once Ram is appointed king?' asked Urmila, looking searchingly at the cold visage of the queen. 'Ram would have never allowed any sort of injustice within this family. You know that. He would have loved and protected us as is expected of him. You saw how Bharat was unwilling to participate in the competition against Ram, so how can you imagine he will accept the crown that belongs rightfully to Ram? Oh, queen mother, think! And right now you need to save the king...he will die without his Ram! Go and tell him the reassuring words that you have sent back for Ram. Please, oh, please before it's too late!' she stretched out her arms in despair and a final desperate appeal.

Kaikeyi made a move towards her, a tiny flicker of emotion passing on her hard face. Urmila felt a surge of hope. There was a loud clatter of running feet and both of them turned towards the sound. It was a maid, she was panting, her face wet with perspiration and falling tears. She said with a strangled cry, 'The king is dead!'

THE INTRIGUE

The fear of anarchy ruled Ayodhya—both in the city and in the palace. Queen Kausalya collapsed, crumpling into a weeping heap, begging to join her husband in the funeral pyre. But there would be no funeral—not till Bharat and Shatrughna returned to Ayodhya. They had left Kekeya a week ago and were expected to reach Ayodhya either that very day or the next. The king's mortal remains were to be kept in oil till the sons arrived to perform his obsequies.

It had been more than a week since Lakshman had left the palace, and Urmila realized that she had had no time to grieve his absence. She was lost: it was like wandering through a skewed landscape in a state of agonized disorientation, lost and clueless. She was rushing from one chore to another, her mind blank yet chaotic. Urmila found herself spending all her time at Kausalya's palace—initially because of the king's illness and now with the elderly queen having taken ill herself. She lay in bed, alternating between long bouts of weeping and short, fitful sleep, moaning unremittingly for Ram and the king. Shanta had fortunately reached Ayodhya and rushed to her ailing mother. Sumitra and Urmila were faithfully by her side, fearing she would suffer a relapse. Kaikeyi had insulated herself in her palace, waiting impatiently for her son to arrive. Mercifully, the preparations for Bharat's coronation ceremony had been stopped.

'Why was the palace being decorated?' demanded Shanta angrily. 'There's a death in this palace, not a celebration!'

'It was to welcome Bharat, for his upcoming coronation...' began Sumantra weakly.

Shanta went white with anger. 'How dare he? How can he sit on my brother's throne?'

Vasishtha was a worried man. 'The kingdom is without a king. I fear anarchy, especially with the people already unhappy that Ram and Lakshman are in exile, they have no one to turn to,' he frowned. 'And it's not good news considering the enemies on the frontiers, too. They could attack knowing how vulnerable we are.'

Urmila shook her head firmly. 'We are emotionally vulnerable right now but let us not be unprepared for war. Keep the army ready. And it is just a matter of another day or two,' replied Urmila placatingly. 'Bharat should be returning any moment now. Once he has performed the last rites, he can take charge but yes, till then let's not get weak or be caught unawares.'

They were interrupted by a caustic interjection. 'It's a little unusual, isn't it, that the ministers and the royal priest should be discussing the future of the new king and the kingdom with such a young girl, when the royal widow is still alive?' asked Queen Kaikeyi, resplendent in white and gold. She was beautiful and formidable.

'It is customary not to burden a mourning widow,' answered the guru smoothly, unaffected by her biting sarcasm. 'The other queens are in deep mourning and the only person we can now turn to is Urmila, the learned daughter of the learned Janak. And as the royal daughter-in-law, she should know the state of affairs especially when none of the sons and their wives are present in

Ayodhya. As a widow, you are expected to be in mourning,' he added pointedly.

The queen flushed. 'Let me know where Bharat is right now and when he would be reaching Ayodhya!' she said coldly and flounced out of the assembly hall in all her regal hauteur. There lingered a momentary silence in the hall till Sumantra and the other ministers and the learned men of the court—Jabali, Markandeya, Gautam, Kashyap and Katyayana—turned to Urmila. 'O daughter of the wise Rajrishi Janak, please look into the matters of the royal court for we do not want to be accused of power play or otherwise,' said Sumantra softly, bowing his head deeply. 'We shall let you know of all that is happening—and is expected—in the given situation.'

With a jolt, Urmila realized the burden which was now upon her—the affairs of the palace as well as political concerns. The only other person whom she could turn to was Shanta, but she refused to interfere in matters of the state or the court. She was constantly at her mother's bedside, scared that her mother too would follow her father soon. But she made her anger against Kaikeyi and Bharat very apparent.

'Don't come to the wrong conclusion, dear,' warned Sumitra. 'We are in a delicate situation; it won't take much for all to crumble down.'

'How can it get worse? Not after all what has happened!' said Shanta bitterly. 'I cannot believe that matters came to such a head... I always knew things were never too great between Ma and Mother Kaikeyi; but to stoop so low!' she cried. 'How could she throw away my brother from the palace and the kingdom? How could she?'

Leaving the disconsolate daughter with her mother, Urmila walked slowly toward her palace and realized she was all alone. And what surprised her more was that she had been juggling family and formal duties with easy effortlessness since the past few days. Possibly because she used to discuss the courtly matters of Mithila with her father. He had always encouraged her to get involved in the affairs of the state. But it did not mean she could escape the domestic duties. 'If you can run your home well, you can conquer the world!' her mother once told her. It came to good use today, Urmila thought dryly, smiling as she thought fondly of her mother. She sighed. She missed her mother.

Urmila looked up and could not believe her eyes. Her mother was standing in her chamber in person. Her face broke into a smile as she ran to her. She didn't say a word, simply rushed into her mother's arms. It was bliss; it was a relief and Urmila remained long in the comforting embrace. Sunaina gently eased herself from her daughter's gripping hug and searched her face. It was worn and thin, the roundness of her face giving way to sharper, angular lines.

'When did you come?' said Urmila warmly. 'Where is father?'

'Your father shall be here for the funeral. I left Mithila right away, the moment I got to know Sita and Lakshman were accompanying Ram on his exile,' Sunaina answered quietly.

'The funeral shall not take place till Bharat returns.'

'I came for you,' her mother said simply. 'Even in your worst hour, I knew you would not tell me anything. You would rather keep it all to yourself—not always wise or brave, as you think.'

'How could you have helped, Ma? Sita made her decision and I had to take mine.'

'Sita went with Ram to be with him. You did not. You are here alone without Lakshman for the next fourteen years...it's going to be a lifetime. As your mother, can I ask why you took such a decision?'

'Ma, he has gone away; what difference does it make now?'

'You didn't have much to say either, did you? He left you here to be with his brother.'

Urmila winced, the words piercing her sharply, 'Ma!' she said with a catch in her voice. 'Don't! You don't know what you are saying!'

'I do. And I regret that I allowed you to marry such a weak man who forsook his wife. Why did he not take you with him?' her mother demanded. 'And why did you accept it so meekly?'

'Ma, you know very well that I am not meek. I had to accept it,' she replied hotly.

'Accept like a doting, demure daughter-in-law?' her mother demanded, her anger not hiding the worry clouding her eyes. 'You are going to be away from him for fourteen years,' she emphasised the number deliberately. 'How could you allow it? You are being silent and strong now—as you will have to be for all those long waiting years. The pain of separation is intense, it seems interminable. He has gone, but do you know of the emotional suffering that lies ahead? I doubt it. Why did you not use your strength of argument like Sita and go with him? Or dissuade him? Did anyone else try to talk him out of his decision? Or did they forget to advice in the nobility of all that glorified fraternal love? Did anyone stand by you, Urmila?'

Urmila smiled sadly. 'Ma, so many questions and you know all the answers.'

'I cannot bear to see you like this!' she cried, agitated. 'I can't! The suffering, the sheer waste, the injustice of it all...you are my precious girl, my brave princess, but this is not what I groomed you for. Suffering silently is not strength; it is weakness. Why did you not stand up for your rights?'

'As a wife? I did. And I stood by his decision,' replied Urmila. 'Staying behind wasn't giving up my rights, Ma, it was accepting a reality, a responsibility. Sita and I followed the same principle though the outcome and experience are so different—we followed our dharma. Ram had to go to the forest and she went with him. Lakshman considered his dharma to serve his brother so he went with his brother and I agreed to stay back, however much it broke my heart. Father and you taught us, Ma, that our dharma is to support our husbands—never blindly, but to be with them when they are right and to correct them when they are wrong. So, did Lakshman do any wrong? Was he to remain in the palace with me and allow his brother to go for his exile alone?' she sighed.

Urmila took her mother's hand, 'I supported him in this decision. By going with him, I would have simply imposed myself on him; I would have been a distraction. I helped him follow his heart and his greater good. As I see it, he saw his brother needed him more in the forest than I needed him as a wife in the palace. It was not just a sense of duty, or a filial sense of obligation, Ma, it was love. And I accept that love—I love and respect him more for it. This is his defining quality. For me, it is as if he has gone for war with his brother and shall return victorious and...'

'But why should he make you suffer? He could have taken you with him.'

Urmila slowly shook her head. 'It would have killed the purpose. Does a soldier take his wife to war, Ma? And worse, I would have foolishly jeopardized matters and imperilled myself and them as well, don't you see?' she said earnestly. 'And is not dharma all about giving? It can never be about taking or demanding. Our duty cannot just be to the family and our loved ones—what about our responsibility towards society and the world? The promise extracted was a strange one which forced Ram to leave the comforts of the palace for the hardships and challenges of the forest. Clearly, he is destined to perform bigger deeds—I don't know what they are, but I do know that Lakshman realized it and wanted to be there for his brother in his hour of need. Each one here followed his dharma. I am following mine, too.'

Sunaina was still not convinced. 'It kills me that you have been made to bear such pain. I was so wrong, I should have been more firm and not allowed you to marry Lakshman.'

'Just like he would have wanted to,' said Urmila quietly. 'He didn't want to marry me either.'

'A promise he gave me, so can I not take it back?' asked Kaikeyi, her voice low but clear.

Everyone turned to look at her. She stood tall, beautiful and crushed. She was a woman despised, a mother disowned and she sought redemption. And it was her elder son now to whom she turned—the son to whom she had meted out an injustice most foul. 'I have no words to offer any justification. I have sinned for which I cannot dare to ask for forgiveness but only repent. But for the sake of everyone else whom I have hurt along with you, I ask you to forgive me for what I did, son, and come back home. All will be well then.'

'Mother, I have no ill-will toward you,' said Ram softly. 'You did what you thought best. Now let me do what has been decided by my father. I blame no one, neither you nor Bharat or anyone else. Please remove any guilt or remorse from your heart. There must have been a reason why this happened; let that reason bear fruit. It will taste more sweet and fulfilling in the end. Also, how can you take back a promise from a person who has passed away?'

'Exactly,' said Rishi Jabali, the learned priest of the court. 'Your father is no more. There is no need for you to carry on his orders considering the changed situation. No one wants you to continue a life in the forest. Come back and rule the kingdom as is the proper duty of a crown prince.'

Angry colour seeped into Ram's otherwise serene face: it was the first time Urmila had seen him like this. He had not been so upset even when he had been banished from Ayodhya for the fourteen-year exile.

'How can you, as the guru, give such advice? Break my father's promise? Shame and woe on the child who does not fulfil his parents' wishes! I would rather die than commit this sin! And don't displease me further by distracting me from my goal. I shall continue with my exile.'

'Then I shall fast unto death if you do not return to Ayodhya as king!' said Bharat, his voice strong and forceful.

'Don't be immature; this is not a game or a time to throw tantrums...' snapped Ram.

'This is neither a tantrum nor a threat—this is my last request, my last resort to take you home, brother,' implored Bharat, his voice breaking.

His brother's plea made Ram more vehement. 'You cannot do this. This is against Kshatriya dharma. Go, Bharat, go back to Ayodhya and rule it well.'

Bharat looked disheartened, his eyes appealing to his elder brother who remained unmoved.

'If it is a question of keeping our father's word, can I not take your place in the forest and you sit on the throne of Ayodhya instead?' he implored. 'I would gladly take your place.'

'I would not,' retorted Ram with a smile. 'I understand your feelings, brother, but I assure you, no one doubts your noble mind or your pure heart. The throne has been thrust upon you unwillingly, but it is yours nevertheless.'

The debate between the two brothers threatened to go on. And it was Vasishtha who saw a glimmer of hope in the current deadlock. He spelt it out, hoping both the brothers would agree to it. 'If you find it unrighteous to accept the throne, Bharat, why don't you rule as Ram's deputy and under his authority?' he said. 'This would make you feel less guilty and Ram would still be king and yet be free to continue with his exile, as he so dearly wishes?'

It was a sensible solution which everyone seemed to approve, though Bharat still looked crestfallen that he had been unable to convince Ram to return home.

'Yes, Gurudev, this is the best answer to all our doubts and worries,' said Ram. 'If that is how it is, dear Bharat, I gift my kingdom to you for the period I am in exile. Take it and rule it as our forefathers would have.'

Bharat bowed before his brother and said calmly, a strange light in his eyes. 'I accept your gift, dear brother, and I shall rule the kingdom for you. But for which, I need a token—your sandals which I shall place on the throne of Ayodhya,' he said. 'Through them you shall rule and I shall administrate the kingdom in your name from Nandigram at the outskirts of the city. I shall await your return and discharge your duties. During these fourteen years while you shall live in the forest, I shall also do my penance as a hermit on the banks of River Sarayu at Nandigram.'

There was a shocked pause and no one spoke a word till Ram finally broke it with a short, 'So be it.' There was a murmur of approval and the matter seemed to have finally been settled.

That murmur was like a scream for Urmila, that brief remark arousing her wrath. Mandavi was going to face the same fate as she. Sita had agreed silently and so had she, now it was Mandavi's turn, her spell of doom. Urmila felt a fury she had never experienced before: it was white hot and smouldering, burning her from within, the flames of which reached her flashing eyes.

'So be it, Bharat, like your brothers, Ram and Lakshman, you too shall live a life of an ascetic, free from the bond of love and worldly care. Who cares whatever happens to your wife and your family?' she asked, each word mouthed with cold deliberation. 'Today, in this room, we have talked about all sorts of dharma—of the father and the sons, of the king and the princes, of the Brahmin and the Kshatriya, even of the wife for her husband. But is there no dharma of the husband for his wife? No dharma of the son for his mother? Is it always about the father, sons and brothers?'

'Princess, how dare you speak such outrageous words?' interrupted Guru Kashyap furiously. 'Do you think this is your father, King Janak's court that encourages free thinking women like that philosopher Gargi to debate and argue shamelessly? This is not so! This is the assembly of the greatest minds of Ayodhya!'

Urmila looked back at him unflinchingly, the heat of her fury fanning her face. 'I am not doubting the great minds, Gurudev; I, as the daughter-in-law of the famous Raghu dynasty of the Ikshvaaku race—and not merely as the daughter of King Janak—ask a very simple question. What is the dharma of the man for his wife, the dharma of a man for his mother? Please give me an answer.'

Kashyap was speechless, apoplectic with fury. He glanced at Vasishtha but the elderly head priest was benignly calm. Urmila looked at him expectantly. 'We are talking about affairs of the state where personal relationships are not taken into consideration,' he said grudgingly.

'Are we now?' she asked politely. 'Then was it not personal when King Dashrath listened to his wife's wishes and stopped the coronation ceremony of Ram and banished him on a fourteen-year-old exile? Wasn't it personal when Queen Kaikeyi asked her son to be made king instead of Ram?'

She heard a slight stir in the room but ignored it. 'Was it not personal when Lakshman, who could have revolted against this royal order and generated public sympathy, decided to accompany his brother instead in his exile?' she continued relentlessly. 'And Bharat coming here to persuade Ram to return, is it not personal? Everything, Gurudev, has been personal here, every single political decision. It's about the father, the brother, the sons; but pray, what about the mothers, the wives? But yes, it is their dharma to follow their husbands' decisions and duties.'

'But you saw what happened when a husband listened to his wife,' cut in Bharat acerbically. 'This current catastrophe is not an act of God, it is the act of one woman!'

'Bharat! Urmila! How can you speak so irreverently?' demanded Ram. 'What is this about?'

'I shall not be irreverent or political now but very personal,' she retorted. 'I asked one question—what is the dharma of the husband to his wife—and I did not get an answer. Our parents taught us that the dharma of the wife is to follow and help her husband in his duties. Sita did it by following you to the forest, I did it by staying at the palace and not following my husband for fear of distracting him from his duties and service to you...'

'Urmila!' she did not turn, but heard the emotion running high in Kausalya's cry.

'No, Mother, let her put forth her thoughts on this,' warned Ram.

'...And now Mandavi too will follow the wife's dharma by staying alone in the palace while Bharat, the ideal brother, does penance and lives as an ascetic at Nandigram. Just as you, the ideal son, lives in the forest in exile and Lakshman as the other ideal brother, follows and supports you in your endeavour.'

She looked at Lakshman steadily; his face was expressionless but his eyes smouldered with suppressed, brooding intensity, his jaws clenched.

'I have not uttered a single, untruthful word,' she continued quietly, refusing wrath to cloud reasoning, unmindful of the backlash. She had to save her sister from a similar fate. She would.

'All I am asking is that does the man have no dharma for his wife? Or his mother? Not taking another wife, is that all this dharma means?'

'This is impertinence, Urmi! How can you?' asked Sita. Her sister was aghast.

'I can because I can't bear it any longer!' cried Urmila. 'I suffered because I was trapped in my own situation, with my own words, my own decisions, my love for my husband. Though he had warned me frankly enough, I went ahead to face and finally accepted this reality. It happened with you as well, Sita, and it has happened again. It is Mandavi this time. Why, Sita? This will keep coming up in our lives and we still won't have any answers. I ask again and again—does the man have no duties toward his wife and his mother? Why are the queens made to suffer the grief of parting from their sons? Can anyone bring sanity and sense into Mother Kausalya's crazed anguish? Does anyone see or recognize the silent tears of Mother Sumitra? Or does one only see the wickedness of Mother Kaikeyi and not her repentance, her private tears? Like the other two mothers, she too shall be suffering the same, endless pain—is that what your penance means, Bharat? Not to forgive your mother? But why are you punishing your wife? What is her sin? That she is your wife and has to follow the dharma likewise of obeying her husband's decision irrespecive of what it entails?'

'This is outrageous!' cried Kashyap. 'How can all of you tolerate this violation, this profanity against the king and his family?'

'Because I am family too,' Urmila reminded him icily. 'Because it is a family tradition here to be silent when someone screams for justice. This royal family is famous for its justness when it comes to its people and the state but it is cruellest to its own family members. Justice here is not just blind—it is deaf and mute. It is easy to spurn her now, but why didn't anyone stand up against Queen Kaikeyi when she demanded her two boons? What were all the elders doing—the other two queens, the ministers, the royal priest and you gurus? No one dared question her till her own son returned to disobey her. Did anyone refute the king's decision, however much he was forced to take it? Did anyone stop Ram from leaving home? Or did anyone try to stop Sita, knowing that the forest would be an unsafe place for her?'

Urmila saw Sita make a movement. 'No, Sita, you will argue it was your voluntary decision. As will Lakshman. And so will Ram—but did any of you think of the people you were leaving behind to discharge of your duties? Your old mothers who won't see you for another fourteen years, living on a slim sliver of hope every single day? Don't you have any duty, any compassion toward them? If you could not keep the vows you made to your wives, why did you brothers marry? You may be the best of the princes, the perfect sons, the ideal brothers, probably the ideal king too, but never the good husband!'

She saw Lakshman flinch and heard Sita gasp in horror. Ram had gone pale.

'You are right, Guru Kashyap, Ayodhya is not Mithila,' rasped Urmila. 'Mithila does not treat her women so shabbily. And unlike Sage Gargi in my father's royal court, I did not receive any answer to my questions. Not that I expected any!'

Urmila looked at each of them in the eye and left the hut abruptly, her throat dry. Anger swamped her and a fresh wave of pain bubbled over. The tears refused to flow, dried by the fire within.

'Mila, stop running away from me!'

She turned around fiercely, ready to confront him. She recalled he had not uttered a single word during her tirade—neither protesting nor protective. Lakshman stood tall, towering and...smiling! Urmila had been prepared for contempt, anger, loathing but not this tenderness—the searching, fleeting emotions spreading on his face, softened by his widening, lopsided smile.

'If I had begged you to stop, you would have ignored my plea. This was the best way to stop you in your tracks, right? Though it's a nice walk if you like grunting!' he chuckled, glancing at the steep slope she had just climbed. 'Don't turn away from me, Mila. You won't get far, remember?' She could not understand his humour, his mood. But he had always been mercurial.

'Why are you smiling? It is not amusing. I am not sorry for all that I said. I said it for Mandavi though I know it is all so wasted!' she started.

He shook his head. 'I am smiling in relief. Finally it's out, you exploded! I knew you would say what you had wanted to for all this while. But frankly, I was more worried of my reaction than yours. I was scared I would hate you for even one unforgiveable word you uttered,' he looked at her searchingly. 'But I found myself simply listening to all you had to say. And could not help but relish every argument of yours, my warrior wife! And I fell in love with you all over again. I had to tell you this before you left— in such a huff!'

Her anguished anger seemed to melt. She looked confused. 'You are not upset...?'

'Both of us at the same time?' he shuddered. 'God forbid, that would be a conflagration! But what you said was true, and only you could have the nerve to say it. I had been expecting it since our tiff that day of the coronation...'

She looked at him long, savouring him, assimilating and memorizing every detail... She felt a sharp tug at her heart: she loved him so. He would be gone again. This would be another farewell.

'Yes, guess I got rid of all my fury, resentment, worries and disillusionment for the next fourteen years. I am spent,' she sighed, stifling a sob. 'I hope I am cleansed. I just want to shut my eyes and be oblivious to any more of this pain, this heartbreak, and simply lapse into a long sleep...'

She sounded tired and defeated. She closed her eyes and could smell the fragrance of his body, the warm huskiness of his voice. '...And take your sleep along with it,' she murmured, opening her eyes and looking at him for a long, last time. 'So that you stay awake and alert all the while as you guard your brother and my sister. In exchange, I give you my rest, my ease, my sleep, my love.'

'Done,' he said softly, caressing her tenderly with his eyes. 'I have always loathed the necessity of sleep—it puts the ablest men on their backs!'

Urmila felt a giggle gurgling within her and could not help breaking into a tiny, tremulous smile.

'Yes, stay smiling always, my love, I want to remember this

forever,' he whispered. And turning his handsome, tormented face from her, he was gone.

His voice had been a caress. He had not touched her but she could feel him in every pore. Urmila shut her eyes, seeing her hopeless future descend into darkness. Her long sleep had begun...

THE SEPARATION

She was painting again, her brush moving rapidly, dexterously, her mind spinning, not forgetting him even for an instant. But she missed his presence behind her back, his warm breath caressing the nape of her neck, the sardonic raise of his eyebrow as he peered more closely at the tinniest details; she missed his gravelly voice as he said, 'Fabulous. Just like you. How do you do it?'

'Just being myself,' she heard herself say.

'That is beautiful and intelligent. Beautiful women, especially those who are intelligent too, make me nervous. They stir a deep feeling within me...'

'And would that be an inferiority complex?' she asked saucily.

And he had demonstrated it was not so.

Urmila stared distastefully at the plate of food placed in front of her. She could not stomach even a morsel. It was well past the lunch time but she still wasn't hungry. It had been the same since the past so many months. Like her, everyone else in the family had almost given up food. Meals together were a thing of the past. Each one of them was interned in their palace, shut away from the world, in an act of voluntary solitary confinement. It had been more than three months since Bharat had stationed himself at Nandigram and the palace still wore a deserted, unloved look. It had become the loneliest place housing unsmiling people—the grieving family and the milling entourage of courtiers, guardsmen and handmaids.

The pall of gloom was stifling. Mandavi had been completely disheartened by Bharat's decision, slipping into a state of melancholia the moment Bharat left for Nandigram. Her flagrant absence on the occasion when Bharat had respectfully placed Ram's wooden sandals on the throne had raised a murmur of disapproval at the royal court. It had been a small, solemn ceremony immediately after which Bharat had left for Nandigram. Looking almost sublime in his self-renunciation and his ascetic bark attire, he bid farewell to all but his mother. Mandavi saw him off with a look of glazed disbelief on her pale, strained face. Urmila did not know what exactly had happened between them. Since that day, Mandavi had simply kept disconcertingly silent, sealing her lips and herself from the world outside. Kirti and Urmila had tried vainly to wean her out from her pensive sadness but she had caged herself in her own private, corrugated hell, alternating between wistful wordlessness and long bouts of fitful sleep.

Shatrughna was the most occupied, mostly engaged with court matters working through the day and touring the city till late hours. But he made it a point to meet the three queens everyday. Kausalya was worse than what she was before she had gone to Chitrakoot to meet Ram; her pessimistic sense of inadequacy compounded by protracted despondence. Sumitra was mostly by her side, a mediator between the other two queens. Kaikeyi was still treated as a pariah and had turned into a recluse, seldom stepping out of her palace, living in her self-imposed exile.

Unhappiness makes us self-absorbed: it makes one think only of oneself—of the pain, and misery one is suffering. Urmila was exhausted of the stifling grief. It made her resigned; she had to shake out of it. That was why, left largely to herself, she tried to find a method in her unhappy loneliness. Her mornings were spent studying the Upanishads and the Vedas under the tutelage of royal gurus, particularly Guru Vasishtha, a teacher she felt privileged to be a student of. At other times, she painted furiously for hours together in long spells, living her thoughts through the smudged colours on the canvas. She was painting their wedding scene yet again—an enormous endeavour she knew would take months to complete. She found herself instinctively skilful, filling the empty white spaces with the right colour, lining the figures with her firm, steady hand, not necessarily in tandem with her unsteady, numb thoughts.

Urmila stared again at the large, silver plate, her meal covered deferentially by a thin muslin cloth. The food must have gone cold a long time ago. Just like their daily course of existence. Cold and tasteless, difficult to digest and taken with a painful swallow each time over. This could not go on. She would have to do something. She glanced again at the gleaming dish and a faint idea started to swirl around slowly.

A situation similar to her painting came fuzzily to her mind; Just a few days after their marriage...

'Don't you people have meals together ever?' she asked Lakshman pertly as the maid, Kasturi, placed two loaded plates before them and left their chamber. Urmila, the self-confessed sensual food lover, as she called herself, promptly removed the muslin kerchief and uncovered the plate to check what was in the glittering small bowls.

'We eat in our respective palaces...' he answered nonchalantly, 'or I drop by at my mother's if the king is not having a meal with her. He usually has his with each one of them. He makes it a point to do so,' he added dryly.

'You mean to say you don't eat together ever? Is this how it is going to be?' she asked aghast, munching on a sliced cucumber. 'I hate having meals alone. It is depressing, and definitely not healthy.'

'I am there, so how would you be alone?' demanded Lakshman. 'I, for one, don't mind this arrangement. I can have you all to myself!' he chuckled lasviciously. 'Or, don't tell me you are one of those militant daughters-in-law who want to bring about immediate change with their battle-axes in their new homes?' he gasped in mock horror.

'Oh, be serious!' she pouted. 'I am ready to eat anything, anytime, anywhere. If you haven't noticed, I love to eat,' she grinned, and saw him looking at her with an altered expression, his eyes lewdly scanning her trim figure, rounded at the right places but she ignored it. 'So while I shall merrily entertain you over breakfast and tea-time with all that hot and spicy stuff,' she said demurely, pausing for dramatic effect, 'how about having the other meals with the family?'

Lakshman shook his head vehemently. 'We have not done it all these years,' he said, but seeing the mutinous expression on his wife's face, he shrugged. 'Is that your next agenda?' he asked resignedly.

'Yes!' she said with renewed asperity. 'I intend to broach the topic soon...'

And she did that when the family met for the Satyanarayan puja the following morning. As she bowed to touch the feet of her parents-in-law with Lakshman, she looked at Dashrath and said softly, 'Bless us that we live and eat together as a family for now and forever.'

Dashrath looked surprised but complied to her wish as he touched her bent head with an involuntary, 'So be it—*tathastu.*'

'You are using this trick far too often,' breathed Lakshman, a smile hovering on his lips.

The old king did not realize the import of her request but Kaikeyi did, and gave a delighted smile. 'That is a lovely suggestion; it starts right away from today's lunch!' she said animatedly. 'I shall look into it immediately!'

The luncheon prepared by Kaikeyi was a finger-licking success. The person most displeased about it was Kausalya as it deprived her with the sole time she sought with her son. Also, whenever Ram decided he would lunch with Kaikeyi—which was often enough, courtesy her superior culinary abilities—meals had, over the years, become another bone of contention between the two queens. By bringing all of them together, Urmila hoped it would ease tensions. The mood at the table now was relaxed, she observed with delight, but what was more gratifying was the sight of all of them sitting together at the long table, solemnly enjoying the food. Urmila frowned; the meal had to be sprinkled with some dialogue, it was too quiet. She would have to start a conversation.

'Ma Kaikeyi, the food is fabulous!' gushed Urmila, heartily complimenting the queen sitting next to her. 'Especially the stuffed potato curry. Sita, you have to learn it from her!' she piped with a bright smile, turning to her sister. 'Sita is a fabulous cook. She knows everything from herbs to the different ways of seasoning to preparing the most elaborate dishes. And Kirti can make the most exotic pickles!'

'And what do you do, child?' asked Dashrath with a twinkle in his eyes.

'Eat well,' she said promptly. 'That's how you show your respect and pay compliments to the cook!'

The small crowd at the table broke into loud guffaw and the conversation flowed as easily as the sweetened lassi making the rounds. The next few minutes were a mix of sweet chatter and even sweeter desserts.

'Bravo, dear girl,' said Kaikeyi, in an awed whisper. 'You smartly achieved what I could not manage for the past twenty-five years! The family eats together...and it is a sight to behold.'

Urmila could still hear the ringing laughter of those happier days, even taste the food in her mouth. But she could not savour the memory any longer: those days now seemed too long ago. But they would have to be brought back, and quickly, she realized. Simply desiring or deciding would not be enough, she would need determination too. Her voice sharp and firm, Urmila called for her maid Kasturi and told her to give a message to everybody—that all of them were invited to the fore-room of her palace at noon tomorrow.

The next day's afternoon did see them all together at her palace, including the busy Shatrughna and the reclusive Kaikeyi. Each looked surprised to see the other but maintained a dignified silence. Eventually, as she served them cool lime juice, Kausalya asked her testily, 'Why did you call us here, dear? What is the occasion?'

'The occasion is that we will start having our meals together henceforth,' Urmila replied quietly, 'as we once did.'

'You can't recreate those days,' snapped Kausalya, her voice hardening. Urmila heard the brittleness and looked at her closely. The queen had not yet forgiven her for her outspokenness at Chitrakoot. She had been frigid with her since then.

'No, but we can't mope and mourn forever, can we? And should we?' riposted Urmila. 'Have some soup, Mother, you have to be strong enough to welcome Ram when he returns!' she added with a smile. 'Let's eat, though I am afraid, the meal won't be as delicious as Mother Kaikeyi's! Mother, please spare me and take over from now on and handle all the other meals!' she said brightly, turning to the silent queen mother, sitting uncertainly next to her. 'I am sure Kirti will be happy to help you out. And Kirti, please make the green chillies pickle; it's been so long!'

'Yes, Kaikeyi,' agreed Sumitra, swiftly taking up Urmila's cue. 'We are missing your heavenly fare; for tomorrow let's have that meat curry you prepare from the herbs you get from your native place. It is glorious! Urmila, the food is not as bad as you said it would be...it's actually very good!'

'Oh, that's Urmi for you, always running herself down and reserving all the praises for her sisters!' said Mandavi suddenly, who had been cold and sullen all the while. The affection for her sister was strong in her voice. She actually smiled, bringing a tinge of life into her wan face.

'Is there an antonym for show-off?' piped in Kirti, relieved that Mandavi had joined in the conversation and at the relaxed mood at the table. 'That's the definiton for Urmi! And Ma Kaikeyi, please teach me your wonderful smoked brinjals, I tried it but failed miserably and Shatrughna still pokes fun at me over that disaster!'

Shatrughna gave a polite smile, 'But you have improved, dear! They were less burnt last time!'

As everyone burst out laughing, Kirti continued firmly, 'Let's do it this very evening, Ma Kaikeyi!' she persisted. 'Help me prove him wrong! And for tomorrow, let's...'

Kaikeyi nodded slowly with her elegant smile and everyone continued with their meal, broken with fits of short laughs and small talk. Urmila felt a hand slip into hers. It was the soft hand of Kaikeyi. She turned to see the queen give her a grateful look, her eyes warm with unabashed gratitude. Urmila gave her hand a reassuring squeeze.

'Let's eat,' she said simply with a smile. They were back eating together at last.

Though Urmila had managed to have all of them sit together for meals for so many months now, she still could not convince Mandavi to step into the thousand-pillared, lotus-domed palace of Kaikeyi. It had been more than a year that Bharat had left the palace for Nandigram, but Mandavi could not bring herself to forgive her mother-in-law. She barely spoke with her except for some cursory civil talk. The wife carried on the husband's resoluteness, but their reasons were different. For Bharat, it was an act of retribution, remorse and repentance; for Mandavi, it was fury. She blamed the queen for separating her husband from her and the burden of that decision was entirely hers.

'How can you forgive her, Urmi, for all that she has done?' she demanded instead. 'You are without Lakshman because of her.'

'For which she has been punished enough. Her son has disowned her, how much worse can it get for her?' said Urmila. 'By all of us hating her as well? I cannot. It would embitter me. And I feel terrible for her. Call it sympathy and a strong trust that a woman who was so affectionate cannot turn so heartless.'

'It was all a pretence!' flared Mandavi. 'She is the evil in the house. You threw away Manthara, but can we throw her out? Each time I see her, I am reminded of the fact that it is because of her that Bharat took that decision. He wanted to punish her, hurt her the way she has hurt others but the person suffering the punishment is me! Why? Why am I being punished for her fault, for his decision?'

'Because you are allowing yourself that luxury of self-pity,' said Urmila brutally. 'Stop thinking about yourself. You are drowning in this self-created sea of misery. She is suffering, too. It is worse for her—everyone despises her, avoids her; she has become an outcast in her own home. But what is killing her is her son's rejection. Which mother can live with the fact that her son has disowned her and has left home to punish her? Look around you, Mandavi, see the others!'

'When I look around me, I see only you—a brave smile on your sad, lovely face...and it makes my blood boil!' seethed her cousin. 'You fought for me at Chitrakoot but did it make any difference? All it did was to earn you the ire of the elders and the gurus. Did anyone come to your defence? You say I am being selfish but what have these people done for us? What have they done to us, Urmi? Don't you ever feel anger against them?' she cried in frustration. 'Don't you ever resent them for depriving you of your freedom, your joy; to have bound you by societal and family rules as the royal daughter-in-law, the wife, the princess?

'I do,' admitted Urmila, her face convulsed with restrained emotions. 'But silently going about my way does not mean I am passive, Mandavi. I said what I had to say, did what I had to do, a woman free to speak freely for herself. I never let them forget what they have done; all of them have been guilty for some reason or the other. They know it each time they look at me in the eye. I make them realize it.'

Mandavi gave her a hard look. 'I did not expect anyone from this family to take your side, but there has been one doubt I have been intending to clarify since long, but circumstances and good sense made me hesitate,' said Mandavi reluctantly. 'But now I ask you—why did Sita not help you? As the senior daughter-in-law who had so wonderfully argued her point and arbitrated her choice to follow her husband in the forest, she could have made Ram, and ordered Lakshman, to take you to the forest with them. And as the elder sister, she should have considered your plight as well, should she have not?'

Urmila was quick to vindicate Sita, 'She barely had the time and opportunity to fight for herself and convince Ram to take her,' she was quick to explain. But her words sounded weak even to her own ears. She was making a frail attempt at justification;

the deep truth was, as Mandavi had realized, that her sister, too, had failed her and Urmila hated to admit it. She had never felt more betrayed, more let down. Mandavi seemed to be going though the same tumult of those tearing emotions.

'Don't defend her, as you always do all those whom you love so fiercely and loyally. She failed you,' said Mandavi, her voice brittle and unforgiving. 'And that is what riles me the most...our family let us down. I have never felt so unwanted, so disgraced—I feel like running away from all of them, from this damned palace so hideous in its beauty. It seems all the walls are trapping me in endless pain. What have I got myself into?' Mandavi shook her head violently, trying to shake away the sorrow stifling her.

Urmila was alarmed, dismissing her own painful thoughts, feeling helpless at her sister's growing grief and desolation. Neither she nor Kirti had been able to comprehend how to comfort their sister. Right now she looked crazed; the raging emotions were eating into her, destroying her slowly. Urmila was, frankly, scared for her sister now.

'Mandavi, of course, it is unjust!' she cried. 'Life always is. We are women, we are wives, we are creatures of circumstances. We make choices we have no control over. You cannot change anything, Mandavi, just try to accept it. We do not have the power to change anything but ourselves; see what has become of you. Oh, please, dear, give me back my old sister, that Mandavi—charming, witty and clever...'

'Oh not so clever really,' interposed Mandavi bitterly. 'If I had been so clever, I would not have married Bharat at all! Ma was right—we sisters should have never married into this family! They have given us just grief, pain and humiliation. Sita is suffering in the forest, you and me here and Kirti, lucky girl, is relatively better off than the three of us! And I am in this situation all because of my dumb ambition to be a queen! I could have got some other king for all my wit and charm! Oh, why did I not marry someone else?'

'Are you regretting everything?' asked Urmila slowly, finally seeing through her sister's frenzied fury.

'Yes! Every single moment!' cried Mandavi. 'Since that day I made the decision to marry Bharat. I thought I had planned it all right and it went all wrong. So horribly wrong! And I feel frustrated that I am the cause of my own misery. I don't love him, Urmila, don't you see?'

Urmila heard the desperation in her sister's voice. Her confession was a revelation—a divulgence of her innermost tormented thoughts—but it shocked Urmila and frightened her a little.

'I didn't marry him for love as you and Sita did; that is where, probably, I went wrong. I married him for all the wrong reasons, in fact!' she said tersely. 'I tried to love him, I tried so hard and if this episode would not have happened I think we could have succeeded... We barely had any time to get to know each other, forget falling in love! And the worst of it all is that he abandoned me as I thought he would and I hate him for that! I have no one to blame but myself and his mother! Who else can I blame? My fate or the choices I made?'

'But he has not abandoned you...he will come back to you! He is repenting for the crime he believes needs to be rectified. He is punishing himself too, can't you see?'

'Bharat the perfect brother, Bharat the virtuous son of the evil mother, Bharat the noble king who abandoned his throne—and his wife—to perform the severest of penances to repay for the injustice on his brother! I am sick of these lofty words. Why is it that I come last in his list of priorities? Like him, I am expected to be noble. But, I confess, I am not. I cannot be as selfless as him. He is great but what about me? Where am I, who am I? His chattel to be discarded or picked up whenever he wishes?' she cried, her hands wringing in nervous agitation. 'And why am I waiting for him to return to me? I do not have the patience and the perseverance to wait for so long. I want love, I want him and not some noble ideals thrown at me to seek solace as a dutiful, devoted wife! I want to feel him, touch him, kiss him, make love to him, talk to him, scream at him but he is not there...' she sighed, spent after the outburst. 'Oh Urmi, how do you handle this despair, this big, terrible void? I know you are going through the same agony but I cannot be as brave, as strong and as forgiving as you! I feel like a mad, caged animal. You are alone, Urmi, but not lonely; you have his love, his memories...and what do I have? A long stretch of wasted years just waiting for a man I cannot love anymore? I am tired of society's definition of me. How long can I conform to its rules? All of these questions keep troubling my mind continuously...they are driving me crazy!'

Urmila felt helpless as she witnessed her sister's violent, crazed despair, but she did not shed a single tear for herself. She could not forget the promise she had given Lakshman—that she would not cry for him. Mandavi's piteous plight broke her heart but all she could do was watch dry-eyed, filled with an impotent anxiety and a pounding pain.

'It is Lakshman. It is his love that helps you get through, isn't it, Urmi?' said Mandavi, her voice suddenly calm and composed. 'It has always been about him—your self-abnegation, self-denial and unflinching will to not give him up. His love gives you strength and hope. That is the power of love...which I don't have...'

Mandavi looked and sounded broken and utterly disillusioned. Urmila walked up to her and gently embraced her. Mandavi held on to her, clinging and trembling, her body wracked with dry sobs. 'Free me, Urmi, free me from this madenning pain!' she sobbed. 'Give me some hope to live on.'

Urmila did not reply. She held her sister closely, waiting for her to calm down. As the sobs subsided, Urmila gently wiped the tears from Mandavi's pale face. 'That hope lies within you, dear,' she said softly, looking deep into her troubled eyes. 'It is there, that light which we can see only when in the dark. See it. Follow it. If you are dark within, you see only darkness around you. Follow the light within you. And learn to smile—that small curve can straighten up a lot of things, believe me. That's what Lakshman told me—smile always and suddenly all goes well. And that's all we have, anyway, the power to smile and make ourselves happy.'

Mandavi sat silent for a long while. Urmila wondered if she had heard her at all. Then she saw Mandavi slowly gathering herself together to strike up a small resemblance of a smile.

'Above all, Mandavi, one has to survive on will, on the convictions that life has to go on irrespective of everything, and not just on hope, love and memories. You are living on memories, Mandavi, and that too the unpleasant ones which are capable of evoking more negativity than nostalgia,' Urmila reminded her gently.

Mandavi's lips trembled. 'I cannot forget what has happened but yes, somewhere along the way I seem to have forgotten to smile, as you just reminded me. Oh, Urmi, what could I have done without you?!' she smiled through her drying tears. 'It would be very mean and selfish of me but I am thankful you are here with me, and not with Sita in the forest. I think I need you more. You are our glue! And that is what you have alway been for us—an adhesive binding us sisters together, holding us up. Not a very flowery praise, but true. You are our binding spirit!' she said with a tremulous smile.

'See, you look so lovely!' exclaimed Urmila, giving her a quick hug. 'Not a sour puss any longer!'

'What do we do now, Urmi?' asked Mandavi simply. 'How do we spend these long years?'

'Good grief, stop worrying about the whole stretch. Take each day as it comes, and get busy!' she said briskly. 'So, what are you reading these days? Did you get some new books?'

'I haven't been reading at all! It's been more than a year, I think,' replied Mandavi dolefully.

'What? But you are such a quick, avid reader. You used to wolf down books! Or else, scour high and low for new ones; that used to be your day's sole goal!' Urmila reminded her gently. 'Do it now—you have all the time in the world.'

Mandavi nodded, her eyes brightening up. 'Yes, I shall. I shall start by searching around here and meanwhile I shall send for my books from Mithila. Ma will be happy to let go of that huge pile! In fact, I think I might just start my own collection here, a full wall-to-wall library stacked with books!' Mandavi's eyes were shining now.

'Yes, do that. You can ask Guru Vasishtha or Guru Kashyap for guidance. They would know the right sources. And check out their collection too...?'

Mandavi flashed her another quick smile. 'Good idea!' she chimed exuberantly, her voice strong with a new vitality, a fresh purpose. 'Right away, today itself before I can push it to another day, I shall meet them this evening after their court meeting gets done.'

Urmila grinned and made a move to go. 'Wait, Urmi,' she said. 'Where's Kirti?'

'In the kitchen, busy with Ma Kaikeyi—they are planning a grand feast...it's Ram's natal day tomorrow.'

'Oh, is it?' Mandavi looked surprised. 'I was completely oblivious.'

'Now you won't be!' she said pertly. 'In fact, I had come here to tell you that. I have already decorated up the palace in whatever way I could. It's time we celebrated these small things and enjoyed living, don't you think so, Mandavi? There is a puja too. Shatrughna is hoping to get Bharat to come for the puja.'

Mandavi's face flooded with colour, a soft glow in her eyes. 'Is he?' she asked after a long pause, 'Will he come?' Mandavi looked anxious.

'Frankly, I am not too sure but if he does, he will come and meet you, Mandavi. He does love you, dear, however much your hurt heart tells you otherwise,' she said. 'He is one of the most gentle, kindest people I know and he could never, ever hurt you intentionally. We said unkind, harsh words for them but the deep truth is that these brothers are too noble, too selfless. Just so good that we are so bad to them! I have said a lot of mean, nasty things to Lakshman too!' she laughed sadly. 'I regret them now...'

Preparing for the next day's celebrations had exhausted her. She was tired—her feet ached from running around the palace grounds, to the kitchen and the great hall where the puja was going to be held. But all this activity could not assuage the ache in her heart. She remembered the preparations for Ram's coronation and was flooded with a deluge of fresh memories... She was dressing up for the ceremony in a hurry, and Lakshman had squeezed in just a minute to peek into their chamber to let her know which sari he would like her to wear, choosing the hairpin for her...

Tomorrow would be the day Ram was born: did they even realize what day it was back in the forest? What were they doing today, right now? It had been more than a year since they had left the palace, walking down these very steps she was decking up with fresh marigolds.

Urmila's eyes still could not forget how Lakshman had left her in her room. Her reminiscing eyes followed as Lakshman walked out of their bed chamber, down the winding marbled staircase, through the tall, carved doors of their palace and out into the darkened dawn of that day. She had wanted to run after him, but could not. Instead, she waited for him. To come back.

THE RIVALRY

The day had dawned pleasantly sunny and bright, streaming in the rays of happiness in the palace afer a long time. It was the celebration of Ram's day of birth and it was a success as Urmila had envisaged, planned and organized. It was after much urging and persuasion that the senior queens had agreed to make that day special and Kausalya was visibly delighted. Enthused with renewed energy and gusto, she had helped Urmila at every step of the preparations. Urmila refrained from being over-ostentatious with the decorations. But each of the carved door frames of the palace was festooned with flaming marigolds; there were rangolis on the marbled corridors and all along the long flight of steps, adding the right splash of colour. The gustatory experience was certain to be as satisfying with Kaikeyi and Kirti taking over the royal kitchen to host a commemorative feast for the gurus, courtiers and family members. It was a closed affair but the jubiliation resounded all over the city as the doors of the royal kitchen were kept open to serve the hungry and the impoverished the entire day.

Kausalya was the lady of the show and she presided over it as only a queen could. From the smallest details to the biggest decision in the kitchen, she saw to it that she had her say, the presence of Kaikeyi notwithstanding. While she fussed over Kirti affectionately, helping her out occasionally, she was clearly displeased at the younger queen's presence in the kitchen. She was unusually imperious: throwing curt orders, nitpicking over inanities. She would look through Kaikeyi frostily, talking to Kirti but addressing her, making the younger queen so distinctly uncomfortable that Urmila thought she would walk off in a huff, as the elder queen would have preferred. But Kaikeyi kept her cool, and took it all silently—a far cry from the majestic queen of last year. The air was thick with tension and Urmila thought it wise to gently divert her attention by taking to her chamber where the gifts were laid to be given to the poor.

But Kausalya was not to be fooled. 'It is my son's birthday today and I don't want Kaikeyi anywhere near!' snapped Kausalya. 'I have decently tolerated her all this while as my dignity does not allow me to be petty. I have even agreed to have meals in her presence as I did not want to disrupt the peace of the house but don't expect me to be so magnanimous as to embrace her in the celebrations. Don't think I did not notice your diplomatic overture, Urmila,' she added sternly.

Urmila was unfazed, and tried to coax her out of her annoyance. 'It is your son's birthday and all the more reason for you to forgive everything and everyone from the bottom of your happy heart,' she explained. 'For the last three days, Ma Kaikeyi has taken pains to prepare all the favourite dishes of Ram—does that not show affection?'

'No, it is just a false demonstration of it,' the queen's tone was waspish. 'If I really had my way, I wouldn't have allowed her to participate in this celebration at all,' she said deliberately, giving her a pointed look. 'It would have been better if she had stayed put in her palace where she had so deviously designed to expel my son from his home, his palace, his throne, his kingdom—and above all, from his parents' hearts. But *that* she failed at, and my poor husband died for that!'

Her eyes glinted, her tone suddenly vicious. 'Am I to ever forget that it was she who first stole my husband and my son with all that shower of love and affection? And still unsatiated, she then drove them away from me through her plotting?' she demanded. 'I never received the respect due to a queen once Kaikeyi came into our lives. My husband had all the respect for me but never any love—that was reserved for Kaikeyi alone! I was no better or worse off than one of her servants!'

Her exaggeration was a magnification of her feelings as well—the seemingly small incident in the kitchen had opened the floodgates of all her bitterness. 'She killed my husband, and exiled my son but I had lost both of them to her a long time ago; that temptress, that witch with her fake smile and fake love!' she said savagely. 'But what still haunts me is that both my husband and my son loved her madly, both were so devoted to her. Almost slavish in their love... What was I lacking as a wife and as a mother?'

'Nothing,' said Urmila quietly, 'just the conviction and belief that your son and husband loved you as dearly, but you could not see it as you allowed your resentment for the younger queen to cloud your judgement.' She said as diplomaticlly as she could. 'Your dislike for her made you dislike her love for them. Your jealousy made you jealous of their love as well.'

'And they have gone, but she continues to affect me!' said the queen, her lips pursed in a thin, bitter line. 'I have suffered her through all these years...yes, in jealous anger, in quiet humiliation and silent indignity. And I see her even today—so beautiful, proud and regal—still so calm after the storm she brought upon us. I cannot bring myself to like her, forget forgiving her. My small solace is that she too is suffering the same grief of separation from her son. But victory is mine for my son will one day come back to me; hers won't ever!' she pronounced with undisguised maliciousness. 'My son loves me, her son hates her. And that is my vindication, my retribution, my justice. It is poetic!'

Urmila flinched. The glee and grief both gleaming in the old queen's eyes made her shudder. Singed, Kausalya was still willing to smoulder in the flames of jealous rage.

'And you derive your happiness from her unhappiness?' questioned Urmila, trying to sound laconic. 'Mother, the tragedy in this happy house did not start with the death of your husband or the exile of your son—it started long ago with you as well...'

She heard the queen gasp sharply but ignored it.

'...And your jealous love and anger strained so many relationships,' continued Urmila steadily. 'Do not consider me impertinent, Mother, but it was that unabated rivalry between you and Ma Kaikeyi that perpetuated all that we are suffering today. Your sole ambition was to see Ram become king. Just as your jealousy made you insecure about your royal position as a queen, wife and mother, Mother Kaikeyi too suffered from the same insecurity that you would be queen mother once Ram became king.'

Urmila saw the look of intense surprise flit across the pained, lined face of the elderly queen. She probably could not imagine her rival as a vulnerable, insecure person. 'It was this emotional vulnerabilty which prompted Ma Kaikeyi to do the unthinkable—demand the rights of her son,' continued Urmila. 'This distrustful, jealous envy between the two of you which was sowed years ago has grown to hideous proportions, ruining everything in its wake—love, family, peace and happiness. And yet you continue to go on heedlessly even when both of you have lost so much in the process. Today is the day your son was born but are you happy?' mocked Urmila. 'You are poisoned with thoughts of bitterness for Mother Kaikeyi. What she did is indefensible, but she is paying for it too. Is that not enough? Have you not lost enough? What more do you hope to lose and gain?'

Kausalya was livid. Her eyes flashed suddenly and Urmila was startled to see how formidable she could look when she let her mask slip. 'How dare you talk to me so disrespectfully?' she seethed. 'Your impertinence needs to be curbed. You should have been reprimanded that day at Chitrakoot when you questioned Bharat's decision. You had the temerity to challenge the propriety of my son, the king, the whole family but it is our goodness that we kept quiet, because we gave you the respect that a daughter-in-law deserves. You are Soumitra's wife, not just the princess of Mithila any longer.'

'Yes, Mithila...where I was taught to protest against injustice,' said Urmila softly. 'I am not just watching the injustice, Mother, I am a part of it. I am also suffering because of the mistakes of the elders in the family. But I am not pleading for myself. All I am asking is for some peace to return in this house,' implored Urmila. 'They are gone but your famous rivalry remains! It insidiously seeped into your relationship with your husband, your son, and even threatened the relationship between the four brothers. But they thankfully remained unpoisoned by it. In fact, their love grew stronger as the hostility between you two grew. Even your petty jealousies could not tear them apart till that fateful day.'

Urmila paused for breath, her face hot. But the queen remained silent, at a loss of words before the girl who was voicing the secret fears and the pain that had tortured her all these years.

'Ironically, in this game of jealousy and powerplay between you both, it was your sons who came out the winners...and the victims. They are paying for your folly. And yet they won, where both of you lost; their love survived and surpassed your hatred bringing them even closer. Lakshman and Bharat sacrificed their personal lives for their brother unhesitatingly to be at his side. Ram preferred to go on exile rather than fight for his rights or usurp his brother's kingship. So, I ask you mother, when Ram returns and the brothers are reunited, will that animosity between the two of you again ruin things for them? Because I am afraid, if this mutual distrust continues to thrive, we shall never ever be together as a family again. Ever.'

Urmila went away leaving Kausalya staring stonily at her caged parrot—a lonely woman with bitter memories tormenting her conscience.

The joyousness of the celebrations lingered for long, ushering a sense of contentment, however wistful. It was like rain after a long, dry spell. And when the rains did come a few months later, they arrived with inauspicious news. King Aswapati had passed away after a long illness. Kaikeyi took the news with dignified composure and immediately left with Mandavi for Girivraja, the capital city of Kekeya. She did not wait for Bharat who was quickly informed at Nandigram. Shatrughna offered to accompany her but she kindly refused, explaining that Ayodhya needed him more than Kekaya did. Kausalya was at her kindest—she looked after every detail of her departure, arranging for the victuals, medicines and escorts needed for the long journey. She came to see Kaikeyi off as she climbed onto the waiting chariot.

Visibly touched, Kaikeyi reciprocated by saying, 'I don't deserve your kindness. I think this is the first time I shall regret leaving Ayodhya,' she said with a whimsical smile, 'and the first time that I shall be happy to return from Kekeya to Ayodhya. Take care, I shall be fine.'

It was just after a day Kaikeyi had left that they received another letter from Kekeya. A maid handed it to Urmila and she took it, surprised and slightly intrigued.

'What could it be? It is not a message. It is a sealed letter,'said Urmila, peering closely at the royal insignia embossed on the letter. 'From the late King Aswapti to Queen Kaikeyi.'

'Open it; it might be something urgent,' suggested Kirti. They were sitting in Urmila's sun-drenched morning room when the maid had arrived with the letter.

'But it's private!' retorted Urmila. 'Between a father and his daughter.'

'But Ma Kaikeyi won't be back before a month! What if the letter has something of time-bound importance? And how private could it be? Open it, Urmi, I am sure Ma Kaikeyi won't be annoyed.'

Urmila opened the letter with utmost reluctance. It was not a very long letter but by the time Urmila quickly managed to read it, her face was drained of all colour. Alarmed, Kirti leaned towards her sister, touching her arm anxiously. She had never seen her sister so shaken.

'What happened, Urmi? What is in that letter?' she demanded.

Wordlessly, Urmila handed the letter to Kirti. She almost snatched it and hurriedly went over it, fearing the worst. 'Oh heavens! How could this happen?' she said hoarsely.

She turned to Urmila urgently. 'What are we to do now? Should we tell the others?'

'No! Wait! Let me think...I wish we hadn't opened this letter but I am also thankful that we did!' she added fervently. 'We got to know what Ma Kaikeyi had been hiding from us all along...' She kept shaking her head, refusing to believe what she had just read.

'I think everyone in the family should know about this, it's shocking!' cried Kirti. 'We should not hide it any longer!'

Urmila perused the contents of the letter again, slowly and surely, making certain she was not missing out on any detail. She frowned, muttering, 'It is unbelievable! I think we need to show this to everyone, especially Bharat,' she said emphatically. 'For now, Shatrughna needs to know this.'

'And the other queen mothers?'

'Yes, they too, eventually,' she replied grimly. 'Let's wait for Ma Kaikeyi to return...'

'Do you intend to talk to her about this? Or should we keep quiet; it is her secret that we are divulging.'

'...but which urgently needs to be divulged; don't you see, Kirti? It has already caused untold damage and if we keep quiet about it now, it would be unfair on all of us.'

Kirti nodded slowly.

'Yes, but only you have the temerity to talk about this with her. Or Mother Sumitra?'

'No, since I was guilty of committing the crime of opening that letter, let me handle this,' said Urmila firmly, filled with a sudden resolve. Kaikeyi would have a lot to answer for when she returned, she thought with mounting unease.

Urmila wondered how she would start the conversation with Kaikeyi. She had arrived the previous evening and the next morning saw Urmila restless to broach the subject. She held the letter in her hands, staring at it but unable to gather enough courage to ask the queen the questions and doubts that were bubbling on her lips.

With grudging and growing respect, Urmila had acknowledged the fact that the queen was an exceptional lady, possibly because she had been brought up that way by her father. He had clearly favoured his youngest daughter over his seven sons. She was his favourite, and not just because of her incomparable beauty but also because she was a scholar, brilliant in music and the arts and warfare. She was his eighth son—he had brought her up as he had his sons, but with a more benevolent, liberal eye. And he hoped to find the finest groom for this extraordinary daughter of his and thus, when King Dashrath placed his request for matrimony

with his lovely child, King Aswapti was acutely displeased and disappointed. For though, the king of Kosala was considered to be one of the mightiest kings of the country, with powerful friends like Lord Indra, the king, the father believed, was too old for his young, lissome daughter who had just turned eighteen. Much to his chagrin, his daughter pleaded her case too—she, too, had fallen in love with him and wanted to marry the middle-aged king, old enough to be her father.

The father reluctantly obliged, but not without reservations and the condition that the firstborn child of Kaikeyi would be the heir to the throne. The besotted king of Kosala agreed readily, and he never regretted his choice. Kaikeyi was young, lovely and adventurous, completely unlike the staid, solemn Kausalya. But like her, this young wife, too, could not beget him a son.

But the consequent birth of the four boys is another story, thought Urmila. What intrigued her was the stronghold her father had over Kaikeyi and which she never attempted to break off, despite her marriage and the huge physical distance between the two kingdoms. In fact, she kept sending Bharat to her father's palace so often that he was mainly educated there. That was another grouse, Urmila remembered, Manthara had against Kaikeyi—that she had neglected Bharat at the expense of her strong affection for Ram. Then how is that a mother who loved Ram so completely suddenly turned against him to protect the interest of that son whom she had largely ignored through his childhood years? Urmila, at last, had got her answer. And it was in the letter in her hand...and it was time the secret was revealed.

With much trepedition, but unfaltering steps, Urmila entered Kaikeyi's chamber. It was still the most luxurious, flamboyant room and described the queen's personality best. Kaikeyi looked surprised to see her, but greeted her warmly.

The smile, however, disappeared when Urmila showed her the opened letter. She lost her pallor as she leafed through it quickly.

'It has been opened!' she said sharply. 'Who dared do that?'

'I did,' replied Urmila evenly. 'And that's why I came to return it to the rightful owner.'

'But that does not justify your action. I thought you had more dignity than being a mere snoop, Urmila!' said the queen scathingly.

But Urmila could see that behind all that blistering anger was a worry, an unease that was gnawing at her. The queen looked restless.

'You may leave,' she said curtly.

Urmila remained where she was. 'I did not just open it, I read it too,' she said softly.

'So I assumed,' snapped the queen. 'But please leave now. I have no intention to speak with you further.'

'Kirti and Shatrughna know about this letter too. They have read it as well.' Kaikeyi went a shade paler. 'And Kausalya and Sumitra?' she asked in a hoarse whisper.

'Not yet,' explained Urmila. 'We were not too sure how they would react...but they will know of it eventually, as will Bharat, Ram, Sita and Lakshman.'

The queen's knees suddenly buckled; she sank slowly to the floor.

'No! Oh, God, no!' she cried.

Urmila rushed to her. 'But why? Why were you hiding this terrible truth from us?' she asked wildly.

The queen shook her head and wept. They were tears of defeat and disconsolateness.

Urmila could not help herself; she wrapped her arms around the shaking shoulders of the older woman, giving her whatever comfort she could.

'Why did you not let us know that you had planned and acted out this entire drama of Ram's exile?' she asked gently.

The queen kept quiet, the silence broken by her soft sobs. 'You knew his exile was preordained and yet you willed it to happen and orchestrated it to look like you had banished him for your greed and for preserving your son's rights. But it was just the opposite. You were actually protecting Ram. And in this masquerade, all you earned was not the goodwill but the wrath and hatred of everyone—even your husband and son! Why? Why did you and your father keep silent?'

'Because that was how it was to be. It is such a long story,' sighed the queen. 'From the day I married the king, I knew what was in store for me. Our family priest, Sage Ratna, had told me that my husband would die of grief for his son. After his death, the throne was to remain unoccupied for fourteen years or else the misfortune would be carried on to the heir resulting in his subsequent death too. I did not believe it earlier but the king once mentioned his curse to me and therefore, to save the family and the Raghu dynasty, I had to play out this entire charade, ensuring no one sat on the throne for this period. Guru Vasishtha knew about this as well and that's why he was the one who suggested to place Ram's wooden sandals on the throne.'

Urmila was shocked.

'He knew as well? And yet he allowed it all to happen and kept us in the dark?'

She recalled that it was the guru who had suggested Bharat be regent of the king and place Ram's sandals on the throne. She also recalled how weakly Kaikeyi had persuaded Ram to return to Ayodhya—she had not wanted him there whatsoever.

'He had to, don't you see? He believed it too. It all had to happen in such a way that things fell into place exactly as fate had ordained...and it did.'

'And you witnessed the entire saga—even watching your husband die, knowing all along?'

'Yes,' sighed Kaikeyi, releasing a long, ragged breath. 'I had to. And I wept silent tears. I was forced to see the man I loved most, die—slowly and suffering—in front of me! But that was as unavoidable as the curse he had to live with.'

'But he died hating you till his last breath!' exclaimed Urmila in horror. 'Why did you not let him know this truth in his last hours so that he could have died in peace?'

'Would he have believed me?' she asked wearily. 'I had completely broken his trust in me. And Urmila, it had taken a lot of effort and guile to convince that I was serious about those two boons for myself—I ranted, raved, raged! He could not believe it, his utmost faith in me telling him that I could not be so ruthless, so loathsome...but I managed to do so eventually with all the cruellest, taunting words I could utter and after that, there was no looking back. I had to sacrifice him, our love, our everything for the future. All I wanted was to save Ram's life and so with all my strength, my moral courage, my self-despication, I extracted the two boons from my trusting, unsuspecting husband and saw to it that Ram was banished—away from the throne and away from further misfortune or possible death.'

Urmila was dazed. 'But did you not put Bharat in danger when you demanded he be the crown prince?'

'No, dear, I knew Bharat would never accept Ram's throne; he would never usurp his brother's inheritance.'

Urmila listened with mounting respect and admiration for the woman sitting in front of her, who had earned herself a stigma for a lifetime to save her family. But she also said it with such burning conviction that Urmila was assailed with a sudden dart of fear.

'How can you be so sure? It all might have gone wrong, or can still go wrong...' she said fearfully.

Kaikeyi shook her head slowly. 'That's what I thought too but when my father came up with the same request but in another manner, I knew all of us were hurtling towards the same end...it was going to happen and I was to be the perpetrator.'

'What did your father actually say?' asked Urmila curiously though from the letter she had got a faint idea what the plan between the father and the daughter had been.

'As you know, my father had this rare gift of being able to decipher the talk between birds, insects and animals but he could not reveal it to anyone for it would mean death for him,' explained Kaikeyi. 'My mother learnt it the hard way and got thrown out from the palace, the kingdom and our lives,' she recalled bitterly. 'I grew up with this legendary reality and I knew it to be true, for my father spent days in the woods and jungles, eavesdropping on the conversation of the creatures there. And from them he heard that the forests were in imminent danger due to the cruelty and atrocities of the powerful Ravan on the sages performing their yagna in the forests.'

'Ravan!' Urmila exclaimed.

'Do you know him?' the queen asked testily, looking equally surprised.

'Yes, somewhat, he was present for Sita's swayamvar and created a terrible scene when he could not lift the Shiv bow and marry Sita,' she shuddered as she recalled his softly leering voice, the way he had looked at her lasciviously.

'So, it's all true...and soon going to come true...' the queen murmured softly.

'What?' asked Urmila in fear and rising exasperation.

'My father got to know from their talk that there was only one person who could stop Ravan and eventually kill him—and that person was Ram.'

Urmila's breath caught in her throat. It all sounded weird, unreal, fantastic. Ram was destined to kill Ravan during his exile?

'Your father explained all this in that letter. But did he not tell you this before?' she asked, puzzled.

'No, he could never let me know the exact details as the moment he did it, he would die. All he told me was to set up some sort of a plan to get Ram out of the palace and banish him to the forest to accomplish his mission. That is all he told me and I followed his instructions, trusting him explicitly...not that it came easy!' reminisced the older woman. 'I initially thought he was protecting Bharat's interests to make him king and I fought with him on that. But he begged me that it was otherwise and implored me to save Ram and the family and the world out there in the forests. He could never give me the details, fearing his own death. He finally did—in that letter—after getting to know how the family, all of Ayodhya and even Bharat had turned against me. That is why he wrote that last letter explaining and making me understand the truth, for which he eventually died, as he knew he would.'

Her mother-in-law suddenly seemed to have aged, shrivelled in front of her, in this short while. Her shoulders sagged, as if tired of carrying the burden of the secret. 'Mother, you lost your father, your husband and even the love and respect of your son and the world at large. But if you had explained all this to the king, would he not have agreed as well? Why this tragic charade?'

'The king would never have let Ram go to the forest. Never,' she reiterated vehemently. 'He could not live without him even for a single day; how would he have the courage to send him to Dandaka to kill the demons and asuras residing there? Last time, he obliged because he feared he would anger Guru Vishwamitra when he took Ram and Lakshman to kill Taraka. I had to do it; it was the only way out. It was when the predictions of Sage Ratna and my father started coinciding, that I realised that Ram's exile was preordained and that I had to be the catalyst to precipitate the event,' said Kaikeyi, touching her twisted little finger, as torn and broken as her.

'You are still bearing the brunt of the misfortune and have

willingly embraced infamy. And yet you don't want to reveal the truth to the family?'

'They wouldn't believe me either!' smiled the queen sadly. 'You precociously opened the letter and read it, that's why you are giving me the benefit of the doubt but who all do I explain to? What do I say? It is just too bizzare and unbelievable. And if I was the one to help it happen, so be it. And more importantly, the idea was to keep all this a secret. No one was to know about this.'

'And Manthara? Did she know?'

'Of course not!' scoffed the queen. 'But she was playing her own game, parallel to mine but both overlapped at the occasion of Ram's coronation. I had to stop it and Manthara, by bringing up the two boons, helped me out inadvertently. I played along, while she thought she was playing on my insecurities...which she did, actually!' she shrugged. 'Manthara always thought she knew me too well but she never guessed either, fortunately. She, unwittingly, showed me the way.'

'And gloated that she had got what she wanted. She wanted you to be the queen mother to strenghten her own position in the palace,' added Urmila.

'But I could not deny her, she was like my mother,' sighed Kaikeyi. 'She nursed me, tended me, did everything for me. I never doubted her love for me—she meant well, but solely for me. She was too possessive and protective and I suspect my father sent her with me, after marriage, knowing full well her wily character and her blind love for me. He knew she would do the needful.'

'That is?'

'Work on my weaknesses so that I would be ready for the day when I had to throw the son I loved most out of the kingdom. I now realize, as Manthara did too, that I had two flaws that I could never overcome—my stubborn ego and my intense insecurity of being abandoned, courtesy my mother who left me when I was six,' recounted Kaikeyi, her face twisting into a bitter smile. 'I was never allowed to forget that by my father. But while it made me cling to him more, it also planted a deep distrust for him in particular and men in general and I grew up with the fear that men left their wives on the weakest pretext...and all these years I lived in the fear that I would lose the love of my husband—either to Kausalya or Sumitra. Or both.'

Urmila felt a small stab of guilt: she had experienced that feeling before. That tearing, irrevocable terror of losing the man you love.

'I realize now how she wonderfully strung me along right from the very first day here in the palace,' narrated the older woman. 'Kausalya was shown to me as my rival—the elder queen whom the king so obviously had deep respect for. She was his chief queen, not me despite all my beauty, youth, love and devotion. And soon, as one year lapsed into another, I could not give him the son he so badly wanted and I realized the bitter truth—that he had married me just to have a son, nothing else,' she recalled, her voice hollow. 'And here, Kausalya had an advantage—she had mothered Shanta—she could beget a child, unlike me. When he got Sumitra, his third queen, home, he confirmed my worst fears. I had never felt so humiliated and demeaned. With that realization, I also understood what Kausalya must have suffered when I was brought in as a bride. But my ego had been bruised; and now with the three of us, I had to be his chief queen, to survive with dignity in this palace or I would be relegated to nothingness. It was when I saved his life at the battlefield, that was to be turning point in my life. I was his forever after that—and I have never looked back since...till I broke his heart when I asked him for the two boons in this very room. It was the day I lost everything,' she said sadly. 'But while I asked for the impossible, I got to know the true nature of those whom I loved dearly. My husband's love turned to ashes and hate. So did Bharat's. But my Ram was the only one who never uttered a single bitter word against me when I was his offender, forgiving me for my crime with his gentle smile. Yes, he is God, for no man can be so good!' she said proudly. 'And, finally, Manthara. I never imagined that someone whom I loved and trusted from childhood, would give me advice that would bring about my downfall. She was espousing for herself, and not for my cause. And while her poisonous words washed over my head, I found myself actually believing her! And a thought struck me— could Manthara have poisoned my mind if there was no fault in me? No greed, no folly, no jealousy, no vanity? The villainy must have always been latent in my heart.

'No, Mother, you were above all this! You might have felt it, identified with it but yet swept it away to listen to your conscience,' refuted Urmila. 'For a higher good.'

Urmila was drowning in a flood of emotions—sorrow, wonder, awe, respect for the elegant, beautiful woman sitting next to her, her face buried in her hands. She saw her in all her shades, muted over the canvas of time—as the tempestuous princess in love, the vivacious bride, the fearful, insecure wife, the ambitious, powerful queen, the fair, loving mother, the maligned widow and finally, the courageous, selfless lady who had braved the contempt of her family and the world. Seeing her thus, Urmila decided that she would reveal this terrible truth of this wonderful woman, at least to the family. They owed this woman that; they should forever be indebted to her.

'I cannot forgive myself for all that has happened,' said the queen, leaning tiredly against the chair. 'And it is when I see you that my heart bleeds the most. I snatched everything from you— your hope, happiness, youth...forgive me, dear, if you can.'

Urmila was horrified. 'I should be saying that...how shall I pardon myself for all those unkind, disrespectful words I said to you?' she cried, with a shake of her head. 'How will the family ever take back all that they said?'

'That is why, it is best they don't know; let it be. Let me live my curse too,' she said. 'As a child I had blackened the face of a sage while he was in meditation, and naturally angry, he had cursed me that I would suffer similarly, and here I am, living with my reputation—blackened and tarnished forever. You can't change that, Urmila. My destiny is at hand.'

'Don't, Ma, are we to be so helpless? Bound, pulled and pushed by the tug of the strings held in Fate's fingers?' she asked desperately. 'That we have preordained destinies and no choices? Don't we make these choices ourselves, Mother?'

'I was a free-willed skeptic like you, Urmila. I had scoffed at Guru Ratna, my father, and even the king. I used to ask him why he was so scared of the curse of the blind father by which he would die of grief for his son when he had no son?!' said Kaikeyi, her eyes dull and distant. 'I tried to assure him that he was lucky he had no son and the curse would never come true...but it did. Everything in my life has happened as predicted...things will happen as they are meant to happen. It is best we don't know about it beforehand. Man is always eager to see his future, but that irrational curiosity never does him any good. Whatever has to happen, will happen' And saying that she carefully placed the letter close to the flickering flame of the oil lamp and watched it slowly catch fire, curling painfully as the flames licked it hungrily, finally crumpling into fine ash to scatter on the marble floor at her feet. Much like her own life.

THE WAITING

He was in her thoughts all day and her dreams in the night. Everyday, she woke up with a sense of pain, of loss. She wanted him near her, wanted him lying beside her, wanted to turn her head on the pillow to look at him gazing back at her with his smiling eyes, to touch his face with her fingers, to smell him, to taste him... She lived it each day, pulled along by her determination to live each day as it came, surviving the rolling days of the years to unfold...

It was the tenth year gone by. Today, she was twenty-seven years old. Another four years to go. When he returned, she would be thirty-one and he, thirty-seven. Urmila looked at herself carefully in the mirror. No longer a girl but a woman—she decided looking at her mellowed face and figure. The girlishness had been wiped out clean, leaving heavy traces of mature feminity. But that would be a cosmetic change. She had most likely grown up from a girl to a woman when she got married into this family and was rushed into the torrent of unhappy events immediately after her wedding. Or did she grow into a woman, when she met Lakshman and fell in love with him with all his complexities?

These ten years had been the longest of her life, but she never let go of him and he was with her through these empty, absent years. She was slowly removing the bangles from her wrists and stopped to stare at them, reminded of his habit of absently caressing them. As she unstrung her ruby necklace, she could see him behind her in the reflection of her mirror, looking at her with that bemused expression as he always did when she removed her ornaments in the night. He had a benevolent dislike for them. 'Granted they make women more pretty but they are too obstructive.' he grimaced. '...and perfect as weapons! Have you noticed how they scratch so murderously? And that hairpin! It actually pierces; it is like a dagger in your bun, hideous and brutalizing your dark, shining hair all tied and pulled back! Let it loose—it's your best feature!'

'Is it?' she said, visibly miffed. She was expecting a better compliment for her large, almond eyes or her full, red lips or her transclucent skin, not her long hair which was nothing unique. 'My grandmother once told me that hair left loose means being wild and wanton and free,' she wrinkled her pert nose, clearly displeased at his lack of praise for the correct object of amour.

'Exactly! That's why I like it that way on you, my enchantress; it should be just like you—wild and free, not to be tied down and so delightfully wanton' he had murmured, his breath warm on her lips as his hands pulled the hairpin out, her silky mane cascading down in a lustrous auburn wave of mounting desire...

She was startled out of her reverie by the shrieks of laughter right below her window. She peered down the ornamented balustrade. Shanta's two sons and her daughter were excitedly climbing the mango tree growing outside her room. Urmila smiled tenderly watching them for a long time. A quick image of her and her sisters attempting the same in the Mithila garden so many years ago flashed in front of her eyes. Mandavi used to curtly excuse herself citing vertigo as a reason for wriggling out of these adventures. Sita happily gave up at the earliest, contentedly perched on the lowest branch, biting on the sourest of the raw mangoes. She and Kirti were always game and tried to reach the highest branch, giggling and hooting in jubilance. That same delighted ring seemed to be echoing now. The boys had given up and were shouting up at their sister to come down. The girl, Smriti, was agile and fast and had almost reached the highest branch.

'You have won, dear! Now climb down a little lower. Be careful,' instructed Urmila from her window, still smiling. The sight and sound of children playing in the palace grounds was a welcoming change and it gladdened her heart. The palace was inhabited and visited by various kind of people, but never children since the princes had grown up. Urmila's smile slipped as she felt a sharp pang—children...would she ever see hers running down the arched corridors some day? When would she hear the soft gurgle of a toothless baby? Urmila bit her lip. She was being silly, she thought with a stab of dejectedness. She could always have them later...but would she have been happier had she had a child to look after now?

Urmila gave herself a little shake—what was she thinking? She heard the happy squeal of the children again and thought of her sisters. They were suffering a similar reality of abstinence. Their husbands were leading the life of ascetics, which forbade conjugality. The brothers shared their pain and sorrow—even the vows of chasity. By leading a life of celibacy like their elder brother, they showed a shared strength and moral purity.

'Sometimes I think I am the most fortunate of us four—Lakshman is not physically here so I don't expect anything from him!' remarked Urmila with a mirthless laugh. 'All of us here are leading an exceptionally unusual variety of marital bliss. We are suffering in common—love and loss, separation and abstinence. Our Fate, besides having a twisted sense of humour, is quite egalitarian.'

'That's good in a way; we don't need to be envious of each

other!' grinned Kirti good humouredly. 'We are all sailing—or should I say capsizing—in the same boat?'

Mandavi was not amused. 'It's called wasted youth! The men have won their moral war, but what about us wives? Forced celibacy is not sublime; I would rather bask in love than such glory. It could be called poetic injustice!' smirked Mandavi, looking up from her book. She shut it and waving it at them, said nonchalantly, 'These books make better companions. They make you live in a world you wish, a world you want to belong to...'

Urmila looked worriedly at Mandavi. Would she be kinder to herself once Bharat was back?

The cold logic of Mandavi's next line reiterated her unease. 'I keep recalling Aunt Sunaina's words, Urmi—that all of us should not have married in the same family,' she remarked thoughtfully. 'We have been married to the same set of problems, that same stock of suffering and sacrifice.'

'But her reason was different, she was wary that it would jeopardize the relationship between us sisters,' said Urmila. 'But I think we did her proud—we managed pretty well so far!'

'Yes, caged in this prison, I think we have progressed wonderfully,' agreed Mandavi casutically.

Urmila felt like surrendering; she was almost indifferent to her sister's rancour. It no longer upset her. Bitter anger and deep ill-will had hardened her sister's personality. Urmila wondered if she would ever soften. Mandavi had always been hard and cold but her ready wit used to often see her through. Her substituted cynicism now made her cruel. Even when she had divulged the secret Kaikeyi had hidden from the family, it seemed to have no impact on Mandavi.

'Does it make much difference to our lives? Will Bharat come back? Or will it bring back your Lakshman, Urmi?' she shrugged. 'Ah, yes, I shall probably hate her a little less! Whatever that means, it is still she who was the harbinger of misfortunes in the family.'

Her bitterness had corroded into her. Hope had deserted her leaving her lonely. Her fairy tale had long lost the romance. But it would probably return once her prince came back to her. Would love reign again? Urmila knew it would; Bharat would win back Mandavi. Or rather, Mandavi would realize his goodness some day. And it was not just her romantic optimism making her hope for the best for her cousin. It was Mandavi whom Urmila knew so well. She would bask in the love and attention, once showered again on her.

But unlike Mandavi, Kirti was content. Requitedly happy with Shatrughna, Urmila could see that. Clearly, humour was her best defence, her safest weapon. Shatrughna's wit seemed to have rubbed on her wonderfully. Did marriage make people grow to be like each other, Urmila thought with amused affection. Each evening, without fail, and however late in the night, Shatrughna sat with Kirti and talked with her about everything—from court affairs to matters of the heart. They reminded her of how she and Lakshman used to spend much of their time in banter. 'Keep it light, Mila, though I can't do much of small talk!' he used to warn her with an engaging grin. 'Our heavy discussions don't seem to be good for either of our tempers!'

She smiled at the recollection. Yes, she and Kirti were happier than Mandavi.

Four sisters, married the same day, living in similar wretchedness but each accepting and acknowledging life differently—Mandavi bitter, Kirti wiser and she catatonic. Urmila was amused at her self-description. But yes she did live—exist—in a certain stupor, enduring on her sheer will to survive. The course of time and events plodded on, as if circling a grindstone, uninterrupted, pausing for none.

Sita was not here but Urmila had gauged from their last conversation at Chitrakoot that she was abundantly happy. She could not have been more content elsewhere—in the forest, in the lap of nature, with the hard soil under her doughty feet. She would not mind the hardship, the rigours of life spent in the forest. Her choice had been clear—felicitous and fortunate with Ram by her side. They lived quitely in the ashrams of the rishis of Dandaka forest, protecting them from the devouring demons. Those who dared attack them, did not live to regret as each of them were killed by the incisive arrows of the two brothers. Bharat had a web of informants who kept him duly acquainted about the whereabouts of the trio in the forest. They had moved from Chitrakoot soon after Bharat and the others had visited them and had travelled through the sprawling dangers of the dreaded Dandaka forest. After having returned from the Vindhyas and meeting Sage Agatsya, they had finally settled at Panchavati and right now lived in a hut off the banks of River Godavari.

In Ayodhya, the people had yet not forgiven Kaikeyi for her transgressions. But her family shamefacedly had. Urmila, without further hesitation, had let them know of the secret of the outcast queen. The three queens for the first time, probably, ate their meal happily together—without rancour and resentment. And that was how it had been for the last few years of that decade. A little peace, a lot of quiet.

Urmila received an unexpected invitation. It was from her father for the forthcoming philosophical conference—the prestigious *brahmanyagna*—which he hosted every year. But what surpised her was that he had not invited her as his daughter. He was requesting her to attend the annual symposium in her own right as an acclaimed scholar. She had long been under the tutelage of Vasishtha and the other gurus of Ayodhya's royal court—Guru Vaamdeva, Markandeya, Katyayan as well as the reluctant Kashyap, who had grudgingly acknowledged her brilliant, questioning mind.

Urmila had grown from being a curious student to an exemplary one to be finally acknowledged as a pandit, a learned scholar, who by long, perseverent study had gained mastery over the Vedas and Upanishads and could proficiently debate on religion and philosophy with the most learned of sages. That was probably why King Seeradhwaj Janak had invited her to the prestigious conference.

Urmila felt a glow of pride. Her father, the most respected of all scholars, had graciously acknowledged her as a peer though he did not always agree with her as a theologist. She questioned the rationality of religion and its influence on the nature of religious truth rather than seeking the divinity in religion as he did. Urmila gave a small smile—it would be an interesting debate especially with Sage Gargi and the controversial Guru Jaabali around.

'You seem strangely esctactic!' said Kirti, watching her sister's radiant face. For a second, she was reminded of the times when Urmila was with Lakshman, gloriously happy.

'Father has asked me to come to Mithila!' smiled Urmila, almost gushing, unable to keep the good news to herself any longer. She thrust the invite in Kirti's hand. Kirti read it carefully and was happy for her cousin.

'It means a lot to you, doesn't it?' asked Kirti softly. 'And I don't mean being able to participate in that prestigious conference; what is more important is that you have managed to impress your father. That means so much more to you.'

Urmila's smile slipped slightly, losing the lilt. 'Am I that transparent?' she asked at last, slowly and thoughfully.

'No you are not,' refuted Kirti quickly, and added gently. 'Others might assume the reason for your evident elation is the conference but we—both Mandavi and I—and Sita, had she been here, know that the true reason for your happiness is the fact that you have exceeded your father's expectations. It has always been that with you—you have always striven to gain their love and respect, unlike the three of us who got it too easy from them. You had to struggle for it and we didn't, for different reasons—Sita because she was the oldest, the privileged first child, the ideal daughter who always did everything right and perfect. We because we were the younger ones and more so because we were motherless. Both your parents were there for us always, sometimes at your expense. You ended up getting ignored often while Sita got all the accolade and we got the affection. That's why you strived so hard, and that's why, though you are so fiercely independent, their opinion matters most to you.'

Urmila looked thoughtful, a sad smile playing on her lips. 'You make me sound so pathetic, Kirti!'

'No, actually the situation was so pathetic!' retorted Kirti heatedly. 'You were entitled to everything but got nothing. And yet you braved it all, never wallowing in self-pity. So, don't think I am feeling sorry for you or worse, cutting a sorry picture of you. It's neither. I admire you. You never showed any resentment because you genuinely never resented us—Sita for being the adopted sister and we as the motherless cousins...'

'Kirti, what are you saying?!' exclaimed Urmila in growing horror. She looked shocked, the hurt evident in her large eyes.

'See? That's what I am saying!' said Kirti. 'Even the mere thought is so repugnant for you! Never were you jealous, angry or malicious. Why, you always played peacemaker between us—patching up our quarrels, diffusing tempers, ironing out differences. You didn't waste tears of self-indulgent sorrow but let it all out so beautifully through your fertile mind and generous heart.'

Urmila pondered over the long praise. She had never been made to feel special, but Kirti made it sound all so magnificently selfless and tragic. 'Kirti, I have always known you to be wise beyond your age but today you seem to be wise beyond words too!' she laughed. 'But you give me too much credit.'

Kirti merely shook her head and smiled affectionately at her older cousin's attempt of dismissiveness. Like pity, she knew Urmila hated praise too. She wasn't good with either. 'I don't really. None of us did or do,' said Kirti quietly. 'But I am happy that there is one such person who loves you for what you are, who recognizes your worth and loves you madly for it. And that is Lakshman.'

Kirti's words floated along with Urmila, even as she travelled and reached Mithila a week later, filling her with the same untold, unquestionable happiness. Doubling that peaceful sense of contentment was the beaming pride she saw shining in her parents' eyes. Her parents had never looked at her that way. That look had always been reserved for Sita.

The conference was as grand as it used to be in her childhood days. But twenty-seven years later, today, it held a new meaning for Urmila. Rishis and learned intellectuals from all over the country came and exchanged, debated and deliberated upon ideas and discourses, searching for the truth, the expanse of the human mind and its quest for knowledge. This time she would be a part of it.

Her father had once told her how the conference had started. King Seeradhwaj Janak was famously known to have four girls in his palace—two were his daughters and the other two his nieces. Yet he never yearned for a son like his friend Dashrath did. Some even advised him to invite Rishyasringa to perform the same yagna he had performed for Dashrath to provide him with a son. The king of Mithila had flatly refused, claiming that he was indeed that lucky man who could be a father to four, lovely girls whom he would raise to be explempary human beings—as beautiful in their minds as in their bodies. His destiny, he reminded everyone, were his daughters. The self, he argued, was not gendered. A lesson he had learned from a woman called Sulabha.

Sulabha was a scholar, a fiery intellectual. She was young,

lovely and unmarried. She wished to have a private talk with the philoshopher-king. King Janak agreed but was clearly uncomfortable about being alone in the room with this beautiful woman. And what she said next was to affect Janak forever. 'You, King Janak, are the king of Videha, which means "beyond the body" and yet as a king of such a land, you cannot look beyond my body and read my mind,' she reprimanded him gently and went on to add, 'the mind is the deity, the body just a temple to accomodate the mind. And it is the mind which is the great leveller, the great egalitarian truth, for it rests in both man and woman. There is no essential difference between them. Each sees the world differently not because of the gender but because of the mind. And each mind needs to search for knowledge and to expand. But for that you have to have a meeting of the great minds, an exchange of thought, a coming together of ideas. Enrich the mind, and that is wisdom. That is Veda.'

Struck by her words, the king decided to provide a platform for free and liberal minds to talk about philosophical issues and ideas. Thus came into being the conference of the most intense, intimate, intellectual conversations amongst the most respected rishis of the country. Over the years, each thought, argument and debate had been amassed; debates, poetry, lyrics and hymns compiled in what was called the Brihadaranyak Upanishad.

At the conference, Urmila sat amongst the brilliant minds of the country as a scholar in her own right, with the famous lady philosopher Guru Gargi, the deformed Rishi Ashtavarka, Guru Vashishta and Guru Markandeya from the royal court of Ayodhya and Rishi Yagnavalkya who had challenged his own teacher and who was also her father's guru. Seated amongst them, Urmila felt a sense of deep humility. It dissolved all false pride, absolved her of trivialities. As she felt the calmness descend on her, she was poignantly fired with a new sense of purpose, a goal she had to strive towards. Each time she recited the Vedic verses or succintly debated with Guru Jaabali, she saw her father listening intently, his brows furrowed, his face thoughtful but in his eyes was a tenderness touched with pride. And in that moment, Urmila felt she was at last her father's daughter. She was Urmila, not just the woman of passion as her name so defined her but one whose heart and mind had come together in intellectual and spiritual enrichment. In this long quest, she had delimitated her persona both as a daughter and a wife suitably, not just complementing but supplementing both the male figures in her life. It would have been a proud moment for Lakshman too had he been here. Urmila felt a sharp pang: she missed him always but today she felt the physical void of his absence. He had always been exhortative, rallying and reassuring her for all her efforts but today she knew he would have been ecstatically proud of her, flaunting her, ostentatious in his pride of her success.

That evening as she touched her father's feet for his blessing, the cursory gesture took on a new meaning. She was humbled, honoured to receive the blessing of such a great man who she was blessed to be a daughter of.

'I knew I have survived so long just to see this day; I have dreamt of it long enough!' said King Janak tenderly.

Urmila was more surprised than touched at this unexpected praise. She had always had an odd relationship with her father—it was neither usual nor ordinary. Possibly because she admired her father more than she loved him.

'You hoped that I would be known as a scholar one day?' she asked, the surprise evident in her voice.

'Yes, dear, always. You had a curious mind, a kind heart and clarity of ideas and expressions which you knew how to use wisely, even as a child,' her father smiled. 'It got honed well as you grew up and I am thankful that you took advantage of the royal rishis of Ayodhya under whose tutelage you so excelled.'

'That was more by default! I had nothing better to do in the last so many years except study and paint,' said Urmila.

'Then the credit goes to Lakshman...' said King Janak softly. 'Had he not gone on exile, you would not have been able to do all that you achieved?'

The mention of Lakshman's name put Urmila immediately on the defensive. 'No, not at all!' she clarified quickly. 'He would not have stopped me, on the contrary, he would have encouraged me. Do you think he would have? Are you disappointed in him?' she asked quietly.

'No, dear, no! You misunderstand. That temper of yours always makes you draw the wrong conclusions!' her father smiled indulgently. 'He is not merely my son-in-law. And I do not respect him for being just that. He, my dear, is that man who brought out the best in you. He fell in love with you because of your mind, because you were different from the usual. Fire recognized fire: the fire didn't want water.'

Urmila flushed with embarassment. 'You think I did not notice that?' smiled King Janak. 'But fortunately for the two of you, your mutual love, not just kindled a fire, but brought about a certain serenity in both of you...it burned to give warmth. As a child you had once asked me if the wife needed to be tamed like Ganga on Lord Shiv's head. You had never seen your mother 'tamed'—she was always fierce and forthright. You are so much like her. To be free does not mean to be wild. And I brought you up in that freedom of thought and action, just as Lakshman did. And he loves you for that. He is the wise man who saw the wisdom in you much before you did yourself. Staying away from him makes your love the highest form of love—the parakiya-rasa—where the two of you share thoughts even through separation.'

Urmila found herself agreeing with every word her father had said. As they rewound a world and time gone by, she could not but admit that they seemed oddly true in retrospect.

'The moment I saw Ram and Lakshman with Rishi Vishwamitra I knew they were no ordinary mortals...' continued the old king of Mithila, '...and that they were destined for my daughters. Or rather, my daughters' destinies would be entwined with those of these illustrious sons of the Ikshavaku clan. They were the disciples of Vasishtha and Vishwamitra, which meant that they were great warriors as well as wise statesmen. Ram and Lakshman are two sides of each other—they are a reflection. They are one atma in two bodies, always remember that, Urmila.'

'I know that, father, I have seen it,' replied Urmila.

'And yet are you sad or glad about it?'

Urmila thought over the strange question for a long time and realized it actually encapsulated her own identity. 'I am glad of it,' she answered slowly. Her initial resentment had long given way to a calm realization, an inner peace which had helped her grow from a wilful girl to a woman of wisdom.

Janak nodded. 'Ram sought opportunity in exile. So did Lakshman—his brother's exile was an exile for him too. And as the wife of Lakshman, it was an exile for you as well—an exile from attachment,' he explained. 'Because only with detachment one learns the value of love versus the range of emotions. These years have taught you that.

'The exile made you understand the meaning of tapasya and thus made you a tapasvi. And as this great tapasvi who has gained great spiritual understanding and intellectual attainment, I greet you today as a scholar. Your scholarship came not just from reciting verses and detailed study but primarily from your pain, your separation, your detachment. Your separation was your meditation, your spiritual rebirth and your love for your husband became your salvation.'

Urmila felt acutely humbled, but not without a trace of helplessness. 'Has it, father? But Mandavi too has had a hard life,' she reminded him strongly.

'But she never realized the greater truth of what and why she was made to experience it. One has to lead one's life through one's own ability and comprehensibility,' said King Janak grimly. 'Did she see the penance of Bharat? Did she see his sacrifice? And why he did it? And more importantly, did she learn from that pain of separation? She is filled with too much anger and hurt, corroding into her very soul. How will she ever get her peace, her wisdom, her deliverance? Agreed, both of you suffered the same destiny, but each eked out a different fate for herself. Destiny is given but it depends on how you take it.'

The truth of his cautious advice rested in her mind as she returned to Ayodhya the next morning. She was coming back home.

THE ABDUCTION

She missed him each morning as she woke up in an empty bed, cold and alone, the dread of spending another day—long and stretched—without him. The nights were more treacherous—interminable and wistful; the void in the bed and her heart felt like an intense, persistent physical pain. She ached for him. To block the tormenting sight of him sleeping next to her, curved and warm against her willing body, she had started sleeping on the hard, cold marble floor, yanking down the silken embroidered counterpane and sleeping on it once the maids had left. But her sleep was fitful, interspersed with short, jumpy dreams—always of him. And that's why, her tired, waiting eyes welcomed them...

Just another few months to go, just another few months for him to return...Urmila felt a warmth kindling her heart, glowing bigger as each day passed bringing her closer to his day of return. The last few weeks, the monsoons had completely drenched the earth, hydrating the dusty landscape into a lush, emerald spread of rejuvenated cheer. The brooding, pregnant clouds had been chased away by the bright sunlight, dappling the clear, azure skies and every verandah running along the palace. Urmila felt a sudden surge of effervescent hope, a burst of unadulterated joy. She smiled as she continued with her painting of the scene of the wedding; it looked almost real and lifelike now, with the smallest expression coming through the minutest detail. She held the brush with a flourish, giving the last touches to the mammoth canvas. That canvas was unusual for her—an entire white wall of the longest hall in the palace. This was the new assembly hall where the newly-appointed king, Ram, would meet with his nobles, courtiers and the people of Ayodhya every day. The hall was huge—long and high-ceilinged—and the running painting dominated the space and the mood, she smiled with unreasonable gaiety.

She heard rather than saw Bharat coming through the palace gates. Urmila frowned. Bharat had not shown his face since the last thirteen years; he had not even attended the puja on Ram's birth anniversary that many years ago. Though that ritual had continued each year, Bharat was missed each time. He had said he would only return to Ayodhya with Ram. Whatever had made Bharat turn down his resolution to hurry up from Nandigram must be sufficiently urgent. She instinctively placed her brush down. He had headed straight to Kausalya's chambers, she guessed correctly, where the three queens would be together. Urmila was still not sure whether Bharat knew about his mother's misrepresentation—so painfully altruistic. She had assumed Shatrughna had revealed the truth to his brother as he met him every single day to keep him informed about the daily court matters. Surely he must have discussed such crucial news with him.

Urmila almost rushed into the room: she had not realized she had been running, her breath coming in short gasps. Bharat looked relieved to see her. She was meeting him after a span of more than a decade. He was painfully emaciated; his face appeared narrower. One look at him and Urmila knew something was terribly wrong.

'I have called for the others too...' he started.

Urmila looked around the heavily curtained chamber of Kausalya. The old queen was sitting upright in her lounge chair. The last thirteen years had especially not been too kind to her. Her hair had gone completely grey but was still thick, puffing up the silver crown as a heavy bouffant. Her face was wreathed in wrinkles, her skin clear and transparent like a dried parchment, her eyes dull, lighting up only at the mention of Ram. With her were Sumitra and Kaikeyi. As if by an inner cue, her two sisters entered the room, along with Shatrughna.

'What is it, Bharat?' asked Urmila impatiently. 'It has to be urgent or you would not be here.'

'I got to know from my spies just today that Sita has been kidnapped from their hut at Panchavati,' began Bharat, failing to mince words. The words hit hard.

Urmila froze, the room slowly spinning around her. How could Sita come to any harm with Ram and Lakshman around? It was all amiss; it could not happen.

'Both Ram and Lakshman were not at the hut—they had gone to chase a deer when Ravan, in the guise of a brahmin, snatched her away as she was giving him dakshina and took her to Lanka in his aerial chariot Pushpak,' explained Bharat, his words coming in short starts. 'Old Jatayu, the king of the eagles, and the protector of the three at Panchavati, tried hard to save her but was fatally wounded. Before dying, he managed to let Ram and Lakshman know that it had been Ravan who took Sita away in his flying chariot and showed them the direction in which he went. Ravan has her imprisoned there in the Ashok garden. Ram and Lakshman are presently taking the help of Sugriva, the vanar king of Kishkindha and his associate Hanuman. They intend to attack Lanka with the help of the vanara army.'

There was a brief, shocked silence, each assimilating the news with disbelief and alarm. 'When did this happen?' asked Sumitra, her voice steady.

'In the summer,' replied Bharat. 'But we got to know only now. My informants knew they were at Panchavati but they lost trace of them when Ram and Lakshman were moving all through the jungles searching for Sita. It was much later that our spies got to know that Sita had been kidnapped,' he added, the agitation evident on his worried face.

'Should we not send our army too to help Ram?' said Shatrughna. 'If he is taking assistance from the vanara army, clearly he could do with more support.'

'No,' Bharat shook his head. 'If he needed so, Ram would have sent us a message and since he has not for all these months, it means he has a certain plan which does not include us or the army of Kosala. No, we can do nothing but wait. And pray.'

'How did it happen, Bharat?' interrupted Urmila, abruptly cutting short the brothers' discussion. Her thoughts were bewildered, her emotions in a turmoil, 'How could anyone dare snatch Sita away with Ram and Lakshman with her? Lakshman used to watch over them even at night so how is that she was abducted in broad daylight?'

Bharat did not answer immediately, searching for words. 'It is a long story,' he started slowly. 'It seems Sita caught sight of a silver-spotted golden deer near the hut and begged Ram to fetch it...'

'A golden deer!' exclaimed Urmila. 'But there are no silver-spotted golden deers! There is no such animal!'

'Exactly. It was part of the subterfuge. The deer was Mareecha the magician and Ravan's uncle,' said Bharat. 'Ram obliged Sita's wish and told Lakshman to remain at the hut till he returned with the deer. Ram chased the deer far into the woods and eventually killed it but before dying, the deer let out a human cry, and in the voice of Ram, screamed out for Sita and Lakshman. Hearing that cry, Sita assumed Ram was in danger and ordered Lakshman to go to his aid. Reluctantly, he left, and Ravan, disguised as a brahmin, having orchestrated this whole scheme, abducted the unprotected Sita in his chariot.'

Again there was a silence, the impact of his words resounding silently within the walls of the room. Urmila found the story too bizarre to believe.

'But why did Soumitra leave her alone in the hut?' asked Kausalya angrily. 'He should have known better! Ram had told him to stay put and look after Sita. Why did he not heed his brother's orders? That was irresponsible and careless of him!'

Urmila flushed, hurt to the quick at the accusation. She bit her lip to stop an angry retort.

'No, Mother, Lakshman would never do that; he would have died protecting Sita,' said Bharat sharply. 'He would never disobey Ram's orders nor would he have left Sita unprotected. Never! The fact that he did means this was all a clever trick, you cannot blame anyone.'

'But how did Ravan get to know of them in the forest?' asked Mandavi puzzled. 'He is the king of Lanka but what was he doing at Panchavati in the Dandaka forest?'

'That is another story,' narrated Bharat. 'For the past thirteen years in the Dandaka, Ram and Lakshman have been eliminating the demons who had been harassing the rishis during meditation and disrupting their yagna. The rakshas often killed these helpless rishis following the orders of Ravan's brothers Khara and Dushan, stationed at Janasthan, near Panchavati, who had started this terror in the forest. One day their sister Surpanakha caught sight of Ram and fell in love with him and asked him to marry him. Ram refused, explaining he was married to Sita. She turned her attention to Lakshman,' paused Bharat, throwing Urmila a look of acute embarrassment. Urmila looked thoughtful, not experiencing the stab of jealousy that would have otherwise left her in agony. She recalled her jealous tantrum the day before their wedding: she was not that girl anymore. Jealousy, she knew, always existed with desire. But it ceased to exist if there was trust. She had implicit faith in Lakshman.

Bharat continued with a red face. 'She went up to him and begged Lakshman to marry her. He, too, politely refused. Spurned twice, the furious Surpanakha saw Sita as the deterrent in her way, and attempted to attack her. But Lakshman was quick, he snatched his sword and sliced off her nose...'

Urmila could not stop her gasp of horror—a woman trying to seduce her husband did not shock her as much as his violence.

Seeing her blanched face, Bharat gently reminded her, 'Remember she was a demon, Urmila, and she was going to attack Sita. Ram killed Taraka, Lakshman mutilated Surpanakha's face—they were acts of self-defence, not violence or disrespect. You will soon realize how this woman was solely responsible for Sita's abduction,' he added and continued, 'More humiliated than hurt, Surpanakha ran to her brothers and sought revenge. The two brothers, as she had expected and wanted, charged with their army but were soon all killed by Ram. Defeated, Surpanakha fled to Lanka to her oldest brother Ravan and demanded he avenge her humiliation by the two brothers. Ravan swore to kill them but when he realized that they had managed to annihilate his brothers and their huge army at Janasthan, he knew he would have to use intrigue to humble Ram and Lakshman—through Sita. That is how he worked out that plan with his uncle Mareecha, who well knew of Ram's prowess. He was the same demon who had dared to disturb Vishwamitra's ashram where Ram and Lakshman had killed his mother Taraka and his brother Subahu so many years ago.'

Urmila heard the narration with a turbulence of emotions rising within her—panic, dread and undiluted rage.

'And it is in this beastly world that my sister went and none of us stopped her,' she said harshly. She turned to Kausalya. 'You accused Lakshman of negligence, and the world too soon will follow and damn him for the same. But why was Sita allowed to go to this demon-infested forest? As her mother-in-law, as the mother who would look after her daughter, how did you allow it?' she cried, the swamping waves of fear breaking into fury. 'You cried for Ram but did you not think of this intrepid, young girl who readily agreed to accompany her husband into the worst of all dangers? I recall Ram dissuading her, pleading with her not to go with him. If you, too, had put in a word, it might have stopped her. But you were more devastated that Ram was leaving for the forest!' her voice grew icicles. 'The fact that Sita was with him, made you feel better that there was someone to look after him. She was the ideal, doting wife who was practising her dharma of following her husband, never mind the danger she would be vulnerable to. But, Mother, it was she who needed to be looked after—not Ram or Lakshman. They are warriors, not Sita!'

Urmila was beside herself with worry, the fear and anxiety rising up in her throat, choking her. She carried on, the anguished fear stark in her voice. 'Lakshman had warned me that the forest was not a safe place for anyone and especially women and it was not his chauvinism speaking. I saw that crazed worry in his eyes— that anxiety for those you love. But didn't any of you see that risk for Sita? She was just a girl in love, a bride, who was vehement about going with her husband. You are our elders whose mere word of caution can become a command, why didn't any of you stop her? Oh why didn't I stop her? I could have, I should have!' she berated herself harshly.

Mandavi had never seen Urmila in such a state; she was almost berserk, her overwhelming worry for Sita and the mounting fear anticipating more misfortune stark in her stricken eyes. She held her cousin's trembling hands; they were ice cold. 'Calm down, Urmi. Why are you feeling guilty?' she implored. 'However much had you pleaded with her, Sita would not have listened to you. You know how adamant she can get. It was not your ignorance or lack of intervention.'

'Then whose was it?' demanded Urmila, implacable, not to be appeased. She continued to address Kausalya. 'Just as Ram and Lakshman were inseparable, so were we, mother! Then why was I not allowed to go with her?' she was shaking, whether in frustration or fury, Mandavi was not sure. 'I have heard of how Lakshman, as a baby, used to cry when he was taken away from Ram and that's why their cradles were always placed close to each other's. So were ours, mother! I do not recall a moment without Sita; we were soulmates, not just sisters. It is my fault—I should have been more firm! Either I shouldn't have allowed her to go or should have gone myself. But I was too selfish, I was deep in my own sorrow and I never thought about my sister's wellbeing. All of us did that!' she said, her eyes flashing. 'We were so involved with our personal grief that we never realized how unsafe it would be for Sita. What must be she going through now?' she swallowed convulsively.

The raw apprehension in her voice frightened Mandavi too. Urmila, standing cold and shaking, next to her, seemed close to a breakdown. 'Who is there for her? Sita, alone, terrified, defenceless, at the mercy of that monster!' she raged, the image of Ravan, firing her with a new terror. 'Who will protect her against him? It has been six months since we got to know of this, how long is she to wait? She hopes with all her will, her faith and her love that Ram will rescue her, but when? Will she sustain till then? Will her will break eventually? What if she does something drastic to herself...tries to kill herself...we'll never know! Oh, help her, please!'

Her panic was contagious. Her sisters were watching her with horror and alarm, helpless and deprived of their strength and power. Urmila had always been their support but the sight of her floundering in despair, paralysed them with the same fear. It was upto Sumitra who placed a firm, gentle hand on Urmila's slight, shaking shoulders. 'Calm down, Urmila. Don't be so hard on yourself, or on the others. None of us could have stopped her. Ram tried, didn't he? If she did not heed his words, she would not have listened to any of us here too. Nor you either.'

'Urmi, you well know if Sita makes up her mind, nothing can move her!' added Mandavi, pleading with her.

Urmila was too distraught to be moved by entreaty but even in her overwrought state, Urmila slowly realized what her sister and her mother-in-law were saying was true.

'I should have been with her. I could have looked after her when the men were away...' she said hollowly in an undimensional voice.

'No. You would have been equally vulnerable,' refuted Sumitra. 'This was a wicked plan and everyone got fooled. Or how would the sensible, rational Ram go chasing a golden deer? You are right, Urmila, it is a fantastic notion—a silver-spotted golden deer does not exist, but yet Sita desired it. Again, this is so against their nature. And what could poor Soumitra have done—he must have been torn between his brother's orders and his sister-in-law's wild pleadings to help his brother whom she believed was in danger. It is all so grotesquely odd as if everyone had lost their minds and good sense to chase the absurd. No, dear, this was to be!'

'No, we brought it upon ourselves! We should have just let the men go. Sita should not have been there at all!' cried Urmila fiercely.

She turned wildly to Kaikeyi, sitting silently, all the while. 'You know better, Ma! Was Sita a part of that prediction? It was to be Ram's mission, not Sita's trial!' she cried. 'Was she to be made a victim? Why was she dragged into this madness, this nightmare which just does not seem to end!'

'I cannot say, dear,' said Kaikeyi, her face composed but Urmila saw her eyes as troubled as the others. 'Because she is Ram's wife and the fact that she went with them was meant for a purpose. If Ram is to kill Ravan, then yes, it is because of Sita. And if that is so, then there is no cause for worry, no reason for anxiety. Ram will win her back and she will return with them safely, a warrior herself to have braved all the hardship.'

The mention of Ravan sent a chill through her as Urmila remembered him raging at Sita's swayamvar. She recalled his raking eyes, his leering grin and his softly spoken threat—'I shall never forget this day, fair lady, I will remember this...!'

Was revenge on Ram and Surpanakha's defence just a pretext and was it this humiliation, this lust for Sita the reason for him having forcibly snatched her? Was it the revenge of a jilted man who could not face rejection? Was it his revenge or lust? Or both? The doubt made Urmila tremble. What would he do to her? Urmila squeezed her eyes shut to blot out the conjured horror. She did not dare to open her eyes...would this endless nightmare ever wake up to the light of a shining day of hope and happiness?

THE WAR

An arrow was coming towards her. She looked at it in speechless horror, as it approached... It swished past her and sped straight—straight into Lakshman's heart, tearing into his chest, flinging him sideways. She saw him falling, his head thrown back, his arms stretched, a scream torn from his throat, bringing the war to a standstill...but before he could fall, someone grabbed his body and started dragging it away from the battlefield. Ram snatched it back, cradling his limp brother in his arms. He was lying still and motionless, his weapons strewn by his side. There were thousands of snakes around him, over him, wriggling, slithering, moving sinuously all over the dead bodies on the battlefield. Ram was next to him, his head on his lap, crying disconsolately, the tears falling fast and thick, dripping on Lakshman's cold, white face, his face drained of blood, of life...

Urmila's stricken eyes flew open. She was staring at the ornate ceiling, the image of him lying limp and lifeless still imprinted on her mind. She heard a loud, thudding sound. It was her heart thrumming. She got up slowly, trembling, straightening herself and her thoughts. It was just a bad dream, she kept repeating to herself. He would come back to her.

The last fourteen years had been a wanton infliction of misery but these last two months had been even more agonizing. The news kept trickling in...how after Sita's abduction by Ravan, Ram, mad with grief, had searched for weeks for Sita and through Kabandha, the one-eyed demon, they were led to Pampa where Sugriva, the exiled king of Kishkindha, was hiding from his brother with his associate Hanuman and a handful of the vanara army. They had found some of Sita's jewels on the forest floor after she had thrown them from the flying chariot. As Sugriva gave him the bundle, there grew a new bond of friendship between Ram and Sugriva. Ram promised to help him regain his lost kingdom and wife from his brother Vali and in return, Sugriva offered his help and the entire army to invade Lanka if need be. Ram killed Vali when the two brothers were in a duel and having his kingdom returned, Sugriva sent Hanuman to search for Sita. Hanuman discovered her in Lanka, in the Ashok garden to be precise, guarded by all the womenfolk of Ravan's family and a host of female guards. Sita refused to go back with Hanuman as she wanted Ram to come to Lanka like a hero to rescue her from the clutches of the arrogant king. But before heading back, Hanuman managed to burn down most of the city of Lanka and openly challenged Ravan in his court that the day would arrive where Ram would kill Ravan in his own country. A bridge was built over the wide expanse of the sea separating Lanka from the mainland by Nala, the son of Vishwakarma, the architect of the gods. After having finally reached the shores of Lanka, Ram had declared war on Ravan.

Ram would kill Ravan as was destined, Urmila was sure, but why was she troubled chronically by these dreams? The prophecy had been about Ram, not Sita or Lakshman, a small voice kept haranguing her. Were they not safe? What harm would befall them? Urmila had no answers and she found herself praying for the first time. She had never been devout like Sita or deeply religious like her cousins. She found herself fervently, silently, calling upon in supplication, communing, entreating, imploring, with a higher force which would keep them both unharmed. When you are without hope, all you have is to will, to pray for a miracle.

Urmila was surprised when she was informed by Sumitra that Bharat had come to visit her. Bharat again, Urmila wondered with a frown. What news had he got now which had made him rush to Ayodhya again? She felt a stab of apprehension—What was he going to tell about Sita? Had Ram killed Ravan? Was Sita finally free?

The thought that Sita was back with Ram brought a smile to her lips but it slipped the moment she saw the expression on the others' faces. All of them were there, all wearing the same stricken look.

Bharat stepped forward, his face ashen, his eyes moist. He finally seemed to gather some courage to break the news. 'Lakshman has been fatally injured by a deadly arrow of Indrajit, the son of Ravan. Shot near the heart, he lies unconscious on the battlefield, and his life is in danger. He can survive only till sunrise...so says Hanuman whom I met just now. What are we to do now?!' he was crying openly, his face wet with tears, his shoulders heaving.

The image of Lakshman lying in the battlefield swiftly erupted through her mind and Urmila understood the import of the dream. That had been a dream; this was for real. Physical danger has a particular tinge to it—sharp-edged, premonition-scented. She had known it was coming her way. The deepest recesses of her brain had screamed in pain and alarm, pounding her heart and flooding the body with a sense of fear needed for fight or flight. But she could do neither. And in that single, slow, unhurried moment, she saw before her eyes her life with him in a flash—her first glimpse of him in the garden, him at the swayamvar drawing his sword out to protect her, he talking about his innermost fears with Ram, he imploring her not to marry him, he teasing her at their wedding, he in her arms, he rubbing his thumb on the inside of her wrist, he removing her hair clip and watching her hair tumble down with smouldering eyes, his last kiss still burning an imprint on her parched lips, he laughing at her at Chitrakoot...and finally he lying still on the battlefield...all of it was real, pulsating with a life gone by. She felt a hot, tearing wrench in her heart, her blood curdling. Was it her heart breaking? Her mind could not take it—swinging tiredly back and forth, from believing to forgetting, from hoping to die to wishing to live. No, it could not be happening. She had waited for him too long. He could not betray her love and her faith. Not now, not ever. He was to return in a few days and he would—her victorious warrior, her faithful lover. He would come back to her...

Encompassed by a sudden sense of calm, Urmila looked in quick concern at Sumitra. She must be devastated. Sumitra was holding on gallantly, leaning heavily on her other son Shatrughna but Urmila could see in both their tortured eyes, the intense grief they were grappling with.

She rushed to her. 'No, Mother, don't be afraid. Your son's heart is filled with the name of Ram. You had said so. So how will Ram ever allow any danger to befall him? He is perhaps sleeping peacefully due to the injury. He will gain consciousness again and will get up and fight! Your Soumitra can come to no harm: he will always remain safe. It must be Ram who would be inconsolable, suffering in pain and worry.'

Bharat looked surprised. 'Yes, he is. He is beyond comforting! He has gone beserk with grief. He has surrendered his weapons and given up hope, accepting defeat. He refuses to pick up his arms and fight the war, claiming what use is victory for him now when he has lost that one person he loves most. He despairs with what face he will meet Ma Sumitra and you and has refused to return to Ayodhya. He sits with the head of Lakshman on his lap and weeps in disconsolate anguish and says he has nothing to live for anymore.'

'No! But he has to save Sita!' gasped Urmila in dread. 'Ram cannot lose hope and give up. Is there no one to assure him that Lakshman will rise and get up? Nothing can happen to Lakshman! I know it! He is a warrior who will not accept defeat. He will win for his brother. He lives for his brother!'

'And will die for Ram too,' said Sumitra softly, her slight shoulders sagging wearily.

'Mother, no, don't believe the worst! Nor should Ram!' said Urmila, trying to pacify the older woman. 'Bharat, you go to Lanka and be with Ram; he needs your help and reassurance.'

'He does not need me, sister,' responded Bharat. 'He has loyalists like Vibhishan, Ravan's estranged brother, and Hanuman. I saw Hanuman flying over Ayodhya holding something dark in his hand and thinking he was a demon, I shot him with my arrow. He alighted and came close and told me he was Hanuman. He was carrying the hill with him as he had been told by Sushena, the vanara doctor, to search for the Sanjeevani herb grown on the Himalayan mountain called Gandhamadan. It is that magic herb which might restore Lakshman to good health before sunrise. The vegetation was too profuse and he could not identify the herb and, running short of time, Hanuman picked up the entire hill and was flying back to Lanka when I forced him down,' said Bharat. 'He too feared for Lakshman's life and was rushing to Lanka...' his voice quivered with fear and the certainty of approaching death.

Urmila calmly shook her head. 'If he could fly to the Himalayas for the magic herb and collect a hill, murmuring Ram's name all the while, nothing can stop him now,' she said, her face serene, without a trace of worry. 'He shall reach on time and save Lakshman. And Lakshman will regain his strength and purpose. He will fight and they will win the war, kill Ravan and shall return home soon with Sita. That is how it will be.'

The icy calm in her voice was both frightening and impressive.

That was how Urmila was in the worst of crises—collected and assuring, thought Kirti, overwhelmed with wonder. But she was apprehensive too, if anything untoward was to happen to Lakshman—as was happening now—how long would Urmila be able to hold herself? She loved him too much; she would not be able to live without him. Urmila had lived through these fourteen years only on that thin sliver of hope—that he would come back to her, later, if not sooner. But return he would. But what if he did not make it? The dread smothered Kirti's heart. Lakshman was fast sinking: Kirti knew that from all that Bharat had told them, the poison spreading slow, sure and surreptitious. But Urmila refused to cave in to any horror or hysteria. Was she in denial? Kirti was getting increasingly worried about her sister.

Kausalya was sobbing but trying to give Sumitra some reassurance. She clung to a pale-faced Shatrughna. Kaikeyi looked unusually fearful; was she, too, dreading the worst? Would Lakshman die? Kirti was again struck by Urmila's unnatural placidity but she knew her sister was breaking inside.

'Urmi, I am going to the temple...to pray.'

Urmila gently shook her head. 'Ma Sumitra needs me,' she whispered, her voice thick with emotion. Kirti gave Mandavi a nod and left the room.

Mandavi looked searchingly at Urmila, troubled by her dispassionate serenity. She had seen Urmila going almost berserk when she had heard of Sita being kidnapped and that, too, had been an unusual reaction. Urmila never lost her wits. And now this remarkable show of self-possession: it was unnerving. Urmila was oscillating between two extremes.

Mandavi had observed her sister through these trying years; she had endured all what Mandavi could not. They had both suffered similar tribulations but it was Mandavi who had preferred to live in her island, surrounded by bitter waters of pain and disillusionment. While she had wilted and withered, Urmila's unshakeable self-belief had made her bloom and blossom, weathering the worst of times.

And each time Mandavi saw Bharat, she was struck by a bittersweet pain. Happy to see him and sad that he could not give her his all. But Urmila could not have even these small moments. Or live in the assurance that her husband was safe and unharmed. In the forest, he was living in danger; here, she was living through danger, dreading and fearing for him, fearful if he would ever return to her. But she never showed it. She hid it well, masking every emotion. Urmila now seemed frozen. Mandavi wanted to rush to her and shake her out of her stupor, make her understand that her husband was dying, force her to face the brutality of that eventuality but her sister seemed to have gone far, far away, living again in her land of everlasting hope. And love. Love knows no fear.

As the war raged on the shores of Lanka, the palace had witnessed within its closed, carved walls, a war of another kind, thought Urmila wryly. Each one of them had their own battles to fight, to combat the demons of their minds. Some were fighting the people around them, some with the situation they were trapped in, some with Fate, some with God and some with themselves. Even the weapons used were different—hatred, angry words, love, patience and faith.

But who all had won that inner battle? Who lost what? Did she lose her innocence for all that she won?

The value of a moment gone and lived often lies in the strength of its memory, sighed Urmila as she gave the final touches to the painting. It was almost done, just like the war. Lakshman had survived his fatal wound with the Sanjeevani brought by Hanuman. He was fighting Indrajit again on the battlefield, more fierce and purposeful than before.

'Indrajit is said to be more powerful than Ravan,' said Shatrughna. 'He is called Indrajit because he had defeated the most powerful god—Indra. And from that day his name got changed from Meghnad to Indrajit. He is said to be omnipotent— all powerful, and none can kill him except a devout celibate ascetic, divinely strong and supremely protected with the love and sacrifice of a doting wife. And that man is Lakshman, my brother, who lives through the power of your love, sister. There is none like you!' he said reverentially, bowing his head in deep respect.

Urmila was embarrassed. 'I did what any other in my place would have done!' she exclaimed. 'It was simply a matter of acceptance.'

'You saved my brother!' said Shatrughna fervently. 'You saved us! All these years, Bharat and I might have looked after Ayodhya and the people, but it was you who looked after us, kept the family together and saved it from a living hell...it is not how it was when Ram left. And it is not going to be when Ram returns with Sita and Lakshman. You made this palace a better place. You made it a home one wants to return to every single day. You blessed it with your patient love, your indomitable spirit and your everlasting hope for peace.'

Urmila coloured a delicate pink. 'She does not take any word of commendation too well,' smiled Sumitra, peering closely at the detailed lines of the figures crowding the canvas. 'But may I praise your work? I wasn't there for the wedding but I feel I am right there, right now! It is as if time had stood and you children have just got married!'

'That was the idea,' agreed Urmila, her tone wistful. 'I want to relive that day each time I look at it. It was a momentous one for all of us, when our lives significantly changed forever...'

'Not for the better, I am afraid,' sighed the old queen. 'You girls from Mithila have suffered more than you deserved.'

'I got your Soumitra that day. And I am grateful to you for that,' said Urmila quietly. 'But I think he deserved me!' she added with a twinkle in her eye, trying to ease the gathering solemness.

'Did he deserve you? I often wonder,' responded Sumitra. 'Did we deserve you? None in the family ever considered your feelings, did they? None of us,' she repeated emphatically. 'But neither did you harbour any resentment for that nor embitter yourself,' she paused. Urmila wondered, with a pang, if the queen was hinting at Mandavi. 'And yet you did not take anything lying down, a woman free to speak for herself, bending the rules but not breaking them, turning the shackles of your feet into anklets, tinkling with serene joy and bringing music to our deaf, saddened ears. We were blind and mute to your pain, your hopelessness. And yet you gave us your all. For years, we were being torn apart by mutual distrust and resentment but all of us pretended that all was well, that denial was the best policy, except you. You made us face the truth. You showed us the mirror to the real us, not a reflection of what the world—and we ourselves—believed about us. I have always been so proud of Soumitra but I am ashamed of my maternal arrogance for overlooking the obvious. You have made me prouder, for you are a finer person. So, don't thank me, dear. I thank you. We thank you for making us happier, better people.'

Urmila was too overwhelmed for words. She simply placed her hands gently on the wrinkled, withered hands of the queen and managed to say softly, 'Soumitra will be back very, very soon. Happier days will be here again...we deserve them at last!'

THE RETURN

He was everywhere around her. She could not forget their fretting arguments, the glances, the feel, the touch, the experience of him being next to her... Each corner of the palace reminded her of him, each wall echoed with his voice, his sardonic laugh, his sure footsteps as he climbed up those steps into the room where she painted. She almost felt that surge of elation when she heard his steps on the stairs. It was a sentiment, it was a memory.

It was the last day of Navratri. And it was the day which saw Ram kill Ravan. Sita was free. Like Goddess Durga, Ram had annihilated evil, thought Urmila as she laid the prasad—several plateful of fruits—at the deity's feet. She folded her hands and bowed her head in deep reverence and said a prayer. Let peace and joy reign in this land, she whispered fervently.

The swarming city was abuzz with tales of Ram's bravery, Sita's capture by Ravan, Ram's frantic quest for Sita, his friendly alliance with Sugriva, Hanuman's discovery of Sita in the Ashok garden of Lanka, the bridge the vanaras built across the sea to Lanka and Ravan's eventual death at Ram's hands in the battle. And as everyone in the palace began the celebrations and preparations for Ram's grand welcome, sidled an uneasy tiding.

When she first heard of it, Urmila could not believe her ears and brushed it off as a rumour—there were always some nasty tongues to vitiate the merry mood.

But the rumours were not wicked hearsay. They were true—an ugly truth that sullied the sacredness of love, duty and faith. The news spread like wildfire that Sita, in a moment of defiance, had walked into a big, brightly burning fire to prove her chastity to Ram and the world. And as she had arrived, pale and beautiful, dressed in splendour, every inch the queen of Ayodhya, the queen of his heart, to finally meet Ram, everyone in Lanka jostled to catch a glimpse of Sita—the woman for whom this war was fought. They wanted to see the princess who had lived in the forest with her husband, who had so enamoured their king and refused to bow down to him; the lady who had walked into the fire to prove her chastity.

Urmila gasped: the scene playing out in her mind's eye after Shatrughna had informed the family that Ram, Sita and Lakshman were on their way home. It had dulled the bubbling joy of their return. How could Ram have allowed it, wondered Urmila. Why would he say it now? Was he not the husband who rescued his wife? Was he not the lover who was waiting to see his beloved again? Or was he the king addressing his queen in front of his subjects?

In the quiet privacy of Urmila's chamber, the sisters remained stunned in subdued silence. The stillness in the room and their hearts was deafening, screaming for explanation. At last it was Mandavi who spoke, the virulence in her voice unmistakable. 'So, as a king, Ram was expected to uphold moral principles and to perform his duty, and thus it was required of him to question Sita's chasity! Was it this overriding responsibility of setting the right standards as a king which was essential to prove her fidelity before the society?' she asked caustically. 'But despite all this, I think the morality of the act is questionable. How can one compel someone to undergo torture and public humiliation for exoneration in the eyes of society?' she demanded. 'Sita was kidnapped, she did not stay at Ravan's palace willingly! Then why this doubt in people's mind? And in his mind?' she added.

Mandavi's biting words reminded Urmila of her unrestrained tirade at Chitrakoot when she had violently denunciated the brothers for not following their dharma to their wives. Her own words echoed back in her seething mind.

She nodded. 'If that was the case, Ram should have renounced his throne and his status as king to protect her rather than be answerable to his people who dared to point fingers at his wife, the queen, for not being "chaste" enough,' said Urmila forcefully. 'It was a dilemma of a husband versus the king—who is higher, is the moral question?' she added bitterly. '...This to a wife who chose to go in exile with him to the forest than stay in the protective luxury of the palace.'

The usually quiet Kirti came out strong. 'Of course, he knew she was true, she was his love!' refuted Kirti. 'It was a calculated, deliberate move on his part. It was his premeditated wish to demonstrate Sita's fidelity publicly so that her chasity could never be quesioned now or later after this trial of fire. Ram did it to preserve Sita's reputation, to preserve the dharma of the world. He did it so that no one later would ever point fingers at his wife, at his queen.'

'Agreed, but he did not stop Sita from walking into the fire lest the people accuse him of favouring and covering up for his wife,' shot back Urmila. 'But what crime had she committed for him to cover up and prove to the world her innocence? And this for his subjects with fickle moods? Can you stop a petty, wicked tongue from gossiping? The best way to remove public misconception is to address it directly, not through trials and tests which can be questioned later. Ram stood up for all those women villified by society—Tara, Mandodari, Ahalya—then why could he not protect Sita from social censure?'

'The agnipariksha was his way of silencing people, Urmi,' maintained Kirti. 'Society has always been hypocritical. Ram shielded these women from social disgrace but exposed Sita to one. Because if he had openly shielded her, society would have also pointed fingers at him and accused him of covering up for his own, favouring his close ones. Society expects their rulers to be more perfect than themselves.'

'If what his subjects believe is so paramount for him, then why did he not listen to them when they begged and implored him not to go in exile and leave Ayodhya?' argued Urmila, recalling the sight of the huge, wailing crowd of people following Ram's chariot all the way up to the banks of River Sarayu. 'They wanted him to be king, but he went to the forest to keep his father's word. So, again, in this dilemma of dharma between king and son, he preferred to follow the dharma of a son. Not the king's,' she reminded pertinently. 'So, why now at the cost of hurting and humiliating his wife?'

'He did it to establish her faithfulness to the world so that they could not malign her later. He did it to protect her!' said Kirti vehemently.

Mandavi shook her head with resolute determination. 'No, she was wronged! But what I fail to comprehend is why did Sita keep silent and not retaliate? And why did she suffer the agony of humiliation by a suicidal action of stepping into the fire?' she asserted. 'It was she who ordered Lakshman to make that fire!'

The mention of her husband made Urmila wince. What must he have gone through hearing his brother's cold, cruel words? Had his hands trembled when kindling that fire for Sita? He had been her protector for fourteen years, shielding her from possible danger and destruction, but he could not protect her from his brother's damaging allegation.

'For all our angry debate here, I think Sita would be the best person to answer these questions once she is here, once all of them are back,' sighed Urmila wearily. 'There's yet so much to be done for the welcome ceremony and the coronation ritual which follows immediately. So it is best we cheer up and get along with the preparations.'

Kirti brightened immediately. 'They are to arrive another five days from today! But, it is amavasya that day—a moonless night!' pouted Kirti dejectedly.

'No bad day is bad, dear,' refuted Urmila. 'They are returning, that's what is so special. If it is a moonless night, the oil lamps will look so exquisite flickering all over the city in the darkness! What a lovely sight that would be!'

'And a lovely sight you should be too! I shall dress you up for that day! Shanta has been informed, so she is certain to doll you up!'

Urmila burst out laughing. 'I am no bashful bride!'

'Oh, you will be bashful for all your intrepidness!' smiled Mandavi, giving her a sudden, hard, affectionate hug. 'I am so happy for you—at last he'll be back!'

Urmila looked into her clouded eyes. 'So will Bharat,' she reminded her gently, giving her sister's arm an assuring pat. Mandavi quickly lowered her lashes but not before Urmila glimpsed a brief flare of hope in the anguished eyes. 'Kirti, how do you intend dressing her up? Definitely no pale shades for our Ice Princess! And hope the feast you and Ma Kaikeyi are planning is both mind-blowing and tongue-tingling! Remember, the culinary queen is arriving—Sita might just head straight for the kitchen!'

Kirti giggled. Mandavi was grinning at their inane garrulousness, pretending to search for her book. She well knew her sisters would not allow her to read now. It was almost like old times, Urmila sighed contented...

They had arrived home. The palace was fully lit up with oil lamps and twinkling lanterns, flickering at every nook and corner, and the fragrance of incense and scented oils lingered heavily in the air. Thick festoons of jasmine, champa and marigold sculpted a colourful mantle at every archway, impregnating the air with their heady fragrance. Kausalya had left for Nandigram to welcome them there and Urmila saw them getting down from the chariot with Bharat and the elder queen mother.

Standing on the same steps where she had bid him adieu, she again held in her hands a gold tray for the aarti to welcome him home. Fourteen years later. Her hands were as unsteady as last time when she had performed the aarti, her eyes as steady. She could not take her eyes off him, gazing deeply as the light of the flickering diya shone in his deeply thoughtful, brooding eyes. They were no longer smouldering with suppressed intensity. Instead there lurked a gentleness, a serenity in them that was deep and unfathomable. The fire burning bright in his eyes seemed to have somehow died. The forest had tamed him. She was quick to notice the dark, angry gash on his chest. That was where the poisoned arrow of Indrajit had struck him...and when she had almost lost him. Her hands shook. Lakshman saw her looking at it and murmured, 'I lived for you. The meaning of my life is you. You got me home, Mila. And my last thought was your smiling face with those large, sad eyes.'

Her eyes were burning with unshed tears and anguish. 'Please let me cry now,' she swallowed convulsively.

He gently took the golden plate from her nerveless fingers. 'No, don't wash this happiness with tears, Mila. I am sure none of these people will allow us to do anything in private for quite some time!' he said with his lopsided smile, looking at Shanta and his mother ready with the vermilion and flowers in their hands. Urmila smiled through her gathering tears as he bent down to touch his mother's feet and the family soon swallowed him in gestures of affection and delighted squeals. But he had managed to grab his small moment of seclusion with her. As incorrigible as always, she could not help smiling. A great emotion of joyfulness, an ineffable esctasy flowed through her veins, injecting her with an infectious blitheness.

As Lakshman was led away with Ram and Sita for further ceremonies in the hall, Urmila noticed them always standing close together, their hands clasped firmly, to never let go. Ram looked weary, severely battle-scarred, but a small smile always hovered on his chiselled, beatific face. Urmila noticed he kept glancing anxiously at Sita, afraid that she would disappear any moment. Her heart constricted; he must have gone mad with grief when Sita had been snatched away. Just as it was for her, Sita and Lakshman were the two most precious people in his life—he had almost lost both of them in his mission and knowing him, he would never forgive himself. For the first time, she felt a special feeling of kinship with her brother-in-law. They both dearly loved the same persons.

Ram headed straight first towards Kaikeyi, regal and lovely as always, the punishing years having added a stoic elegance. He bent down to touch her feet and placing his palms on her feet said, 'I have done what you wanted me to achieve.'

Urmila found his statement vaguely ambiguous—did Ram, too, know what he had been destined for? And was that why he was grateful to Ma Kaikeyi, knowing that she had sacrificed her good name to take on a lifetime of infamy and the stigma of disgrace and despication for him?

Kaikeyi's answer confirmed her doubt. 'Fate is funny. It makes us shape our own destiny. And you have done the greatest duty of all—you have relieved the nation of great danger and a greater enemy. You did it. Not I.'

Ram smiled at her gratefully and it was Bharat's turn to face his mother. For the first time, he did not see through her or cast her a look of contempt or a word of anger. His eyes soft with love, and sorrowful with remorse, he could not utter a word. He sought her blessings and she enfolded him in a gentle embrace. Both did not need to say anything; their wordless embrace spoke for them, for all that they had lost, and all that they had gained.

At last her son had come back to her—she had got back Bharat. Being her son's mother had redeemed Kaikeyi in the eyes of the world. As the mother of a virtuous, selfless son like Bharat her lost honour had been restored considerably.

Urmila felt a tug on her arm. Sita was nudging her urgently. 'I need to talk with you. Right now,' she whispered.

Urmila scanned her sister's face anxiously. She was lovely, the ethereal quality still strong but the prettiness had shed way to be tempered with an emotional hardness.

'Let's go to your chamber,' she answered briskly. 'You need to get dressed up and I am supposed to supervise your scented bath anyway.'

The moment Urmila shut the door of the inner chamber, she turned worrriedly to her elder sister. 'What is so urgent?' she asked.

'I had to talk with you before Lakshman gets to speak to you about it.'

The glow of pleasure abruptly dimmed. Urmila could not stem the unease curling up inside her. What now?

Sita seemed to summon all her courage and convictions. 'I have done the most unpardonable. I accused Lakshman of an unutterable crime!' she whispered, barely managing to get the words out, wringing her hands in apparent nervousness.

Urmila wanted to still Sita's trembling hands but she remained silent, afraid to interrupt, fearful of the next words.

'...I made the most heinous accusations at him...' cried Sita.

'Sita, please come to the point,' said Urmila, preparing for the worst. 'What happened?'

Sita gave her a helpless look. 'It all started with the wretched golden dear! I saw it and fell hopelessly for it—I had to have it! It was like a spell—I was compleltely mesmerised. I requested Ram to get it for me. Lakshman immediately warned us that this could be a ruse as the demons in the forest excelled at disguises. I saw Ram hesitate at Lakshman's warning and I got indignant. I was more petulant. I implored, I begged Ram to give me that one gift which I could take home and keep in the palace. Ram relented, much to Lakshman's horror. But I felt vindicated. I thought I had won. Again Lakshman cautioned him but Ram agreed to fetch that beautiful deer. He ordered Lakshman to stay behind as he hunted down the deer. With great reluctance, Lakshman acquiesced, pleading yet again with Ram not to go. His constant admonishments infuriated me but finally Ram left, leaving us in the hut. I could barely hide my annoyance with Lakshman but waited eagerly for Ram to return with the deer. And soon we heard that eerie, inhuman cry of Ram screaming for Lakshman for help. It made my blood curdle but Lakshman remained unperturbed. I could not believe my eyes. The faithful Lakshman seemed so calm, so unfazed at his brother's agonized plea. I had expected him to hurry off to save him but when he remained stoicly silent, I orderd him to go seek his brother. He refused citing that he could not disobey his brother's orders. Besides, this was a trick to fool all of us and he assured me that Ram was safe. I did not believe him: I could not believe him. Each passing moment was making me go wild with worry, crazed with what must have happened to Ram. All I could do was stand helplessly and beseech Lakshman but he seemed to be in a strange, stubborn mood of not listening to me at all. He stood his ground and remained unmoved despite all my imploring. And I lost my temper, mad with anxiety and anger. I shouted at him to go and look for his brother. I scolded him, I screamed at him, but he kept reassuring me that Ram would come back safe and unscathed.

Crazed with worry and driven insane by now, I don't know what came over me to say the unspeakable...'

Urmila saw Sita hesitate, and gave her an imploring look but she did not prompt what Sita had to say. She waited with a heavy heart. What had Sita said to Lakshman that made her so ashamed of repeating the words?

'Agitated and exasperated with fury, I lashed out at Lakshman that he did not wish to help his brother as he wanted him dead as he had designs on me,' she blurted, her face flaming a deep red.

Urmila's heart lurched painfully, thudding hard at every word her sister had enunciated. She couldn't have said that, she wanted to shout in disbelief and horror.

Sita's voice faltered but she went on, determinedly. 'I accused him of plotting with Bharat to get rid of Ram at an opportune time so that Bharat would get the throne and Lakshman would get me...'

Sita could no longer go on, her words dying in her mouth, her face flaming hot with shame. She could not look into her sister's eyes. She buried her face in her hands.

He must have been shattered, was all Urmila could think of—hurt, heartbroken, disillusioned, mortified. He must have died a thousand deaths in that moment. What must he have gone through?

What must have Sita gone through to be able to utter those words? A frightened young wife gone crazy imagining her husband in grievous danger. Going slowly out of her mind, demented with fear and grief, desperate and deranged. Urmila could imagine the state of her sister, mad with despair and hopelessness, searching for any means and words to rouse Lakshman from his apathy. In her frantic desperation, she would have said anything to goad him. These were the insults she could fling at him, to shake him out of his perceived indifference, to prod him to rush to Ram's aid.

'I could see the shock on his face, his sorrow, his anger, but I was relentless. Yet he refused to leave me alone in the hut, refusing to disobey his brother's order,' continued Sita, trembling at the memory of her words. 'Finally, I threatened to kill myself if he did not leave and go to Ram. Humiliated and helpless, he agreed but before leaving he warned me again, and with his Agni astra, he drew a long, mystic line all around the hut. Lakshman forbid me to cross it warning me that if I did, I would be unprotected by human social law, and be just another creature in the wilderness where the jungle law prevailed. I heard his admonishment, but did not listen to him. Had I not crossed that line, Ravan could not have touched me. Ravan realized the power of that protective Lakshman rekha, for he could not step inside. I crossed it and was abducted because of my foolishness. I unwisely coveted the golden deer and, made Ram leave me to hunt for the deer and the biggest sin of all, I suspected and made the most crass insinuation against a virtuous man like Lakshman. A man who had forsaken everything to come to the forest and selflessly served and guarded me till that moment. I insulted his very being, his soul. I consistently ignored his warnings, I disobeyed him. And the abduction and the aftermath is my punishment for hurting the honour of that good man. I had to pay for my sin, didn't I?'

'Haven't you suffered enough, Sita?' asked Urmila, taking her hand in hers. 'Why do you insist on inflicting yourself with this punishing guilt and self-remonstration?'

Sita shook her head violently 'But I cannot forgive myself! Ram has not forgiven me and I dare not ask for Lakshman's forgiveness either,' she said wretchedly. She threw Urmila an uncertain look. 'Do you? Are you not upset with me?'

Urmila pressed her hand assuringly. 'No, why would I be? It was an abnormal, terrible situation and you reacted violently saying things in the heat of the moment. The words were offensive and seriously hurtful,' she started slowly, 'and it was unbecoming of you and yes, you must have grievously hurt Lakshman but he must have forgiven you too. Those were trying times, let them be,' she gave a long sigh. 'It has been difficult for all of us. Don't rake them and relive them. They will only destroy us. In fact, Sita, you need not have let me know. Why did you tell me?'

'To allow you to know the sordid truth before Lakshman shared it with you.'

Urmila gave a small, sad smile. 'He would probably have not told me at all...' her voice trailed uncertainly.

Sita looked shocked. 'Why would he not? I know he shares everything with you!'

'To protect you,' said Urmila quietly.

Sita was dumbstruck. 'Lakshman would have never spoken poorly about you or revealed anything about you that would have distressed me. Or made me choose between you and him. Never!' Urmila said fiercely. 'He loves me too much to force that choice.'

'...but now I made you do so,' whispered Sita, horrified.

'No, you made me love him more, which I thought would not be possible,' said Urmila, her eyes soft with a deep, stirring emotion.

'And made you despise me for what I did!' cried Sita.

'No, is our love so weak that it cannot encompass our transgressions, our faults, our flaws? We love each other too much to not know all what each has been through,' she sighed sadly.

'I created this mess and I suffered for it! Had I heeded Ram in the first place and not forced him to take me with him, had I listened to Lakshman and Ram and not been so stupidly stubborn about possessing that deer, had I not goaded Lakshman with my insults...Urmi, how do I undo what I did?' Sita was weeping, her face wet and wretched, the tears burning down her pale, hollow cheeks.

Urmila held her shaking shoulders in a warm embrace, trying

to protect her from further pain. 'We made mistakes...let's just learn from them and not keep searching for justifications. Life is too short to have regrets. And too long to endure the tribulations,' she said, gazing at her sister long and searchingly. 'And you are too precious for me, I went crazy thinking the worst when you were kidnapped. And now I have you back inspite of everything. I couldn't have asked for anything more. I don't want anything more! For I don't dare lose you again.'

Urmila felt the hot prick of her welling tears and she at last allowed them to flow freely, washing away the bleakness, the agony and anguish, the despair and desolation of those last so many years. There was still so much to be said. The sisters wept in each other's arms, holding on to each other, holding on to a new hope, expecting the best possible outcome from the past they had suffered and yearning for some possibility of fulfilment.

Their bedchamber was like the one on their wedding night. The soft warmth of the scented oil lamps basked it with an alluring glow. Shanta and Sumitra had strewn the pillows and the silk sheets with rose petals, making a soft flower bed, fragile and fragant. But Urmila barely glanced at it, her eyes were riveted on the man in her room. He was here after years of lonesome days.

Lakshman turned around to look at Urmila. She did not eagerly rush to him and fling her arms around him to passionately kiss him as she had so many nights ago, after their wedding. She stood there still, watching him, her eyes aged, weary. He would do anything to reinfuse the mischievous sparkle back in them. He felt a rush of emotions. She looked different; she seemed different. It was her face which now dominated her personality; it shone from a serene loveliness, the wide, large eyes having lost the twinkling vivacity. She was quiet and contemplative, a small smile hovering around her lips, making her look all the more forlon.

'Did you get to talk to your mother?' she asked falteringly.

He nodded. She was unusually quiet, desperate to talk with him, yet finding herself tongue-tied. She had never been inarticulately shy with him. But seeing him again—leaner, thinner, darker—in such close physical proximity, in the privacy of their chamber, made her suddenly feel awkward. His mere presence in the room overpowered her; the long, frozen years refused to melt away. She was disconcertingly assailed with a fit of nervousness, faintly unsure of herself and flooded with self-doubt. She frantically groped for words to say something: she had so much to tell him, so much she wanted to know yet her churning mental chatter remained unspoken.

'You have been crying,' he said gently, his sharp eyes taking in the slightly swollen red eyes. He took her trembling hands in his. She felt a dart of sharp pleasure. She felt pleasantly warm, the heat spreading and fanning her face: she had not experienced his touch for so long.

'Never remind a woman she has been crying!' she retorted, wishing she had washed her face more thoroughly to cleanse it of any traces of tears. She had not wanted him to know she had been weeping.

'I know you hate tears and you hate it more being discovered with them and I am not talking of your temper tears of the tantrum variety,' he laughed softly, rubbing his thumb on the soft skin of her unexposed wrist.

Mingled with the erotic frisson of pleasure was a new sensation. His fingers were scratchy and rough. She took his hands in hers and turned them palm outwards. They were badly calloused, the pink skin now bleached, tough and hardened. These were the hands that had chopped wood, fetched water from the river, strung arrows to kill animals and demons. These were the hands that had shown no mercy while killing Indrajit and more. These were the hands which had collected wood to kindle the fire for Sita's agnipariksha, these were the hands that had begged her to let him stay back to guard her till Ram returned. These must be the hands which must have clenched in mute pain as Sita had hurled those insults. And these were the hands to draw the mystic line to protect her in his absence. Urmila saw in a quick flash, the entire fourteen years in the deep, webbed lines of his blistered palms.

Her vision suddenly blurred and she blinked her eyes hard. Drawing his hands close to her and resting her head on his chest, her face turned away so he could not see the gathering tears. She did not want to mar this moment with any more sad thoughts. As he gathered her in his arms, sculpting her against his hard frame, allowing her to regain her composure, she relaxed slowly against him. They remained wrapped in each other's arms, he holding her close and she hearing the steady beat of his heart against her, both washed by a long wave of pleasure and peaceful fulfilment. She could not believe she was holding him at last, that she could feel him, touch him, breathe him in. She clung to him closer to reassure herself and felt his arms tighten around her as if to never let her go. He swiftly unpinned her hairpin and let her hair fall loose, burying his face in its silken fragrance. She turned her head slightly to inspect the wound on his chest. It still looked fresh and raw against all the scars on his chest. She ran her fingers lightly over each of them, wondering about the history of each. Gently laying her lips on it, she caressed it softly, hoping to drain the pain away.

'You must be exhausted,' she murmured as she edged him towards the bed. It looked large, soft and welcoming. She sat down waiting for him. He stretched down on the bed and gave a long sigh. He looked at her long and languidly, and then he held out his arms for her. He was still holding her in his arms, sometime later, when he fell asleep through the longest, peaceful stretch of a starless night lit up with fireworks still bursting outside the palace.

The early morning rays flooded his sleeping face, the thick lashes flying open immediately, his eyes alert. She looked up at him, her eyes smiling, 'Now will you tell me how was that my sister got kidnapped in spite of you being there?'

And Lakshman settled down to tell her the whole story.

EPILOGUE: THE LOSS

Urmila and Lakshman had two sons—Angad and Chitraketu—almost a year after a pregnant Sita was banished by Ram into the forest, a few months after their return to Ayodhya. Urmila remained Ram's most outspoken critic and could not bring herself to forgive him for choosing his people and his country over his wife—Sita, her sister. It was Lakshman who was entrusted with the task of abandoning Sita in the forest—a deed for which he derided himself all his life, his guilt-ridden self-flagellation as impotent as Urmila's anguished fury. Things were never the same after that...

Lakshman died as he had lived—for Ram. Ironically, for one who had obeyed his elder brother all his life, Lakshman died for disobeying Ram. Having acted against a royal decree, his brother's orders, Lakshman too had to bow down before the laws of the land.

Decades after a distraught Sita had descended into the bosom of bhoomi devi, her mother earth, Lord Yama decided to pay King Ram a strange visit. While he was in a closed-door conversation with Ram, Rishi Durvasa too sought an audience with the King of Kosala. Lakshman asked him to wait as Ram was not to be disturbed. Enraged, Sage Durvasa threatened to destroy Ayodhya, forcing Lakshman to disobey the royal command and suffer the death penalty of intruding into the room when the king was in private conversation with some one else. Fully realizing the fatal eventuality, Lakshman forced the door open, choosing to die rather than watching his city being destroyed. And as per the laws of the land, which even Ram could not alter, Lakshman accepted the death order and beheaded himself with his own sword.

Unable to bear the grief of losing his dear brother, Ram decided to relinquish the throne to his twin sons, Luv and Kush, and give up his life through jal samadhi, by walking deep into River Sarayu. The remaining two brothers followed him into the river, as the people of Ayodhya stood horrified and repentant, wondering if they had deserved such a king and their long-gone queen.

The kingdom was judiciously divided between the young princes. Luv and Kush were crowned the kings of North and South Kaushal Pradesh in Ayodhya. Bharat's sons, Taksha and Pushkal, ruled Gandhara with Takshashila as the capital. Shatrughna gave his kingdom of Mathura and Vidisha to his two sons, Subahu and Shatrughati. Lakshman's sons, Angad and Chitraketu, ruled over the kingdom of Karupadhadesha, a Himalayan kingdom near Mithila—the land of their mother Urmila.

ACKNOWLEDGEMENTS

I come from a family of three sisters, and am fortunate to be a mother of two daughters and an aunt of three nieces, besides having four aunts myself. And thriving amidst such feminine obviousness, I often wondered how it might have been with Sita and *her* sisters. It is for and because of all these lovely ladies in my life that I have written this book; and of course, Aai, my doughty mother, who brought up three distinctly dissimilar daughters so beautifully. Possibly, because she had two sisters as well! I am indebted to all these interesting host of women in my family.

Talking of such wondrous women-bonding, I could not have gone much ahead with this book had it not been for the constant verbal editing and proofing, debates, doubts and discussions with friends—Priya and Sarika, who were impatient enough to comb through the book, whilst still a draft, twice. Priya's constructive comments and arguments extended to the title of the book as well.

Many thanks to Niloufer, another good friend, who, being an illustrator-artist, was indulgent enough to come up with a fetching cover design, something far more creative than what I had in mind. Urmila could not have looked more pensive and wistful...

Thanks again to my niece, Maithili, for making a short trailer of this book. I say *again*, since her debut attempt at film-making, previously with *Karna's Wife*, was pretty much a success, it prompted her to dare another.

More thanks extended to the Rupa team and to Kadambari for editing this book. A special thanks to my editor, Ritu Vajpeyi-Mohan, for shepherding the publishing of this book so wonderfully.

The only study on Urmila that I could gather were a few scarce, random articles and a treasure of interesting quips, once recounted to me by my grandmother.

And lastly, had it not been for His blessings and the good will of those well-wishers, I would not have been able to write or complete this book.